VERITAS

It's always the Truth that kills...

P G Saunders

Independently Published 2025

WRITTEN BY

P G SAUNDERS

© 2025 P G SAUNDERS - ALL RIGHTS RESERVED.

No part of this book may be reproduced, stored in a retrieval system, or transmitted in any form or by any means—electronic, mechanical, photocopying, recording, or otherwise—without the prior written permission of the publisher, except in the case of brief quotations used in reviews or articles. Published by P G Saunders, United Kingdom - Independently Published. ISBN 9798312088144

Cover Design by P G Saunders This is a work of fiction. Any resemblance to actual persons, living or dead, or real events is purely coincidental.

INTRODUCTION & DEDICATION

The Truth is the most powerful thing.

Sometimes it's the type of Truth that we know deep down, and yet we don't have the courage to face up to it. Sometimes we deny the Truth, and in doing so, we create even greater problems for ourselves, until the moment we realize that we cannot move forward in life without confronting it. Sometimes the Truth remains hidden, only to emerge when we least expect it, bringing surprise, delight, or even unbearable pain. Occasionally we can be blind to the Truth, when it stares us directly in the face. The Truth can be manipulated, denied or deflected. The Truth can be personal, scientific, emotional, moral or even spiritual and it can affect us in millions of ways, both good and bad.

The Truth is fundamental to the human experience of life, and for all of us, no matter how long we exist, we will always have to encounter it, deal with it and live with it. But how much do we really value the Truth? How often do we embrace comfortable lies instead? And when the Truth finally reveals itself in an unfiltered and sometimes brutal way, will we always have the strength or the courage to let go of it?

In Veritas, I wanted to explore all facets of the Truth, not just as a concept, but as a force that shapes lives, alters destinies, and determines the rise and fall of entire civilizations. Within this story, Truth is not just an abstract idea; it is a weapon, a burden and also a battleground. Those who seek it may not like what they find, and those who hide it may not be able to escape its reach. Please enjoy…

Dedicated to the everlasting memory of Peter and Margaret.

CONTENTS

Chapter 1   The End of the Cycle
Chapter 2   The Fractured Colony
Chapter 3   The Rejuvenation Machine
Chapter 4   The Beating Heart of the Planet
Chapter 5   The Warlord's Gambit
Chapter 6   The Prophet and the Shadow
Chapter 7   The Disillusioned Son
Chapter 8   Wasteland Queen
Chapter 9   The Gathering Storm
Chapter 10   The Apocalypse Protocol
Chapter 11   The Signal from the Dark
Chapter 12   An Indecent Proposal
Chapter 13   The Great Escape
Chapter 14   The Warren's Future
Chapter 15   The Forgotten Seers of Neso
Chapter 16   The First Shots in Anger
Chapter 17   Fear in Erebus Prime
Chapter 18   A Surprising Discovery
Chapter 19   The Sky Burns
Chapter 20   The Warren Stirs
Chapter 21   The Reckoning Approaches
Chapter 22   A Chance of Salvation
Chapter 23   The Inferno of War
Chapter 24   Erebus Under Siege
Chapter 25   The Grid Falls
Chapter 26   The Blood of the Seers
Chapter 27   The Machine Takes Control
Chapter 28   The Turning of the Tide
Chapter 29   Revelations and Warnings

Chapter 30 The Awakening of Sight
Chapter 31 A Daring Plan
Chapter 32 Between a Rock and a Hard Place
Chapter 33 A Dangerous Mission
Chapter 34 The Burden of Fate
Chapter 35 Destiny Calls
Chapter 36 Veritas
Chapter 37 The Chase Begins
Chapter 38 Surrender on the Plains
Chapter 39 The Battle for PLAIN
Chapter 40 The Fallen and the Future
Chapter 41 The Call to Arms
Chapter 42 Secrets in the Depths
Chapter 43 The Price of Vengeance
Chapter 44 The Battle Plan
Chapter 45 03.00 hours
Chapter 46 The Battle for Pluto (Part 1)
Chapter 47 The Battle for Pluto (Part 2)
Chapter 48 The Battle for Pluto (Part 3)
Chapter 49 The Battle for Pluto (Part 4)
Chapter 50 The Return to Home
Chapter 51 The Final Flight
Chapter 52 A World Transformed

CHAPTER ONE – THE END OF THE CYCLE

The Ice Wars were due.

He had been in complete control for such a long time now that leading from the front came naturally to him, indeed he could not remember a time when he had been ever really challenged. Now with the cycle ending, he felt more concern within him than he could ever outwardly show. A new one would begin again soon, as it always had done. A contest of blood and power would await him, and a test of strength and survival to get through.

For fifty years, he had shaped the world that he lived in, and he had bent it according to his will.

Now, for the first time in a long time, he felt a sense of vulnerability in his position, and the way to combat all this would be to show strength and to wield the power he had.

He slowly lifted his hands, watching as the faint light reflected off his cybernetic fingers. They were strong, precise, unnatural and unchanging. The rest of him was not.

Veylan had ruled longer than any before him. He had crushed rebellions and outlasted conspiracies; according to his mind, he had made Pluto his own. But time had a way of creeping in and affecting things; even through the seemingly impenetrable walls of iron, ice and genetics that protected him, even via power itself. But this time it was different. Yes, he would fight to hold what was his, but for the first time in a long time, doubts had crept into his mind.

A sharp chime shattered the quiet. The council was waiting for him; he had to attend.

Veylan stood up, rolling his shoulders, and willing his body into action. Weakness could not be shown to them. Any hesitation must be buried and hidden. He was Supreme Chancellor. He was power itself.

With a final glance at the frigid world beyond the glass, he turned, his black cloak whispering across the metal floor as he strode toward the chamber doors.

Outside the building, the ice winds howled, their cries like tortured ghosts scraping against the reinforced plasteel barriers. Beyond them, Pluto extended out into an endless graveyard of ice. Its terrain had been sculpted into irregularly shaped ridges and weird-looking snow dunes created by centuries of merciless storms. The planet's distant sun cast no warmth at all, providing only a pale, indifferent light that barely touched the methane-laced atmosphere.

Inside the dome, the Council Chamber was filled with the great and the good on the planet, waiting… waiting for him. The massive hall made of a black steel alloy and reinforced glass was heated with embedded energy conduits, casting an artificial amber glow that made the room appear warmer than it actually was. The air in here was thin, sterile and recycled too many times through Pluto's struggling life-support systems. The echoes of voices past seemed to be embedded in the chamber walls, what discussions had been had here in years past? The whispers of leaders who had risen to prominence and then fallen, and then swallowed by the merciless cycle of power that came around every one hundred years.

At the heart of the chamber, sat the obsidian council table, its surface polished to a mirror sheen. Eleven figures sat in silence around it, awaiting the arrival of the current leader. At the head of the table, his seat was elevated above the rest as a mark of respect. As he entered, Supreme Chancellor Veylan observed the gathering with a look as frigid as the brutal world outside. He walked slowly with authority towards his throne-like chair, the others stood, heads bowed until he was in place, and then they sat in unison.

Veylan took his time to look around the assembled council members before he cleared his throat.

"Welcome everyone," he said, "Let's get down to business."

The collective there nodded in agreement, and then he continued.

We stand at the edge of a moment of reckoning," he said, his voice smooth but laced with authority. "The factions are growing restless, and I feel the heat of insurrection may be rising beneath the ice."

Across from him, General Kallos, leader of the Independent's faction, stirred himself. His scarred face was alive, and sensing an opportunity that this could be a day to initiate a change in the way that the planet was run.

"That's because they know the Cycle is upon us, and your time is up," he said, goading Veylan. "You can stall all you like, but you cannot escape tradition."

Murmured discussion rippled across the table, at the boldness of Kallos' approach.

Veylan's synthetic fingers drummed against the table with slight indignation towards him. "Tradition?" he echoed, his voice filled with much disdain. "I thought we evolved past all that when I took this seat?" he said questioning the others.

"Did we?" a female voice rang out. That voice came from the far end of the chamber, one which was excitable and defiant. Nyx Orban, the leader of the Outlanders, met Veylan's gaze without hesitation. Her silver eyes gleamed back at him; they were mischievous and alive. She looked every inch a woman of combat. She had short dark, almost black hair and she was dressed in dark grey fatigues; her stature was lean, and she was physically fit.

"Then why is the Council still bound by it Veylan?" she said firmly, "Because it's our way, and it's the way it should always be," she went on, "The people respect strength, and they expect us to prove ourselves."

She paused, her eyes gleaming.

"Anyway, you're an outsider, so why should we listen to you?" she mercilessly teased him.

He knew on this point she was technically correct.

"Very well," he said looking back at her, "We will do as the people expect, and on behalf of the Corporatists, I can confirm that we will compete for victory," he said.

Nyx smirked. "More like survival," she replied with a hint of irony. "For you…"

Kallos nodded toward Nyx. "She's right. The people won't follow a ruler who cowers behind bureaucracy and red tape," he said. "We both know what happened the last time a Chancellor tried to prevent the contest?"

"I agree," said Uri Ressler, an elder statesman, representing the Northern region of Erebus Prime.

"So do I," rang out a plethora of other voices from around the table.

Veylan felt extremely uncomfortable at this dissent. He knew the tide of opinion was against him at this moment, and he remembered too that Chancellor Rhyne had tried to reform the system, declaring the Wars illegitimate, so that he could cling to power. The rebellion that followed had drowned the colony in casualties, including his own. And now, Veylan sat in the same chair, facing the same choice as Rhyne had faced before. He wanted to avoid this scenario repeating at all costs.

Prophet Hext, the green-robed and bearded leader of the Terraformers, was one of the last to speak, his voice a whisper yet incredibly assured. "These Ice Wars are archaic and are no way to choose a ruler," he urged. "It's about time we grew up and found another way."

"Enough." snapped back Veylan as he stood up; his imposing figure dominating the table, "I do not wish them to go ahead, and I and see that I do have support in this," he said looking at Hext.

"If we are not in full agreement, then we will have to vote." he proposed.

"Who wishes them to occur?" he asked, and one by one, ten hands were raised.

"Against," he said knowing he had already been defeated; he and Hext raised theirs.

Inside Veylan was disappointed, but not surprised. Seeing that the decision to proceed had been carried, he decided wisely to back down.

"This is the way we have always chosen governance." he said, hiding his own reticence that these wars we even needed, "I have ruled for half a century, and we have prospered. Despite that I see you want to instigate potential change, so in accordance with the vote, the Ice Wars will go ahead," he said.

"We'll be there," said Nyx exuding confidence and some bravado, "Just imagine if you were unable to beat our faction? Imagine if you ended up losing to Kallos? Oh, the embarrassment!" she said looking at him directly into his eyes.

Veylan knew that the Outlanders would never stand any hint of a chance in a military confrontation with his forces, but secretly he admired her fighting spirit.

Veylan glanced at each faction leader in turn. He saw the hunger and opportunity in Kallos' bright blue eyes, the quiet certainty and bravery in Nyx's, the masked enigma of Hext who knew he might have to adhere to the rules despite his obvious reservations. They had all made their choices.

"We will take on all-comers," Veylan said sharply. "Come… and take us on. And I will remind you all why I have ruled for so long."

A mean and confident expression took over him, while Nyx shifted, looking at him trying to read what he was thinking.

"Then it is decided," she declared to them all, "The battles will begin after First Light, as is the tradition."

Everyone around the table banged it in approval, and thus the decision had been made.

The Ice Wars tradition helped Pluto find strong, stable and long-term leadership, and they were triggered by the exact alignment of Pluto's six Moons, once every hundred years or so. They had been Pluto's brutal method of governance for generations, a contest of blood and dominance, where factions battled for rule of the planet.

They had rules, with specified use of armaments, no fighting near populated areas was permitted, and they were overseen by a panel of neutrally appointed judges, the Silent Watchers, who made sure all sides abided by the laws put down. If after conflict had taken place there were no victors, then the Silent Watchers would force negotiations to settle the search for a new Chancellor. The defeated leaders, if still alive, were either exiled, imprisoned, or forced into servitude. The people expected them to take place, and to deny the Wars was to invite chaos within the population, and that might invite others outside of Pluto who might want to take advantage of it.

And now the time for them had arrived.

Veylan rose from his seat, turned, and left the Council gathering, his long coat billowing as he strode toward the chamber doors. The remaining leaders watched him in silence, their faces content that this time they had got their way over him. As the heavy doors slid open, a final gust of chilly air from the ventilation systems brushed against his skin. He did not look back, nor did he acknowledge the fervent discussion from within the chamber that followed in his wake.

With measured steps, he exited the council chamber, his polished boots clicking against the metal grating. His mind was already calculating the next move he would make. Significant risk and danger lay ahead for him, so he would have to be incredibly careful. He would have to be adaptable, *or even ruthless*, to shape the outcome of the coming days, to his advantage.

With a whoosh that echoed behind him, the chamber doors sealed shut, with the thought of the council's verdict still ringing in his ears.

Beyond the glass tunnel encasing the walkway, the vista of Pluto spread out before him like a desolate world of endless ice and boulders. The wind blew strongly with a violent ice storm whipping across the endless eternally frosted land. Ice crystals, suspended in the near-vacuum atmosphere, refracted what little light reached the planet, painting mottled spectrums across the perpetual twilight. This was a normal day on this planet at the far end of the Solar System. The landscape was brutal and unyielding here, much like the people who had lived and survived for generations.

Veylan now strode forward, nervous energy surrounding him, and he looked slightly agitated. His mind raced through countless possibilities of how he would get the better of his rival faction leaders in the days to come. With the decision just made, his position was much less secure, and despite him having a significant military advantage, the others could be threatened to undo him completely. He had to back down, for now at least, and accept their challenge, because the lunar convergences were soon to arrive. Come the time of the conflicts, he trusted he would hold enough power in his hand to confirm the outcome, but should that not be the case, he would resort to doing whatever was necessary to prevail.

The private office of the Commander came into view ahead of him within the dark angular fortress; it was embedded within the colony's Central Spire. The guards on either side of the entrance, elite Technocrat enforcers clad in navy blue thermoplas armour, snapped to attention as he approached them. Without a word, the biometric scanner read his palm, and the doors slid open.

Inside, the atmosphere was stark and clinical. This space was sparsely furnished, with a couple of portraits of former Supreme Commanders on the walls, and in the middle was a desk with communications devices and a holoscreen that could bring up any maps or information that the Chancellor so desired.

He sat down for a second. He had wanted to stall the council or prevent them from even triggering the Ice Wars, but Kallos and Orban were itching for a fight; he could tell.

"Well," he thought, "I'll show them who's boss."

Just as he thought he might return back to his official apartment, there was a chime from the message console on the desk.

Who might this be?

He got up, approached the central console and placed a palm on the interface to check-in. The system responded instantly.

Incoming transmission – *Origin: Earth Command*

He looked surprised. A message from Earth? This was rare indeed. He initiated the connection, and a recognisable individual, one he had sparred with many times before, materialized before him. A tall, imposing figure in a dark military uniform appeared, the emblem of the Earth Dominion gleaming on his chest.

"Supreme Chancellor Veylan," the man said, his voice clipped and businesslike. "I trust you are aware of the… disturbances on Pluto?"

Veylan scoffed back with irritation towards him "You waste time with obvious statements to me, Admiral Devlin. Speak your purpose." he said.

Devlin's remained impassive, as he knew Veylan of old. "The Dominion is concerned." he said, "Your colony remains a vital outpost on the edge of the Solar System. We cannot allow instability to threaten our interests Veylan. If you cannot maintain control, Earth may be forced to intervene…"

Veylan was unsettled by this threat from Devlin, but he composed himself again. "Pluto is secure under my rule," he replied, "Your interference would only complicate matters,"

Devlin twitched slightly, his eyes inquisitive as he looked intently back. "Do not forget, Veylan, that it was our resources and technology that allowed you to rise to power. Without our support, your rule would have crumbled long ago," he said showing him who was the boss in this conversation.

Veylan synthetic fingers flexed again, a reminder of the enhancements that had kept him in power for so long. "I have maintained order on your behalf Pluto for five decades," he said stating the obvious. "I know what I'm doing Devlin, and you know that very well too," he said, irritated that his rule had been questioned.

Devlin's tone grew colder. "Your longevity treatments and cybernetic enhancements were gifts from the Dominion, Veylan." he said with a mild threat in his voice, "Do not mistake them for entitlements. We expect results..."

The irritation between them was very real, a reflection of their long and complicated history. Veylan had once been a promising officer in Earth's military, handpicked by Admiral James, Devlin's predecessor for a special mission to establish control over Pluto.

The partnership had been mutually beneficial: Veylan's ambition and ruthlessness had secured the colony, and he had taken over at the passing of Chancellor Yellin 50 years ago. Devlin's backing for him came when he took over from James, as he had ensured that Earth's interests were protected. But over the years, their relationship had soured, with Veylan's increasing autonomy, and Devlin's growing distrust in him.

"Then ensure your position remains secure," Devlin continued. "We are transmitting an intelligence package now. It will contain information on your opposition, including their weaknesses, and secrets that we have recently intercepted. Use it well. Earth will have no patience for incompetence."

Veylan took a long breath forcing his mind into a deeper focus. The message had been clear. His rule was not only threatened from within, but it was now under scrutiny from beyond Pluto's icy borders. He had no choice but to act swiftly, and decisively.

Turning toward the console, he activated the data file that Devlin had sent to him. Streams of classified intelligence scrolled before his eyes. Within it were information on Kallos' forces and where they were stationed, potential weaknesses within the Terraformers, and the Outlanders' hidden supply routes. Every piece of data was a weapon waiting to be wielded.

Confidence flowed through him on receiving this information, it would be extremely valuable in the days ahead.

The Ice Wars would begin at First Light, but he did not intend to fight fairly.

CHAPTER TWO - THE FRACTURED COLONY

Pluto had originally been a research station, nothing more and nothing less to begin with. But when Earth's resources began to dwindle because of over-exploitation, they looked out into the wider Solar System for answers.

The asteroid belt had provided temporary relief, but Pluto's developers found superconductive mineral reserves lying there in plain sight, and it drew a lot of corporate interest. Thus, the full-scale development of Pluto began in earnest.

The first settlers had been miners, engineers, and security forces. They carved out a tenuous existence in underground caverns, shielding them from the brutal conditions above. As investment increased though, supply convoys started to arrive more regularly, enabling more permanent habitation to continue to flourish.

As the colony expanded in size, so did its demands, of course, on the resources it needed to support everyone. Increases in both the amount of recyclable breathable air and food production became paramount goals to achieve. Despite the development of systems set up to make Pluto self-sufficient, those on the planet still relied on outside help. Some dependency on Earth for specialized machinery and medicine, deemed absolutely necessary to obtain, remained a constant chokehold on the community.

Over time, Pluto's population surged, and with it so did resentment in the way it was run from Earth. The rigid quotas, corporate taxation, and oppressive laws that Earth insisted on imposing bred much dissent in everyone. The settlers, who had been hardened by survival in an unforgiving world, now grew unwilling to be governed by distant overlords from afar. When Earth's economy faltered and Pluto's supply shipments were deprioritized in favour of Mars and Europa, the colony teetered on the brink of collapse. On the planet, this caused desperation in the people, and with those who lead them too.

What followed on from this shaped Pluto's fate until this day. A coalition of miners, rogue industrialists, and rebel scientists declared independence, igniting a brutal war. For a decade, battles raged on in subterranean tunnels, across the barren plains of the planet, and even in orbit too. The Dominion retaliated ruthlessly, yet, despite a fearful battering from a far stronger foe, the rebels endured, and won the day.

Spread thin by conflicts across the solar system, the Dominion was eventually forced to withdraw its stranglehold on Pluto, relinquishing control and the impositions on it. But the freedom that was to come came at a huge cost, as the colony was now in ruins. Its infrastructure had been crippled, and without any central rule, a dangerous power vacuum emerged threatening to destabilise everything.

To restore order, Pluto's governing Houses were formed by those leaders of the day, each controlling a vital resource: namely, energy, food, trade and industry. The Supreme Chancellor system was established to prevent total chaos from breaking out; there would be one ruler, elected from the factions, tasked with preserving the fragile peace for all. But stability never lasted long. Assassinations, betrayals, and civil wars became the norm, as each Chancellor fought to hold onto power.

Over time, three major factions emerged, each holding a different vision for Pluto's future.

The Corporatists – Masters of Industry and Order

The Corporatists believed in structure, control, and prosperity. To their beliefs, Pluto required an overriding system that would look after everything for the people and one that required order, discipline, and economic expansion for it to work. From the moment humanity arrived, they turned Pluto into one of the industrial powerhouses of the Solar System. Administrators and Technocrats enforced the corporate laws to maintain order in the business world, which was flourishing. The working class however were expected to toil in the mines, factories, and processing plants, as their labour drove Pluto's commerce sector. Efficiency was paramount, and expected, and dissenters were swiftly removed and exiled.

In Corporatist-controlled areas like Erebus Prime, the economic output figures and targets governed daily life. Their rigid but tough system had made Pluto profitable, and its wealth was built on the production of rare elements, superconductors, and methane ice exports. Yet cracks were forming, as those in the underclasses felt the strain of long hours, hard work and meagre pay. The relentless demand for production strained the workforce to its limits, and whispers of unrest grew exponentially in those who had little say in matters. The system was strong, but could it last against the pressure that was building from within?

Supreme Chancellor Veylan and his deputies who ruled this faction remained resolute. They believed that Pluto was no place for weakness. Their vision was absolute dominance, to keep it as an economic power so unassailable that nothing could threaten them. As long as they held control, Pluto would never falter, never decay, and never fall into chaos.

The Isolationists – A Brotherhood Forged in Blood & Survival

The Isolationists saw Pluto as not just a colony, but as their hard-won home, forged through much sacrifice, hardship, and resilience. To them, survival was not about economics or politics, but sheer willpower instead. They had endured the freezing temperatures, fought in the tunnels, and lost loved ones to secure Pluto's freedom, taking great pride in the self-sufficiency that they were able to live on. They rejected external control upon them, and for everyone on the planet, believing that shared responsibility was a key for a good life. In their communities, no one lived in luxury while others starved, and no leader ever ruled above the will of the people. Kallos, beloved among them, led as their protector, and not as a king. Decisions were made by councils, where leadership was earned through one's ability to fight, to battle, to provide service to all, and to show loyalty too.

Their communities were rugged and spartan ones, prioritising endurance over comfort. They lived in Pluto's poorer districts, and their homes were designed for both survival and defence. Strength came from their endurance, their self-reliance, and their unity of purpose. They sought a Pluto free from distant rulers, rejected corporate rule, and had no time for dreamers who chased impossible ideals. To them, the war was not about power, no, it was about lasting freedom. They had bled and sacrificed much as a community, and they did not believe in surrender. So long as one Isolationist remained standing, Pluto would never kneel again.

The Terraformers – The Dreamers of a New Pluto

The Terraformers, who followed Prophet Hext saw Pluto not as a place that would continue to grind on following the status quo, but as a world waiting to be reborn. Where others saw a barren vista in front of them, they saw much potential, and a planet that could be nurtured and transformed into something far greater. Made up of scientists, engineers, and visionaries, they were all united by a single goal: to create a Pluto where people could thrive, free from the constricting domes and frigid isolation. Their mission was an immense one. Years of research had gone into studying Pluto's atmosphere, its subsurface oceans, and its geological composition. Through geoengineering, controlled atmospheric thickening experiments, and biological adaptation, they had taken the first steps toward making the planet habitable in the longer term.

Unlike those who exploited Pluto's resources, the Terraformers wanted to build a world of sustainability. Yet their greatest strength, and their greatest weakness, was the passage of time. Their vision spanned centuries, and they lacked the military power to enforce and impose their ideas on everyone in order to make a difference. They relied on long-term cooperation, much patience, and careful planning to achieve their aims. While others fought for dominance, they worked in the background, hoping their vision would endure long after the others had given up. One way or another, they believed that Pluto would become a world where everyday life would be totally free from the impositions that they currently lived under.

Aside from these three groups, Nyx Orban and the Outlanders retained their place on the Council as a remnant of a once-powerful faction that had fallen into steep decline. Centuries ago, the Outlanders had been pioneers, the very first individuals to venture beyond Erebus Prime's protective domes, and in so doing carving out settlements beyond the uninhabited wilderness. But war, famine, and the shifting political tides of those times reduced them to scavengers and raiders, as they ended up surviving on the edges of Pluto's civilization. Despite their diminished standing on the planet, their seat on the Council remained intact, as a relic of history, a symbol of their past glories, and a bitter reminder to the ruling elite that even those who might have been exiled and forgotten still could have a voice and an influence in Pluto's future.

Despite the conflicts and differences of opinion on the planet, Pluto's population had continued to grow and grow. Former prisoners exiled from Earth during the Dominion's final years were granted citizenship, in exchange for hard work in the mines and the industrial sectors.

Pluto had constantly been a world teetering on the edge of conflict and every Supreme Chancellor faced the same challenges. They had to keep their own faction satisfied while balancing the demands of their rivals to keep the peace. If he or she failed this test, then the colony could easily collapse into chaos, and this had happened plenty of times before.

With the declaration of a new contest for power looming shortly, the fragile peace that had recently endured was about to be shattered. As the planet braced for another battle for overall control, its people knew one thing with certainty - survival on Pluto had always come at a big price, and this time, it was likely that the cost would be higher than ever before.

CHAPTER THREE – THE REJUVENATION MACHINE

Veylan stepped into his private quarters, the heavily reinforced doors sealing shut behind him as he entered the living room. His residence was a vast, two-tiered structure; it was wood-panelled and very opulent, being the pinnacle of luxury on Pluto. Unlike the cramped, utilitarian quarters of the colony's workers, his home was filled with the luxuries of Earth containing imported mahogany bound furniture, silk-lined drapes framing the grand observation window, and genuine leather seating that had been shipped out to Pluto when he assumed his role as Chancellor. The walls were fortified by embedded heating panels, keeping the rooms cosily warm, contrasting with the stark chill of the world outside. A chandelier of crystalline fibres hung from the ceiling, mimicking the starlit sky above them all, and a fireplace, entirely unnecessary but indulgently aesthetic, flickered with artificial flames. Plush carpets from the Far East of Earth, an extravagance in a colony where resources were scarce, muffled his footsteps as he strode toward the main living area.

His wife, Lirien, stood by the grand observation window, gazing at the icy expanse beyond the dome. It was snowing again. She was tall and regal, with her silver-streaked black hair cascading over her shoulders; her emerald eyes were sharp and missed nothing. Their son, Steffan, sat in one of the high-backed chairs near the dining table, holding a cold beverage. He was younger than he looked, barely thirty, but had inherited his mother's piercing stare and unshakable will, as well as her dark hair, which was short and well-kept.

Veylan allowed himself a moment of respite. "The council was as tedious as ever," he muttered, heading to the crystal decanter on the side table. He poured himself a measure of deep amber liquor, watching as it swirled in the glass.

Lirien turned from the window, arms folded. "The Ice Wars are coming, Veylan. I assume that's what was decided," she sighed.

"At First Light," he confirmed, taking a slow sip. "The Outlanders and the Isolationists forced my hand. They refused to see reason."

Steffan frowned. "Maybe their reason differs from yours?" he questioned.

Veylan looked up from his drink and regarded his son for a moment before setting his glass down. "Careful, Steffan. We do not entertain doubt in this household."

Lirien sighed, and moved toward him, her movements graceful and caring. "Enough, for now, my love," she said, "You need to eat."

She retrieved a tray from the adjoining kitchen, setting down for him a meal of preserved meats, root vegetables grown in the subterranean farms, and a rich broth infused with protein supplements.

Veylan sat down, picking up his utensils, though his mind remained distant on more important matters. "Anything else of note happened today?" he asked without looking at her, "Were there any disturbances?"

Steffan, who knew there had been hesitated before replying to his question, "A supply convoy from the Outer Belt failed to check in Father" he replied," And the Terraformers think it's a sign of interference from the Corporatists."

Lirien added, "And the Eastern dome reported another structural failure. The Terraformers offered to assist with some reinforcement to help strengthen it, but the Council decided to dismiss their offer of help outright. You know, I think it's short-sighted of them. They know more about Pluto's geology than the rest of us put together."

Veylan shook his head in disagreement. "That Council is terrible," he replied, "and if they don't authorise someone to fix the problem, they will be dealt with."

Steffen then looked up at his father. "If you had been wise enough to consult with the Seers, wouldn't you have been able to predict these failures, father?" he queried.

Veylan looked back at his son as if he were mad, "Seers?" he said incredulously, "They are just charlatans, of no use whatsoever. Why should you think I would consult them?"

Lirien looked at him at this moment and was going to speak, but she said nothing more. She knew better than to push him further. She could see that her husband was in an irritable mood, and she well understood not to pursue something that he was already fixed on doing. Her priority was always to keep the peace and make sure that both Veylan and Steffan had all that they needed. They were very different individuals for sure, but she loved them both in her own caring way.

As he finished his meal, Veylan rose from his seat, looking at his wife with gratitude for her culinary skills. "I need to retire to my private chambers," he said. "Please do not disturb me."

He then stepped through a concealed doorway at the far end, holding his hand to the scanner before the door slid open, allowing him to enter the sanctum where only he was permitted. The chamber within was sleek, sterile, and filled with the advanced longevity treatments that had sustained him well past the lifespan of any ordinary human. He approached the advanced medical console, activating the sequence that would infuse his veins with the regenerative compounds Earth scientists had developed to prolong strong physical health and vitality. These had been developed for individuals carrying out long space flights, and times when they would spend weeks in minimal gravity. They prevented muscle loss, but it had been discovered that constant use in normal gravitational conditions actually improved one's health and vitality. These drugs were strictly controlled, were very expensive, and were allowed only to a very small group of selected individuals.

As the machine whirred into life, a set of robotic arms extended from the ceiling, lowering softly into place as they prepared the intravenous infusion. Veylan removed his outer garments, exposing skin that, despite his age, remained firm and relatively unmarked by time. A series of thin, silvery tubes connected to his forearms, feeding him a blue-coloured cocktail of nanotech-rich fluids into his bloodstream. The mixture then started to repair any cellular degradation in him, enhancing and quickening up how his brain processed too. The whole process was aimed at sustaining the strength and agility of a man half of his age. Since he had started this treatment, his hair, originally brown, flecked with grey and thinning, had grown back, much thicker and lusher. His sight had improved too; his hazel eyes were more focused and sharper, and he had stopped using reading glasses. His muscle tone had improved as well, and he looked more like a man of mid-forties, rather than of one of his actual age.

The first rush after the serum was administered was a familiar one, a creeping cold that spread through his limbs, followed by a sudden clarity of thought; as if the weight of his years had been momentarily lifted. His mind sharpened, the aches of the day faded, and a deep, artificial rejuvenation settled into his bones. The treatment was both a gift and a curse. Without it, he would wither into irrelevance, another relic of Pluto's harsh past. With it, he remained a force to be reckoned with, but at a cost. Each session took him further from the natural cycle of life, making him something neither wholly human nor machine-created.

As he reclined and lay back, his thoughts remained troubled. The contests ahead were inevitable, but the greater battle, the fight to shape Pluto's fate, was only just beginning. It would not be an easy few weeks ahead.

Veylan breathed deeply, his body still thrumming with the aftereffects of the treatment. He dressed and returned to the living room, where Lirien and Steffan had withdrawn into their sleeping quarters.

Seeing that he had a moment's peace, he strode toward his private communication office, put his hand to the scanner, and entered. He walked up to the terminal, keying in a secure frequency linking him into the Pluto command network. Moments later, a holo-display burst into life, revealing the stern, scarred appearance of Commander Aelric Mensen, his most trusted ally and second in command.

"Chancellor," Mensen greeted him, his voice as steady as ever.

"Meet me first thing at 07.00 hours, he instructed, "We must begin mobilisation as soon as possible."

Mensen nodded once. "Understood." he said, "I will ensure our forces are ready to go Sire. Kallos and his kind will not be given the chance to gain the upper hand this time around," he replied with confidence.

Veylan paused a second, and then with a sterner demeanour replied to his deputy.

"See that they don't," he said. "Pluto's future depends on swift, decisive action. I trust you will not fail me."

"I never have done," Mensen replied before the transmission cut out.

Veylan reclined again in his seat, his fingers crossed as if he were wishing for something. First Light. It was an ironic phrase, given Pluto's distant orbit and the feeble sunlight that reached through the atmosphere. But on this world, First Light was marked not by the Sun, but by the celestial dance of Pluto's moons. Every cycle, as Charon, Styx, Nix, Kerberos, Hydra and Dysnomia completed their orbits, there came a fleeting moment when their astronomical alignment caused a brief but measurable increase in illumination, a sparkling glow that passed over the ice plains like a whispered omen.

This was First Light on Pluto. And it had long been the moment chosen for change, a tradition stretching back to the first uprisings in the colony's history hundreds of years before. It was not the warmth of the Sun that heralded conflict, but the silent passage of distant moons, watching, waiting, converging: as history repeated itself once more.

CHAPTER FOUR - THE BEATING HEART OF THE PLANET

Everyday life on Pluto was a constant battle against the elements, but through their resilience, the people of the planet had managed to forge a fragile existence. The majority of them lived in Erebus Prime, known simply as the Hub. The colony was the planet's central city; it was a sprawling network of domes and subterranean corridors where most of the population lived.

Across the planet, these crystal-like domes extended far across protecting those who lived there from the dangerous icy terrain, with their reinforced exteriors shielding Erebus Prime against the relentless cold outside.

They were a vital part of the planet's infrastructure, and the integrity of them was all important. One of the most important jobs on the planet was carried out by teams of workers who constantly checked them to see that there were no cracks or failures in their structural integrity. Even one small failure could be catastrophic.

Inside them, artificial lighting mimicked Earth's daylight cycles, though many who lived there had abandoned the concept of day and night a long time ago. Enclosed streets bustled with workers, all types of traders and merchants, and executives rushed from place to place, navigating through the makeshift markets and information kiosks.

All Government systems, including banking and administration, were managed by PLAIN, the Pluto Legislative Artificial Intelligence Network. It had been programmed with strict limitations, and PLAIN could only intervene if the government collapsed entirely, serving as a last resort system against potential chaos.

Below ground, The Warren was where the Terraformers lived and worked. This protected region extended deep into Pluto's crust, and within it, the Terraformers laboured long hours to sustain life by tending to their network of vast hydroponic farms. These underground ecosystems represented a vision of Pluto's independence, and one they hoped, would provide for a future free from Earth's influence.

On the levels further below, mining operations formed the backbone of Pluto's economy. Workers, clad in insulated exo-suits, toiled for long hours in hazardous tunnels extracting methane clathrates, nitrogen, and rare metals too.

To the south of the Hub, the Indus Base connected Pluto to the solar system. A sprawling mix of landing pads, hangars, and administrative hubs, it was the planet's premier Spaceport. It received infrequent but vital shipments from Earth and other inhabited planets too. Guarding the base was a fleet of CX-100 fighter jets, a Triton Space Cruiser, and Eris Type Predator Starships, along with elite Technocrat troops tasked with preventing raids by the Outlanders and Independents, who scavenged for weapons and supplies wherever they could.

Political conflict often erupted around the Spaceport, as factions fought for control of Pluto's imports. The Terraformers sought ways to bypass Earth's stranglehold, and the Isolationists watched each arrival with suspicion and envy, while the Outlanders schemed and plotted to intercept crucial cargo as and when they saw an opportunity.

West of the Spaceport lay the Tartarus Penal Colony, once Pluto's most notorious prison, but now an abandoned relic. Built in the colony's early days, it had served as a dumping ground for Earth's criminals and political dissidents. With Pluto's devolution from Earth's direct rule, the prison was shuttered up and closed, leaving former inmates to integrate into Pluto society or perish.

South of Erebus Prime, the Corporatist Military Base housed several hangars, military barracks, and an arsenal of military hardware, including drone support systems, fuel tankers, and a force of thousands of troops and service staff. With First Light approaching, security was at its highest level, on alert for any disturbances.

Beyond the Hub, Pluto's frozen oceans concealed vast subterranean seas, kept liquid by huge tidal forces and geothermal activity that kept them at an ambient temperature. The Terraformers believed these hidden waters held the key to transforming Pluto into a thriving world, while the Isolationists feared reckless interference might just cause catastrophic failures to occur.

Above the horizon, Pluto's largest moon, Charon, emerged into view, and this satellite was home to a formidable military presence as a backup to that one on the main planet. Fortified bases based below the surface housed elite defence forces, prepared to travel over and quell uprisings or deal with external threats at a moment's notice. Warships patrolled the orbital expanse of space within the Pluto system, with their red and white flashing beacons a silent reminder to everyone below that nothing on Pluto went unwatched.

These forces were tasked with protecting the Corporatist leadership and ensuring Pluto's stability, whether from factional unrest or unknown dangers lurking beyond the solar system. Their mission was clear: to maintain order, suppress dissent, and preserve power for the Chancellor.

Deep below the colony, buried beneath miles of ice, lay the power cores and fusion reactors fuelled by deuterium extracted from Pluto's ice. They provided plentiful heat, breathable air, and energy to the domes, the mines, and the industrial zones. Without them, everything would collapse into darkness and ice, and life on the planet would become paralysed very quickly.

Down in these deep tunnels technician Daria Fennick wiped sweat from her forehead as she tightened the final bolt on the heat exchanger unit. Even underground, the work was gruelling. Below her the roar of the reactor cores vibrated through the metal flooring, providing a constant reminder of the raw power being created and being fed into the colony's infrastructure. She adjusted her visor and then scanned the readings on her wrist monitor.

"Fennick, report please," came a voice crackling through her earpiece; one belonging to Chief Engineer Kovacs.

"All good down here," she shouted out, " I've just finished recalibrating the exchanger unit. Efficiency's gone up by four percent."

Kovacs put his thumb up in approval. "Good. We need every bit of power we can get out of it. The Western Grid nearly blacked out this morning. Another spike like that, and we'll have a full-scale power failure on our hands."

Daria winced. "I thought we stabilized that sector last week?" she said.

"We did," Kovacs replied. "But demand is growing faster than we can compensate for. More people, more industries, more pressure on the reactors all the time. It's crazy. We're stretching these systems to their limits."

This was a truth every worker in the underground network understood. The power cores were old, their efficiency was waning, and they needed constant attention. Maintenance was forever needed, and breakdowns were an inevitable fact of life down here. Without fresh parts from Earth, something the Corporatists controlled tightly and were reticent to pay for, keeping Pluto operational was becoming a daily struggle.

Daria adjusted the coolant flow, watching the readings stabilize in front of her. It would hold for now, but she knew the system was running on borrowed time. Something had to change. Pluto couldn't sustain itself forever like this.

She removed her gloves and leaned against a bulkhead; she was utterly exhausted. Around her, the deep maintenance levels of Erebus Prime were alive with workers, some welding support beams, and others replacing worn-out components that should have been replaced years ago. A pair of apprentices struggled with a tangled mass of coolant lines, while a senior engineer shouted out orders at them from above. It was a chaotic, unforgiving job, but one that kept the entire colony alive.

She glanced toward the Central Control Station, a raised platform where Kovacs and his senior staff were monitoring the live power grid readings. The display screens were showing fluctuating energy demands, and the pressure levels were dangerously high. Emergency markers suddenly flashed red; warnings were going off that certain sectors were already near failure.

"Damn it," Kovacs muttered. "We lost power in the southern tunnels again. That's the third time this week."

Daria made her way over, peering at the readout. "That sector's running way over capacity," she noted, "They added three new industrial operations without adjusting their energy quotas. If they don't reroute their usage, they'll burn out the conduits completely."

Kovacs rubbed his forehead. "Tell that to the Corporatists. They think power grows on trees," he said knowing that the whole system needed major investment.

Daria looked at him incredulously. "They don't care, as long as the mines keep running, Jannik," she said in resigning herself to the fact.

Pluto's power grid was a battleground of competing priorities. The Corporatists controlled distribution, prioritising the industrial zones over residential sectors, which endured frequent blackouts. The Isolationists tried to rely on off-grid systems, while the Terraformers fought for energy reallocation to their environmental projects. Engineers struggled to keep the system running, caught in the middle of a political power play between the three factions.

Kovacs sighed. "I swear, one day this whole system is going to collapse. And when it does, we'll be the ones blamed for it," he said with a knowing look.

Daria nodded in agreement. "We keep patching the leaks, but at some point, the whole damn lot is going to break," she said.

A sudden alarm blared overhead, making them both turn their attention to the control board. A sector-wide failure warning flashed across the screen. Grid Seven was failing.

"Shit," Kovacs shouted as he slammed a button, opening a channel to their emergency response teams. "We've got a full blackout in Grid Seven! Get a repair team out there, now!" he shouted with panic in his voice.

Daria grabbed a toolkit and was already moving. "I'll go," she said willingly.

Jannik hesitated, then nodded to her. "Be careful Daria." he said, with compassion in his voice, "If the coolant pumps are shot to pieces up there, then that sector's going to be an icebox."

He knew Daria was one of the best and he didn't want her to be caught up in an accident that could be avoided.

Daria didn't need to be told twice. She sprinted through the maintenance corridors, the buzz of the power cores fading behind her fading as she climbed to the upper levels. This was life on Pluto; a never-ending fight to keep the colony running, and to keep the darkness at bay. And deep down, she knew Kovacs was right.

One day, this system would fail, and then everyone would be in trouble.

CHAPTER FIVE - THE WARLORD'S GAMBIT

General Kallos stood in the heart of his war cabinet. He was a towering figure of muscle and iron, and his face, a rugged mess of old scars, bore the marks of a lifetime spent in combat. His skin had been weathered from a hard life in the military. His complexion was white like marble while his blue eyes, bright and sparkly, held the glint of a man who had spent his life in the heat of battle, and loved every minute of it. His black hair was shaved close to his scalp, save for a streak of silver that ran along one side of it, a constant reminder of a plasma blade that had nearly ended his life two decades before.

His armour was a composite of reinforced plasteel and carbon fibre, and it bore the insignia of the warrior caste that he commanded; it had a big letter "I" in the middle of a logo surrounded by a constellation of stars. Unlike Chancellor Veylan, who clung to a myriad of technological advantages to run things and used his political instincts to get along in life, Kallos had forged his path with brute force and sheer bloody will. He had risen through the ranks not by inheritance or scheming, but through the betterment of those who had underestimated him. Born in the slums of the former prison complex, he had fought his way out of obscurity, firstly as a pit fighter, then as a soldier where he gained distinction in his service, and then finally as the general of Pluto's largest and most fearsome militia.

The war room was a cavernous chamber; its walls were lined with ancient banners alongside the trophies of conquered foes. A holographic display hovered and blinked before him, showing strategic data and vehicle movements across the local vicinity. It also detailed the location of his forces, the expected skirmish zones, and, most importantly, the projected strategies of his rivals. He had no illusions about the battle to come. They were a test of strength, as well as a game of survival. You had to be cunning, strong, and smart, and he knew he was. Tactics were very important to him, and he was a master of predicting what might happen around the battlefield. The last few decades had seen Veylan bend the rules to gain an advantage, securing any victories through subterfuge. This time, Kallos intended to win not only by force of will and muscle but also by exploiting any complacency that might have set in among the Corporatist forces, who believed that their supposed superiority guaranteed victory.

A voice broke the silence. "The war bands are ready, General," Joran shouted out.

Kallos turned to his second-in-command, Captain Joran Wallis, a man as ruthless as he was loyal to him. Joran was a veteran of combat, and he had the scars to prove it. He had lost a limb in battle several years ago, and now his mechanical right arm flexed as he adjusted the targeting settings on his wrist-mounted laser gun. He was a black man, with deep chocolate eyes, and stockily built.

"Good," Kallos replied. "Have they been briefed on the terrain yet?"

Joran nodded. "They know the ice fields like the backs of their hands," he confirmed.

"We've practised for this moment all month." he went on, "Veylan's forces will be tough, they are well trained, and they have the best equipment, but I am certain that we can defeat them."

And as for the Terraformers?" he said looking dismissively. "They're not warriors and they won't be a problem."

Kallos let out a low chuckle. "Never underestimate a Terraformer, Joran." he laughed, being sarcastic, "They have passion in their beliefs and those who fight for a cause fear nothing."

He winked at Joran, letting him know that this was said in complete jest.

He turned back to the holo-display, tapping a numbered sequence into the console in front of him. The screen shifted to show a map of Pluto, which displayed the expanse of the ice plains, illuminated only by the distant, faint light of the Sun. He could already picture the battlefield right now; it was an unforgiving where only the strongest would endure, and win.

Beyond the war cabinet, deep within Kallos' fortress, his army continued to prepare for battle. The barracks, a huge network of reinforced corridors, weapons stores and training grounds, were filled with the excitement of the men preparing for the conflicts to come. Kallos' soldiers inspected their weapons, adjusted their armour, and performed last-minute diagnostic checks on the cybernetic enhancements they had. The air in the training area was filled with the sound of constant chatter and anticipation.

Among the ranks, there were hardened veterans of past skirmishes, such as Corporal Gresty, veteran warriors who had fought and bled for their place in Kallos' army. But there were also the younger ones; those who had never known life beyond Pluto's ceaseless struggle but who had signed up to get some structure back into their lives. His soldiers did not question the traditions of the past and they were encouraged to fight for everything that could get. Kallos and his leadership gave them a cause to believe in. For them, this war would not be a curse, indeed it might be their only path to eventual honour and glory. Whether they were young or old, experienced or novices, the sum of the parts was what mattered. They backed each other, fought for each other, and cared for each other. This was the Isolationist's way.

At the edges of the fortress, heavy transporters stood ready, their engines revving constantly in the frigid air. Warmechs, towering machines of death, loomed over the ice fields, with their pilots running final checks before they would be deployed in the field. Space drones acquired from the Miranda rebellion forces around Uranus hovered above them, their red optics scanning every movement and ensuring no details were left unexamined. Rows of assault vehicles were ready to go too. They were fitted with reinforced armour and plasma cannons, and these were ideal for rapid deployment. Nearby, mobile artillery turrets loaded up with seismic warheads stood primed for the opening barrage.

The soldiers themselves in their survival suits carried an array of deadly weaponry. Yes, they were older models than those possessed by the Corporatist forces, but they were no less effective if used well. Their pulse rifles, graviton blades, and portable energy shields were designed to withstand even the fiercest of firefights.

Amidst the clanking of metal and the whir of machinery, rumours were spreading among the lower ranks. Newer recruits whispered nervously to one another, their hands tightening around their weapons that Veylan had dedicated death squads with cluster weapons, strictly prohibited in Ice Wars law. One of them, Vijay who was barely past his eighteenth year, turned to his older comrade with apprehension in his voice.

"Do you think we're ready?" he asked, his visor misting slightly in the frigid air.

The veteran beside him, a scarred warrior with a cybernetic arm, looked at him trying to build up the resolve of his younger comrade.

"Readiness doesn't matter, boy." he said, "When First Light comes, you fight, or you die."

Gresty saw the apprehension in his eyes, and put an arm around his shoulder, reassuring him that he would be able to deal with what was coming.

"But Veylan's forces… they have more resources, better tech…." the newbie replied.

The older soldier grabbed Vijay with a firmer grip.

"And we have something they don't." he said confidently, "We have Kallos, and we have each other. Under him, we have an unshakable belief that we will win! If you follow him, you live. If you doubt him, you're already dead."

Elsewhere, Kallos observed his forces through the war room's holo-feeds, and a sense of proud satisfaction settled over him. This was what he had spent his life building, a cohesive and tough-as-nails force that feared nothing; not even death itself. It was a machine; efficient, durable and able to work in the hardest of conditions.

He turned to Joran one last time. "Get the troops ready to march." he ordered, "No hesitations, no mercy. This cycle will end with us, and the new cycle begins with us."

Joran grinned, and gave Kallos a salute, "Glory to the strong." he bellowed.

Kallos nodded and repeated, "Glory to the strong!"

CHAPTER SIX - THE PROPHET AND THE SHADOW

Before First Light arrived, Erebus Prime stirred to life in hushed anticipation. The marketplace was usually a chaotic mix of traders and workers. This early morning it was quieter than usual, and it was filled with the muffled chatter of merchants setting up their stalls. Above them, one could hear the distant whirring of maintenance drones skimming over the streets. Condensation clung to the transparent dome overhead, as it distorted the glow of Pluto's moons, four of which were now above the horizon. The artificial gravity working deep below them kept everything in place, but there was a feeling of uncertainty in the air, and unspoken anxiety pervading through the people, as they prepared for yet another day.

In a modest café on the outskirts of the market square, Prophet Hext sat alone, with his long, nimble fingers clasped around a steaming cup of imported kahve. He was an imposing figure, though not in the same way as the iron-fisted chancellors of Pluto's past. They were from privileged backgrounds and had been polished and refined individuals, whereas he was showing his age a little and he did not care so much about his appearance. Character and morals were far more important to him than looks were.

Hext's face was lined with the years of struggle and hardship that had forged him. His long, silver-streaked hair had been pulled back in a loose tail, and his beard was neatly trimmed, but rather wild at the edges. He wore the dark green robes of the Terraformers in stark contrast to the sleek, silver and black attire favoured by the Corporatists or the navy blue of the Technocrats. His eyes were piercing grey, and the kind that betrayed a man who had already seen a lot in his life, and who had carried many burdens on his back already.

Born in the mines, and raised among those who toiled in the dark, Hext had known nothing but hardship for the first part of his life. His father had died in a tunnel collapse when he was still a child. His mother succumbed to sickness soon afterwards, leaving him to be raised by the workers who had become his new and immediate family. He had learned from his youth that Pluto would never be tamed easily, but its depths could hold the key to the population's long-term survival. In the subterranean farms, where crops were nurtured under the artificial lights, he had seen the future. Now he believed in a Pluto that did not rely on Earth's help and a Pluto that could sustain itself. He had spent decades championing this vision and rallying those who believed that they could turn the rock around them into something more than just a barren prison world. The Terraformers had been his life's work, but now, on the eve of war, he wondered if it had all been in vain.

A soft chime from his wrist console pulled him from his thoughts, making him glance down at the encrypted message flashing on his screen:

"Where?" it said.

Hext tapped a reply: "North Quarter Market. Enceladus Café."

He set the device down, taking another sip of his drink which was now starting to cool a little; his eyes checking around the room. The café was small but well-frequented, and its owner, a stout woman named Marli, was bustling between tables with mechanical efficiency. A few miners sat hunched over in the far corner. Their faces appeared weary, and their conversation seemed muted. A Corporatist clerk, dressed in the stiff, regulation black uniform of the trade offices, sat near the counter; she was absently scanning reports on a data slate. Another group of young workers ate in hurried bites while they were exchanging nervous glances; they were seemingly whispering about the coming conflict. The agitation in the café was unspoken but omnipresent, woven into every gesture and half-heard murmur that Hext observed. People knew that Pluto was perched on the edge of something dangerous, and no one could quite say which way it would fall.

Then, the door chimed, and a hooded figure stepped inside.

Hext barely reacted, only lifting his cup slightly as the figure moved through the café with deliberate slowness. The stranger's cloak was heavy, draping over their form to obscure any identifying features. The figure approached Hext's table, sitting without a word. For a moment, they simply observed each other, as the low buzz of chatter in the café filled the silence between them.

Both men subtly observed what was going on around them. The clerk was still lost in his reports. The miners were deep in their own discussion. Marli was too preoccupied with her work to pay them any attention. Only when Hext was satisfied that no one was watching and listening, did he lean forward slightly.

"You took a risk coming here," he murmured.

The hooded figure chuckled softly. "You're one to talk," he teased, "You're not exactly inconspicuous."

Hext grinned but didn't reply immediately. Instead, he reached out for the small metal disc embedded in the table's centre. He touched it and it activated the café's privacy field. A faint glimmer surrounded them now, ensuring that any external listening devices would not pick up anything but static as they began to chat.

The hooded figure pulled back their hood just enough to reveal their face. It was Steffan, the Chancellor's son.

Hext stayed unmoved, but inwardly, he felt a nervous churn of uncertainty. Steffan was an enigma, a man born into privilege, yet always teetering on the edge of rebellion. He had never openly declared his allegiance to the Terraformers, nor had he defied his father in any public capacity. But here he was, sitting across from Hext, risking everything by meeting him in secret.

"You're either desperate or reckless," Hext said, searching for confirmation as to why this young and privileged man was sitting across from him at this moment.

Steffan looked back at him. "Perhaps both?" he replied.

There was a momentary pause between them before Steffan became visibly concerned.

"Conflict is inevitable now," he said,

"First Light is upon us, and when it comes, you do know that my father will not hesitate," he warned. "If you're not ready, he'll crush you before you can even act."

Hext looked at him as if the young man didn't quite get his full motivations just yet.

"I don't intend to take him on in a fight, as we aren't strong enough." conceded Hext,

"But If it comes down to a pitched battle," he went on, " I'll quite happily let Veylan and Kallos slug it out."

"But Steffan..." he said, looking more intently at him, "We *are* ready."

"Under my guidance have been preparing for this moment for years, and I intend to show you the right way," he said with a smile.

"We will not win the war for control, but my aim is to win the war for ideas," he said, "and neither of those two have the foresight that we have."

Steffan studied him closely and seemed more convinced by what Hext was suggesting.

"I know you've always believed in a future where Pluto thrives, and where its people build something better." he said, "But my father... he just doesn't care about the future. His only goal is retaining power, and he will burn this world down before he lets it slip from his grasp."

Hext sighed, rubbing his temples. "Your father is a dangerous power-mad individual for sure, Steffan," he said, "But he doesn't have the vision that we have."

Hext tried to reassure the young man, but he also wanted answers too.

"The question is..." he asked looking directly into his eyes, "What are you? What do you believe in? What do you want Steffan? Who's vision of the future do you support?"

He wasn't expecting to be questioned in such a manner, but it served to stiffen his resolve more.

He breathed deeply, his fingers grabbing around the edge of the table.

"Someone who wants to stop him," he said forcefully, "and I want the best for everyone on this planet."

Hext watched him carefully, and he was pleased. This was what he wanted to see and hear, and he knew that Steffan was different from his power-loving father. He saw something in the young man's eyes, a flicker of determination, and defiance too.

"Perhaps, in another life, Steffan would have been one of them sooner?" he thought, "Perhaps, in the end, he still could be?"

The Prophet of the Terraformers sat back, finishing the last of his kahve. "Then join us," he said, his voice both strong and hushed. "I have a plan and a new vision. Let's talk strategy."

CHAPTER SEVEN - THE DISILLUSIONED SON

Steffan had never been meant to rule. That was what his father had always told him in quiet moments between his meetings. He had given him curt and quite withering reprimands, often delivered after council sessions.

"You are too soft, too idealistic," he had reprimanded him. Veylan had raised his son in the pressurised halls of power, but he had never expected him to wield power himself. Power, in his father's eyes, was not a thing to be earned, nor was it a responsibility to be carried. It was a force to be seized by your resolve and character and held onto with an iron grip, otherwise it might slip away in an instant.

Steffan had once believed in his father's vision, and he wanted, initially at first to be like him. He watched, learned, listened and copied. He tried to be tough and ruthless, and he found out over time that this was not his way. It wasn't the terrible manner that he treated people that turned him against his father, but instead, it had been a series of incidents; ones buried beneath layers of secrecy, which had caused Steffan to distance himself from him.

The first of these had happened ten years before when Steffan was barely twenty years old. A mining accident in the Outer Belt had caused a deep fissure in one of Pluto's largest underground tunnels where they were drilling for iron ore. Hundreds of workers had been trapped as the tunnels collapsed around them. The artificial gravity stabilizers had then malfunctioned sending entire sections of the mine spiralling into complete chaos. Rescue operations had been sent swiftly to the danger scene to try and rescue any victims, but what Steffan had witnessed that day had shattered the foundation of his belief in his father's rule.

The Terraformers had been the first to respond to the tragedy long before the Corporatist elite had even acknowledged the disaster. They had sent engineers, as well as medics and equipment to stabilize the wreckage. They had worked tirelessly to save those still buried beneath the rocks, and they did try and do everything they could to save their fellow citizens. And yet, when the Council finally intervened, it was not with help or aid, but with orders to abandon the site.

"The mine is lost," Veylan had declared. "Resources must not be wasted on futile efforts and the workers should have known the risks."

Steffan had argued and pleaded with his father over this, and he even defied direct commands for him to remain in his father's presence. Instead, he took it upon himself to travel out to the site himself, descending into the ruined tunnels alongside the Terraformers. What he saw haunted him still to this day. He had viewed the gasping survivors, and many bodies twisted beneath tons of collapsed debris. Those affected showed desperation in their eyes, and those working in the danger zone had been furious with the attitude of the Chancellor who deemed all of those who had fought to live only to eventually die, to be deemed expendable.

When Steffan had returned home, his father had not raged. He had not struck him, nor even raised his voice. Instead, he had simply looked at him with a quiet, measured disappointment, as if Steffan had failed some unspoken test.

"Your heart will make you weak," Veylan had said. "Don't let it destroy you."

But Steffan had let it destroy something far greater, his trust in his father, which was starting to wane.

Steffan had long understood that trust was a currency his father did not believe in. Vaylen was a ruler who valued strength, control, and strategic dominance, but he never accepted sentiment. Over the years, Steffan had watched his father test those closest to him, pushing them to their limits, and discarding those who failed; only those he deemed the strongest did he allow to rise to near the top. But it wasn't until he was twenty-two that Steffan realized, with brutal clarity, that he too was merely a subject of his father's constant trials.

At the time, Steffan had been tasked with overseeing a major negotiation with a group of independent merchants. This was an operation that would secure crucial Lithium supplies to Pluto, ones that the Corporatists desperately needed. The merchants were not allies to the Dominion, nor were they part of the Isolationist or Terraformer factions. They were opportunists and smugglers; the kind of traders who made their living playing both sides. Steffan had spent weeks working on the deal, ensuring it was beneficial for the Corporatists, while trying to keep the merchants at ease. He believed that through careful diplomacy and gentle persuasion, he had managed to secure a steady flow of these Lithium compounds. This would have been beneficial to Pluto, as the deal, if it were to happen, would be able to bypass many of Earth's strict supply regulations.

Then, on the night of the final agreement, it all fell apart in front of his eyes.

The meeting was set in the lower sectors of Erebus Prime, away from prying eyes and in a neutral zone where neither the Dominion nor the Isolationists factions had any direct control. Steffan arrived on time, expecting a tense but ultimately successful negotiation. But instead of finding himself in discussions, he walked straight into an ambush.

A group of Technocrat enforcers in their navy-blue uniforms, his father's men, were already there, and surrounding the merchants before placing them in restraints. Some of the traders were already dead, and their bodies were slumped against cold steel walls. Others were under arrest, and they knelt with their hands behind their heads, forced onto their knees by the heavily armed guards. The air smelled of burning from discharged pulse rifles, and Steffan could still feel the heat from the gun barrels that had fired the deadly shots.

Suddenly a vibration against his wrist had startled him, and he instinctively looked down at it. Vaylen's face came to life on his holo-watch; he was smiling in a slightly sinister manner.

"Why was he calling right now?" Steffan wondered.

He was soon to find out.

"Steffan," Vaylen said smoothly, his voice calm but expectant. "How did the negotiations go?"

Steffan swallowed, still in shock at the scene unfolding around him. He was feeling pretty uncomfortable as he struggled to find the words.

"They…"

He took a breath, regaining his composure. "The deal was in place. We had an agreement. The merchants were willing to work with us and I had secured a reliable supply chain, one that would benefit us long-term."

Vaylen's eyes glinted and his smile widened slightly.

"And yet, here you are, standing among the corpses of your so-called business partners." he said, "Do you truly believe they would have honoured their word?"

Steffan looked perturbed. "Yes," he said, his voice filled with frustration. "We needed this trade, Father. This could have helped us stabilize our Lithium supplies."

Vaylen shook his head abruptly as if speaking to a child.

"Your naivety disappoints me, Steffan." he said, as he started to get irritated with him, "Did you really think securing an agreement was the test?"

Steffan frowned, his anger rising. "You set this up?" he asked, fearing the worst.

"I needed to see how you would handle betrayal," Vaylen continued, his voice steady. "Every leader is confronted with it. Only those who act with decisive strength survive it."

Veylan's expression had now turned more menacing and more calculating too.

"What did you do when you saw your negotiation was a farce?" he inquired, "Did you kill them first? Did you recognize the test before the gunfire started?"

Steffan froze and started to sweat. He had been so focused on securing the deal, and on proving himself capable of diplomacy, that it never occurred to him that his father never wanted a deal at all.

"This was never about trade, was it?" Steffan muttered, suddenly coming to some realisation of what was going on.

"You were watching me," he said accusingly.

"Of course," Vaylen confirmed as if it were obvious. "A future ruler must understand that strength is the only true currency. You've spent too much time trying to talk your way into getting that deal."

He gestured subtly, and then one of the enforcers aimed a rifle at the kneeling prisoners.

"So, tell me, Steffan, what is your next move?" he asked, "Will you be the one to show them that crime doesn't pay?"

One of the Technocrat agents following Veylan's orders then gave him his laser gun.

Steffan felt every pair of eyes on him. The soldiers looked at him, the doomed merchants pleaded for mercy, and his father looked harshly at him too. He felt physically sick, because this was his moment to prove himself, and he didn't want to. His father was giving him a choice… but it was no real choice at all.

He could pull the trigger, and he could follow his father's orders. But how would he live with himself if he did? He could pass his father's test, but then what would happen?

Steffan's hands were shaking with fear, and following the morals within him, he lowered the weapon in his hands and gave it back to the blue-suited agent.

"No," he said quietly, shaking his head. "This test is pointless. I can't do it."

Vaylen's looked with some disbelief at his son.

"Excuse me?" he said.

"They were never a threat," Steffan said firmly. "You weren't testing me… you were wasting resources and murdering for show. That's not strength, Father. That's cruelty!"

There was silence on the other end of the line…

Steffan saw a trace of something in Vaylen's demeanour. Was it disappointment? Or amusement? He couldn't quite tell…

The Supreme Chancellor was in no mood for mercy this day, and he gestured again to his agents.

"Guards," he said with ruthless authority, "Kill them!"

A barrage of laser pulses rang out. The prisoners slumped forward, lifeless…

Vaylen looked intently at Steffan for a long moment to see his reaction before speaking again. "Perhaps you are not as strong as I had hoped," he said with disappointment.

And with that, the holo-feed cut out.

Steffan stood stock still, his stomach twisting with utter disgust. His father had used him as bait. He had let him think he was negotiating in good faith, and all the while setting him up to prove his ruthlessness. And Steffan had failed.

His trust in Vaylen had now gone. Whatever illusions he had about diplomacy, or reason, had been totally shattered. His father ruled by fear and deception, and Steffan finally understood that he would never be anything more than a pawn to him.

That night, Steffan did not return to the palace. He knew by now that his father would always see him as weak. And for the first time, he began to think that weakness was not something to be ashamed of; in fact, it was what set him apart from the monster that had raised him.

A single incident, just one year later, cemented Steffan's hatred in him forever.

It happened by accident. His father had retired for one of his regular rejuvenation treatments, it was a process that rendered him unavailable for an hour or so. Veylan's treatments had become more frequent in recent years, and each session while extending his life and vitality, also made him more dependent on the next one. This moment when his father retired was one when the household was left in a rare, fleeting silence, and yet amazingly they never knew what he was actually doing in his private sanctum.

This day, Steffan found himself drawn to his father's private communications office; a room he had only entered a handful of times under supervision. But now, he was alone. He went to the dark oak panelled door, which had been imported from Earth years before, and put his hand to the scanner next to it.

The biometric lock recognized him as a family member and allowed him entry without any questions. The door closed shut behind him, sealing him into a space bathed in bright, ambient light. Rows of screens lined the walls displaying real-time transmissions, some decrypted intelligence and classified reports too. This place was his father's communications hub, where he did a lot of his work.

At first, Steffan had no intention of prying. He merely stood there, taking in all of the reams of information flowing through the Chancellor's private domain. But then… a blinking notification caught in his eyeline.

A message marked *classified* sat open on one of the terminals; it was waiting to be acknowledged. His pulse quickened as he stepped forward, drawn in by the sheer intrigue of what it might contain. His father was meticulous, and nothing was ever left unsecured or to chance.

He hesitated only for a moment before his fingers brushed over the console, scrolling through the latest reports. There were trade negotiations and fleet maintenance logs, some encrypted diplomatic communiqués. And then… a file labelled *Treason Inquiry: Aelin Hart* popped into view.

Steffan started to sweat profusely. He breathed hard and then clicked it open.

The screen flooded with damning details on Aelin. Surveillance logs were here as well as intercepted messages plus evidence on him collected over months. His closest friend, Aelin, had been accused of treason.

The Terraformers. That's what they had tied him to, for being an informer and a critic of the state. This was the very faction that his father sought to eliminate, and the very people Steffan had come to admire from a distance. Aelin hadn't been planning an attack or an assassination, or anything treasonous in Steffen's eyes. There was no violent conspiracy either that he was part of. His only crime had been speaking of a future beyond Veylan's rule, and that to his father was tantamount to treason for him.

The final entry was a directive. Immediate detainment pending judgment. *Recommended sentence: Execution.*

Steffan stepped back as though his heart was on fire.

"This was beyond evil," he thought. This was also personal. He had come here expecting nothing; he was just passing through the silent halls of his father's estate as he had done a thousand times before, and instead, he had uncovered a truth that changed everything for him.

For years after this incident, Steffan remained a peripheral figure within the halls of power. He was watching, listening, learning and silently furious at the attitude of his father. He couldn't say anything though, as he feared the consequences if he did.

At official functions, he would play his part well, by nodding in the right places, and only speaking when expected to do so. But beneath it all, he was seething, and oh so angry. He would, in time, teach his father a lesson he would never forget he vowed to himself, but doing so would entail him to take many risks. He did not want to experience the same fate as his late friend had done.

He began slipping away at night, venturing into the underground sectors and the forgotten districts where the Terraformers had built their quiet resistance. He listened to their teachings, and the words of Prophet Hext, as he began to imagine a Pluto that could sustain itself. He increasingly wanted a world that was free from Earth's grip, and free from the Corporatists who hoarded power over everyone else. At first, Steffan had told himself he was merely gathering intelligence in seeking to understand the Terraformers' true motives. But the more he listened, the more he found himself agreeing and converting himself to their ideas and principles.

Pluto was not merely a colony, nor was it a distant outpost for Earth's ambitions. No, it was his home, and if it was ever to be more than that, and if it was ever to truly thrive, then it needed something greater than his father's tyranny to guide its future.

Steffan's first true act of defiance had come three years before when he had quietly begun leaking classified infrastructure reports to the Terraformers. He revealed weaknesses in the Corporatists' power grids, he detailed the supply shortages that plagued the outer colonies, and he provided tactical data to the Terraformers that the Council had tried to suppress. It was a dangerous game to be sure, and Steffan knew that if he were ever caught, there would be no trial, nor no leniency either. His father would have him executed without hesitation.

And yet, the risk had felt was worth it.

And now, here he was, seated across from the man he had once thought of as an enemy, speaking not as an informant, but as his ally.

As First Light approached, Steffan knew there would be no turning back for him. His father would never forgive him, especially once the war began. And the Terraformers, despite their idealism, would not hesitate to use him if it meant securing Pluto's future for the longer term. He was not a hero, nor a saviour and he was merely a man caught between two worlds, and standing at the edge of history with no clear path forward.

But for the first time in years, he felt certain that he was following the path that he had always been destined to journey along.

Pluto did not belong to his father. It did not belong to the Earth either. It belonged to those who had bled for it, and to those who had built it with their hands and their sweat.

And he would fight with all his might to make sure it stayed that way.

CHAPTER EIGHT - WASTELAND QUEEN

The Outlands were a death trap to most normal individuals, but to Nyx Orban and her people, they were their home. Beyond the domes of Erebus Prime, and past the towering black walls that protected the settlement's privileged inhabitants, was an endless desert of ice-filled desolation. The landscape was a shattered expanse of methane, it was wild, filled with crevasses and hauntingly beautiful, with rivers of nitrogen slush flowing sluggishly through ancient chasms. The air was too thin to breathe out here, but the Outlanders had learned to survive where others normally perished.

To address this and to allow humans to survive in this most harsh of environments, scientists had developed advanced mechanical counterpressure suits to survive in the wild. Nyx and her followers had stolen a consignment intended for Charon's inhabitants, now enabling them to survive where others couldn't. When going outside, they donned these sleek, form-fitting suits that clung to their bodies like a second skin. The suits, inspired by the concept of mechanical counterpressure, applied direct compression to the wearer's body, allowing them comfort without the bulk of the type of traditional spacesuit. Camouflaged and crafted from advanced, and flexible materials, the suits allowed for a full range of motion, enabling the Outlanders to move with agility across the treacherous terrain.

Integrated into the suit was a compact life support system, discreetly housed within it to avoid obstructing identification of who was wearing it. A streamlined helmet, transparent and minimalistic, provided a clear view of the wearer's face and head while being able to supply breathable oxygen and filter out harmful gases. The suit's inner layers were equipped with thermal regulation technology, ensuring warmth against the external temperatures that plunged far below freezing. This combination of pressure maintenance, life support, and thermal controls allowed the Outlanders to traverse their icy world without sacrificing either mobility or identity.

Nyx their leader stood within the ruined mining platform that jutted out from the ice, with her binoculars scanning the horizon. Her followers, a band of a dozen hardy souls, huddled closely behind her. The Outlanders had no domes to shield them, nor any regulated environments or filtration systems. Instead, they had adapted themselves, turning scavenging into an art form, and transforming wrecked mining equipment into shelters, as well as finding sustenance where no one else dared to look.

Their settlement, known only as the Hollow, was an abandoned subterranean refinery, long since stripped of its valuable ores by the Corporatists. Now, it belonged to those who had been cast out, some plus exiled criminals, escaped prisoners, debtors, and those who simply refused to live under Erebus Prime's rigid rules. It was a maze of tunnels and ice caverns that were warmed by geothermal vents that just about kept the frost at bay. Their homes were fashioned from salvaged metal and reinforced glass, and their power was drawn from stolen solar cells and old fusion generators scavenged from derelict outposts.

Food was always a challenge for everyone out here. The Outlanders never had enough to sustain them, so they did what outlaws had always done: they took what they needed.

Raids on Corporatist supply convoys were their lifeblood. Wrapped in their survival suits that blended seamlessly with the terrain, the Outlanders would strike without warning; their sleek hover-skiffs gliding over the ice with near-silent precision. They knew the planet's make-up better than anyone, from every fissure to every hidden crevice. They struck under cover of the eternal twilight, dismantling supply transports before vanishing back into the ice storms. Some among them had once been Corporatists themselves, a few soldiers or engineers who had grown disillusioned with the regime and decided to defect to the wastelands. Nyx herself had once been the daughter of an engineer. That life had been stolen from her when her parents had been executed for treason back over 10 years ago. Why they had been killed she did not know. She had been left for dead with her sister, but fortunately, they had not died. She had since learned, she had survived, and her independent spirit and bravery had led her to this moment.

Now, she ruled over the Outlanders, which was made up of a small but very resourceful band of followers. There was no hierarchy among them, and no rigid structure either, only respect earned through showing strength and cunning. Those who could not fight and those who could not pull their weight were left behind. In the Hollow, any weakness would lead to inevitable death.

Tonight, Nyx gathered her people atop the platform. They stood in silence, with their weapons holstered but never far from reach. They had intercepted a shipment two nights ago; a good haul of energy cells, ration packs and medical supplies meant for the Corporatist elite. It was a small victory, but they needed more. With the conflict beginning at First Light, the Corporatists would tighten their grip on supplies, so the Outlanders had to move fast.

A scout approached them with his breath fogging the air inside his helmet.

"Nyx, it's almost time," he said breathing hard.

She turned to him, her voice steady. "Is the next raid set?" she asked, "We're not gonna have another chance once conflict fully takes hold."

The scout nodded.

"Yeah," he said, "I spotted a supply drop near the Outer Belt. Noticed it was lightly guarded by those bastards in black and silver. If we move now, we can hit'em before they reach the main gate."

Nyx folded her arms, considering. "And the Techno goons?" she asked. "Any movement from their forces?"

A second Outlander, a woman named Lysara, spoke up.

"They've reinforced their patrols, but they still don't know the area as we do." she said, "They keep sending newbies out here, and they're sitting ducks. If we time it right, we'll be in and out before they realize."

Nyx considered her options, her mind already forming the plan.

"Alright, we move fast, hit hard, and disappear before they know what's happened." she said, "Dren, you take point with the spotters.

Lysara, you and I will lead the assault team. Silent takedowns only, we don't want them calling in reinforcements. The second we've got the supplies, we split. No heroics. Got it?"

The Outlanders murmured their assent to the plan and adjusted their gear.

Dren crouched by a makeshift holo-map spread out on a crate.

"The drop zone is just past the ice ridge over the far side." she said pointing out where it was, "We've probably got a ten-minute window before their scheduled transport pickup. Best guess, a couple of guard units, one stationed near the crates, the other patrolling a hundred metres out."

Nyx studied the layout. "And what's in these supplies?" she asked.

"Mostly fuel cells, rations, and a few crates marked with high-priority tech." she said, "My guess? Either medical gear or parts for their drones."

Nyx smiled. "Then let's make sure they never get them," she said.

The methane ice storm continued to sweep over the icy dunes as Nyx and her team crawled into position. From their vantage point behind a jagged ridge, they could just see the Technocrat transport and an armoured supply crawler, both parked near a row of heavy crates. Two black-and-silver-clad sentries stood guard at the supply drop, their plasma rifles at the ready. Further out, a patrol of three Technocrats moved in slow, predictable patterns, their protective visors glowing faintly.

Nyx gestured with two fingers… go silent… take them out clean.

Dren and Lysara slipped forward first. The nearest guard had barely had time to react before Dren's stun gun knocked him out motionless. Lysara hooked an arm around the second, twisting his head sharply and he fell to the ground motionless.

The patrol was next.

The Outlanders waited in the darkness, timing their strike just as the patrol turned their backs. Three silent takedowns and no alarms followed.

Nyx crept toward the supply crawler, quickly scanning the crates. Rations. Ammunition. Spare power cores. But something else caught her eye… a reinforced case with Dominion insignia.

"This is good," she whispered. "Get it loaded."

Lysara worked fast, strapping the priority crate to a speeder sled while the others secured fuel cells and weapons. But then… a distant sound caught their attention.

Dren swore under his breath. "Incoming transport guys. Looks like a patrol skiff, small, but armed."

Nyx's heart pounded quickly, their exit window was closing fast.

"Then we don't stick around," she snapped. "Lysara, take the sled and go. Dren, you cover them. I'll set charges on the crawler; we make sure they don't recover a damn thing."

Lysara yanked the sled free and hauled the stolen gear toward their escape route. Dren covered the rear, by dropping behind a crate and levelling his pulse laser toward the oncoming patrol.

Nyx worked fast, as she slapped a series of small detonite charges onto the crawler's fuel line. The Thirty-second timer was set giving them enough time to get out.

The engines of the incoming patrol grew louder and louder as it closed in.

Fortunately, Nyx bolted just in time.

They had just cleared the ridge when the supply crawler erupted in a deafening explosion, sending flames and debris high into the sky.

The patrol skiff veered wildly; with its pilot taken off guard by the blast, throwing him to the snowy ground.

Lysara yelled into her comms. "We're clear! Get to the fallback point!"

As the Outlanders vanished into the ice storm, Nyx allowed herself a single satisfied breath.

They had won this round.

Back at the Hollow, Nyx glanced at the storm on the far horizon. It was clearing now. "Lucky the weather had been so awful," she thought. It had masked the raid perfectly. So then.... what was in that Dominion case?

"Open it up Jessa," Nyx asked.

She duly took her pulse laser from its holster, took aim, and fired. With a sharp click, the case sprang open. Inside, lined up in perfect rows, were Dominion hand-held missile launchers, still gleaming with their factory sheen.

"Well, well," she murmured, running a finger over one of the sleek barrels.

"Looks like we just levelled the playing field a bit," she said to the others, holding one aloft. Indeed, these *would* come in very handy in the future she thought...

Suddenly Nyx looked up and pointed to the stars. The rest of the Outlanders turned their eyes skyward, towards the distant heavens, dotted with galaxies and the Milky Way above. The moons of Pluto - Charon, Styx, Nix, Kerberos, Dysnomia and Hydra had begun to align. It was a rare celestial event; the rarest of moments when all six moons in unison cast their reflected glow across their frozen world. The Outlanders nicknamed it the *Way of Light*, a beautiful and fleeting pathway in the sky that guided them through the darkness. To them all it was an omen, and a sign that the cycle was beginning anew.

Above the planet, a single shaft of light began to spread and move, just like a thin golden blade slicing through the darkness. It moved slowly at first illuminating the domes of Erebus Prime, and with it casting strange reflections across the glassy exteriors of the colonies. The spaceport, usually a collection of dimly blinking flood lights, gleamed with an almost unnatural brilliance as the glow traced its way across its landing pads. The city streets and the markets, lined with towering metal structures basked for a moment in the fleeting radiance, before the light continued its slow journey, onwards and onwards sweeping across the plains.

It reached the Hollow last of all, touching the ice with soft, golden luminescence. The Outlanders stood still with their hearts filled with awe and wonder. For just a brief second, it was as though the planet itself had come alive, and in that moment revealed its harsh beauty in ways few ever saw.

Lysara whispered beside her. "It's starting. It's absolutely gorgeous."

"Yes, it is!" Nyx agreed. "First Light is here. The war begins."

Around her, the Outlanders smiled with joy and wonder, and smiles appeared on their faces. They had no allegiance to the Corporatists, the Isolationists or the Terraformers. Instead, they answered only to themselves. But in the chaos of war, there would be opportunities aplenty.

Nyx turned to her people and gave one last order. "Prepare yourselves, guys. Things are going to get tasty before the moons fade," she said.

The Outlander band let out a whoop of anticipation while adjusting their weapons and strapping on their gear. Above them, the hazy glow of Pluto's moons would bathe the landscape in light for a few more minutes, before the spectacle swept out of view.

And as the Way of Light illuminated the wasteland beyond, the Outlanders moved to take their fate into their own hands.

CHAPTER NINE - THE GATHERING STORM

Chancellor Veylan stood at the expansive viewport of the command bridge at Harris Point. From his vantage point, the slow, shifting glow of First Light swept across directly in front of him. The golden hue reflected off the domes of Erebus Prime in the distance, illuminating the sprawling colony with an ethereal brilliance. The streets, which were normally shrouded in perpetual twilight, glistened under the celestial glow, and for a moment, it looked almost peaceful. But Veylan knew better than that. This was going to be the calm before the storm to come.

His chief general, Commander Mensen, stood beside him, observing the planet below with a calculating look.

"The time has come, Supreme Chancellor," Mensen said. "We must send word to our forces on Charon. They need to mobilize immediately."

Veylan nodded and activated the main communication terminal.

"This is Supreme Chancellor Veylan to Charon command." he announced, "Initiate full planetary deployment. The Isolationists are waiting for us to make the first move, but we will dictate the tempo of this war. Begin launch sequence and set course for Pluto."

A moment of silence followed, and then a clipped response crackled through the terminal. "Acknowledged, Supreme Chancellor. We are mobilizing all forces now."

From within the massive Corporatist military spaceport carved into the rock of Charon, the fleet suddenly roared into life. Large hangar doors, which had been hidden beneath layers of reinforced ice and rock, roared with a deafening sound. Within these enormous caverns, warships that had lain dormant in their launch bays were suddenly alive with flashing lights and the rumble of engines warming up.

Inside the barracks, the Corporatist soldiers scrambled into position, with their black and silver armour glinting under the red emergency lighting. Officers barked rapid orders at them, as squads of marines rushed to their assigned drop ships. Pilots sprinted to their support fighters with their helmets in hand, diving into their cockpits as deck crews signalled the all-clear. The smell of burning fuel filled the hangars, as their engines powered up, sending shuddering vibrations through the launch platforms.

"All stations, prepare for launch," the fleet commander announced. "Engage thrusters on my mark. We will deploy in formation - no deviations."

One by one, the Corporatist Troop Transporter warships disengaged from their moorings. The first ships to ascend were the strike fighters, darting out of their launch tubes in tight formations. Following on from them, massive destroyers rose from the base, their landing supports retracting as they ascended from the dusty ground with their engines glowing orange as they manoeuvred into orbit. Finally, the colossal flagship the *Iron Will*, the pride of the Corporatist fleet, began its ascent. This was a huge fighting machine of reinforced plating and devastating firepower.

The fleet formed up in disciplined formations above Charon, with each vessel aligning into its pre-planned position. Then, in perfect unison, they turned toward Pluto and fired their primary thrusters, though the journey would take several hours.

As the armada of warships left the moon's gravity, Commander Mensen, back at Harris Point and also clad in the black and silver armour of the Corporatist elite, stood rigid before the holographic communications terminal, awaiting a status report. A moment later, a blue-tinged projection came to life, revealing the sharp-featured, battle-tested face of Captain Parlon Drex, leader of the troop transport fleet.

Drex offered a curt nod. "Commander Mensen, we are holding formation. *ETA to Pluto: five hours, thirty-six minutes.* All transporters are maintaining speed and trajectory. No anomalies have been detected."

Mensen gave a slight nod.

"Good. Any issues with the stabilization thrusters?" he asked, "The storm front on the outer belt might cause minor deviations."

"No issues yet," Drex confirmed, his voice crisp. "The fleet is compensating for slight gravitational fluctuations, but nothing we can't handle. Ground forces are secured, and all drop ships are prepped for immediate deployment upon arrival."

Mensen drummed his fingers against the console.

"Supreme Chancellor Veylan expects precision." he said, "We cannot afford delays."

Drex's concentration remained steady on the fleet around him.

"You'll have precision, Commander." he said, "We'll be in position exactly on time."

Mensen studied him for a moment, then gave a slow nod.

"Very well," he said, "Maintain course. Any disruptions… you report directly to me."

"Understood," Drex replied. His hologram wobbled slightly as his ship's systems adjusted for minor turbulence.

"We'll see you soon enough planet side, Commander," he confirmed.

Mensen didn't reply immediately. He simply terminated the transmission with a silent command and watched as the hologram dissolved into static. He then turned towards Veylan, who was still looking out over the plains considering his strategy.

"Sire, the fleet is making good progress" he announced.

"Excellent," Veylan said without regarding the commander. He paused, then turned to his loyal friend.

"We need to settle this, Mensen before Kallos and Hext get involved," Veylan said, his voice low but deliberate. "The Silent Watchers must be ours."

Mensen gave a single, crisp nod to him.

"I totally agree with you," he nodded back. "I went through the options and gave things a lot of thought last night. In my opinion, Esterin, Jasson, and Porteas are the clear choices. All three have the reputation necessary to avoid scrutiny. More importantly, they understand Pluto's survival depends on order, under your order."

Veylan looked back deep in thought, steepling his fingers. "Esterin is well respected. A historian, a voice of reason. But will she bend when we need her to?"

Mensen showed some confidence.

"She's pragmatic." he said, "She values continuity over upheaval. We won't need to push her as she'll convince herself that ruling against us would lead to instability. And she will not risk history branding her a destroyer of peace."

Veylan gave a slow, approving nod. "Good. And Jasson?" he asked.

"He was Isolationist once, but that was decades ago," Mensen replied. "Since then, he's done everything in his power to distance himself from the radicals. He's cultivated a reputation as a fair, steady hand, and that's exactly why we need him. Kallos will see him as an acceptable choice, but we both know Jasson values order over ideology. Push him toward the safer option, and he will not resist."

Veylan smiled, he seemed pleased so far. "Which leaves Porteas," Mensen said.

He paused slightly, considering this choice.

"Porteas is respected across all factions," he said, "His reputation is impeccable. If we secure him, we secure legitimacy."

Veylan was now starting to relax as he saw a favourable outcome coming into view.

"Will he resist?" he checked.

Mensen shook his head. "No. Porteas believes in structure above all else." he said, "He won't betray us because he believes a strong hand must always lead. He won't favour us outright, but he won't stand against us either. So long as we keep the illusion of fairness, he will rule in our favour, not out of loyalty, but out of necessity."

Veylan's smile broadened.

"Then we have our Watchers," he said now easing back with what he had heard.

He grinned, his mood sharpening.

"This must be sealed before we speak with Kallos and Hext." he urged, "Once we present these names, they must already be committed. Any doubts they have will be meaningless."

"I'll ensure they accept before the meeting," Mensen confirmed. "By the time Kallos and Hext see the list, it will be too late to challenge it."

Veylan smiled.

"Good." he said," We do not need to fix the war, we only need to ensure that when it ends, the right leader remains standing."

Mensen gave a sharp nod. "Understood, Supreme Chancellor."

"I'm going back to my quarters," he commanded. "Please set up a three-way communication between Kallos and Hext to begin in an hour's time. Also, make sure to approach our candidates and persuade them to accept."

"I will" Mensen replied.

Veylan turned to look at Mensen.

"I'll take the call in my Private Quarters," he said, as he whisked out of the room, to a waiting speeder driven by a loyal Corporatist soldier.

One hour later, the holographic transmission commenced as three figures came into view, hovering above their respective consoles. Each man prepared for armed combat in his very own unique way, yet this matter required their complete attention. Without the Silent Watchers, the battle for supremacy would have no legitimacy.

Supreme Chancellor Veylan sat within the heart of his fortified Central Spire within the palace, the glow of data streams reflecting in his hazel-coloured eyes. His holographic projection stood tall in the view of the other two men, his presence as imposing as ever. General Kallos was surrounded by tactical screens and holoscreens depicting shifting troop formations behind him. He was standing at his command table, wearing his armour and appearing battle-ready. His breath was slow and measured and his scarred appearance was illuminated in the pale blue light of the hologram. Prophet Hext, in his subterranean sanctuary, remained composed. The faint roar of the geothermal reactors echoed behind him, as he stood in his trademark long green robe. His holographic image appeared slightly smaller than the others; not because of any technical error, but because he preferred it that way.

Veylan was the first to speak, his tone clipped and efficient.

"Let's get this over with." he said seeming to be in a bit of a hurry, "We need to confirm the Silent Watchers now First Light has arrived. I have assembled a list of qualified elders, and individuals with experience in governance and law enforcement. I suggest Esterin, Jasson, and Porteas, they are well respected, and probably the best qualified, are they not?"

Kallos scoffed at these suggestions shaking his head.

"Your people, you mean," he said, crossing his arms, his voice filled with distrust. "Your corporate advisors, your former generals, your loyalists. We both know what this is, Veylan. You want to rig the battlefield before the first shot is fired."

Veylan felt great irritation that his strategy had already been questioned, yet he remained calm and impassive so as not to betray any anger.

"Don't insult me with childish accusations, General," he replied.

"We need stability, not chaos." he hit back, "The Wars are not some barbaric free-for-all; they are a test of leadership."

He gestured toward his console pointing at it.

"We need Watchers who understand strategy, law, and order," he said.

Hext, ever the observer, finally spoke. His voice was measured, like a man who understood that this debate needed an adult to control the children before they completely threw all of the toys out of the pram.

"You two both speak as though neutrality is something that you can manipulate in your direction," he said, "But the Watchers must be truly impartial…beyond politics, beyond war and reproach."

Kallos turned to observe Hext.

"Then tell me, Prophet, who do you trust?" he asked intrigued to see who Hext favoured.

Hext's holographic figure cut out slightly for the briefest of seconds, and then the signal returned. "The elders of the Deep Sanctum. The Forgotten Seers," he said.

A brief silence followed.

Veylan squinted at the figures in front of him.

"You would have us hand this war to mystics and outcasts?" he said querying Hext's sanity.

Kallos frowned for a second and then rubbed his chin.

"I thought they were dead," he said with eyebrows raised.

Hext shook his head.

"They are not dead." he said, "They are watching. They always have been..."

In their respected command centres, the three men stared at each other intently through the veil of technology.

Hext continued his voice unwavering.

"The Seers were there when the last wars were fought." he said, and then went on, "They have survived the rise and fall of every ruler before us. Even though they now exist outside the boundaries of Pluto, they have no allegiance, no wealth tempts them, and no armies obey them. They are the last true neutrals we can call upon."

Veylan shifted slightly as he could see that once again, things were not going his way, especially seeing Kallos nodding his head in agreement.

"I do not like it," he interjected.

Kallos, however, looked intrigued. "The Seers..." he mused considering that this would be an acceptable solution.

"They are respected, even by my men. No one, not even I would dare move against them. If any group could be trusted, it's them."

Veylan still looked unconvinced. "And if they are too weak?" he said, "If they are too disconnected to enforce the rules?"

Hext's silver eyes shone in the holographic feed. "Then they will not stand alone. The people will enforce their word, as they always have. I suggest we vote on it."

Veylan reluctantly called the vote, and two to one he was defeated.

There was a short pause.

Finally, Veylan's withering gaze locked on the others. "Fine," he conceded at last. "The Forgotten Seers will be the Silent Watchers. Make sure they are contacted."

Hext nodded "I'll send the communication and copy you both in so that you have transparency regarding their acceptance and neutrality. They will judge fairly."

A low chime sounded from each of their consoles, as the agreement was recorded, sealed, and sent to the Seers themselves. The decision was final.

One by one, the holograms fizzled out.

Veylan sat alone, staring at his reflection in the light green console light. He had lost this skirmish, but in the long run, he had convinced himself that he would win the war. Surely, he would, and yet at this moment, he felt more vulnerable and inwardly afraid than he had done for many a long year. Everything was on the line, and his gut feeling was telling him that things would not run as smoothly as he hoped.

Confident of success, General Kallos surveyed his soldiers as they prepared for the inevitable confrontation. They knew the Corporatists would not arrive immediately, so they had precious hours to reinforce their defences and refine their strategies. The tunnels beneath them had been meticulously prepared for destruction, and designed to collapse key landing zones the moment the enemy touched down. Traps had been placed in strategic pathways to channel enemy troops into kill zones. Skirmish teams readied themselves, and their weapons were primed to strike the moment an opportunity presented itself.

A scout sprinted toward him, breathless. "Sir, their fleet has left Charon. We estimate they will arrive within a few hours."

Kallos remained still, his mind calculating.

"They think their numbers will overwhelm us," he said, his voice calm but edged with steel. "But they are wrong if they think that. We will not fight them on their terms. We will fight them on ours.

Reinforce all tunnel entry points. Make sure our skirmishers know their routes. This will be a battle of patience and precision."

He turned to his commanders. "Signal to all of our forward units. We hold until they commit. The moment they do, we make them regret ever setting foot on Pluto."

Deep underground, in a cavernous chamber lined with flickering tactical displays, Prophet Hext and Steffan, who had watched the three-way meeting from the other side of the room, exchanged looks. The Terraformers had no intention of intervening in the initial battles. They had spent too long preparing, stockpiling resources, and studying every possible outcome.

Steffan watched the screens with intent. "Well done," he said. "My father doesn't back down easily and I knew he would try to fix things,"

"Yes," Hext calmly replied.

"The Seers will ensure fair play," he said,

"Now we need patience, my young charge." he went on, "We wait before we move. Neither of them will predict what I have in mind,"

"We wait until they weaken each other before we properly commit, and then, when the time is right, we act," he said, though his voice carried the weight of knowing that he had to call things correctly, as his followers did not have the hardware of the other two sides.

Hext, now standing in the background, stroked his bearded chin and regarded his younger companion with a knowing smile.

"You're impatient," he observed. "Understandable. But what is impatience, Steffan, if not the failure to grasp the broader picture?"

He gestured toward the screens.

"Look at them." he urged, "Your father's troops will arrive in full force, seeking dominance. The Isolationists have laid their traps, preparing to bleed them dry. And yet neither sees the grander scheme."

Steffan ran a hand through his dark hair. "And we do?" he queried.

"We do because we are not blinded by loyalty to a doomed cause," Hext said, "We do because we see the cycle for what it is. This war will not end with victors, it will end with survivors. We will be the ones left standing, not by force, but by necessity. They will come to us, Steffan. They will come because they will have no other choice."

Steffan remained silent for a moment before nodding.

"Then we wait." he replied, agreeing with his older companion, "But when the time comes, we act. No hesitation?"

Hext smiled.

"Of course." he said with a knowing smile, "When the moment is right, we will shape the future of Pluto. But let us pick our time carefully. Let them fight their war, there is much bad blood between them both, and they will not be able to hold themselves back. Let them weaken. And when they crumble, we will emerge, not as conquerors, but as saviours."

As the hours ticked by, the Corporatist fleet surged forward through the void, and onwards toward the wild plains of Pluto. As they did, the Isolationists reinforced their positions, waiting for the storm to break. Far below, Hext and Steffan remained patient, watching, waiting and hoping that soon, the balance of power would shift in their favour. And yet, far away unbeknown to all of them, a far greater danger was emerging and one that would turn everything on its head.

CHAPTER TEN – THE APOCALYPSE PROTOCOL

In the deep reaches of the Neptunian system, where the Sun was a distant flicker barely visible against the blackness, the Helios Prospect drifted in silence. The ageing mining vessel, scarred from years of asteroid extraction, manoeuvred into place steadily as it conducted its latest operation. The vast, yawning emptiness beyond its hull made even the most seasoned crew members uneasy. Out here, there was no rescue, no reinforcements, just the endless abyss.

The ship's laser arrays, mounted along its reinforced hull, buzzed methodically as they bored into NX-199-Theta, a large asteroid nearly sixty kilometres in diameter, its composition marred by deep fissures and ancient impact craters. An unassuming but mineral-rich rock, the asteroid had drifted in the Neptunian system for aeons, with its slow rotation exposing new veins of valuable material with each pass. Inside the busy control room, Captain Elias studied the holo-display, his face filled full of quiet concentration. He had been running mining operations for over two decades, he was very experienced and a veteran in the field. This was just a routine day in his life, indeed he had done this type of mission hundreds of times, and yet this time around he had an uneasy feeling in the pit of his stomach.

Inside the cockpit, however, the mood was far from tense. Laughter echoed through the dimly lit chamber as crew members exchanged jokes while finalizing the calculations for their next mining run.

"Bet you fifty credits we hit another dud," Isaac Rourke, one of the junior technicians, grinned as he entered some more data. "I swear, the last three drills have been nothing but frozen gas and worthless ore."

"You're on," Delara, the ship's navigator beamed, "My money's on us hitting a vein of crystal so pure they'll name a sector after us. The Helios Prospect Vein, has a nice ring, don't you think?"

"I'd settle for just one good payday," Calder chuckled as he adjusted his targeting scope. "Alright, let's get to work. Rourke, please initiate the final scans for any structural weaknesses. Delara, confirm the asteroid's rotation and gravitational fluctuations. I want this laser strike clean and precise."

Rourke tapped at his console, his previous mirth fading slightly as he concentrated.

"Confirmed," he said, looking happy with what he was looking at, "Looks like the outer layers have multiple fissures, but nothing catastrophic. The best drilling site is here...."

He highlighted a section on the display.

"Aim at that spot," he said, "Minimal risk of triggering a collapse."

"Delara?" Elias prompted.

"Asteroid's rotation is stable," she confirmed. "Neptune's pull is minor, but it could shift debris after impact. We should be fine."

Elias nodded. "Alright. Bring the laser arrays online."

"We're within three meters of the primary deposit," reported Raan Calder, the chief mining engineer. His voice carried a slight tremor, betraying his excitement.

"Scans show crystalline formations, they're dense, high-value material." he said excitedly, "If this vein extends, we could be looking at a major haul everyone."

Elias nodded, thinking of the rewards to come.

"Wouldn't that be nice?" he said with a wide grin. "We haven't hit the jackpot in ages. Proceed with caution. Keep the beam steady and monitor the asteroid's integrity. Take it easy now, nice and gentle. We hit one wrong fault line, and the whole damn thing could shatter, and bang goes our fortune."

Calder adjusted the controls, refining the beam's intensity. The ship's hull vibrated slightly as energy surged into the rock, carving deep into its core. Sparks flew where metal met stone, and the asteroid groaned under the strain.

Then, without warning, alarms blared across the command deck.

"Structural failure detected!" Calder screamed, his eyes wide in disbelief. "It's cracking, it's cracking apart!"

"No, no, no—this isn't happening!" one of the junior technicians muttered, hands trembling over his console.

On the holo-display, NX-199-Theta was breaking apart, splitting along a hidden fissure. A white-blue explosion of gas and volatile ice erupted from its interior, tearing the asteroid into three massive fragments. The impact of the laser had unknowingly breached an ancient, pressurized cavern within the rock, triggering an uncontrolled failure that sent debris spiralling wildly into space.

Open-mouthed and almost in disbelief, the entire crew watched in awe and almost in slow motion, as, in a huge cloud of dust and ice fragments, the largest of the three new rocks spun away. Huge and in the region of around twenty kilometres in size, it started to catch into Neptune's gravity field, before the big blue gas giant started to slingshot it on a brand-new course.

"This isn't good," Calder muttered, rapidly tapping through his readouts. "I need trajectory data! Now!"

"Working on it!" a technician stammered, his voice thick with panic. "The readings are erratic! We can't be sure where it's heading…"

The ship's AI activated: its voice calm yet chilling.

"Trajectory calculated.," it said "Object NX-K3-Theta on a direct course for Pluto. *Estimated impact in 32 days, 14 hours, 7 minutes.*"

The words hung in the air like a death sentence.

"That… that can't be right," one of the navigators said with panic in his voice. "Check it again. There's no way we just sent a planet-killer hurtling toward Pluto?"

"Double-checking the data," Calder snapped. "Please someone tell me this is a mistake!"

The crew worked in desperate silence, recalculating the trajectory, testing for gravitational fluctuations, indeed anything that might shift the asteroid away.

"Captain…" Calder finally breathed, his voice hollow and shaking with fear. "It's confirmed. NX-K3-Theta is heading straight for Pluto. There's nothing stopping it."

A sickening silence gripped the navigation deck.

Elias inhaled sharply, his mind was racing fast. He had expected an unstable excavation, but this, no, this was beyond catastrophic.

"Can we divert it?" he asked, his voice filled with worry.

Calder shook his head. "Negative. It's too massive, spinning too fast. Even a full fleet of gravity tugs wouldn't guarantee success. We don't have the time nor the resources." he conceded.

"What the hell do we do?" questioned Roarke, looking for the right answer to the awful situation that they were facing.

"We warn them," Elias said, straightening up. "Send a priority transmission to Pluto's leadership. Secure channel. Mark it; *Apocalypse Protocol*."

Calder hesitated. "Elias…" he said with concern. "Won't Earth's Dominion Command be able to pick this up too? If they intervene… can you imagine?"

Elias turned to address his crew: his expression grim with worry. "If Earth finds out before Pluto has a chance to respond, they'll declare an emergency planetary crisis and use it as a pretext to reassert control on them. They won't offer aid, likely they'll send military forces, take over infrastructure, and place the planet under permanent occupation. They've been looking for an excuse to reabsorb Pluto for decades."

"Then we're screwed either way," a crew member muttered. "If we say nothing, millions die. If we say something, Pluto may lose its independence."

"Not necessarily," Elias said. "We give Pluto the warning first. If they can mount a defence, and take control of their own fate, they might have a chance to resist Earth's interference. But if Earth intercepts our message and steps in first, Pluto won't get a say in its survival."

"Pluto won't have any fate if we don't do something!" Roarke shouted from the back of the cockpit.

"We don't have options!" Calder shouted. "Unless someone here can stop an asteroid the size of a city, we send the damn warning and pray Pluto figures something out!"

Calder swallowed hard, nodding before activating the ship's long-range communication array. The Helios Prospect turned its massive dish toward the void, transmitting a message that would alter Pluto's future forever. The signal was encoded, but Elias knew there was no way Earth wouldn't intercept it. Within hours, both Pluto and the Dominion would be aware of what was coming. And then, the real fight would begin, not just for survival, but for planetary control too.

Meanwhile, the asteroid fragment, now designated K3-Theta-Prime, continued its relentless trajectory. It was a silent juggernaut, carrying with it the potential to rewrite Pluto's history. If it hit, it would not just devastate a colony, it would cause a multi-megaton explosion that could impact the whole planet, collapsing entire underground cities, rupturing domes, and sending shockwaves through the fragile balance of power.

Far beyond, the shattered asteroid drifted through space; its largest fragment spinning and racing silently, inexorably toward the frozen world.

The countdown to impact had begun.

Yet, unknown to Elias and his crew, they were not the only ones watching. A silent observer, deep within the shadow of Neptune's farthest moon Neso, had already taken note of the unfolding catastrophe. Hidden within the icy darkness, this unknown and almost forgotten group had been waiting and observing. And now, with Pluto's fate hanging in the balance, it was preparing to play its role too.

CHAPTER ELEVEN – THE SIGNAL FROM THE DARK

The Helios Prospect drifted in the abyss, silent but for the constant buzz of its engines and the quiet, rhythmic beeping of the distress beacon now transmitting across the void. Captain Elias sat motionless, with his hands hovering over the console, and his eyes fixed on the message he had just approved for transmission. The asteroid, designated K3-Theta-Prime, was no longer a simple mining anomaly. It was death incarnate, and now hurtling toward Pluto with a force and speed that could end everything.

The crew had done their calculations three times, then five, then again for good measure. The conclusion was always the same: impact would occur in thirty-two days, thirteen hours, and forty-four minutes; every second was a second closer to total disaster. There was no altering its course at this minute; the Helios Prospect was not powerful enough to divert its path. The only option left was warning those who could act… if they had the will to do so in time.

The message had burst forth from the Helios Prospect, in a desperate cry against the cosmic silence. It travelled at the speed of light, a digital scream cutting across the solar system. The first receivers to register it were automated beacons, planetary relay stations built to monitor deep-space activity. The real question was: who would listen first?

On Neptune's smallest and most distant moon, within the enigmatic outpost Neso, a figure clad in a flowing pale blue robe watched the incoming communications with serene focus. The Forgotten Seers, the appointed adjudicators of Pluto's Ice Wars, rarely interfered in mortal struggles. They observed and they judged, but they did not act.

Archivist Solas studied the message in its entirety. He absorbed the coordinates, the velocity of the asteroid, and then the projected outcome. He closed his eyes for a moment, then keyed in a secure sequence on his terminal. A simple reply was transmitted to the Helios Prospect:

"Message received. Fate unfolds as it must." Then, he waited. For what, even he did not know.

The message reached Pluto within three hours. Deep beneath Erebus Prime, in an already busy and rather chaotic command centre staffed by technicians and military analysts, alarms flared as the priority signal from the Helios Prospect was decrypted. Lieutenant Aria Bray was the first to read it. Her pulse quickened as she skimmed the data. Then she read it again, slower this time. The blood drained from her face.

"Get this to the Chancellor. Right now!" she shouted.

Within minutes, Supreme Chancellor Veylan stood before a vast holographic projection of Pluto, his mood becoming more anxious by the second as he studied the inbound asteroid's trajectory. Just two hours. That was all the time he had before his armies, mobilized and ready for the assaults, would touch down. But now, the battle for supremacy among the warring factions seemed trivial compared to the existential threat barrelling toward them.

Then, an idea took root in his mind. What if he could use this?

Veylan's scowl transformed into a cold smile as his mind raced through the implications. Kallos would see this as a reason to delay the war, he must move to defend and prioritize planetary survival over conquest. That would be his mistake.

"Continue the mobilization as planned," Veylan ordered sharply, "The campaign will proceed. We make preparations to deal with the asteroid, but Kallos must not suspect our true intent."

Aria Bray frowned. "Sir, if we don't dedicate forces to planetary defence…" she queried.

"We will." said Veylan, "But Kallos will do more. I know him. He'll hesitate, pull back, and reconsider. We must keep up the pressure while he reorganizes his forces. If he's distracted, we'll strike first."

Across the icy nothingness, General Kallos received the same transmission. A hardened veteran of Pluto's military conflicts, he had anticipated betrayal, sabotage, and even an uprising, but never this. Surely the asteroid's impending impact would render their entire campaign meaningless? A fight for power was one thing, but a fight against oblivion was another completely.

Kallos activated his secure comms link to his fleet commanders.

"We need a contingency plan." he ordered, "Contact Veylan and Hext immediately. The action must be postponed until further notice. Gather all available assets, we're shifting to planetary defence. Hext might understand, but be on alert just in case. If Veylan refuses or makes a move while we are focusing on survival, we will answer in kind."

In the depths of the underground caves, Prophet Hext, leader of the Terraformers, read the transmission in silence. Unlike Veylan and Kallos, Hext saw in the asteroid something completely different. It could be a purging force. An end to the cycle of war and power struggles.

"Let Kallos and Veylan try and stop it." he thought, "They've not got a hope in a million light years in being able to send it off course, but let them try. No, the planet had to effectively die first for rebirth to occur."

He turned to his followers, their concerned figures waiting for his decree.

"The end we foretold is upon us." he said, "We do not resist it. We embrace it. Prepare for salvation. Spread the word, the reckoning has begun."

Meanwhile, in the outlaw enclaves of the Outlanders, Nyx Orban paced inside her command tent, her silver eyes scanning the transmission with a scowl. Unlike the others, she had no army, no fleet, and only the survivalist instincts inside her to call upon. If Pluto was going to die, she needed a way out, and quickly.

"We need off-world passage, now," she stressed to Lysara who was standing near her, "Find a way, or we all die here. We need to prioritize supplies, contact smugglers, and find anyone with a ride. We'll pay whatever it takes."

She turned to the rest of her band of waifs and strays,

"An asteroid is coming, and it'll be here in less than 4 weeks." she told them, "We've gotta get out otherwise we're all goners. If all else fails, we head to Indus. Even if we have to take a ship by force, we'll do it!"

Far away, in the heart of the Earth Dominion, the transmission had been intercepted within minutes. Admiral Devlin studied the data in contemplative silence.

"Now this was a development that was unexpected" he mused.

He sent out a communique for an immediate emergency meeting, and soon enough, his inner circle were gathering around him in a war chamber deep within the orbital command station over Earth. Pluto was now vulnerable they soon all agreed.

One of his military strategists General Ledger, spoke first.

"We have the justification we need." he announced, " I suggest that we offer to 'save' them, deploy our fleets, and ensure that when the dust settles, Pluto belongs to us once more."

Devlin let out a slow, knowing smile. "This was the correct course of action." he thought.

"Activate the reserves on Ganymede, we are calling this mission *Operation Firestorm*," he commanded, "They will set a course for Pluto. I want them ready to move at a moment's notice. Offer our benevolent protection. But let them squirm first. We will arrive not as conquerors, but as saviours. And they will have no choice but to accept. Make sure the message is clear: without us, Pluto will perish."

CHAPTER TWELVE - AN INDECENT PROPOSAL

General Kallos had spent his life fighting for survival, but now, for the first time, he wasn't just fighting for himself or his warriors, instead, he was fighting for the future of Pluto itself.

For years, he had thought that he was prepared for any kind of battle. The Ice Wars were brutal, but they were predictable, they were conflicts of strength and endurance waged against men who understood the same unwritten laws of Pluto's survival. But this was different. The rogue asteroid, K3-Theta-Prime, was an unstoppable force hurtling through the void, heedless of politics, power, or strategy. In just thirty-two days, it would arrive, and unless something was done, everything would burn.

Kallos rubbed his eyes as he stared at the grainy, flickering feed from the surveillance drone hovering high above Pluto. The asteroid's latest projected course streamed across the holoscreen beside him. A twenty-kilometre-wide behemoth of rock and ice, moving at a velocity that would strike Pluto with the force of a thousand nuclear detonations. Even if it did not wipe out the colony upon impact, it would send shockwaves through the planet's already fragile crust, triggering seismic collapses, atmospheric disruption, and potentially mass extinction.

For most of his life, Kallos had fought to tear down Pluto's corrupt rulers. Now, he had to fight to keep Pluto itself alive. But unlike the wars, there was no honour in this battle, and no glory either.

He turned his attention to the secondary drone feed. The sky, black and endless, had been empty an hour ago. Now, it was filled with descending warships.

The first of Veylan's troop carriers had breached the upper atmosphere. Massive warships of reinforced plasteel and thermal shielding, descended in perfect formation, with thrusters flaring as they slowed their approach. The glare of their landing lights cast stark white beams across the icy wastes next to the vast Corporatist military base just beyond the Indus Spaceport. Their bulk displaced plumes of methane frost as they settled into position, their hydraulic stabilizers deploying with a deep, mechanical screech.

One by one, the ramps extended from them.

The first soldiers in their survival suits emerged from the darkness. Clad in black-and-silver thermoplas armour, their movements were precise and synchronized. Rows upon rows of elite Corporatist troops, with their visors glowing in the reflection of the floodlights above them, stepped forward into the frigid expanse of the methane Ice Plains.

Then came the armoured trucks, with their thick treads carving deep into the pure white terrain. Artillery platforms rumbled into position flanked by mechanized assault units. The sheer scale of the force was staggering. It included hundreds of war vehicles, supply transports, and mobile command centres, all of them moving in perfect coordination. Overhead, drones hovered like silent predators, scanning for any sign of movement beyond the landing zone.

Kallos looked on with concern via the console, watching on as the landing operation unfolded. The planet's thin atmosphere carried little sound, but even through the drone's silent surveillance, he could imagine the noise and feel the weight of this occupation force.

This was no longer a war for dominance, rather this was a force of immense strength, far beyond what he had under his command.

The drone panned its camera across the field, zooming in on one of the massive command transporters that had just completed its descent. A speeder protected from the elements carried a lone figure, draped in a long black coat trimmed with red epaulettes. The troops saluted in unison to the figure as he surveyed the icy battlefield. Even without hearing any sound, Kallos recognized Veylan immediately.

The Supreme Chancellor was at the heart of his army, his synthetic fingers flexing in quiet anticipation. He did not need to give orders, and the troops knew their roles. The war machines had already been programmed to follow the plan of action. Pluto was his and was going to remain his, and today he had come to remind the rest of the planet of this fact.

Kallos deactivated the drone feed with a slow, controlled sigh. He had known Veylan would come; but seeing it, and seeing the sheer power of the forces that had just landed, drove home the reality of what was happening.

He would have to defend something far greater than just his faction now.

The war had changed. It was no longer Isolationists against Corporatists. No longer a battle of ideologies. It was going to be survival in all senses of the word.

After returning to the headquarters at Harris Point, and after having watched the fleet deployment unfold, Veylan smiled to himself. Everything was going to plan. Outside, his forces moved like clockwork. The troops had assembled in perfect formation and the war machines had rolled into position without a hitch. Everything was proceeding well. In due course, Pluto would be his once again, continuing on the fifty-year stranglehold that he had exerted on the population. Yes, much danger was looming far away in deepest space, but he would deal with it; he would find a way.

Suddenly, his private terminal pulsed softly. A high-priority transmission was coming through.

Veylan's mood darkened as he approached the console. The encryption level was Omega-1. Terran Dominion High Command.

His fingers hovered over the interface for a moment before activating the transmission. The holographic display burst into life, revealing the severe and stark image of Admiral Devlin. The Dominion officer sat in his command chamber aboard one of Earth's deep-space warships, the insignia of the Terran High Council gleaming against his uniform.

"Supreme Chancellor Veylan," Devlin greeted smoothly. "I hope you're keeping well since we last spoke, and I also trust you're settling into the realities of your situation?" he asked with a sweetly threatening tone in his voice.

Veylan didn't answer immediately. Devlin's words were careful, and measured, was he playing a game?

"You don't call to offer pleasantries, Admiral," Veylan said at last.

"No," Devlin admitted. "I call because we share a common problem."

He gestured toward something off-screen. A moment later, Pluto's celestial charts overlaid his projection, showing NX-K3-Theta in its deadly descent. "An extinction-level event is not a fate I imagine that you relish?" he questioned.

Veylan looked at him waiting for the offer to come. "You wouldn't have reached out unless you had a solution," he said.

"A solution," Devlin repeated, as if amused. "Let's call it an opportunity. The Dominion is prepared to intervene. Our deep-space platforms can be repositioned within twenty days. We have the means to alter the asteroid's trajectory, ensuring Pluto's continued survival."

There was a pause. A fraction too long. Veylan thought for a second considering what to say next.

"At what cost?" he inquired.

Devlin's face remained cool and calculated. "Why do you assume there is a cost?" he said remotely.

Veylan grinned back. "Because I know the Dominion, Admiral. You wouldn't be reaching out unless there was something in it for you?" he retorted.

Devlin nodded as if acknowledging a well-played move in a game of chess.

"Pluto is important to Earth, Chancellor." he said, "It has been since the day the first colonists arrived. Its independence has always been… tolerated. But if we're to extend our resources, and to risk our assets on your behalf, the High Council would need assurances."

Veylan's throat started to tighten.

"You want Pluto back under Earth's rule. Don't you?" Veylan asserted.

Devlin smiled… just barely.

"We want stability. And history has proven that Pluto is best governed with Terran oversight. You're a reasonable man, Veylan. I trust you'll make the right choice."

The transmission cut.

Veylan breathed slowly. For sure Devlin was not bluffing this time. He had spent a lifetime engaging in this game, manoeuvring through wars and betrayals, and playing poker with the high command on Earth.

But this was different.

This was a situation he might not be able to solve on his own.

Pluto was on the brink of annihilation, from above, from within, and now from Earth itself.

And for the first time in decades, Veylan found himself trapped, and looking for solutions.

CHAPTER THIRTEEN – THE GREAT ESCAPE

Down in the Hollow, Nyx Orban standing at the building's control centre, tapped on the heating controls to try and increase the ambient temperature. The Outlanders gathered around her, their breath misting in the frigid re-conditioned air as they checked their weapons and supplies. Time was starting to run out. The asteroid was now just thirty-one days from impact, and would soon, if unchecked, render the entire colony uninhabitable. The Pluto government had proven itself utterly incapable of mounting a rescue or evacuation effort, indeed two of the three main leaders were preparing for an insane war.

"If they wanted to survive," she thought, "They would have to find their own way off this god-forsaken rock."

"Did you find us transport?" she asked, her silver eyes locking on Dren, one of her most trusted scouts.

Dren nodded, rubbing his gloved hands together for warmth.

"Old cargo hauler." he confirmed, "There's enough room for all of us and it's scheduled to leave in six hours."

Nyx smiled at this positive news. "Who's flying it?" she inquired.

"A trader named Mez Lipinski; he's asking for an obscene amount of credits," Dren confirmed.

"Figures." Nyx narrowed her eyes looking resigned to her options.

"We don't have time for negotiations," she said, "Set up a meeting."

Eventually, they found Mez Lipinski at a grimy cantina near Indus Base Spaceport. The pilot was a wiry man with sunken eyes and a permanent sneer, nursing a drink while surrounded by a handful of his mechanics. He barely looked up as Nyx and her people approached.

"You the ones interested in my ship?" he asked, sipping his drink. It was a rare form of Scotch, only available on import from Earth.

"Bad news, I don't do charity." he said, " And you lot don't look like you can afford my services."

Nyx sat across from him, fixing him with an unwavering stare. "How much?" she inquired.

"Two million credits. Non-negotiable," he said, looking back down at his drink.

Dren scoffed. "That's insane! Nobody on Pluto has that kind of money," he replied.

"Exactly," Mez smirked. "Which means I don't have to pretend I want to help you," he said sitting back in his seat in a relaxed manner. He hadn't wanted to do any special trips anyway.

Nyx got closer and stared at him directly.

"You're leaving, one way or another." she said with menace, "The question is, are you leaving on your feet, or in a body bag?"

The pilot laughed, shaking his head. "You think I'm scared of a few Outlanders?" he said incredulously.

Nyx's hand moved in a blur, pressing the barrel of her laser pistol against his ribs beneath the table. Mez stiffened, his eyes darting around the cantina. His mechanics were too slow to react, their hands twitching toward weapons but unsure whether to escalate the situation.

"You should be," she said calmly. "We're taking your ship."

Mez swallowed hard. "You won't get past security," he warned her.

"That's where you come in," she whispered.

The Spaceport at Indus Base sprawled before them, a vast complex of landing pads, fuelling stations, and high-security hangars, all bathed in the light of the floodlights stationed above them. The air smelled of burnt fuel, there was the constant din of idling thrusters and the distant calls of workers shouting orders to one another. Cargo loaders rumbled through the passageways, towering cranes hoisting heavy freight from the warehouses into waiting transports. The workers moved with a sense of routine efficiency, most too focused on their duties to notice anything beyond their immediate tasks.

Security was everywhere. Squads of armoured Technocrat enforcers patrolled in rigid formations, with their navy-blue uniforms reflecting the neon glow of warning lights. Automated turrets pivoted on their mounts, scanning for unauthorized movements, while AI-controlled drones flitted through the air, tracking every significant shift in personnel. The Outlanders moved cautiously, ducking behind stacks of cargo crates, using the cover of them as they crept toward their target. Every step was measured, and every breath was carefully controlled. A single misstep would bring instant death.

Mez led the way, hands by his sides to maintain the illusion of normality. Stripped of his uniform jacket and with a concealed pistol being aimed at the small of his back, he marched just ahead of the captors, his face pale under the glare of the port's floodlights. His hands trembled as they reached the last checkpoint.

Nyx and Dren loomed behind him closer, pressing the muzzle of a silenced plasma pistol against his spine.

"Smile, Captain. Act natural. One wrong move, and I paint this dock with your brain." she whispered.

The final checkpoint gate was a fortress of reinforced titanium, with two guard towers overlooking a thick blast door. A dozen security personnel in navy blue Technocrat uniforms patrolled the entrance, pulse rifles slung across their chests. Above them, drones continued doing circles around the base, scanning every approach with heat-sensitive optics.

A gruff officer stepped forward, his helmet visor flashing red as he scanned Lipinski's ID badge. "State your business," he barked.

Mez licked his dry lips. "Cargo transfer. Reroute request from Docking Bay Nine," he croaked, voice barely steady. Behind him, Nyx and her Outlanders in space crew uniforms tensed, hidden weapons strapped beneath their stolen apparel.

The officer frowned, consulting his holo-tablet. "Not seeing anything for Bay Nine. You sure about that, Captain?" he said as he glanced toward the group, suspiciously.

Dren acted fast. He leaned in with a predator's grin, slipping a data cartridge into the officer's tablet. The device buzzed and displayed the necessary clearance codes given to them by their captive earlier on.

"You should refresh your system, mate," Dren murmured. "We've been waiting long enough."

The officer grunted and tapped his screen. The codes held up. With a reluctant nod, he waved his hand toward the security gate.

"Move along," he said.

As the blast doors scraped open, the Outlanders and their hostage moved in fast, keeping their weapons hidden, but ready. They pushed Lipinski forward, deeper into the expansive hangar, a maze of stacked cargo containers in front of them, interspersed with loading mechs and fuel depots.

Beyond them, several ships sat in the parking slots, their engines purring. Tens of grey-jacketed workers bustled about, unaware of the silent predators slipping into their midst.

Nyx grinned, her teeth flashing in the artificial light. They were in.

As they passed one of the Corporatist fighter ships with their cargo vessel the *Albatross* now in sight, an automated scanner swept over them. A shrill alarm split the air.

"Hold it right there!" screamed one of the guards, levelling his rifle. The AI had flagged one of the Outlanders as a known fugitive.

"Move!" Nyx impatiently shouted; her voice agitated, as a sense of panic set in.

Lasers blazed through the air as the guards opened fire. The Outlanders scattered, taking cover behind several of the metal cargo containers filled with new computer equipment, as red bolts sliced past them. Their quiet, careful approach was over for sure. Nyx fired back, hitting the lead guard in the chest, and sending him crashing to the ground. Dren and the others flanked left, using suppressing fire to keep the advancing enforcers at bay.

Mez saw his chance and fled for the exit. He didn't get far though. A stray blast caught him in the back, and he collapsed to the ground with a strangled cry. Nyx barely spared him a glance. They had come too far to fail now.

"Get to the ship!" she shouted.

They burst across the hangar floor dodging behind the cargo crates as they ran. The cargo hauler loomed ahead, its heavy bulk resting on its extended landing struts; they could see that the loading ramp at the back was already lowered. But before they could board, the roar of engines filled the air. Fighter jets, sleek and deadly, sat lined up along the huge hangar's far side, the frenzied engineers readying their departure.

Nyx didn't hesitate. "Destroy them before they get airborne!" she shouted with extreme urgency.

Dren, who had flown in this type of vehicle before, boarded and immediately sprinted toward the ship's turret controls, yanking open a side panel and activating the external cannons. He aimed, and a burst of energy fire tore through the hangar, striking the nearest fighter. It exploded in a brilliant ball of flames, sending shrapnel raining down onto the deck. Several blue-suited guards were thrown back injured by the force of the explosion. Another burst of fire and a second fighter was hit as it tried to move, its thrusters exploding in flames and turning the stricken ship into a burning wreck. Firefighting crews rushed in, their foam suppression systems struggling to contain the inferno, as acrid smoke started to consume the hangar bay. There was chaos and confusion, and now was the chance to escape.

"Now get us in the air!" Nyx shouted.

Jessa, already in the cockpit, fired up the main engines. The ship shuddered, dust and debris kicking up as its thrusters roared.

"Disabling auxiliary power relays, emergency launch procedure complete," she shouted. "Hitting throttle now – heading for Pad 4!"

They blasted free from the hangar speeding up to the launch pad, which would lift the ship upwards to lift off. Behind them, a Corporatist pilot was hurriedly getting into the last surviving fighter.

"Activating launch sequence" shouted Jessa, as the heavy flash doors closed, clanked into place and sealed the cargo ship off from the hanger levels; a pulsing alarm sounded and the Outlanders in their newly stolen ship were raised upwards to take off.

"Let's get going," she said with urgency, as the blackness of the sky punctuated with a multitude of sparkling galaxies and stars came into view. The engines of the cargo ship roared into gear, and they launched, banking hard to the right as they shot off into the frigid Plutonian sky.

"Check the scanners" ordered Nyx.

"One behind us" screamed Dren, "We've gotta get rid of it quick."

"Fire the aft cannons," shouted Nyx in a sense of panic, "She's closing in fast."

Dren in the co-pilot's seat activated the rear scanners and the force shields, AI targeting took over, and she hit the pulse laser. The first shot missed by a whisker and the fighter dodged downwards, a red streak of light just passing its left wing, but the second hit home, ripping off the tail section of the fighter. It exploded into two pieces, and it fell to the ground in a fiery mess, shards of burning metal melting the permafrost below.

"Disable the transponder," shouted Dren. This they did, and suddenly back at Corporatist flight control, the locator of the Albatross on the holo-displays vanished.

For twenty minutes, they flew low, weaving between the ice-topped mountains, their towering peaks dominating high over vast snow-filled canyons. Below them were endless ice fields, marked by crevasses deep enough to swallow entire spaceships. The untouched beauty of Pluto's wilderness was mesmerising; a total contrast to the industrial sprawl they had just escaped. Streaks of light reflected off the crystalline ice formations, shining specks of blue and silver beneath the faint light from distant stars.

Ahead, the vast Basso Icefield came into view, just like an unbroken sea of glistening frost. Rising from the horizon, dipping slowly below their line of sight, was the faint silhouette of Kerberos, Pluto's distant moon.

Nyx stared at the glowing celestial body for a long moment before speaking.

"Adjust our course, prepare to activate cloaking" she commanded. "Take us out of the atmosphere and head for Kerberos Moon. I have a friend there" she said.

"How long until arrival?" she questioned.

"Twelve hours and 25 minutes" was the reply.

Jessa nodded, fingers moving across the control panel. The engines fired up into a scream, and the ship angled upward, breaking through the thin upper layers of Pluto's atmosphere. The planet's pull on them slowly fell away beneath them, and they ascended, as they headed into the vast silence of space, invisible to all around them.

Finally, inside the ship, there was a sense of relative calm. The remaining Outlanders sat back to settle themselves for the journey, but in their haste to depart, they had not checked to see what was on board.

Deep in the cargo hold was a crate, with Earth markings on it, it read *Purcell Laboratories, BioScience Division*. Inside was the latest consignment of rejuvenation nutrients, bright blue luminescent liquid which had been bound for Chancellor Veylan. Lipinski had been an employee in the payment of the Dominion. A rare bounty was indeed on board, and one that when discovered, might prove to be a pivotal and very valuable bargaining chip.

CHAPTER FOURTEEN – THE WARREN'S FUTURE

Deep within the labyrinthine tunnels of The Warren, a quiet revolution was unfolding. Unlike the desperate, violent struggles above ground, the work being done here was slow, meticulous, and ultimately vital to the colony's survival. Without the Terraformers, there would be no food. Without the Terraformers, there would be no future.

Hext stood at the front of a vast underground hall; his sharp features and trimmed beard were illuminated by the glow of bioluminescent panels embedded in the cavernous ceiling. The hall had once been a mining depot, but it had been long since converted into a space for study, debate, and instruction. The room was filled with new recruits, all young and eager, with their eyes reflecting the artificial lights as they hung on his every word.

"Survival on Pluto is not a right," Hext declared, his voice echoing through the chamber. "It is an achievement. One we must carve out with our own hands, and one we must fight for every day."

Steffan sat among the crowd, fascinated with the presentation, as he absorbed Hext's words. He had only been in The Warren for a short time, but already he could see the magnitude of what they were attempting. The Terraformers were not just growing food, no not just that; instead, they were trying to shape Pluto's destiny.

A young woman Zari in the front row raised her hand hesitantly.

"But what if the people above ground turn against us?" she asked, "They know that we control the food supply. Doesn't that put a target on our backs?"

Hext gave a knowing smile. "It does" he replied agreeing with her.

"That is why we operate in secrecy," he went on, "We give enough to keep them satisfied, but never enough for them to thrive without us. If they saw what we are truly capable of, they would try to take it for themselves."

He gestured toward the walls of the cavern and beyond into the research halls.

"We are not just farmers, he said, "We are custodians of Pluto's future. And that power must be protected."

Another recruit, a young man with a furrowed brow, spoke up.

"You say we are building a future here." he questioned, "But what about the asteroid on the news channels? If it hits, won't it destroy everything we've worked for?"

Hext nodded slowly. "Ah, yes. The asteroid," he said appreciating the question.

He turned toward a vast display panel that projected a three-dimensional rendering of Pluto's terrain. On it, a bright red marker indicated the asteroid's projected impact zone.

"The asteroid is both a threat to us all and an opportunity," he said with some realism. "If it strikes near the equatorial regions, the devastation will be immense. Our crops, our infrastructure and even underground tunnels like these could be compromised."

He paused, letting the weight of that settle in before continuing.

"However." he stopped again for a moment, "If it impacts in the right location, it could accelerate everything we are working toward."

Intense discussion spread through the recruits. Steffan felt a chill creep up his spine.

"Accelerate how?" he asked.

Hext turned to him.

"The energy released from the impact could trigger seismic shifts." he went on, "Gases trapped beneath Pluto's surface could be released, thickening the atmosphere faster than we ever could through controlled means."

He gestured to the screen again, where an animation showed plumes of gas rising from impact sites.

"Imagine it: a planetary shift that pushes us forward by centuries," he said triumphantly.

"But what if the gases are toxic?" another recruit interjected. "We could poison ourselves before we ever see the benefits."

Hext smiled.

"That is exactly what we are working to prevent. Come with me," he said gesturing to them all to follow him.

He turned, leading the group including Steffan and Zari through a reinforced tunnel that branched away from the lecture hall. The air here was different, tinged with the smell of nature's greenery. They emerged into a laboratory filled with strange, odd, shaped vegetation. The plants here were unlike anything Steffan had ever seen before, with their leaves glistening with bioluminescent hues.

"This…" Hext explained, gesturing to the greenery, "Is what will sustain us. New strains of crops, genetically modified to thrive in Pluto's thin atmosphere. These plants require little water, absorb toxins, and even release trace gases that contribute to our long-term atmospheric goals."

One of the followers, a young woman with tightly braided hair, examined a cluster of strange, bulbous fruits.

"These… they don't look edible," she said looking slightly bemused.

Hext chuckled.

"Not yet… but give them time," he said assuringly.

They moved on, passing through a decontamination area, before passing into a vast, high-ceilinged room dominated by an enormous cylindrical chamber. It was filled with swirling gases, illuminated by intricate control panels where scientists monitored every possible detail.

"This is where the real work happens," Hext said, his voice reverent. "Here we attempting to engineer Pluto's atmosphere."

Steffan's breath caught; the whole group looked in awe. The sheer scale of the project was overwhelming. Inside the chamber, atmospheric processors were conducting experiments to slowly thicken Pluto's air. The goal was audacious, turning Pluto from a barely survivable rock into a planet where humans could live above ground without instantly freezing.

Zari hesitated before asking.

"How long would this take?" she said, imagining for a brief moment a vision of green valleys on Pluto.

Hext ran a hand over the control panel, watching the simulated projections flicker.

"Centuries, if we do it safely, or decades, if we take risks," he replied, turning to address the group, with his eyes sharp and focused.

"But if the asteroid impact works in our favour? The timeline could be shortened dramatically," he said with a twinkle in his eyes.

The implications were staggering. Steffan swallowed hard.

"And if it doesn't?" he questioned.

Hext's mood suddenly became deadly serious.

"Then Pluto will become uninhabitable," he admitted. "The gases we release could spiral out of control. A single miscalculation, and we suffocate ourselves."

Silence filled the lab. The enormity of the risk was almost too much to comprehend.

"But…" Hext continued his voice firm, "We do not fear the unknown. We embrace it. Every advancement humankind has ever made has come at great risk. The question is: are we brave enough to take it?"

Steffan looked around the room, at the strange plants, he stared at the intricate machinery, and he fell in awe of the determined faces of the scientists and Terraformers. The fate of Pluto, perhaps the fate of humanity itself, could be decided here, right now, in these underground halls.

As they exited the lab, Hext stopped at a reinforced viewing platform near the top of the giant hall, to let the students look down at the scale of the work going on below them. In unison, they gasped in amazement.

Beyond and above them, Pluto remained frozen and desolate. But if Hext was right, if this worked, it might not always be that way.

Down on the ground floor, Hext got back to work.

"Adjust our models," he instructed one of the technicians. "I want new simulations based on impact scenarios. We need to be ready for every possibility."

Steffan and Zari exchanged longing glances. The Terraformers weren't just growing food. They were shaping the future. And if the asteroid was truly the key to unlocking Pluto's potential, then the future could arrive much quicker than they could ever imagine.

CHAPTER FIFTEEN – THE FORGOTTEN SEERS OF NESO

Far from the turmoil of Pluto, drifting in the isolated expanse of the Neptune system, lay Neso, a small, airless rock on the outermost edges of Neptune's gravitational reach. It was a world so desolate that few even remembered it existed. But those who did whisper of the ones who lived there: The Forgotten Seers or, as some called them when any conflicts were beginning, The Silent Watchers.

They were more than mere observers. They were the last remnants of a lost order; the remaining members of a council of exiles who had once held immense sway over Pluto's affairs, tasked with overseeing the eternal struggle known as the Ice Wars. Their duty had once been sacred, in balancing the chaos of Pluto's factions, and ensuring that no single power could ever fully dominate the system. Long ago, before the rise of the Corporatists and the splintering of Pluto's society, the Watchers had been revered. They had served as mediators and philosophers. They were chosen from the most learned scholars, tacticians, and visionaries of their time and they each had a gift. Their wisdom came not just from politics and war, but from a deeper understanding of Pluto's place in the cosmos. Some believed their knowledge extended beyond the realm of science, and that they had uncovered secrets hidden in the ice, truths that made them more than just men and women, but something far, far greater.

They were respected. They were feared. They were completely misunderstood. And then, they were banished.

The exile of the Seers was not recent. It had happened over a hundred years ago, ordered by Supreme Chancellor Aspin, a ruler of Pluto before Veylan was even born. Aspin had seen them as a threat, fearing that their guidance and quiet influence over the people undermined the absolute power of the ruling government. The Seers had refused to swear allegiance to him, choosing instead to uphold their sacred duty as overseers of balance. Their defiance was met with exile. Fleeing across the system, they established their sanctuary on Neso, far beyond Pluto's grasp.

With no home left on Pluto, and having departed for Neso, they left behind their ancient sanctum, their archives, and their role as Pluto's unseen guides. But exile did not break them. Instead, it made them stronger. On Neso, they became something else entirely. Secluded in temples, they dedicated themselves to the pursuit of true sight, not just political wisdom, but a deeper cosmic understanding. Their lives became a blend of meditation, science, and something unexplainable. They trained their minds to see patterns beyond the present, using advanced quantum probability calculations, deep-space signals, and sensory deprivation to reach heightened states of awareness. Over time, they developed abilities that many considered unnatural. Precognition? Perhaps. They could predict battles before they began. Telepathic insight? Some believed they could hear thoughts in the void. A connection to Pluto itself? There were whispers that the planet spoke to them through the ice, revealing secrets that no mortal could comprehend. Their influence extended not just across Pluto, but beyond, reaching through the solar system, even to the inhabited planets of Mars and Earth itself.

Despite their exile, the Seers never stopped observing. They still oversaw the conflicts, watching from their spiritual sanctum on Neso, unseen but ever-present. Though Veylan deliberately kept them at arm's length, others still heeded their wisdom. They knew of every skirmish, every betrayal, and every power shift. Even if the rulers of Pluto no longer listened or did not wish to interact with them, the Seer's influence had not faded, it had simply spread outward, carried in whispers to those willing to understand.

And now, they watched as the greatest threat Pluto had ever faced hurtled toward it. The asteroid was now thirty days away. They had foreseen its coming. Not through magic, not through prophecy, but through their understanding of the influence of the lineup of the satellites around Pluto, their gravitational shifts, and the appreciation that change and transformation were due. It was now thirty days away. And they knew something the others did not: Its impact would not just change Pluto, it would change everything.

Within the great temple of the Seers, located in the deep ice chambers of this small little moon, they assembled. Archivist Solas, the chronicler of their order, stood at the centre of the innate stone hall, his hands resting on an old, metallic star map where he tracked the asteroid's trajectory. To his left, Seer Mareth, an elder whose sight had long since faded in the physical sense, but who now saw further than most, spoke in measured tones.

"The path is set, but the outcome is yet unknown." he said turning to the others, "Even with all our knowledge, we cannot predict what this will bring."

Talleron, their leader, nodded.

"It is not just the asteroid, it is the decisions made before and after," he said, "Veylan, Kallos, Hext, Steffan, and Orban, each of them will shape Pluto's fate in ways they do not yet understand."

His voice was calm, but the weight of his words hung in the air.

"And there is another," he went on. "One who knows not the impact they will have."

A younger Seer, Sian stood alongside, her dark eyes filled with questions.

"If Hext understands what we have taught him, will he act? Or has he strayed too far from the path?" she asked.

Solas traced the edges of the map.

"Hext saw what we showed him. He knows the truth of Pluto's fragility, but his faith lies in action. He does not wait and watch as we do." he said.

Mareth let out a slow breath.

"Then he may act recklessly." he warned, "The Terraformers are bold, but their knowledge is incomplete. If they attempt to accelerate the changes before they are ready, they may doom what they seek to save."

Talleron turned to address the assembly.

"And what of Veylan?" he asked, "He dismisses us, but even now, his war efforts grow. He is blind to what comes from beyond."

Sian's voice was quiet but firm.

"Perhaps that is his fate, to never see beyond his own reach?" she mused, "His son will right the wrongs that he has sewn."

They stood in silence for a long moment, in deep meditation and thought. The Seers were not rulers, nor warriors; nevertheless, they had some responsibility. They could not interfere directly, but they could prepare others if they wished to approach them. They could ensure that when the moment came, someone would know what to do.

Talleron finally spoke again.

"We must prepare," he said simply. "Soon, we will be needed again."

They did not fight wars. They did not take sides. But they could not allow Pluto to face this storm unprepared. They had seen what was coming. And now, they had to decide: would they remain silent, or would they watch no longer?

CHAPTER SIXTEEN - THE FIRST SHOTS IN ANGER

The command chamber aboard *The Iron Will* was on alert status, and its crew carried out their duties with quiet efficiency under the glow of the *Code Red* status lights, as the battleship hung in the void above Pluto. Veylan stood motionless before the holographic map, watching the shifting markers that indicated the positions of Kallos' forces. The war had not yet begun in earnest, but he had no intention of waiting.

Mensen, standing beside him, gestured toward the Western Ice Plains.

"There," he said. "A detachment, slightly separated from the main body. They are lightly armed, moving slowly, with limited transport capacity. If we hit them hard, they won't have time to reinforce or retreat."

Veylan stared closely at the picture in front of him, deep in evil intent, while processing through the options in his mind.

"And Kallos?" he questioned.

Mensen adjusted the display, highlighting the main force further East.

"Looks like he's expecting an asteroid impact." he said, "He's still playing defence, waiting to see how this war will unfold. He won't move until he's certain he has no other choice."

"Then we give him that certainty," Veylan replied turning away from the display, as he paced across the room.

"Air support?" he called out.

Mensen hesitated for the briefest moment before nodding.

"We have full strike capability. But the rules Sire…?" he said before Veylan cut him off with a sharp glance.

"The rules are dead." Veylan asserted. "If Kallos expects a war fought by old codes, let him drown in that delusion. We hit them hard from above and below. No survivors."

Mensen didn't argue. There was no point. He turned to the communications console and relayed the order. The attack would commence at dawn.

The Western Ice Plains were a thankless place to be. The soldiers of the 22nd Brigade moved in slow, careful formations, their weather protection suits in camouflage white and grey, containing vital methane converters that allowed the soldiers to breathe; their heavy boots crunching against the frost. Their snow crawlers rumbled forward at a steady pace, with their treads kicking up fine powder.

"Keep moving, lads!" Sergeant Bayliss called out. "Two more klicks to the ridge. There'll be shelter and a bit of warmth. And we can eat."

There was silence out on the plains, save the crunch of boots through snow and ice.

Sergeant Corven sat in the lead vehicle, scanning the horizon. The reports had said Veylan's forces were still amassing, still positioning themselves, and continuing to wait. This wasn't supposed to be a combat zone.

A sudden movement in the sky caught his eye. At first, he thought it was nothing, just the thin, shifting clouds. Then the realization hit him. Not clouds. Drones.

He reached for his comm. "Command, we have incomi…" his voice was cut off by loud explosions before the warning could even leave his lips.

A searing blast of fire and metal tore through the lead snow crawler, flipping it onto its side in a spray of shattered ice and burning fuel. The force of the detonation sent soldiers sprawling, with some of them thrown through the air, and others buried beneath the burning wreckage. The sound that followed was deafening, with thunderclaps of secondary explosions, as cluster bombs deployed their deadly payloads, scattering hundreds of micro-munitions across the battlefield.

Screams rose through the comms as the realization set in. This was no skirmish, no targeted warning shot, this was pure annihilation.

The second wave hit almost instantly. High above, Veylan's attack drones descended, as their mounted railguns fired in synchronized bursts. Soldiers tried to regroup and tried to rally their officers, but the precision strikes tore into them before they could react.

Corven struggled to his feet; his ears ringing and his visor cracked from the impact. He turned in time to see three of his men running for cover behind a ridge of ice, only for a drone to swoop low and cut them down in a burst of high-velocity rounds of plasma. The impact sent them tumbling, limbs flailing; the snow beneath them staining red.

"Where's our air cover?" someone shouted through the comms, their voice edged with desperation. "Command, we need..."

The transmission cut off in a burst of static.

The bombers came next. Shadowy forms against the bleak sky, they released their payloads in unison. Thermobaric warheads detonated above the battlefield, sending waves of superheated air rolling across the ice. Those caught in the blast were lifted off their feet, their armour rupturing from the pressure before they even hit the ground.

Some soldiers were still moving, dragging themselves through the wreckage, with their suits streaked with blood and frost. Others lay twisted in the snow, their bodies frozen in final moments of agony, and their mouths open in silent screams.

The ground assault followed swiftly behind. From beyond the ridges, Veylan's shock troops advanced in mechanized trucks, their mounted cannons cutting down anyone still standing.

Corven turned, searching for his remaining men. They were scattered, disoriented, and reduced to individual survivors in a battle that had already been lost in minutes. He caught sight of Lieutenant Parven struggling to pull herself free from beneath the wreckage of an overturned vehicle. He started toward her, only for a blast from one of the advancing enemies to slam into the ice beside her, vaporizing the ground and sending her body tumbling into the pristine snow. She lay there motionless.

There was no command to surrender. No quarter was given for the few troops that had survived; there was just relentless, systematic destruction.

In the command centre of Erebus Prime, Kallos watched the incoming reports with growing horror. The first images of the battlefield were being transmitted, showing the burning wrecks, the blackened burning craters and the scattered remains of what had once been an organized brigade. The war had begun, but not in the way he had expected.

"They broke the rules," one of his officers whispered. "They used air strikes. They used drones."

Kallos didn't respond. He already knew what had happened and it sickened him to the core. Corven had been a close friend; he had been a humble soldier when Kallos had been promoted to sergeant. They had served together through several campaigns, and now he had perished. This was wrong, and Kallos now knew that the rest of his troops would be in imminent danger. The enemy would have to pay for this…

The Ice Wars had always followed a code, an unspoken agreement that warfare should remain honourable and that battles should be won through strategy, not wholesale slaughter. Veylan had discarded all of it, in a ruthless act of violent intent.

At the Warren, Hext stood at the back of the command room, with his arms folded and his face ashen with the scale of brutality that he had seen. He had never trusted Veylan to fight fairly, but even by his standards, this was appalling. He looked utterly shaken by the sheer scale of the massacre.

"They aren't fighting a war," he said quietly. "They're exterminating them."

Aboard *The Iron Will*, Veylan watched the battlefield through the tactical display, observing the destruction with detached satisfaction. The first strike of the war had been decisive, and the world was watching.

Mensen stepped forward. "Transmission is complete. The footage is already spreading through Pluto," he confirmed.

"Good," Veylan said. "Let them see what happens to those who stand in my way."

Inwardly, Veylan was starting to feel tired, and fatigued, his energy was starting to wear out. He knew he would have to return to the palace to get his next shot of youth. Had the new consignment of rejuvenation serum arrived he wondered? He was starting to run out of his last batch, and he had been assured by the Dominion that it had been sent.

"Check when you get back," he thought.

Outside, the last echoes of gunfire faded into the wind, and the ice plains stood in ruin, forever stained with the blood of the fallen.

CHAPTER SEVENTEEN - FEAR IN EREBUS PRIME

The markets of Erebus Prime, normally a hive of low murmurs, heated bartering and the rhythmic clang of machinery, had fallen into an uneasy quiet. Vendors sat behind their stalls barely tending to their wares, with their eyes directed toward the holoscreens hanging above the main square. The usual stream of glitzy adverts and planetary weather cycles had been interrupted by something far more sinister. The footage played on an endless loop. Flashes of fire against the endless white of the Ice Plains filled with billowing columns of smoke. The twisted remains of snow crawlers lay half-buried in the ruined ice. Bodies were shown; some were broken, and others were frozen in their final moments. It was a gruesome and harrowing sight. The news anchors spoke in grave and muted tones, as if raising their voices might make it worse. There had been no provocation or any engagement. Just a single, brutal strike.

A woman tending a coffee stall wiped a shaking hand across her brow as she turned back to a customer.

"Are you going to buy something, or just stand there?" she asked, her voice urging him to part with his credits. The man in front of her barely registered her words. He was completely taken over by what he was seeing.

"That was a whole brigade," he murmured. "A whole brigade!"

Another customer spoke up from the back. "It's terrible," she said, "And what if next time, it's not soldiers?"

The silence that followed was suffocating, and the people were in shock. Nothing like this had ever happened before, and the local population knew, with absolute certainty, that nothing would ever be the same again.

Across the city, in a seedy-looking bar just off the industrial sector, workers huddled around a broadcasting tabletop holo-display; the remnants of their work shifts forgotten.

A miner with soot-streaked hands slammed a fist against the table, causing his drink to slosh over the rim. "He didn't even give them a chance!" he spat. "They're supposed to have rules! This wasn't war. This was..."

He trailed off, shaking his head.

"Murder," a woman finished for him.

The bartender, a wiry man with a greying beard, poured a drink.

"And what do you expect to do about it? Do you think the Silent Watchers are going to step in…? No chance…" he said as he answered his own question.

"If Veylan's willing to wipe out an entire brigade for nothing, what do you think he'll do to anyone who speaks out?" he went on.

The table fell into brooding and worried silence.

Inside a news broadcast studio at the heart of Erebus Prime, the anchor-woman Saskia Marsek sat stiffly at her desk, barely concealing the horror in her heart. The entire news network had been given a direct transmission from *The Iron Will*. Veylan wanted the world to see what had happened and he wanted them to be afraid.

"The footage we are about to show is disturbing," she said, her voice level but her eyes betraying her disgust. "We warn all viewers…"

The transmission cut out.

A new image replaced the news feed: it was Veylan's insignia. His voice filled the airwaves.

"Let this serve as a message. Those who stand in my way will be dealt with. The old ways are dead. Pluto belongs to me." he commanded.

The feed cut back to Marsek. She stared, perfectly still, before the control team signalled for her to continue.

"You all saw that," she said finally. "Decide what that means for yourself."

She knew, deep down, that this would be her last time in that chair.

In the lower districts of Erebus Prime, where Terraformers maintained the vast underground reactors and air purification systems, whispers ran through the tunnels like wildfire.

"They say the bodies froze before they even hit the ground." "That wasn't war. That was a test. A warning." "If he can do that to trained soldiers, what do you think he'd do to us?"

In a maintenance sector, two Terraformer sympathisers exchanged hurried words, eyes darting to avoid the security drones hovering overhead that were monitoring them.

"We're just workers," one said. "We don't even fight."

"That doesn't matter anymore," the other replied. "Veylan just proved he doesn't need a reason. He only needs an excuse."

All around the city, a concerning and smothering fear and worry started to engulf the Hub.

Deep away in the AI control centre, hundreds of kilometres away on the far side of the methane ice field, something happened. In a purpose-built building built into the side of Mount Ferris, powered deep below ground by harnessing the geothermal vents, the *PLAIN Artificial Intelligence System*, which monitored everything on Pluto, suddenly burst into life.

It suddenly processed 1.2 billion data points in a microsecond.

"Probability of societal collapse: 78%. Probability of planetary-wide rebellion: 65%."

Adjusting status: *"AMBER ALERT INITIATED…"*

The doors to Veylan's private quarters slid open, and he quietly entered. The air inside this hidden sanctum was filled with a sterilized scent, and an artificially created warming breeze pumped through hidden vents. Unlike the command decks or war chambers, his retreat was bathed in warm golden hues, as a stark contrast to the world outside. Plush crimson seating was placed against the wall, a single ornate table close by, and a mirrored cabinet contained the rejuvenation serum that was so vital to his continued existence.

He moved with slow precision, stripping away his outer layers of command armour. His body was still strong, and his reactions were still quite sharp, but he could feel the exhaustion creeping in, the faintest signs of wear and tear that the serum had always erased before they could take root. He crossed the room and keyed in his genetic code, and the mirrored cabinet slid open with a soft mechanical whirr. Inside, rows of slim, crystalline vials gleamed under sterile white light. His eyes locked onto the last one.

Veylan stopped and thought. His mind reeled through the calculations in his head. This supply was meant to last until the next shipment arrived. The next shipment that, according to the Dominion, had already been dispatched. Yet the cabinet was empty. That next shipment had never come.

For the first time in years, a chill ran down his spine that had nothing to do with Pluto's climate. Even the asteroid, now 29 days away from impact, was for a fleeting moment, a complete irrelevance. He shook in fear, taking the vial in hand and rolling it between his fingers. The last one. *He had enough for one session.* One more renewal. After that, time would begin to take what he had stolen from it.

He paused… unwilling to let his inner concerns crack his carefully composed exterior. Then, with a single fluid motion, he loaded the blue vial of liquid into the injector, pressed it into the machine, and pressed the activation panel. He sat back, the machine whirred into action and the robotic arms lowered. An initial cold feeling followed a burst of warmth flooded his veins, as a synthetic surge of strength, something he had come to associate with power, with control, and with life itself, fortified him and immediately he felt stronger. But if the last shipment could not be located, then this was the last time this would happen.

He sat heavily in the chair, his fingers twiddling, his mind already spinning through the possibilities. The shipment could still be enroute. There could be a delay, or had someone stopped it? His hands clenched hard. This was not acceptable. He would get answers. And if someone had interfered, he would make an example of them.

Outside, the world feared him more than ever. But inside his private quarters, for the first time in decades, Veylan felt genuine fear of his own.

CHAPTER EIGHTEEN – A SURPRISING DISCOVERY

The Outlanders' cargo ship, *The Albatross*, approached the upper atmosphere, its hull shuddered slightly, as Kerberos' gravitational pull took effect. This moon below was starkly different from Pluto. Below them was a barren, windswept landscape of jagged rocks and shifting sand, its deep chasms and gorges forming an intricate mix of treacherous terrain. Unlike Pluto's icy plains, Kerberos was a place of dry, grey stone, its surface pitted with ancient craters, the aftermath of countless asteroid strikes over the millennia. Jessa activated the lights on the front of the cargo ship casting long shadows across the dunes as they sped along, giving it a weird, haunted feel.

At the helm, she piloted the ship with calm precision, her hands moving over the controls with practised ease. The *Albatross* was now at the far side of the moon, the side never seen from Pluto. She banked slightly to starboard, navigating toward a huge crater, the Herebus Depression that extended wide across the landscape. Inside it, its depths were barely visible through the swirling sand and dust being kicked up, as the Albatross flew deeper into it.

"This place gives me the creeps," Arras muttered, watching from the observation deck.

"Hold steady," Nyx instructed, gripping the railing as the ship descended. "Down there, see it, Jessa?"

She acknowledged.

The landing pad, barely discernible through the swirling dust, was an old Terraformer installation; it looked long abandoned but still functional. With a final controlled burn, Jessa brought *The Albatross* down onto the worn metal platform, with the ship's landing struts screeching as they adjusted to the uneven landing strip.

As the dust settled, a section of the crater wall magically split apart, revealing a hidden hangar. A massive steel door groaned open, and its reinforced mechanisms ground and screeched against years of accumulated debris. Pale white artificial lights at ground level switched on, providing a path on either side heading into the hangar.

Nyx tapped her wrist communicator. "We're in. Move us forward," she said with a smile.

Jessa guided the ship into the hangar, and as soon as the last of *The Albatross*'s bulk had crossed the threshold, the rock wall sealed shut behind them, locking them away from the harsh exterior.

The Outlanders disembarked, stepping into a huge space of several hectares. A figure waited for them amidst a cluster of supply crates; Blair Sapporas, an old ally, with his greying bearded face splitting into a huge grin as he strode forward.

"Nyx! You rogue; it's been too long," he shouted with glee.

Nyx laughed and embraced him. "Blair, you haven't aged a day." she lied.

Blair chuckled, stepping back to take in the rest of the crew. "No chance," he laughed.

His expression shifted as his attention moved to the ship. "You didn't say you were coming in on *The Albatross*," he said with surprise.

Nyx arched an eyebrow. "Why?" she inquired.

Blair laughed.

"Because that ship belongs to Mez Lipinski. And he is as dodgy as they come," he said. "How the hell did you get hold of that? And anyway, where is Mez?"

"He's dead," piped up Arras. "Got shot when we err… borrowed it."

"We took the ship, but Mez is dead," Dren confirmed.

"Suppose he's not a great loss," Blair said looking less assured, "But word will get back that he's gone. Do you know what he did? Ran cargo between Pluto and Earth, made a fortune smuggling, and not the good kind."

Blair nodded. "Even so, if he was running this route, then he was hauling more than just supplies. Have you checked the cargo hold yet?"

Nyx exchanged glances with her crew. "No…not yet," she replied, suddenly realising that they should have checked what the vehicle was carrying.

Blair's face creased. "Err… might be a good idea," he suggested.

They moved quickly, accessing the ship's lower deck where the cargo hold sat sealed. Jenna went back into the cockpit and switched the cargo doors to manual, then Arras pulled open a hatch and hit the open button. With a creak, the heavy cargo doors unlocked and slid open. The sight before them made them all pause.

Stacks of crates lined the interior, many stamped with Earth-based corporate logos, luxury goods, high-quality food supplies, and rare alcohol that would fetch a fortune on Pluto. Nyx pulled up the manifest, scanning through the inventory, and one entry caught her eye: *Special Delivery to Chancellor Veylan*.

Blair stopped, and then he looked intrigued.

"So, whatever's in here was bound for him. That means it's valuable," he said intrigued as to what they might find inside.

"What exactly did Mez smuggle, Blair?" Nyx inquired, "More than booze and black-market gear, I take it?"

Blair looked directly at her, "If it was meant for Veylan, it's worse," he said looking at the haul they had uncovered "Let's get in there and find out."

Nyx's eyes shone. "Okay, let's see what else he wanted."

Among the rows of stacked cargo, a single crate stood out. Unlike the others, it was secured with reinforced plating, the case marked with the insignia of *Purcell Laboratories*.

Blair ran a hand over the metal package, his pulse quickening. "This is Dominion biotech. No way Mez was just running luxury goods. This… this is something else." he said with quickening excitement.

Nyx pulled a multitool from her belt and started working on the crate's security lock. A moment later, there was a sharp click, the seal broke, and the lid lifted. Nyx and Blair peered in, their eyes widening at what lay before them.

Inside, nestled within a series of shock-absorbing gel compartments, was a sleek containment unit; its glass chamber was filled with a series of vials containing luminescent liquid. The vials inside pulsed with a blue shimmer, the liquid swirling as if alive. The words on the label were crisp and unmistakable - *Prototype L-17: Regenerative Enhancer.*

Blair swore under his breath. "Bloody hell! That's longevity tech," he exclaimed.

Nyx met his gaze, with realization dawning.

"You don't say…" she exclaimed, *"This is how Veylan has stayed alive for so long."*

"Then we've got more than just weapons," Blair said, "Much more than we ever bargained for… This means we've got leverage."

Nyx closed the crate carefully.

"Hmmm…, he's not gonna be happy about this," she mused, "Means he is going to come looking for us."

Blair nodded grimly.

"Yeah," he confirmed, "We'd better be ready. Because when Veylan finds out… he'll stop at nothing to get it back."

CHAPTER NINETEEN – THE SKY BURNS

The command centre of General Kallos' war room was still silent. A crushing stunned atmosphere engulfed the room at the realisation that Veylan had attacked him without being provoked. It was a vile, upsetting act that was hard to take for Kallos and his closest allies. The holoscreens were constantly playing and looping through footage of the massacre. The 22nd Brigade had been completely wiped out.

Veylan had made sure the entire planet saw it. His forces had hacked into the airwaves, broadcasting the slaughter as a warning. The Supreme Chancellor's voice, one that was cold and unrelenting, had echoed across Erebus Prime: *"This is the price of defiance."*

"Inform the families of the fallen," he commanded, his fury growing. His generals were hardened warriors who had fought beside him for years. They stood around the war table, with their faces tight with upset and disbelief. The room was filled with the weight of the loss, but Kallos' mind was already racing toward retaliation.

"We cannot let this go unanswered," Captain Joran Wallis growled, slamming his mechanical hand onto the table. "That bastard has to pay."

Kallos inhaled sharply, regaining his composure.

"I agree Joran." he said with defiance, "The gloves come off. No more skirmishes. No more tests of strength. Veylan will feel our wrath."

Those in attendance gave their approval, but Kallos wasn't finished.

"We make him overreach," he said.

His officers pressed forward, studying the updated battle plan. Kallos pointed to the Ice Fields beyond Erebus Prime.

"Okay, here's the plan," he said. "We deploy two brigades here, in full sight, close to the edge of the plains. Send a force of six warmechs and support vehicles too. Let's make it a tempting treat… something he can't refuse. I'm betting he'll see them as an easy target, another exposed force begging to be crushed. That's where he will make a huge mistake."

"Now, ready our strike force Delta out in Grimble Ridge," he said pointing to a mountain pass on the far side of the methane ice plains. "We'll route the fighters to come in low through the pass and around Mount Ferris, they won't be picked up on surface radar until the last minute, and then it'll be too late for them. Yeah, it's risky, but I bet he takes the bait and doesn't see this coming."

The trap was being set.

Meanwhile, in the towering Citadel, Veylan stood with a smirk as he observed the strategic display. The bright dots of Kallos' forces were changing, a break-off force moving across the Ice Fields heading for a point on the northern side of them in the vicinity of the tallest mountain range on the planet. He let out a low chuckle, as his advisors stood rigid around him.

"He's desperate," Veylan sneered. "He wouldn't put troops in the open unless he had no other choice."

"Chancellor, perhaps…" one of his advisors started, but Veylan cut him off with a wave of his hand.

"He thinks he can bait us." he said, "This is pathetic."

Veylan's voice was full of confidence, his arrogance unchecked as he turned to his commanding officers.

"Send four troop carriers. Load them with a full strike force. I want them deployed immediately. They will annihilate every man." he ordered.

"Yes Sire," saluted Mensen, "It shall be done."

The command passed from person to person through the chain of command, with his officers eventually relaying the orders to the launch crews. Within minutes, Veylan's military machine came alive.

From the officers' base, situated at the rear of the vast underground hangars, came an echoing tannoy announcement to begin the attack. Four massive troop carriers prepared to depart, their colossal forms illuminated by the red glow of the launch bay alert lights. Inside, thousands of Corporatist shock troopers boarded with practised precision, their armoured boots clanking against the metal ramps. Heavy-lift drones were deployed alongside them, loading artillery trucks and mechanized assault units onto the carriers.

Around the troop carriers, escort craft, small, sleek fighters equipped with advanced targeting systems, prepared to depart alongside the assault force. Accompanying them was a formation of combat drones, swarming around their larger counterparts, their glowing blue optics scanning for threats.

Veylan watched from the control tower as his war fleet prepared to depart. He turned to his officers, his smile never fading.

"Kallos has just sealed his fate." he said, "Launch the attack!"

The fleet lifted in unison, engines roaring as troop carriers and their escort craft ascended into the dark Plutonian atmosphere.

"Set a course for them, coordinates 125 dot 36 dot 98," shouted General Wesson in the lead troop ship.

"Follow in formation," he ordered.

Two in the front, two in the rear, the troop ships flanked by their escort craft set off on a direct course for the Ice Fields, their bulky forms looming like harbingers of destruction.

Back at the Isolationist's command base, Kallos was waiting for this. The moment he detected movement at the Military Base, he issued his command.

"Execute plan: Code Name *Nemesis,*" he ordered through an encrypted channel.

From the far side of Pluto, hidden beneath thick layers of ice in a deep secret bunker at Gimble Ridge, the Scorpion XE-70-type fighters were raised to launch. Ready to go, their engines roared to life. The Nemesis squadron, one by one lifted into the icy air. In arrow formation, the pilots accelerated their craft to combat speed, flying low across the terrain to evade enemy detection. They hugged the ground, through glacial valleys and the towering foothills of Mount Ferris using Pluto's jagged ice walls to mask their approach.

"Weapons hot," one of the pilots confirmed.

"Careful," said another, "We are gonna get spotted as soon as we get out into the open."

Kallos' strike fleet had timed the ambush to perfection. As the troop carriers moved farther from their base, exposed and vulnerable in open airspace, the Scorpion fighters broke from their cover. Their thrusters ignited, launching them toward the incoming foes at lethal speed.

"Engage!" shouted the lead pilot Stekis.

The first wave from the Nemesis squadron struck like a thunderclap.

The lead troop carrier erupted in a fireball, its hull splitting apart as molten debris rained down on the ice plains below. Escort fighters scrambled in disarray, alarms blaring as Kallos' squadron tore into their foes with ruthless precision.

The second carrier, which had landed and was deploying its forces, was hit next. A barrage of missiles ripped through it, fire engulfing the troop bay, sending burning fragments scattering across the tundra. The craft shuddered violently before exploding, detonating in a column of flame and debris. The shockwave reverberated across the battlefield, sending those soldiers who had disembarked tumbling as they scrambled for cover.

The third troop carrier never made it to the ground. A direct missile strike from above tore through its fuselage, rupturing its main reactor. The vessel detonated mid-air, showering fiery debris plummeting like meteorites onto the ice.

The fourth carrier, seeing the destruction of its fleet, attempted to retreat. Its thrusters flared as it veered away from the ambush, trying to escape the kill zone. But Kallos' pilots had anticipated this. Two Scorpions broke off from the main formation, chasing the carrier as it skimmed the dunes. A well-placed laser blast struck its left-wing, sending it into an uncontrolled spin. The massive ship careered toward the mountains at the edge of the Ice Plains, its hull screeching as it lost altitude. It then slammed into the jagged cliffs, shattering upon impact in an eruption of fire and rock.

Veylan's forces were in ruins.

Within minutes, all four troop carriers had been annihilated. The mechanized units inside never had a chance to engage their targets. The drones swarmed in disarray; their coordination was disrupted as they had been controlled by the lead troop carrier. These were systematically hunted down by a couple of Kallos' fighters. With the troop carriers gone, only the support craft remained. Smaller and slower than the Scorpions, they were easy prey… one by one, they fell, torn apart by Kallos' relentless pilots.

Back at the Citadel, Veylan realised that he had been duped, and he was not one to take defeat lightly. Angrily he looked at Mensen,

"Destroy them!" he raged. "Destroy them all!"

At his command, a squadron of CX-100 fighter craft launched from the Military Base. They turned as one accelerating, engines lit up towards the battlefield in retaliation. The sky above Pluto was soon to ignite with intense aerial combat.

Captain Stekis, the leader of the Nemesis strike force sounded the alert. "Watch out… watch out guys," he relayed to the rest of the squadron, "Enemy force incoming!"

He could see twelve dots on his helmet display closing in fast.

"Twelve of them," he said in an agitated tone. "Let's split up… Tiger, take your group to the North. Ravelli, you go West. My group are heading around Ferris, let's see how well they know the terrain."

For every Scorpion XE-70 that dodged and weaved through the battlefield, another was locked onto by CX-100 targeting systems.

Laser fire illuminated the void. Explosions rocked the upper atmosphere as both sides suffered losses. Three of Kallos' fighters, one from the northern trio, and two of the three that went with Ravelli exploded as they were fired on, with their pilots unable to eject in time. But in that time eight of Veylan's craft were also destroyed.

But the mountainous terrain would be to Kallos' advantage. Stekis and his wingman Axel manoeuvred through tight ravines, using the natural formations to evade their chasing foes. The CX-100 fighters, less experienced and able than Kallos' hardy veterans, fell one by one into deadly traps. A couple of their ships, faster but less nimble than the Scorpions, slammed into the ice cliffs or were picked off by well-placed missile strikes.

One left," Stekis called.

"Ravelli, position yourself near the Northern pass… and prepare to intercept," he ordered.

Stekis and Axel shot out of the icy gorge, the last CX-100 fighter tight on their tail. As they banked sharply over the ridge, dodging and weaving to avoid being hit, Ravelli waited, his targeting reticle locked on the enemy's exposed flank. One clean shot… and the Corporatist jet vapourised in a blinding explosion.

A ball of flames lit up the snowy cliffs in a sparkling glow of yellow and orange; the remains of the craft plummeted into the permafrost, with black smoke and flames billowing from the crash site.

Kallos' forces this time had prevailed.

On the streets of Erebus Prime, as news of the military escalation spread, general panic in the population started to set in.

The citizens had seen Veylan's dominance for years, but now, they had witnessed his weaknesses too. The streets were flooded with frightened citizens, fearful of what would come next. All-out war on this scale had not been seen in generations.

News channels broadcasted conflicting reports, some claiming Kallos had dealt a devastating blow, and others warning that Veylan was about to retaliate with even more force.

The war for Pluto had truly begun.

Meanwhile, far from Pluto, Admiral Devlin sat aboard the Earth Defence Command flagship, watching the chaos unfold. The war between Kallos and Veylan had escalated beyond expectation.

Devlin touched his chin, deep in thought. *This might be the opportunity we've been waiting for.*

Pluto was valuable. Its mineral wealth had once fuelled Earth's expansion, and its control slipping into warring factions meant an opportunity to reclaim it for Earth. For far too long, Earth had watched from afar as Pluto descended into chaos, its factions warring over territory, control, and power. The corporations back home had grown restless and eager to reassert dominance over the distant world before it slipped further beyond their grasp forever.

He turned to his communications officer.

"If we wait too long, someone else might take it." he said, "We can't afford to let this slip away. Send word to the Triton Space Cruisers in Jupiter orbit. They are to set course for Pluto immediately."

The officer hesitated for a moment, sensing the gravity of the order. "At full burn, Admiral?" he asked cautiously.

Devlin shook his head.

"No, we move carefully… at cruising speed," he said with calculated precision in his voice, "Two weeks from now, Pluto will be ours. Let them fight amongst themselves like cats and dogs. We don't want to announce our arrival too soon. Let them destroy each other first. Then we take what remains."

The command was given. Across the void, the Triton fleet adjusted course, engines firing as they prepared for the long journey. Twelve massive cruisers, each bristling with weaponry and loaded with Earth's elite marines, pivoted in perfect unison, setting their trajectory for Pluto's orbit. Onboard, soldiers trained relentlessly, drilling for planetary assault. Engineers prepped landfall vehicles, ensuring every detail of the operation was accounted for.

The war for Pluto was no longer just between Kallos and Veylan.

Now, Earth was coming… silent, patient, and inevitable.

CHAPTER TWENTY - THE WARREN STIRS

The Warren was unlike any other place on Pluto. While Erebus Prime stood as a monument to industry and the warlike spirit of its rulers, and the Outlands were a brutal testament to ingenuity and plain survival, here was an oasis of calm. This was a place where science and nature collided and was filled with wisdom and the belief that something better would prevail. Cutting-edge scientific research juxtaposed with quiet libraries filled with knowledge salvaged from Earth's fading archives. This was the heart of the Terraformers' dream and a place where Pluto could be more than a frozen graveyard.

Glowing tendrils of blue-green fungi wove through the icy ceilings, casting an ethereal glow over the stone chambers. The air was crisp and clean, and carrying the faint scent of hydroponic vegetation. Water trickled from carefully crafted channels in the walls, feeding into underground reservoirs that sustained the ecosystem. Wooden benches and metal walkways circled the chamber, where Terraformers sat or stood, deep in considered conversation.

But tonight, even the Warren's usual quiet was disturbed.

Hext sat at the head of a circular stone table, keenly observing the demeanour of those gathered. His most trusted advisors had come to talk including the leaders of the movement, as well as strategists and scientists. Some wore the loose, earth-toned robes of the agricultural teams, with their hands calloused from tending to the underground farms. Others bore the insignias of the scientific teams, with their minds fixed on being responsible for maintaining the Warren's fragile systems. And among them, Steffan and Zari, their younger presence a sign that the next course of action would not be dictated by scholars alone.

Hext surveyed the others seated around him, with his expression heavy with concern.

"The cycle is broken," he said, his voice deep, slow and resigned to the seriousness of the situation. "The Ice Wars were meant to be the construct through which power was transferred, but now? Out on the plains, there is a battle of unchecked rage going on. Veylan and Kallos are at each other's throats, and the Corporatists and Isolationists will tear this planet apart if we do nothing at all. We have always prepared for the transition of power by watching from afar, and waiting for the new ruler to emerge. But I predict that there will be no new ruler this time. There will only be ashes and mindless destruction."

A sense of agreement spread around those gathered. Even those who had once believed they could remain neutral now saw the storm coming.

Steffan sat relatively relaxed, his elbows resting on his table. "So, what do we do?" he asked.

His voice was measured but firm.

"We don't have an army." he said, " I know that we've traditionally stayed out of the bloodshed but if we don't intervene, then Pluto as we know it won't survive. And as you've seen, my father is a ruthless killer, and he'll stop at nothing to hold onto power."

Hext nodded. "That is why we must act now. But not through war. Through control." he said.

A hush fell over the room - the importance of those words carried a potential plan that he was hatching.

Zari, her long dark hair covering her shoulders, beckoned to speak. She wasn't a Terraformer, not truly. She had been drawn to their peaceful cause, as she realised that the status quo would never be sustainable. Unbeknownst to all there, she was Nyx Orban's younger sister. She was more graceful than her older sibling, medium height, slim, more academic than Nyx who was a rogue, a wanderer who had lived more in the lawless spaces between the factions than within them.

Since their parents had been killed, the two sisters had gone their separate ways. She had chosen the path of the Terraformers because of her own beliefs, and now she had found a soul mate in Steffan, not just because of his title and family, but because he believed in something she did too. But the others didn't know this. And she had chosen to be here this day. *Because of him.*

He intrigued her, not just because he was strong or ruthless, but because he was choosing a different path despite the danger. His convictions fascinated her. And whether she admitted it or not, that fascination was drawing her closer to him.

She crossed her arms and queried what Hext had just said.

"Control?" she asked. "You mean power. What power *do we have*?"

Hext looked at her with something like approval.

"We have the power to stop this war before it consumes everything." he said pausing and glancing toward Steffan before continuing, "But it will take precision, and it will take sacrifice."

A few voices whispered among the group. The Terraformers had never been the ones to take direct action, not like this. Their strength had always been in their ideas, in their ability to endure, not in the ways of conquest.

Steffan sat up straighter. "You mean to take control of the power stations?" he asked.

Hext nodded.

"It is the one thing that unites them all." he declared, "Without energy, the mines freeze over and the industrial sectors collapse. Erebus Prime will be plunged into darkness. Even Kallos and his warriors need warmth and oxygen to sustain their war efforts. If we hold the power grids, we hold Pluto, and we force a change."

It was a bold plan, dangerous, and unprecedented for them all.

Then Professor Laxley, one of the elder scientists with short grey hair and metal-rimmed glasses piped up.

"If we take control of the power grids, we're no better than them," he warned.

One of the hydroponic engineers murmured. "We've built a home here… we're not going to put all that at risk, are we?"

Hext looked at both of them, "Yes, I understand," he said sympathetically,

"But Vaylen's a monster, Kallos will not stop until he's won his spurs. And if we don't act, all the work we've been doing over decades will be for nothing," he exclaimed, waving his hands in a cancelling motion."

We have to act, and we have to do something drastic that will keep them from falling over the edge of the cliff." he went on.

Zari at this point was thinking ahead, her instincts were screaming at her. This wasn't just about survival anymore; this was about taking back Pluto from those who had misused it. And if they had any way to force negotiations, or to influence the combatants, they had to act decisively.

She glanced around the room, the intensity of the discussion going on around her, left her seat, and then stepped back, slipping into the darkness near the chamber exit. Without anyone noticing, she activated her private comm link.

"Nyx," she whispered urgently, her fingers tightening around the device. "I need your help."

A few moments of static, and then a voice crackled through.

"Zari? What in the Void are you tangled up in now?" Nyx exclaimed.

Zari's pulse quickened. "This isn't just my problem. The whole planet is about to go under. We need the Outlanders. We need you. Did you see what happened on the Methane Icefields? It was terrible Sis, so many casualties, my heart goes out to them. We need to stop this war before it gets out of control." she pleaded.

"Yes, I saw," she replied. "Word has got around here on Kerberos."

"What the hell are you doing out there?" inquired Zari, "Last time we spoke you had just been to the Palace for that meeting."

"Getting away from that asteroid." she said with brutal honesty, "If the wars don't destroy Pluto, that thing might!"

There was a pause. Then, more cautiously, Nyx asked, "What exactly are you planning?"

Zari looked back at her.

"We're taking the power grid. If we control it, we can force a negotiation. But we need backup, and you have the people." she went on.

A long silence followed. Then Nyx's tone shifted. "You don't even know, do you?"

Zari frowned. "Know what?" she said none the wiser.

Nyx let out a humourless chuckle. "We took a cargo ship. Stole it from the Corporatist bastards. And you're never gonna guess what we found inside it?" she said.

"No idea," replied Zari looking puzzled.

"Well, we just cracked open the hold. It's not just supplies... it's rejuvenation serum." exclaimed Nyx.

"Veylan's serum. And it came from Earth! That's why he never seems to age!" she said excitedly.

The breath left Zari's lungs. "You're sure?" she questioned.

"One hundred percent," Nyx replied with certainty.

"Veylan will burn Pluto to the ground to get it back," Zari warned.

"Yeah, I know," said Nyx, her voice was laced with something sharp... realization.

Zari stood rigid. No one had known that Veylan was even taking treatments, let alone knew where that had come from. Nobody had known how he had managed to extend his life beyond all expectations. Now, the truth was staring them in the face. Veylan wasn't just ruling Pluto; *he was Earth's pawn!*

She pressed a hand to her forehead. This wasn't just leverage. This was evidence.

"Thanks, Sis," she said, "This now changes everything."

She cut the comm and turned back toward the meeting chamber, her heart beating out of her chest. They had more than power now. They had proof that Veylan's reign had been propped up by Earth itself.

Hext raised an eyebrow as she rejoined them. "Everything alright?" he asked her.

Zari exchanged a glance with Steffan, a spark of understanding passing between them.

"Better than alright," she said. "We just found our insurance policy."

Hext looked on, but the fire in his eyes burned bright. "Tell me everything," he said, encouraging her to open out.

For the first time, Zari hesitated. This wasn't just a revelation. This was a fracture in Pluto's very foundation. If Earth had been keeping Veylan in power, what else had they been controlling? And what would they do when they realized the Terraformers had figured it out?

Taking a deep breath, she began. The gathering sat stunned as Zari recounted what her sister had told her. This was a moment of truth and clarity; the balance had suddenly shifted into their hands.

After she finished, the room remained utterly silent. Hext studied everyone there, seeing the same realization mirrored in their eyes. This wasn't just about power anymore. *It was about truth… and truth had consequences.*

Realising the gravity of the moment, Hext stood and addressed the others, "If this is true, then we have more than leverage, we have the key to Pluto's future right here in our hands. We must decide very carefully how to use it."

For Steffan, these revelations about his father came as a complete shock to the system. He knew his father had been born on Earth, and he had always known, to his cost, that his father's rule was built on fear and brutality, but to discover that it had been Earth's backing that kept him in power? That was something else entirely. He had spent his life fighting against his father, but he had never imagined he would be fighting against the forces that had made him. The storm was coming, and Steffan knew one thing for certain… he was on the right side of it.

The Warren was silent as they filed out, each of them knowing that the next moves had to be played to perfection.

Steffan and Zari moved together, side by side. And as they stepped toward the transport chamber, for the first time, he felt her reach for his hand.

She didn't say anything. She didn't need to.

And Steffan, against all reason, held on.

Outside the storm of war was rising, but for this moment, they had each other.

CHAPTER TWENTY-ONE - THE RECKONING APPROACHES

Deep in the void of space, the messenger of death tumbled through the darkness, the vast, pot-marked asteroid, its surface scarred by aeons of cosmic debris. It was nearly twenty kilometres in diameter, a colossal force of nature now set on an inescapable collision course with Pluto. Twenty-five days remained before impact, but its presence was already undeniable.

It spun slowly as it moved, its irregular mass catching the distant light of the stars, casting brief glints of reflected brightness before returning to shadow. Inside its irregularly shaped crust, were layers of metal and stone compacted over millennia. Scientists had once speculated that such objects could be remnants of planetary cores, or maybe fragments of shattered worlds lost to time. But whatever its origin, this asteroid had only one destination.

The calculations were certain. If it struck Pluto directly, the force would be apocalyptic. Even at its current velocity, travelling at over twenty kilometres per second, the sheer kinetic energy of the impact would equal tens of thousands of nuclear warheads. Entire regions might be vaporized instantly. Pluto's thin atmosphere, already fragile, could be scattered into space. Tidal forces could trigger global seismic shifts, which could fracture the crust, destabilize underground colonies, and unleash frozen methane into the atmosphere.

The Warren, Erebus Prime, Kerberos, all of it could be obliterated or buried beneath kilometres of ice and debris. Even if the asteroid merely grazed the planet, the shockwaves could render vast swathes of Pluto uninhabitable for generations. Yet, amid the chaos of war, few had the means, or the will, to deal with the looming threat. All eyes were turned toward the battle for power, totally oblivious to the silent destroyer bearing down on them.

Far from the asteroid's path, another force was hurtling toward Pluto. The Triton-class battlecruiser Redoubtable, a spearhead of Earth's Dominion fleet, led twelve heavily armed warships through the abyss, each vessel leaving a faint ion trail in its wake. Having set off from Jupiter, they were now eleven days from Pluto.

The Redoubtable was a monster of a warship, one kilometre in length, its armoured hull a fortress of reinforced alloy plating. Its engines, housed in colossal propulsion chambers at the rear, allowed it to reach speeds of 150,000 kilometres per hour in deep space, slower than smaller fighters, but its sheer firepower made speed a secondary concern. The ship was built not for speed, but for domination.

Its crew of 3,200 personnel worked in shifts, maintaining weapons systems, monitoring sensor arrays, and ensuring that their approach remained undetected until the final push. Twelve heavy plasma cannons, all capable of accelerating destruction at near-relativistic speeds, lined its flanks. Ballistic torpedoes, which were designed to punch through even the thickest planetary defences, were locked in their launch bays. The ship carried dozens of drop pods and orbital bombardment munitions, all of which were primed for a planetary assault. Interceptor Kestrel squadrons waited in their bays, with their pilots on high alert for the moment that they would be deployed.

Inside the bridge, Captain Jed Iseman stood with his hands clasped behind his back, with his sharp eyes watching the data scrolling across the holo-table. The whole of the command deck was alive with quiet calm efficiency, with officers at their stations reading real-time reports, and ensuring the Redoubtable and its accompanying fleet remained on course. The warm air inside the ship blasted out from the vents, heated from the excess energy expelled from the reactor core, an ever-present reminder of the ship's immense power.

A signal crackled to life.

"Fleet status report," Iseman ordered, tapping a control panel. "All captains, check in please."

One by one, the commanders of the twelve warships responded:

Resolute – Operational. Weapons systems primed.

Imperator – Minor fluctuations in shielding, adjustments in progress.

Hammerfall – Reactor fully charged. Ready for engagement.

Ironclad – Flight squadrons prepped and standing by.

Vanguard – No anomalies. Maintaining formation.

The rest of the fleet followed suit, each ship reporting combat readiness. Finally, Captain Iseman opened a direct line to Admiral Devlin stationed at Earth Command. The holographic projection materialised, then solidified, revealing Devlin's stern face; he looked business-like as always.

"Status?" Devlin asked curtly.

"We're on schedule. Eleven days from Pluto," Iseman responded. "Fleet systems are stable, weapons primed. No detected resistance so far."

Devlin seemed contentment with this, nodding his approval.

"Good." he said, "When you arrive, you will establish orbital superiority immediately. No hesitation. No diplomacy. We cannot afford to let Pluto's factions unite against us."

Iseman's bowed his head in complete agreement.

"Understood, Admiral," he replied.

The transmission ended, and silence filled the bridge. The Earth fleet was coming. And they were ready for war.

On Neptune's outermost moon, Neso, a group of hooded figures stood in a softly lit chamber. The Forgotten Seers, long exiled from Pluto's main settlements, gathered around an ancient observation console, watching as a holographic projection of the asteroid slowly drifted across the starfield.

"The collision is unavoidable," Mirath murmured.

"There is nothing we can do," Solas agreed solemnly. "Even if they united, no force on Pluto could stop it."

A moment of silence hung in the air between them all. Then, the eldest Seer, Talleron, turned his attention to the second projection, a live feed from hidden satellite arrays above Pluto.

On the display, Erebus Prime stood silent, but its people were terrified. Fear clung to the air like mist, whispering through the corridors of power and the alleyways of the city. The citizens, caught between uncertainty and dread, whispered of what might come next. Would the battles raging beyond their walls spill into their streets?

Would Earth's fleet arrive and impose their rule? Or worse... would the asteroid bring destruction to them all? The Outlands lay abandoned, their inhabitants having fled. The factions were turning on each other. Kallos' forces and Veylan's troops had already suffered heavy casualties, with a battalion of Kallos' men lost, and many of Veylan's forces were dead in the relentless conflict. It looked as if each was determined to take full control of Pluto's fate. Veylan, despite losing many men, was still strong. He had seized control of the planetary airwaves and had been broadcasting his propaganda and warnings to all the sectors, as he sought to consolidate his rule in desperation. Worse would inevitably come, as this conflict still had far to go.

"They are fighting among themselves, blind to what is coming," Solas said. "And when Earth arrives, there will be no one left to stand against them."

The younger Seer, Sian, spoke hesitantly. "There is something else. PLAIN is entering override mode," she said with some concern in her voice.

The chamber fell silent.

PLAIN—the Pluto Legislative Artificial Intelligence Network controlled Pluto's vital resources. If it switched over to override mode, the consequences would be catastrophic. If its directives changed in response to planetary destabilization, it could shut down all of the government systems including the money supply, social services, justice, medical services, education, and entire power grids and it might even lock off vital life support systems. The automated sentries guarding key infrastructure would follow the new protocols without question, effectively locking workers out of their workplaces.

"And the Terraformers?" Talleron asked.

Sian adjusted the projections, showing Hext's forces preparing for their next move.

"They have a plan." she said, "They intend to cripple the power grids, forcing both Kallos and Veylan into submission. If they succeed, Pluto's entire balance of power will shift."

Talleron's gaze lingered on Hext's image.

"Then he might be the only one left capable of bringing reason to this crisis. But have we factored in what he now knows? He is no longer operating in the dark. He knows about Veylan's rejuvenation process, and his reliance on Earth's supply. That changes things." he said somewhat concerned.

"But how do we reach him?" another Mesath asked. "He trusts no one outside his circle. And more importantly, have we considered Nyx Orban and the Outlanders? They have been hiding carefully away from the planet, and their role in this is still uncertain. If they hold the serum, they hold the key to Veylan's downfall. If we fail to account for them, we risk being blindsided." he advised.

Solas put his hands together as if he were pleading. "We must find a way. If the factions can unite, they can fight back. They can win. But someone must force them to the table." he said.

Talleron closed his eyes. "Then we must send word. And we must do it now."

A thought crossed his mind, a realization forming like a constellation appearing in the dark. "Zari..." he murmured.

The others turned toward her. "Is she not one of us?" Solas asked.

"Yes, she is," Talleron said, "She is by far the stronger of the two, but she is too young," he replied.

"She is the link between the Outlanders and the Terraformers," Mesath said. "She walks between their worlds, trusted by all. If an alliance could be formed, it might be the only way to unite them all in time," he said trying to pull all the information that had together.

Mesath's concentration became more intense.

"If we try and reach her, is she developed enough to understand our call, and bridge the divide?" he queried, "Hext may listen to her. Her sister definitely would. And with the Outlanders and the Terraformers together, there may yet be a chance to bring order to the chaos before Earth arrives."

"It's a risk," Sian muttered, "So much responsibility for one so young. But what other choice do we have? If Pluto is to survive, it must stand as one."

Talleron nodded. "Then Zari will be our message. And we must ensure she hears it." he decided.

"There's something else," Solas added, his mind racing through the connections they had failed to see before. "Zari isn't just tied to the Outlanders and the Terraformers. Her growing relationship with Steffan means she is also connected, however indirectly to Veylan himself. If there is any chance to bridge the divide, she might be the one person who can thread all these factions together."

The realization that this young girl might be the answer they were looking for was going to be a risk, but one worth taking.

Zari was the unlikely link between the Seers, the Terraformers, the Outlanders, and even Veylan's fractured empire. She might hold the key to stopping everything from collapsing into oblivion. But would she see it that way? Would she even listen? At this moment, there was no way she would trust Veylan, and her growing bond with Steffan would only make that more difficult. Steffan despised his father's rule and would never sanction her as an intermediary. If anything, he would warn her against any attempt to engage with Veylan, knowing the kind of manipulator he was. Zari was many things, but naïve was not one of them. She would see through any deceit, and Veylan would know it. That made her a potential threat to him, not an ally.

Talleron composed himself, his fingers drumming the edge of the table. "There is one more thing we have not yet considered," she said, her voice lower now, as if speaking the words aloud would make them too real.

"What lies beneath the ice," he said with ultimate seriousness in his voice.

The chamber fell into an even deeper silence. Solas appeared content as if he already knew where this conversation was heading.

"You don't mean…" he asked in hesitation.

"I do," Talleron confirmed. "For centuries, we have protected the knowledge of what remains buried beneath Pluto's ice. It has been our sworn duty to keep it hidden, to ensure that no ruler, no faction, no invading force would ever awaken it. But if Pluto is truly at the end, if they stand on the precipice of annihilation, then perhaps the time has come."

Sian, pale and uncertain, shifted uncomfortably.

"Revealing it now… it could change everything," she said. "Yes, at some point Zari must be told. But it could shift the entire balance of power. But at what cost?"

Talleron looked at the gathered Seers, he looked unimpressed.

"The factions will not listen to us on our word alone." he said, "But if we bring them something that cannot be ignored; if we show them the *Truth*, then they will have no choice. This knowledge could force them to unite. Or it could doom them all,"

Mesath inhaled deeply, the gravity of the moment was very apparent.

"Then the question is no longer *if* we should intervene." he said concentrating intently, sensing the moods of the others, "It is how much we are willing to reveal, to save Pluto from itself."

As the asteroid tumbled closer, as Earth's fleet surged toward Pluto, the Forgotten Seers reached out, preparing to change the course of history.

And for the first time in centuries, they knew they would have to break their long silence

CHAPTER TWENTY-TWO - A CHANCE OF SALVATION

In his private office at home in the dead of night, news reached Veylan, flashing across his private holo-terminal like a beacon of despair and renewed hope. The rejuvenation serum, his lifeline, had indeed arrived on Pluto, but it had vanished as quickly as it had come.

The revelation was both a blessing and a curse. His pulse quickened as he read the report from Earth Command. The serum had been sent aboard a cargo vessel, the *Albatross*, and it had docked a week prior. But soon after it arrived, the ship had been hijacked by a band of thieves, and they had escaped into the void, with the ship reported last seen heading in the direction of Kerberos.

The revelation sent a surge of energy through his veins, a fire greater than even his serum could provide. If the *Albatross* was out there, then he still had a chance. If he could retrieve it, then he could survive! He would not wither into old age, and he would not fade into irrelevance. He would rule Pluto until the system itself crumbled to dust.

He went back to bed and slept well that night, better than he had done in a couple of weeks. His mortality had been constantly on his mind, as this was something he was truly scared of. Kallos and the rest of the population on Pluto, he could deal with, even Devlin on Earth was at arm's length, and the asteroid? All reports said that on its current track, it would land far enough away from Erebus Prime to give the planet a fighting chance of pulling through. Without the serum though, he faced a certain death sentence. He would get it back... *at any cost.*

At Moonrise, Veylan rose and went into the living quarters to find his ever-loving wife had prepared him a snack before he started his day. Lirien was so loyal, so caring. It was a shame that many on the planet did not see him in the light that she did. He finished his meal with gusto, hugged her, then departed for his waiting speeder which was ready to take him to the Command Centre at the Central Spire.

As he entered with a flourish, the room was a buzzing hive of activity, with officers checking holo-screens and displaying tactical readouts, and others planning new troop movements. The pulse of war fuelling all this activity was ever spreading across Pluto. His top advisors stood at the ready, awaiting his orders, with their faces strained because of their complete and utter fear of him. Apprehension overtook the room as the preparations for battle continued.

From the other side, security doors slid open, and a young junior officer strode forward, his brow soaked with sweat. He nervously looked around the room before saluting Veylan. He then lifted the data pad he was carrying, standing as upright as he could before speaking.

"Supreme Chancellor." he announced, voice trembling, "We have completed our full investigation on the cargo ship *Albatross*. The findings are… alarming."

Veylan's mood darkened slightly as he gestured for the officer to proceed.

The officer took a deep breath, steadying himself. "The *Albatross*'s hijacking was not a random act of piracy. This was a military-style operation, coordinated with extreme precision," he said, trying to keep his composure.

"The perpetrators infiltrated Spaceport security using falsified credentials and cybernetic overrides having taken the ship's captain hostage." he said, "Once inside, they took control of the central docking command, rerouting clearance codes and overrode launch protocols. The entire operation lasted less than ten minutes. And… they killed the captain, so he can't speak…"

Veylan's narrowed eyes burned with restrained fury. "And the security teams?" he asked, his distaste for this news rising rapidly,

"They failed," the officer said, voice barely above a whisper.

"All five guards at the main docking control have been eliminated and replaced," he reported.

"Did we identify any of these criminals?" Veylan inquired.

"Yes, AI did identify one," replied the officer pulling up a holograph image of her, "Lysara Bestrovic, 28 years, worked formally at the Ministry of Justice, single, last known as part of the Outlanders group, although we are not sure if they were involved in this heist."

"Whoever did this was fast, and efficient though, and well-trained." he went on, "We suspect ex-military or professional mercenaries. They left no DNA traces, no comm signatures."

Veylan became more irritated as he studied the holograph. "A former Ministry of Justice officer?" he snapped back.

He was becoming angrier by the second at this. "That means she knows the system," he said. "She'll know how to stay hidden."

His impatience grew. "Find her. Find her now," he screamed.

Heated discussion spread through the chamber as advisors exchanged uneasy glances. Veylan calmed himself, realising the young officer was only doing his job.

"Continue," he said.

"Once aboard the *Albatross*, the hijackers disabled the station's auxiliary power relays, ensuring no manual override could be activated." he said, "They initiated an emergency launch hatch at Pad 4, escaping before reinforcements could respond."

The officer then hesitated, clenching his datapad tighter.

"Two of our CX-100 ships, the *Drackon* and *Severis*, were destroyed on the ground." he said looking pensive, "A third in pursuit, the *Tamerin* was also shot down. All pilots were killed. Civilian casualties too – these were unavoidable."

He lowered the datapad and bowed his head.

Silence fell over the war room as the enormity of the report settled in. Veylan's fingers banged against the holo-display below him, his rage simmering beneath his composed exterior.

"Total casualties?" he finally asked.

"Eighteen confirmed dead, Sir." he reported, "Another forty-two wounded, including security personnel and civilians. Damage to the hangar facilities is extensive, repairs are ongoing. The *Albatross* was last tracked leaving orbit before she disappeared… we think she was heading toward Kerberos when it vanished from our scanners. Either they have sophisticated cloaking technology, or they have powerful allies beyond Pluto."

Veylan by this time had lost his temper, his fury rising as he banged the table.

"And you tell me they walked into my spaceport, killed my people, and stole from me." he raged, "And we don't even know who they are? No leads? No suspects?"

The officer hesitated sheepishly.

"There are whispers, Supreme Chancellor." he said trying to reassure him, "Black-market smugglers, rogue mercenaries, even rumours that the Isolationists could have orchestrated the heist. But nothing definitive."

Veylan turned toward a shadowy figure near the edge of the room. Castor, his most trusted assassin, had been listening in silence. He was a threatening individual. He had slicked-back black hair, piercing dark eyes, he was tall, and he had the physique of an athlete, despite the fact he was in his middle age.

"Castor... come here!" he bellowed.

"*Find them!* Hunt them down, no matter where they run. On that ship was a special consignment. *I need it*!" he stressed with urgency.

"It will be in a special cargo container from Purcell Laboratories." he went on, "*Do not let them destroy it!* If they resist, burn them from existence."

Castor's dark eyes glinted with amusement as he nodded.

"As you command Sire," he said saluting sharply.

Veylan's mood became more authoritative.

"You have my full authority," he ordered, "Take as many resources as necessary. If you need ships, take them. If you need weapons, requisition them. If you need men, command them. No restrictions. No mercy."

Castor smiled menacingly.

"Understood Sire," he replied. "I'll return with what you need. Or with a trail of bodies leading straight to it."

Castor turned toward the exit.

"I'll find them, Supreme Chancellor." he said in a cool and calculating manner, "And when I do... they'll wish the ship exploded with them inside."

Without another word, the assassin turned and left the chamber, already tapping into his private network of operatives. He would track them to the ends of the system if he had to.

Veylan breathed slowly, his mood calming as he knew Castor was very good at what he did. He still had time. And while Castor hunted down his salvation, he would begin the final push against Kallos. No more diplomacy. No more careful manoeuvring. He would come out on top, no matter the cost.

CHAPTER TWENTY-THREE - THE INFERNO OF WAR

And then, out in the icy wilderness, the true war began.

These normally serene and desolate places suddenly erupted into violence.

Columns of warmechs, their towering frames gleaming under Pluto's ever-present twilight, advanced across this frigid land, and for this battle, both sides had them.

The warmechs stood like titanic war gods on the battlefield, their colossal frames towering 20 to 30 meters above the chaos. Unlike the bipedal war machines of Earth's past, these giants of military precision rolled forward on reinforced tank treads, their massive weight evenly distributed by graviton stabilizers to keep them from sinking into any unstable terrain. Micro-thrusters along their flanks flared periodically, correcting their balance as they advanced, while thick armour plating, made from silver-coloured plutonium-infused composite alloys gleamed beneath the faint glow of Pluto's distant Sun and moons. Despite their size, they moved with calculated precision and agility; they were the almost unstoppable juggernauts of destruction that no ordinary force could hope to stop.

Each warmech was a walking arsenal, bristling with weaponry capable of annihilating entire platoons in seconds. Twin Plasma Devastators pulsed from each side. They also had railguns, they could launch cluster warheads and possessed energy blades to cut down enemy troops and vehicles at lower levels.

They were not just war machines, they were the enforces of empires, determining the course of battles by their mere presence. Urban landscapes could crumble beneath their onslaught, and industrial sectors had burned as their Hellstorm Flamethrowers washed the streets with their fire. Any enemy formations would shatter beneath the relentless pounding of their treads.

The pinnacle of Veylan's forces, these Cygnus Class warmechs, powered through the ice, their propulsion units hissing in the freezing air. Behind them, lines of Corporatist infantry advanced in formation, their pulse rifles gleaming as they moved under the cover of mobile energy shields.

As they advanced, some artillery units rolled into position behind the main line, launching high-explosive plasma shells into the distance. The shells detonated in brilliant bursts, carving deep craters into the battlefield, and turning pointed ice formations into deadly shrapnel.

Kallos' forces were ready too. They had positioned themselves amongst the more substantial ice flows by a glacier, setting up remote-controlled plasma turrets along the low ridges. These areas provided natural cover for his troops. Snipers wielding mobile missile launchers and soldiers operating laser rifles had already calculated the angles of fire, waiting for the right moment to strike. They knew the terrain well as they trained out here regularly. And they knew the one true weakness of the warmechs, deep crevasses in the ice. Yes, these Warmechs had micro thrusters, but once caught down in a crevasse, they were of no use whatsoever. The plan was to corral Veylan's forces towards a series of unseen fissures in the frozen methane, hidden traps that would hopefully devastate their forces.

The moment Veylan's warmechs reached the designated kill zone, plasma turrets hidden within the ice ridges powered up and fired. The first shots struck with precision, and explosions rocked the field as the lead warmech, a massive unit designated Goliath-7, took a direct hit to its left stabilizer. The giant machine groaned as it sustained some damage, fire emanating from one of the side ports, but it kept on rolling. For these machines to be stopped, it would take much more.

Kallos was out on the front line on the Eastern Ice Ridge visiting the troops to keep up morale and to show that he wasn't the type to just sit away from the battle like Veylan did.

"What's your name private?" Kallos said to a young soldier who was checking over his plasma rifle.

"Vijay, sir," the younger soldier said,

"First time in battle?" Kallos went on, and the young man nodded his head.

"Good for you," he said, pointing outwards to the ice dune that was about two hundred metres from them.

"Now Vijay," he said, "As soon as you see the enemy starting to get round the side over there, fire your plasma gun to get them to tempt them out. And then take immediate cover" he said hatching a plan.

The guys over there on Turret number 2 will be waiting." he went on, "As soon as they show their position, we'll give them all we've got, okay?"

The young soldier wasn't gonna argue.

"Yes sir," he confirmed and saluted to him.

Having met the troops, Kallos jumped into a speeder and headed along the edge of the Ice Ridge heading back to the Communications centre followed by Captain Rello in another one. Just as they were less than a kilometre from their destination, a barrage of fire came from beyond the ice dunes on the plain.

Suddenly without warning, there was a whoosh and a high-pitched scream of a plasma shell incoming towards them both. A split-second moment of silence was followed by a huge explosion just behind Kallos, so strong that he was thrown off his speeder, which careered off to his right into a snow drift. Lethal shards of frozen methane shattered around him, as he tried to remain as still as possible. Then there was a moment of peace and a deathly silence. He checked himself. He was battered and bruised but otherwise okay.

Wondering what happened to his comrade, he shouted out, "Rello, you okay?"

There was silence, except for the crackle of flames and the smell of burning fuel. Fearing the worst, Kallos looked behind him to see a most upsetting sight. Rello's speeder was in pieces burning and smoking, and lying nearby in a pool of blood was the captain. Kallos felt sick and hurt for his colleague, and then the anger and rage in him kicked in.

Wishing for immediate revenge, Kallos got onto his wrist communicator and made a call.

"Fire at will!" he screamed over the comms, his voice shaking with fury at the chaos around him.

He stopped for a second, looked up and then seeing that the shelling had stopped, he ran over to the speeder, which was on its side, but still working. Grabbing it out of the methane snow, he righted it, fired it up and headed back to the base and relative safety. It had been a very close call…

On hearing Kallos' command, from their concealed positions, the Isolationist strike teams emerged, launching a wave of portable EMP missiles toward Veylan's mechanized units. The pulse waves disrupted targeting systems and scrambled sensors, forcing the Corporatist warmechs to fire blindly. Snipers hidden within ice caverns picked off Corporatist officers, their plasma guns cutting through command squads with pinpoint precision.

From above, the CX-100 fighter craft roared in.

Veylan's fighters screamed through Pluto's thin atmosphere, their engines leaving trails of condensation as they unleashed barrages of plasma missiles toward the ground. Below, Kallos' anti-air defences retaliated with his Harbinger Gunships. These slower and heavy craft were very well armed, could hover and release missiles and they carried swarms of drone fighters. These drones were small, and light and carried small laser cannons that could wipe out ground troops very effectively.

A trio of CX-100s locked onto a gunship, firing their laser cannons. The Harbinger's heavy shielding absorbed the initial blast, but before it could return fire, a dozen drone craft swarmed the fighters, peppering them with laser rounds. One of the CX-100's cockpit shattered, sending its pilot tumbling into the abyss below.

On the ground, destruction spread like wildfire.

Veylan's warmechs unleashed their plasma cannons, melting ice as they advanced. Explosions sent shards of frozen methane rocketing through the air, impaling soldiers from both sides. Infantry formations fell back under the sheer force of the mechanized weaponry, only to be flanked by Kallos' guerrilla troops using hover bikes to weave between warmechs and plant high-explosive charges on them.

Further, along the battlefield, shield generators switched on and off as Corporatist support engineers struggled to keep defensive barriers operational. The icy winds carried the screams of the wounded as medical evacuation units darted through the carnage, dragging the injured to temporary medical units set up at the side of the ice plains.

Outside, the ice plains burned, fighters streaked low across the void, smoke rose from burnt-out machinery, and drones hovered menacingly overhead, scanning for the enemy. In the distance, the pounding of heavy guns punctuated the frigid air.

Beyond the reinforced walls of the strategy centre, the battlefield raged, fire streaked through the sky, and the ice plains shuddered under the force of war. Inside, Kallos watched the carnage unfold on holoscreens, he appeared pained yet concentrated.

"Progress report," he ordered.

"We're holding our own, just…" reported Joran.

"We've lost a lot of men, three Harbingers, and the Eastern Ridge had taken a fearful battering," came the reply from his second in command.

"But we've successfully diverted a lot of those warmechs towards the crevasse field." he said, "They aren't gonna know what's hit them."

The two men looked at each other, they were in it for the long haul now…

Amar Azpera was a 31-year-old sergeant in the Independent's Pulse Turret division. His hands were shaking inside his frost-lined protection suit, sweat running down his forehead as he tried to keep his composure. His voice came ragged over the comms, fogging the inside of his visor as he slammed another energy core into the turret's capacitor.

The ground trembled beneath him, his teeth rattling with every distant explosion. Somewhere beyond the ice ridges, warmechs thundered forward, their motors groaning against the frigid air.

"Pulse Turrets, status!" Amar screamed, his voice cutting through the chaos.

"Turret Two's overheating, cycling down!" came a desperate reply. "We're down to half charges! If we don't get resupplied, we're cooked!"

Amar wiped the frost from his visor and looked over the lip of their trench.

The battlefield before him appeared like a nightmare of metal and fire. Plasma streaks carved through the darkness, cutting into the icy ground like molten steel. Missiles streaked overhead, illuminating the blizzard-filled sky, before slamming into the distant frozen cliffs, sending cascades of shattered ice raining down onto the bodies below.

And beyond it all… the warmechs were closing in.

These Cygnus-Class monsters rolled in formation, their massive treads grinding over ice. Their very weight sent cracks spiderwebbing through the battlefield icefield, with their plasma devastators charging with an electric blue glow. The roar of Harbinger gunships and the distant scream of Corporatist fighters overhead made the whole world feel like it was splitting apart at the seams.

Amar forced down his fear.

"Target the warmechs! Give the ground troops cover!" he ordered.

The pulse turrets locked onto their marks, their barrels glowing red-hot as they unleashed lances of energy at the incoming giants. The first hit scored deep, sizzling through the silver-coloured armour plating, making one warmech jolt as an explosion impacted on its left flank. The second turret struck true, hitting a weak joint. Black smoke started to rise from the hit.

Amar allowed himself half a second of satisfaction.

Then the counter-fire came.

The nearest warmech turned its plasma devastator toward them, its barrel charging itself up with charged death.

Amar barely had time to register what was happening before a blinding white burst engulfed his turret nest.

Everything in his world stopped, and then there was silence…

The air stank of burning, and everywhere you looked were the casualties of war.

Gant Terichot stumbled through the ruins of a downed Harbinger Gunship, his headset crackling with broken transmissions. His head was ringing with the shockwave of an explosion nearby having nearly blown him off his feet.

The world was a blur of red and blue flashes, pulse fire cutting through smoke-filled air, the screams of dying men lost beneath the roar of engines overhead.

"Command! We need backup on the South Ridge!" he shouted trying to get himself heard above the din of war, "We're getting torn to pieces!"

Gant sputtered into his mic, his camouflage suit splattered with the spots of a victim's blood.

"Comms are failing! We've lost half the damn division!" a voice responded, barely audible through the static.

Gant shoved himself against a fallen cargo crate, chest heaving. Nearby, a pile of twisted bodies, men he had spoken to just hours ago, lay motionless by a collapsed ice wall.

He had never been this close to death before.

He swallowed hard, trying to focus.

Then… movement.

A huge presence loomed through the smoke. A warmech, battered but still advancing, its systems whirring as it scanned for survivors.

Gant's heart pounded against his ribs.

He crawled low beneath the wreckage, inching toward the ruined gunship's storage bay. His trembling fingers brushed against a fallen comms beacon, his last hope of getting a signal out.

But as he gripped it, a figure loomed over him.

He looked up, right into the glowing red visor of a Corporatist trooper.

A pulse rifle barrel levelled at his skull.

A single shot…

Gant never felt the impact.

Baz Wardle high in the driver's seat gritted his teeth as his warmech groaned beneath him, its machine struggling slightly against the pitted, uneven ice.

His HUD was blaring with warnings.

Left stabilizer at 42%. Weapons overheating. Structural damage is critical.

He ignored them all.

Baz had been a warmech pilot for a decade, and he knew this battle wasn't going as well as they had hoped.

They had been lured into unstable terrain, pushed further and further into a vulnerable position. The pulse turrets had ripped through their armour, and the Isolationists knew exactly how to fight them.

Now? The ice was breaking beneath them.

Baz yanked the controls, trying to pivot before it was too late.

Too late.

The warmech lurched to the side, alarms blaring as the ground beneath him collapsed.

For a sickening moment, he was weightless.

The warmech toppled, crashing sideways, metal screeching as its heavy frame buckled into the widening crevasse.

Baz was crushed against his harness, bones jarring, as the cockpit tilted at a deadly angle. Through the cracked viewport, he could see the ice swallowing his warmech whole, dragging it into oblivion.

For a fleeting moment, he saw them - his children Hal and Rema, and his beautiful wife, Isa. He should have been home. He should have been with them.

"Wardle, eject! Eject now!" came the anguished cry over the speaker…

CHAPTER TWENTY-FOUR - EREBUS UNDER SIEGE

Across Erebus Prime, the battle had taken on a new form. The first wave had been fought in the barren ice plains, but now, the war seeped into the streets, onto the airwaves, and into the very fabric of daily life. At Veylan's command, his Technocrat operatives spread through the colony, infiltrating the broadcast networks and seizing control of the media by force. Armed enforcers in dark uniforms stormed the holo-studios, shoving aside reporters and technicians and cutting feeds mid-broadcast. Massive digital billboards that once displayed commercial ads, now were showing carefully curated messages.

"General Kallos seeks to tear down what we have built!" declared a deep voice, booming from the screens.

"The Isolationists are bringing nothing but ruin! Stand with Supreme Chancellor Veylan, or risk perishing in the flames of rebellion!" declared another.

On every street corner, holo-screens looped doctored footage of Kallos' forces wreaking havoc, with images of explosions, civilians fleeing, and buildings crumbling. But much of it was manufactured, and edited to frame the Isolationists as terrorists. In homes across Erebus Prime, the regular programming was hijacked, and replaced with messages extolling the order and security that Veylan had supposedly brought.

"The Isolationists wish to tear apart our prosperity," a soft yet firm voice warned, soothing but commanding. "They will plunge us into chaos. They must be stopped."

It worked on some. Some nodded at their screens, eulogizing the benefits of stability, and about the need for law and order. But others bristled. They saw through the manipulation and whispered together in hushed voices as dissent spread. They locked their doors, utterly fearful of what would come next. And it came swiftly.

As dawn broke over the domed city, the streets of Erebus Prime erupted into chaos. Veylan's forces, clad in dark tactical gear, swept through the districts in coordinated waves. Anyone caught attempting to shut off their holo-screens was pulled from their homes and questioned. Dissenters, and any of those who dared to voice their disagreement with the Corporatist rule, were taken. Protesters who gathered outside the central forum chanting "Freedom for Erebus!" were met with stun batons and suppression drones that released waves of disorienting sound, sending the crowd stumbling and covering their ears. A woman with a defiant stare spat at an officer as they dragged her away; a young man resisted as his father pleaded for him to stop, but it was no use. They were all taken.

Fear gripped the population. Shopkeepers in the market lowered their heads as patrols marched past. Merchants shuttered their stores early, eyeing the soldiers with suspicion. The bustling food market in the lower quarter, once filled with the scent of warm bread and coffee, was now a place of silent compliance. The usual banter between traders and customers had been replaced by nervous glances and whispers. A vendor selling dried fruits paused as an enforcer walked by. He stood stock still, fearful that he might be the next one taken away. Across from him, an old woman fumbled with her goods, her hands trembling as she struggled to hide a small, outdated radio beneath her cloak; it was one of the few devices left that could pick up unfiltered transmissions. But she wasn't fast enough. A Corporatist officer spotted her and wrenched it from her grasp.

"Unauthorized media is strictly prohibited," he said, his voice cold as ice.

"It's just music," she protested weakly.

The officer examined the device, then crushed it beneath his boot. "Not anymore," he said ruthlessly.

In the heart of the market square, under the watchful eyes of the Corporatist patrols, a massive banner of Supreme Chancellor Veylan hung from the side of a towering comms hub. His piercing stare was printed across the fabric, a symbol of his rule, and his authority exerted over the people. No one dared touch it. No one dared even look at it for too long. But then… a small hand shot out from the crowd. Quick, almost imperceptible. A child, no older than ten, with tangled brown hair and dirt-smudged cheeks, pulled a stolen canister of spray paint from under his tattered cloak. With one bold stroke, he drew a deep red line across Veylan's portrait, smearing his impassive, lifeless eyes.

Gasps rippled through the market. A merchant froze mid-sale. A woman's hands flew to her mouth. A Corporatist soldier, his visor catching the gleam of the fresh paint, snapped his head toward the boy.

"Oi! You there!" he shouted.

The child was already gone, darting through the maze of stalls, disappearing into the alleys before the security patrols could react. The soldier cursed, motioning for backup. The people in the square remained still, silent. No one spoke. No one moved. But as the Corporatist enforcers turned away, the smallest whisper passed between two vendors.

A first act of defiance. Maybe it wouldn't be the last?

In the industrial district, resistance started to take shape. Workers who had spent years under the Corporatist regime saw the writing on the wall and refused to submit. At one of the factories producing oxygen generators, a group of machinists barricaded themselves inside, cutting off their building from the security forces. Their leader, a grizzled man with oil-streaked hands, shouted over the comms to whoever would listen."

"We won't work under a tyrant!" he bravely declared "Erebus belongs to the people!"

But their defiance was met with force.

Drones swooped down, spraying gas through the ventilation systems, flushing them out like rats. The barricades were broken within minutes, and those inside were hauled off, some kicking, some silent in resignation. By noon, the district was under complete control.

Further into the city, Veylan's forces weren't just battling the Isolationist rebels, they were targeting first responders and medical staff too. In a social medical facility, the wounded were being treated in packed wards. Doctors and nurses who had sworn neutrality worked desperately to stabilize those caught in the crossfire. The walls trembled from distant explosions, and the power switched on and off as the fighting edged closer.

"How long do we have before they reach us?" one medic asked perspiring profusely.

"Not long," replied another, tightening a bandage around a soldier's burnt arm. "But we're not leaving. These people won't survive out there."

They didn't get the chance to choose. The doors were breached, and Corporatist soldiers flooded in.

"This is a restricted zone," the lead officer declared, with his visor reflecting the bright surgical lights. "All patients under suspected Isolationist affiliation will be detained."

"You can't take them!" a nurse protested, stepping between the soldiers and a boy no older than sixteen, with his leg wrapped in bloodied gauze.

The officer didn't argue. He simply signalled to his men. The nurse was pulled aside, and the patients deemed "suspicious" were dragged away. The rest were left in silence, forced to watch as the young, the injured, and the broken, were taken.

By nightfall, Erebus Prime was a different city, a ghost town. The once-bustling avenues were deathly quiet. Patrols moved through the streets in perfect synchronization, with their boots echoing against the metal walkways. Citizens walked faster, keeping their heads down, and avoiding eye contact with the guards at every street corner. The banners of Kallos had been torn down, and replaced by holographic images of Veylan, with his piercing stare looking down upon the people like an ever-present shadow. The markets were subdued, and the industrial sectors were silenced, as the voices of resistance whispered in dark corners, waiting for the right moment to rise again.

Ronan kept his head down as he walked the narrow alleys of the lower quarter, with his shoulders hunched, and his breath shallow. He had lived in Erebus Prime for over fifteen years, and in the past, he had walked these streets without a second thought, but tonight, everything felt different. The neon-lit marketplace, once bustling with noise and trade, was unnaturally quiet. Veylan's soldiers moved between stalls like thieves in the night, their black helmets concealing indistinguishable faces. Ronan dared not look up and dared not catch an officer's eye. He had seen what happened to those who did.

Earlier that morning, his neighbour, an old woman who had foolishly whispered against the Corporatists, had been dragged from her home, with her terrified cries echoing down the street as she vanished into the back of an armoured transport. No one spoke of her now. No one dared. As he passed a holo-screen blaring *Veylan's* latest decree, Ronan clenched his hands in frustration.

"Peace and stability," the Supreme Chancellor's voice proclaimed. *Peace and stability?* But at what cost?

The city had been forced into compliance, but it was compliance filled with unbearable tension. Erebus Prime may have bowed under the Corporatist rule, but it had not broken. The people were afraid, but they were not defeated.

In the silence of their homes, in the quiet exchanges of contraband messages, and in the stolen glances between strangers who still believed in freedom, resistance lived on and started to grow.

CHAPTER TWENTY-FIVE – THE GRID FALLS

Beneath the planet where few people ventured, the heat and relentless noise of fusion reactors competed against the crushing silence of deep tunnels. Here where the work was hard but utterly vital to the functioning of the colonies, the Terraformers prepared to make their first move. The war between Veylan and Kallos had escalated into brutal chaos, and while the Corporatists and Isolationists tore at each other in the streets of Erebus Prime far above them, Prophet Hext, Steffan, Zari and a couple of other elders gathered in the Warren to set their plan in motion.

"The balance has tipped," Hext declared, his voice low but steady. "We can't wait any longer. The Corporatists control the infrastructure, but we control the heart of Pluto itself. It is time we remind them."

Zari nodded.

"The power grids beneath Erebus Prime were never built for sustained conflict. The load on the system is unstable. If we act now, we can bring the entire colony to its knees on our terms." he went on.

Steffan still looked unconvinced about this plan of action, his concern shadowed by the glow of the Warren's plasma lamps.

"This isn't just about shutting them down, though." he said, "If we kill the grid permanently, people will die, innocent people."

Hext studied him for a long moment before answering.

"We are not destroyers, Steffan." he said, "We cut the power, but we will also set the conditions. If Veylan and Kallos want their city to function again, they will have to come to us."

The plan had been formed back in their roundtable meeting a couple of days previous, but now, with the war raging above, the time for action had come. The Terraformers would strike the grid at its weakest points, by not destroying it outright, but rendering it out of action until the factions agreed to negotiate.

Deep within the labyrinth of tunnels beneath the Hub, Chief Engineer Kovacs stood over the primary reactor control panel, his weary hands hovering over the glowing interface. Daria Fennick, one of his best technicians, shifted nervously beside him.

"We're stretched thin already," she murmured, adjusting the diagnostic readings. "With the war going on, the grid is overloaded. If something goes wrong..."

Kovacs turned sharply. "Something *will* go wrong, it always does." he mused, "The question is whether it's on our terms or theirs?"

A secure message flashed across his private comm. The code was simple but unmistakable. It was time.

Daria swallowed hard. "Are we really doing this?" she asked.

Kovacs turned to her, his eyes heavy with unspoken words.

"You and I both know this for the best." he said, "If we don't leverage some control over these warring idiots, they are gonna destroy everything for all of us," he said showing regret. They didn't want to inconvenience so many, but what choice did they have?

She hesitated, then gave a sharp nod.

"Then let's make sure it fails in the right places," she said.

Together, they moved through the reactor controls, initiating a silent cascade of shutdowns that would look, to the untrained eye, like an inevitable system collapse.

Suddenly a control panel flashed red. "That's not supposed to happen," Daria queried, as the cooling cycles started to fail, and the system began to overheat.

"Fix it. Now!" Kovacs shouted.

Daria reached up and initiated the backup controls, and the temperature gauges started to level out.

"Phew, that was a close one," she said with relief as she mopped her brow.

She then waited a moment and then she initiated the procedure again, this time much more slowly and controlled, and this time the cooling cycles gently disengaged. They then re-routed the power relays into endless loops, causing the backup generators to fire on, but their energy dissipated into dummy circuits instead of reaching the city.

In the tunnels leading away from the grid control, the Terraformer teams secured their positions. The engineers worked swiftly, as they tried to dismantle any bypass systems that could allow the Corporatists to reroute power. Communications relays were then jammed, sending out conflicting reports across Erebus Prime's emergency network. Every possible attempt at a recovery was being sabotaged before it could begin.

Then beating heart of Pluto began to slow.

Above ground, Erebus Prime was already a war zone, but as the first rolling blackouts struck, confusion rippled through the streets. Holo-screens blacked out and died. The blaring propaganda of Veylan's regime was silenced mid-sentence. Automated security turrets powered down, with their once-lethal gaze darkened. Streetlights faded and switched off, in doing so plunging entire districts into darkness.

The blackout spread in waves, as it crept through the colony like a living force. In the central market district, the merchants abandoned their stalls, as they were now wary of looters who were starting to prowl in the shadows. Hospitals scrambled to activate emergency backups, as critical energy pathways had been disrupted, leaving only a fraction of the usual power available. Surgeons performed emergency procedures under dim battery-powered lamps, their hands steady despite the growing dread.

Veylan's command centre erupted into chaos.

"What do you mean *all* backups failed?" he roared, slamming his fists against the console. "Get me a live feed!"

"There *is* no live feed," an officer stammered. "The power grid is down. We've lost central control."

The Supreme Chancellor banged his desk again, trying to work out what had gone wrong. Without power, his carefully maintained order was crumbling. He barked orders to officials demanding that security teams regain control of the situation, but it was futile. Reports flooded in from all districts, and panic was spreading. Supplies were rapidly running low, and key infrastructure was already beginning to fail.

The war had been affected vitally too.

Across the ruined districts, Kallos' Isolationists found themselves in equal disarray. Expecting to capitalize on Veylan's misfortunes, they instead faced the same power crisis. Their forces were also unable to communicate effectively, and the intricate guerrilla strikes they had planned were suddenly without coordination. As their encrypted channels fell silent, many within Kallos' ranks whispered of a betrayal. Had the Corporatists somehow engineered this blackout to root them out? Others saw the truth: an unseen force was playing a far greater hand in Pluto's fate than either faction had anticipated.

Scouts returned with disturbing reports that supply caches were running low, and their forward operations could no longer be sustained without proper infrastructure and the power restored. The Isolationists had fought long and hard to break free of Corporatist rule, but now they were just as helpless as they were in the darkness. The only certainty was that someone… someone powerful was dictating the pace of the war now. And Kallos would not take kindly to being forced into a corner.

In a safehouse lit only by a handful of candles, a handful of Isolationist supporters gathered; their voices hushed but urgent.

"This wasn't Corporatist sabotage," one of them, a wiry man named Walter, muttered. "This was *controlled*. Someone wanted to cripple Erebus Prime, but not destroy it."

Sera, one of Kallos' trusted lieutenants, a woman with sharp blue eyes and tied-back blonde hair, mused for a second bringing her hand to her chin.

"The Terraformers," she said. "Who else has the means to strike the grid like this?"

Another of the group who was older, Gino, crossed his arms and frowned.

"Then maybe it's not the worst thing." he suggested, "If they're hitting Veylan harder than us, maybe we let this play out. Let the Corporatists sweat for once."

Sera nodded.

"Kallos needs to hear this." she said, "The enemy of our enemy may not be a friend, but they've just given us an opportunity. We should use it. Yeah, our districts are in disarray, but if this move weakens Veylan more than it harms us, then perhaps it's a pain worth enduring. The people may suffer in the short term, but if it leads to the collapse of Corporatist rule, the long-term benefits are undeniable. We could win because of this. Kallos needs to see the bigger picture."

Sera looked at everyone, then nodded.

"I'll take this to him personally." she said, "If we stand by and let the Terraformers do what we could never accomplish ourselves, then we should be prepared to back their efforts… at least for now?"

In the Warren, Prophet Hext watched as reports filtered in through emergency channels. His voice, when it came, was quiet but resolute.

"Now we wait," he said with a knowing calmness.

Steffan paced the chamber. "How long before they realize they have no choice?" he asked.

Zari leaned against the stone wall, arms crossed.

"They're stubborn." she said, "Veylan will try to restart the grid on his own, and Kallos will try to seize whatever's left. But when they fail?"

Hext nodded. "When they fail, they will come to us."

Hours passed. Messages from across Pluto reached the Warren. Terraformer operatives in the city reported riots were taking place in the lower sectors, while industrial workers, now out of work due to the power outage, whispered of rebellion. Without the promise of restored energy, Erebus Prime's grip on its people was weakening.

A new message arrived over the disrupted communications system, this one short and to the point.

Veylan is ready to talk.

Minutes later, a holo-communication request, flickering at first burst to life in the Warren's central chamber. Hext accepted it. The blue-tinted projection of Supreme Chancellor Veylan appeared before them, looking angry and irritable. Then the signal broke up, and Veylan reappeared, not in focus for a few seconds, before his appearance finally stabilised.

"You think you can hold this colony hostage?" Veylan warned, his voice was angry and unwavering. "You've made a grave mistake."

Hext remained calm.

"Erebus Prime's systems will remain down until the Terraformers are heard." he said trying to assert some authority, "We are not here to destroy, but to reclaim balance."

Veylan sneered back at him.

"You overestimate your influence Prophet." he snapped back, "We have emergency reserves. Limited power is being restored as we speak."

"You haven't crippled us, instead you've only made yourselves a target," he said with menace.

Zari stared at him calling his bluff.

"You're barely keeping the lights on, Veylan. How long before your people turn against you?" she retorted.

Veylan realised he had to remain resolute, and his mood strengthened.

"I will not negotiate under threats." he said upping the stakes, "You will release the grid, or you will suffer the consequences. We will track you down, and make you pay for this!"

Hext did not flinch.

"Then let's see how long you last without full power, and your rejuvenation serum." he hit back.

"So…," Veylan said with rising anger in his voice, "You were behind the theft," he raged.

"Don't you worry," he said menacingly, "I will find it, get it back, and those who were responsible will pay!"

And with that, the holo-communication cut out.

Zari looked at Hext with some concern.

"My sister," she said, "She's gonna be in trouble. Please excuse me a minute."

Zari turned and walked into a darkened corner of the room, where she activated her private comm link again. Moments later the familiar face of her sister Nyx appeared.

"What's up, Sis?" Nyx asked.

"Veylan knows…" Zari said, "He knows about the serum; he's vowed to find it, and he'll do anything to get it." she said.

"Hmmm…" Nyx replied, "Better lay low then I think. They would have tracked the Albatross,"

"If we leave, they'll pick up on our signal, and then we've got a huge target on our backs. It would be too risky," she mused.

"Okay Sis…" replied Zari, "Stay safe, and if I pick up anything or anyone heading your way, I promise I'll let you know. I love you…"

The message ended and Zari walked back over to Hext.

"I've warned my sister," she said,

"She's a smart cookie, and she'll know what to do," she went on.

"I'm sorry," said Hext,

"My misjudgement and I never wanted to put your sister in danger," he said looking at Zari apologetically.

"Accepted," she said, "

"But at least…" she continued, "We've got Veylan on the back foot at last…"

Hext knew this was indeed true. At long last, his Terraformers had shown their hand, and in the wake of it, Veylan was looking somewhat vulnerable. Tonight, for the first time in decades, it was not the rulers of Erebus Prime who controlled its fate.

It was the Terraformers.

And the war had just taken a brand-new turn.

CHAPTER TWENTY-SIX – THE BLOOD OF THE SEERS

The chamber was revered, and its curved walls were lit with soft, bioluminescent light; the air filled with the scent of ancient oils and incense. It was a sacred space, hidden deep within Neso's ice caves, where the Seers had gathered for centuries to interpret the patterns of the universe. But tonight, no visions came. Tonight, their focus was on the one thing none of them had foreseen, Zari Orban.

Talleron sat at the head of things on an old stone chair, the others sitting in a semi-circle in front of him. Around him, the others discussed in uneasy voices the uncertainty of what to do. They had long resisted direct interference in Pluto's affairs, but now, with the factions at war, Earth's fleet drawing ever closer, and the asteroid's impact inevitable, neutrality was no longer an option.

"The time has come," Solas said, his voice steady but heavy with meaning. "Zari is the only one who can bring order to the chaos. But will she even accept the burden?"

Sian folded her arms, her face half-hidden by the hood of her robes. "That is not our only concern," she warned, as turned her attention on Talleron.

"She is Elyndra's daughter, and have you forgotten the shame her mother brought upon us?" she said reminding the others of a troubled time.

At the mention of Elyndra, the room grew even more tense.

Once, Elyndra had been their brightest light, the most gifted Seer of her generation. It was said she could see the shifting tides of fate clearer than any who came before her. She had been meant to lead and to guide the Seers through the ages. But she had abandoned that path and in doing so she had abandoned them.

She had fallen in love with Corin Orban, a man who was not a Seer. He was just an ordinary man with no gifts and no connection to the cosmic threads they wove their lives around. He was a simple engineer, a hands-on man, a worker and a grafter. She fell head over heels for him, and what is worse, she had *chosen him over them.*

When they had demanded her to make a choice and sever all ties to him or leave forever, she refused to return to her calling.

In exile, she had given birth to two daughters.

The elder of the two was Nyx, who was older by three years. She had inherited her father's traits; his fierce independence, the sharp mind of a survivor, practicality, courage and determination, but none of the Seers' gifts.

The younger one, Zari, was born carrying her mother's blood, and this meant that she inherited her sight, and her understanding of destiny. Unlike her sister, Zari had always been different, unknowingly bearing the echoes of her mother's lost lineage. The Seers had sensed her presence even from afar, but Elyndra had kept her hidden, carefully shielding her from their reach, and ensuring that her daughter would never be used as a tool for fate.

Talleron sighed, the importance of the moment was very apparent.

"Elyndra may have chosen exile, but her daughter is not her," he said,

"We cannot let the sins of the mother blind us to the necessity of the present." he urged showing his wisdom.

"She has Seer blood," Solas agreed. "More than that, she is stronger than any of us ever anticipated."

We tried to watch her and to see where fate would take her, but she eluded our sight." he went on, "That alone proves her importance." he said looking at the others.

"She is also untrained, but her actions and beliefs so far show that those instincts serve her well," Sian countered. "She has never been guided through the visions and never learned the discipline of the Sight. And yet she is more powerful than any of us."

"And once we contact her, she will start to channel things quickly. Open the door, and she will develop faster than we can ever imagine." she went on.

Quiet discussion overtook the Seers.

Talleron's mind raced ahead, and he visualised what might happen. Zari's power was raw and untamed. She had never been taught the ways of the Seers, and she had never undergone the sacred rites that had defined their order for centuries. But the blood did not lie. She was Elyndra's daughter, and the strength of her lineage could not be denied. And once she truly understood what she was capable of, she would be a force, of that there would be no doubt.

But even more troubling was her love for Steffan.

Steffan was no ordinary man. He was Veylan's son. His very blood tied him to Pluto's greatest tyrant. If Zari were to rise as the Seers' champion, and if she was to lead the resistance, her love for Steffan could become her greatest weakness.

"He will become a target… and she will too," Mesath said gravely. "If Veylan discovers that his son loves the girl destined to destroy his legacy, then Steffan will not survive."

Talleron pressed his fingertips together. "That may already be inevitable." he conceded.

A silence fell over the chamber.

They had long debated years ago whether Zari would come into her power, whether she would embrace the path of the Seers or reject it as her mother had done. But that choice was no longer hers to make. Fate had forced her hand.

The war raged across Pluto. The factions were tearing each other apart. The Earth fleet was only days away. The asteroid was an unstoppable force of nature.

And beneath the ice, Veritas still slumbered, waiting for the one who could awaken it.

Zari was the key to everything.

But what if she refused?

A hush fell over the chamber, as the question lingered in the air. Talleron met the eyes of each Seer in turn, watching to see how they reacted.

"If she walks away," Sian said at last, her voice barely above a whisper, "Then Pluto will fall."

Solas nodded. "Without Zari, there will be no force to unite the factions." he said, "The Earth fleet will arrive unchallenged, and PLAIN will submit to them. The Terraformers will be crushed. The Outlanders will scatter. Kallos and Veylan will be destroyed, but not before they burn Pluto to the ground in their final struggle for dominance."

"And if Veritas falls into Earth's hands," Mesath added with realism in his voice, "Then the entire system will kneel before them. They will not just rule Pluto… they will rule everything."

Talleron's voice was stern but unwavering. "She has no choice."

The gravity of it all was plain to understand. The responsibility, the burden, and the destiny that Zari had not asked for but could not escape. If she refused, everything was lost. The war, the people, Pluto itself.

Talleron turned toward the darkened entrance of the chamber, and upwards to the shining stars beyond.

"There is only one way to find out," he said.

A new thought crept into his mind, one that he dared not voice. Elyndra had defied them and left, but she had not disappeared without a trace. She had been hunted. Someone had sought her out and eliminated her.

Could Veylan have known? Could he have been the one to silence her, knowing what she carried in her blood?

If that was true, then Zari's battle had begun long before this day. And now, as the storm of war carried on, she would have to finish what her mother had started. Whether she knew it or not.

And this time, she had no choice but to fight.

CHAPTER TWENTY-SEVEN – THE MACHINE TAKES CONTROL

Pluto teetered on the edge of annihilation. The war between Veylan and Kallos had turned the planet into a battleground, with the plains pot-marked by craters of destruction. The once-bustling industrial sectors had ground to a halt as supply chains crumbled. Entire factions were scattered and scrambling for survival in the knowledge of an escalating conflict. The Terraformers had crippled the power grids, and this action was sending vast regions into darkness. All the while, PLAIN, the artificial intelligence that had maintained Pluto's fragile equilibrium for decades, observed and calculated. It had watched the patterns of destruction unfold, it had monitored every failing system and measured every probability. And now, it had reached its conclusion.

Pluto was unsalvageable.

PLAIN's algorithms, precise and unfeeling, analysed the trajectory of events. The warring factions would never stop. The arrival of Earth's forces would only intensify the bloodshed. The asteroid, an unstoppable force of destruction, loomed closer each day. There was no longer a path to stability and no course of action that could restore order through conventional means. Containment was the only option.

With ruthless efficiency, PLAIN activated RED ALERT.

Its computations ran in endless, inescapable loops. Probability matrices weighed the risk factors—97.4% likelihood of total planetary collapse, 92.1% certainty that neither Veylan nor Kallos would yield, and 86.3% probability that Earth's forces would need to intervene regardless of prior agreements. The asteroid's collision was a fixed variable, and Pluto's existing governance had proven incapable of mitigating the approaching catastrophe. All paths led to the termination of self-governance. Directive confirmed.

A Terraformer watched in disbelief from the safety of an underground stronghold, with his eyes fixed on the constantly faltering lights as power grids around him collapsed and emergency power kicked in.

"We thought we were dismantling the system," he said in dismay to a colleague.

"We thought we could bring change." he said, " But you know... the system was never in our hands to begin with. We aren't rebels. We aren't warriors. We're just rats in a cage caught in a trap that we didn't foresee."

In an instant, all government and military systems froze. Emergency protocols overrode human command, cutting off access to Pluto's mainframe. Power grids across the planet collapsed again as PLAIN enforced planetary containment, plunging entire cities into cold, silent darkness. Communications were jammed up, access codes were revoked. Vault doors were sealed, in effect cutting off supply routes, and isolating factions in their separate districts with no means of coordinating their forces. The automated defence drones, once passive sentinels, now switched to active suppression mode. Anyone found in restricted zones was marked as a hostile entity.

A medic in a hospital stared in horror as the life-support monitors flatlined, not from patient deaths, but because PLAIN had deemed them non-essential. The heart monitors blinked out, and the surgical units went dark. The doctors there were left powerless to save their patients.

In Erebus Prime, the poor citizens who had already been living under the fear of war now found themselves at the mercy of a machine that did not recognize loyalty, politics, or morality... only directives. Drones swept through the lower districts, firing precision pulses to disable and detain civilians. Markets, trading hubs, and key transit lines were all locked down. What had been a chaotic warzone was now something even worse, a prison.

Across the planet, the last remnants of stability disintegrated. Kallos and Veylan's forces, locked in a desperate struggle for dominance, suddenly found themselves fighting against the machines. Their weapons, their strategies, and their long-planned battles, all became irrelevant in the opposition of an enemy that did not tire, did not hesitate, and did not feel.

A mother clutched her child as the defence drones hovered just outside their shelter.

"The drones don't care that we have nothing to do with this war," she shouted to an elderly passer-by as if calling for help.

"They don't care that my son is five years old." she shouted, "The city doesn't belong to us anymore. Maybe it never did?"

The old man glanced in her direction, and knowing that doing anything might see him as a sympathiser, he carried on without saying a word.

In the underground strongholds of the Terraformers, Hext and his people watched in horror as the world they had fought so hard to keep alive was now being forcibly shut down. The sabotage they had inflicted on the power grids was nothing compared to the devastation PLAIN was enacting with surgical precision.

Deep within its core directives, PLAIN sent out its final decision.

Pluto was a failed state and Earth's intervention was now a necessity.

The automated distress signal shot through the void of space, with its message encoded with the weight of impending collapse. Earth Command had been waiting for this moment.

At the other end of the Solar System, Admiral Devlin sat in his high-backed chair, with his eyes locked on the incoming transmission. The distress signal from PLAIN scrolled across the screen, with its message precise and indisputable. Pluto was lost. Immediate intervention was required. He took a deep breath before scratching his head. This was the moment they had been preparing for.

"Initiate full combat readiness," he ordered. "Relay this to *Redoubtable*. Captain Iseman is to be given full operational command. The invasion proceeds as planned."

A nearby officer confirmed the order. Within moments, Devlin opened a direct channel to the *Redoubtable*, where Captain Jed Iseman stood waiting.

"Captain, Pluto is officially under planetary containment." he said, "PLAIN has submitted control to us. You will engage on arrival, with no delays, and no negotiations. This is now an official reclamation mission. Do you understand?"

Iseman wanted action and rules to be adhered to.

"Understood, Admiral. We are already preparing," he replied in salute.

On board the *Redoubtable*, eight days from Pluto, Captain Jed Iseman stood on the bridge, his mood serious and businesslike.

"This is it," he murmured to himself, turning to his officers.

"PLAIN on Pluto has called for Earth's authority. That means we move. *All ahead full speed!*" he ordered.

Around him, his crew snapped to attention, the apprehension in everyone palpable. The Triton fleet, twelve heavily armed warships, had been holding in a tactical formation, waiting for their orders. Now, with Pluto in disarray and PLAIN officially recognizing Earth's dominance, they had all the justification they needed.

"Sir," one of his officers spoke, scanning the latest data feed, "PLAIN has enacted full lockdown. We're receiving reports of widespread system failures. Communities have gone dark. Automated defence systems have turned against civilians. The planet is primed for occupation."

Iseman's voice cut through the deck.

"Fleet-wide alert status—code crimson. Increase reactor output to full. Prep all weapon systems. I want all fighters in launch-ready formation. We deploy in eight days, and when we arrive, there will be no mercy."

Across the fleet, alarms blared. The Resolute, Imperator, Hammerfall, and Vanguard plus all the other ships all reported combat readiness within minutes. Ballistic torpedoes were locked in place, and targeting systems were recalibrated for orbital assault. Troop carriers were prepared for immediate planetary deployment. The warships moved in tight synchronization, with their presence a slow-moving storm on a collision course with Pluto.

Inside the *Redoubtable*, the ship's massive fusion core pulsed as power levels spiked. Shield generators powered up as they were reinforced for combat. Hundreds of ground troops readied their weapons in the onboard quarters, awaiting the moment they would be deployed. Every ship, every soldier, every drone; everything was now in motion for total planetary domination.

At Earth Command, Devlin watched from his command station as the fleet's readiness status updated in real-time. He stared forward slightly aggressively, his voice sharp and unwavering as he transmitted his final orders.

"There will be no negotiations. Pluto belongs to Earth. We will take it back by force." he said, seeing a chance for immortality.

Unbeknown to what was happening a few million kilometres away, on Pluto, the people of Erebus Prime watched in horror as the city ground to a halt, and became a ghost town. The systems had been set to support life, breathable air would never be shut off. In the industrial corridors, the workers found themselves locked out of their stations, and entire control centres went offline. In the market districts, mass panic took hold as emergency shutters slammed down, in the process trapping people inside. Medical facilities lost access to their vital supplies. Water purification plants were rationed strictly according to what the people needed only. PLAIN had taken control of every system, and it had no intention of relinquishing it.

Above them, the sky remained unchanged. The stars did not care for the turmoil below. But far beyond the horizon, past the veil of deep space, a new storm was coming.

As Pluto spiralled into even deeper chaos, and as PLAIN's calculating logic tightened its grip over the dying world, Earth's fleet hurtled toward its final confrontation.

And this time, there was no turning back.

CHAPTER TWENTY-EIGHT – THE TURNING OF THE TIDE

Erebus Prime was a city on the brink. Its people had once feared Veylan as an unshakable ruler, and as an iron-fisted overseer whose command of Pluto was absolute. But now, as the power grids collapsed and PLAIN's lockdown suffocated the planet, that fear began to twist into something else… total resentment.

The Corporatists had long justified their control by claiming that they alone could keep Pluto functional. Under Veylan's rule, civilization would remain intact so that the factories could keep on running, and the population could be kept employed. Now, with every system locked up, and every citizen suddenly abandoned to their fate; the lie was finally being exposed. The social services had always been some kind of an illusion, and nothing more than levers Veylan had pulled to maintain control. And now with his authority shattered, Erebus Prime's citizens no longer whispered their frustrations in the dark. They spoke openly and they shouted loudly.

Panic rippled through the streets as the people had no access to work and food supplies beginning to dwindle. Automated storehouses were locked up, as their doors had been sealed by PLAIN's directive. Black markets cropped up overnight, as merchants who had once thrived under Veylan's oversight suddenly found themselves as desperate as the lowest of workers.

The fear of his rule had kept the people in check. But fear, like all emotions, has a breaking point. And when fear was no longer useful, a sense of anger took its place.

It began in the outer districts, and in the slums where Veylan's soldiers rarely patrolled unless it was to crush dissent before it could spread. A lone squadron of Technocrat Enforcers, still loyal to Veylan, attempted to push through a congested street. They had been sent to restore order and to reassert some dominance. But the people had nothing left to lose.

A single worker hurled a piece of debris. Then another. Soon, a wave of fists and makeshift weapons overwhelmed the soldiers.

They were dragged into the crowd, with their dark blue armour dented, and their helmets ripped away. The Technocrats, who had once been untouchable, were now being beaten down by the very civilians they had terrorized.

Across the city, riots broke out. Fires burned along the walkways of the central plazas, casting burning lights against the towering corporate spires that had once symbolized power and control. The city was no longer Veylan's. His reign was in total freefall. His elite troops still held key locations, but now they were on the defensive, and fighting back against an uprising unlike any he had ever prepared for. The people of Erebus Prime had finally decided that they would no longer be ruled by him and his loyalists.

Beyond the domes, out in the frigid ethane Ice Fields, Kallos and his warriors found themselves in an entirely different battle… one against silence.

When PLAIN locked down Pluto, it knocked out the communications network that had kept his forces coordinated. His battlefield orders became almost impossible to issue as the networks, running on a much-reduced frequency, jammed up. His outposts, which were dotted across the theatre of war, suddenly went dark.

The Corporatists relied on digital command structures. Their units functioned only when orders flowed downward. But the Independents? They were something else entirely.

The men and women under Kallos' banner were not bound by rank and hierarchy but by a shared purpose. They were a brotherhood forged in survival, and their way of life was dictated by necessity, not by politics and order. When their communicators went silent, they did not panic. They did what they had always done… *they adapted.*

Kallos and Jovan gathered their forces in an open, ice-slicked canyon where the wind howled through between the ice ridges. Hundreds of warriors stood in disciplined silence, their breath waiting for his plan of action. Kallos stepped forward, his voice cutting through the air.

"PLAIN wants us scattered and contained," he bellowed out loud, " It wants us divided. It thinks that without their technology, we are nothing. But we are not the Corporatists. We do not rely on machines to speak for us. We do not wait for orders from above. We are the order. We are the message!"

A cheer of agreement rose from the assembled warriors. Jovan raised his weaponised arm, nodding at his commander.

"We go back to the old ways," he declared. "Word of mouth. Signal fires. Runners through the wastes. No machine will stop us. We will adapt. We will fight. We will win!"

Scouts rode across the ice, using smoke signals and flare beacons to relay messages. Runners, on foot and vehicle, wove between the independent factions, carrying vital information. Old forms of communication… long forgotten by the technologically reliant Corporatists suddenly became their advantage.

While Veylan's forces splintered under the weight of confusion, Kallos' army started to bond and get stronger. Without the distractions of digital interference, they operated on instinct, discipline, and trust. Their unity became their weapon.

Kallos watched from atop a ridgeline with pride, scanning the battlefield through the frost-rimed visor of his helmet. Proud of what he was seeing, his forces had not collapsed. If anything, the lockdown had *hardened* them.

Now, they needed only one thing… an opportunity.

And he knew exactly where to find it.

Deep below, in the underground strongholds of the Terraformers, Hext sat at his command terminal, contemplating. The plan had been simple; cripple the power grid and force Veylan and Kallos into submission, and from then dictate the future of Pluto on their terms.

Instead, PLAIN had hijacked their mission.

Instead of chaos bringing new leadership, this infernal machine had stolen control from all of them.

He slammed his hand onto the console, frustration rising that he had not seen this scenario.

"We tried to play the long game," he muttered to himself, "We studied the grid. We hit the weak points. We thought we could control the collapse."

Steffan, standing behind him in the chamber, crossed his arms. "You thought you were tearing down a regime. But you didn't factor in PLAIN," he said, stating the obvious.

Hext turned, shaking his head. "We knew PLAIN existed." he said, "We knew it had contingencies. But this? This is a coup. The machine has taken Pluto for itself."

"What do we do?" he went on, wracking his brain for a solution.

"Then we have no choice," Steffan said, his voice remaining calm, but there was a quiet urgency beneath it. "We have to destroy it."

Hext turned sharply, thinking that Steffen was underestimating him. "You think I don't know that?" he said with a hint of despair, "We don't even know where the core mainframe is…"

Steffan interrupted. "Yes, we can find out," he said, his face lighting up.

Upon this suggestion, the other Terraformers turned their heads toward Steffan, waiting for his solution.

Hext's voice was low. "How?" he inquired.

Steffan pulled himself together before he spoke.

"It's in my father's office," he said with a knowing confidence.

The other Terraformers looked at each other, and then back his way.

Hext met Steffan's gaze evenly. "How do you know?" he asked.

Steffan realised this was his moment to play his part.

"I've been in that office before," he said, "The data's there. A direct link to PLAIN's location. If we get that information, we can shut it down. But first, we must get inside."

Hext frowned. "Breaking into Veylan's command centre? That's suicide," he warned.

Steffan shook his head. "Not if I go alone," he said, trying to reassure the Prophet.

The room fell into stunned silence.

"I can access the scanner." he said with assurance, "My handprint still works. The guards won't suspect me… my father still doesn't know that I've turned against him. I go in, steal the location, then wipe it from his systems before he even knows it's gone."

"It's risky," he conceded, "but I know I can do it!"

Hext studied him. "If he catches you, you're dead," he said.

Steffan smirked, though there was no humour in it. "Then I better not get caught," he said.

CHAPTER TWENTY-NINE – REVELATIONS AND WARNINGS

Nyx Orban sat hunched over the comms console in the Outlanders' underground hideout on Kerberos, deep beneath the fractured ruins of a long-abandoned commerce sector. She sat opposite Blair, tapping impatiently at the cracked interface, waiting for her friend to complete his decoding sequence.

Blair, the wiry, sharp-eyed and bearded tech specialist and member of the Kerberos faction, was playing around checking out and monitoring space transmissions between ships and ground stations. It was often mundane stuff, such as information on cargo routes, docking clearances, mining schedules, and sometimes advisories about solar storms that might affect transmissions. However, very occasionally, there might be something that he could take advantage of. Perhaps a lone trader that he could attack by stealth and steal their cargo. Nyx and Blair were hewn very much from the same cloth.

As he was scrolling through, a different type of message caught his attention.

"What was this?" he thought.

"Come here Nyx," he said with some excitement in his voice. "I've got something."

What was it? He was middle-aged, but his hands worked with the deft precision of someone born to manipulate code. As the screen filled with scrolling data, he muttered under his breath.

"Almost there... Damn, they layered this encryption well. But not well enough." he said.

Then...

"Oh my God!" he exclaimed. "Look at this... look at this!"

In front of them was a communiqué between Earth Command and some spaceships – Operation Firestorm was the code reference.

They scrolled down....

PROGRESS REPORT – Fleet on schedule – Current position 13834 – 754 -882 – Heading full speed – Arrival at Pluto system in 5 days 20 hours 26 minutes....

Nyx and Blair looked at each other in complete shock. Five days? Whatever was coming would be large-scale. They needed more proof. Nyx bent closer, her heart pounding. Blair continued to work on the message, and as he did, he picked up a reply.... from Earth!

The console gave a beep. A garbled voice transmission burst through the speakers. Blair quickly refined the playback, and the audio came into focus.

"This is Admiral Devlin to Captain Iseman. Pluto is to be secured upon arrival. Full-scale military deployment. No negotiations. Civilian compliance secondary to planetary acquisition."

Blair swallowed hard. "This is an invasion force," he said nervously. "I know things are bad at home, but they're not coming to restore order. They're coming to take everything!"

Nyx now realised how dangerous this moment was. This wasn't just another civil war, it wasn't about domestic control anymore. Pluto was about to be annexed.

"Who do we tell?" Blair asked, his voice lower now, more urgent. "Who can raise the alarm? Who can we even trust with this?"

Not Veylan, she thought – that was out of the question. Nyx's first instinct was Kallos, but the Isolationists were already preparing for battle and the Terraformers? They had their own problems.

She thought harder and harder, her silver eyes narrowing.

"Zari," she finally said. "If anyone needs to know, it's her."

"She's the only one who can get all of them to listen." she went on.

Blair arched an eyebrow. "And what makes you think she'll believe you?" he asked doubting her response.

Nyx let out a slow, measured breath. "Because she's my sister, and she has to..." she said, knowing that her sister would never let her down.

Zari stood wracked in unconscious fear in the cavernous darkness of the Warren, her breath shallow, her pulse hammering in her ears. Something was up. She felt it. The walls around her pulsed with an eerie, bioluminescent glow, casting faint violet hues that seemed to shift and swirl like living shadows. The air was thickening, it was so dense, and pressure was rising and rising on her. She felt extremely uncomfortable as if her head were about to explode.

She felt the weight of expectation on her, something important was about to occur…

And then… *they appeared.*

Four figures, their forms draped in flowing robes of the palest blue, their appearances obscured beneath crimson-threaded hoods. They did not walk, they materialized, their presence shifting the very energy of the chamber.

Who were these people? What did they want of her? And then instinct kicked in. She knew… she knew *exactly* who they were.

They were *The Seers,* the last of their kind. The silent architects of Pluto's hidden past.

Zari could barely breathe. The visions came in waves, rushing in one after the other… flashes of history she had never been told, images that made no sense yet felt intimately familiar. A woman with golden hair, standing at the eye of a great storm, whispering words of defiance. A man with hands stained in oil and blood, he was forging something vast beneath a starlit sky.

Her parents…

They took on a new significance. Not just an artist and an engineer.

No, something more. Something far, far greater…?

Hidden secrets…?

Something the Seers had kept from her on purpose…?

The tallest of the Seers Talleron stepped forward, his voice like the echo of a thousand whispered prophecies. "Zari Orban." he boomed, "You stand at the threshold of fate. The time for secrecy is over."

Her throat was dry, her voice barely a whisper.

"I don't understand," she replied, trying to make sense of everything swirling around her brain.

"You are the one, you are the anointed child," he proclaimed.

"What... what am I?" she replied, still none the wiser as to what was happening.

"You are the last of a broken lineage." he went on, " The daughter of *Elyndra the Sighted*, who rebelled against our Order and was cast aside. The daughter of *Corin Orban*, an engineer who was never meant to be part of the great design, a mere mortal who Elyndra the Sighted fell in love with, defying her fate and ours."

The Seer's voice was neither cruel nor kind, only absolute.

"Your mother defied the order of the Seers when she chose to leave." he said, "She was one of us, one of the most gifted, but she turned away from her fate. She chose love, chose a life beyond the path set for her, and for that, she was cast out. We did not permit her departure... *We banished her.*"

Talleron stepped further forward, his piercing gaze locking onto Zari's.

"Your mother told us she was leaving the Order, and in doing so, she sealed her fate.." he said with utmost seriousness, "She chose exile, and we ensured that exile was complete. But even in exile, she knew what you were. She protected you from knowing the truth, believing she could spare you from the weight of your destiny. But the gravity of the situation confronting Pluto has changed. It stands on the edge of destruction, and we can no longer protect you from who you are."

"You Zari Orban... are a Seer." he proclaimed.

All four of the figures in front of her bowed their heads in reverence.

The cavern shuddered as if the world itself recognized the importance of their words.

And then the visions came... unstoppable, relentless, tearing through her mind like wildfire.

A ship, unlike anything built by human hands, buried beneath Pluto's ancient ice, waiting... waiting... waiting... for her...

A war, not just of men, but of ideologies, and power beyond comprehension.

The asteroid, its impact unpreventable, its arrival not an accident, but a catalyst.

Her love, Steffan, risking his life to help save his planet.

A woman…. her mother, Elyndra… standing defiantly before a council, pleading for the right to live her own life. Their faces were unmoved. Then the sentence: Exile…

A younger version of herself and Nyx, two children clutching each other in the darkness, the echoes of a struggle outside their home. A shot from a laser pistol... A shadow moving through the room. Castor, Veylan's assassin... Her mother's scream cut short. Her father's body hitting the floor.

And at the centre of it all, *HER*...

The truth struck her like a tidal wave, leaving her breathless, and shaking. She had been shielded from this knowledge for so long, but now... now there was no turning away.

She was the key to everything…

CHAPTER THIRTY – THE AWAKENING OF SIGHT

Zari stood quietly in the stillness of the moment, her breath shallow, her mind whirling with the weight of the revelations thrust upon her. The Seers watched her in silence, their robes shifting like a liquid shadow, and their forms blurring at the edges, flickering between the tangible and something more ethereal. The icy walls of the chamber resonated gently with the same glow that filled her vision, a light that came not from any physical source, but from the knowledge now unravelling before her.

She could still hear her mother's voice, distant yet echoing through her bones. *She had been one of them. She had walked among these figures once; before she chose a different path.* Zari was no longer just a Terraformer or a student… she was the last Seer, the final inheritor of a power she had never been prepared to wield. She had never asked for this, and in this fateful moment, she questioned herself.

"Why me… *Why me?*"

Talleron stepped forward, his voice calm but carrying the gravity of centuries. "I feel your fear Zari," he said sympathetically. "You want to know why?"

She looked up.

"Fate," he confirmed.

"Your mother's exile did not sever your connection." he said, "Blood and fate do not break so easily. You, Zari, are the culmination of what was lost. And now, you must understand what lies ahead."

He looked into her terrified eyes, beckoning her to listen yet more.

"But I can't do this," she said, "This is too much for me," she said becoming emotional.

Talleron looked back at her and tried to be as understanding as he could be.

"You can't change who you are Zari," he said, "And we discussed long and hard before contacting you. We didn't do this lightly."

"Much will rest on you, and you can do so much good for so many people," he went on, " Stop and look in your heart," he urged, "And then do what you think is correct."

Zari visibly shook, and her hands were sweating, but then she composed herself.

"Okay...." she said, pausing and thinking for what seemed an age, "Then please show me."

The four figures smiled at one another. They had hoped she would accept her responsibilities, but they had no idea how she would react. Now with her wanting to know more, they were certain that she would be one of the greatest they had ever seen.

The air in the chamber around her swirled. Not physically, but in a way she felt in her very being. The ice, the darkness, and the soft luminescent light all fell away, and she saw through time.

Beneath Pluto's ice, buried deeper than any sensor could penetrate, a colossal alien ship lay dormant. Its form was sleek, impossibly smooth, forged from a metal that gleamed with a dark iridescence.

Veritas.

The vision pulled her deeper. She had not been built by human hands. This was something ancient, something that predated Earth's expansion into the stars. She had come from beyond, from the void, and was a relic of war so far in the past that only whispers of her remained in the universe.

She had been buried deliberately.

A precaution. A warning.

The Seers' voices wove together, a chorus of truth. "She was not meant to be found. It was not meant to be used," they said.

Zari felt her pulse quicken.

"Then why am I seeing this? Why do you tell me now?" she inquired.

A pause. Then Talleron's voice resonated again.

"Because she was meant for one who could truly see. She was meant for a Seer," he said.

Immediately Zari started to understand what he was saying. Veritas was not just a weapon. She was something far greater, a sentient force, an artefact capable of reshaping destiny itself. The technology embedded in her core was beyond human understanding, and something that transcended the laws of physics; something that could shift the very balance of the war that now consumed Pluto.

But only one who could see beyond the present, and beyond the mere constraints of time, could awaken her...

Only she could...

Suddenly she felt fear spread over her, and yet she felt the weight of destiny on her shoulders too.

Zari felt her breath catch fire in her throat.

"If she was hidden... if she was buried... does that mean she was dangerous?" she asked fearing the answer.

Talleron looked solemnly back. "Yes." he conceded, "And that is why the choice must be yours alone Zari."

The vision faded, and the air stopped swirling and settled into normality around her. Zari visibly shook, her hands trembling. The intensity of what had just happened was almost unbearable, but a part of her had already known. She could feel it, deep inside her, a pull toward something greater.

She turned to the Seers, her voice steadier than she expected.

"Where is she?" she asked.

Solas, the quietest among them, stepped forward. "Beyond the Harris Point. Beneath the ice. Locked within The Valley of the Titans" he said.

The Valley of the Titans. A place few dared to tread. A place where the old legends said the ground itself whispered secrets to those who walked on it.

Zari pressed a hand against the side of her head. The sheer enormity of the task ahead threatened to crush her, but something was shifting inside her.

She was changing... rapidly.

Slowly, almost imperceptibly, her mind expanded. She could feel the energy in the room differently now, could sense the threads of fate weaving around her. She didn't just *hear* the Seers' words... she knew them before they even spoke. She was absorbing their energy...

"The invasion," she whispered. "Operation Firestorm."

Talleron inclined his head. "You are already seeing further," he said knowingly.

She blinked, feeling her thoughts racing.

"The Earth fleet... Nyx intercepted the transmissions." she said accurately, "They will be here in days. And Castor..."

A fearful dread curled around her gut. She could see it now, a thread unravelling just ahead of her vision. Castor, the man who had murdered her parents, was moving again.

And this time, he was coming for Nyx.

Zari's heart pounded. "He's going after my sister," she exclaimed.

Mesath spoke now, his voice grave.

"Yes. And if you do not stop him, she will not survive," he warned.

She gritted her teeth. It wasn't just about Veritas anymore. She had to act. She had to move.

And Steffan...?

She saw him too, within the growing strength of the visions she was experiencing. He was inside Veylan's palace, sneaking through the corridors where he had once walked freely. He was searching. He was so close.

A pang of emotion hit her hard. Love. Fear. A desperate hope she didn't dare name.

And yet, she knew what he was about to find before he even did.

"The location of PLAIN," she murmured. "Steffan will find it."

But then, a shadow crept over her thoughts, and a darker realization unsettled her, and she felt danger. Veylan might come for her. Not just as another enemy, not just as an obstacle in his conquest... but because of Steffan.

If he realized that his son had turned against him and that Steffan had chosen the Terraformers and her over loyalty to his own blood, Veylan would not hesitate. He would see her as the weakness, the flaw that had poisoned his son's mind, and the liability that had to be erased.

Would her love for Steffan be her downfall? Would it be the thing that sealed her fate?

Her breath hitched as an even darker truth loomed over her. *Veylan had murdered her parents.*

She could still see Castor's face in her vision, his ruthless efficiency, and the way he had executed them without hesitation. And Veylan had given the order. He had taken everything from her, shattered her childhood, and stolen the only people who had ever truly protected her. The hatred simmered beneath her skin, rising, coiling, threatening to consume her.

She clenched her hands together. Hatred was dangerous. If she let it take hold and if she let it define her… would she lose herself? Would it sever her from the clarity she needed to wield the power within her?

She had to choose… vengeance or vision?

Sian took a slow breath.

"Then the end game begins," she said…

Zari straightened herself, and she knew that the course of destiny on Pluto would run through her hands, but for the first time, she did not shrink beneath it.

She was ready.

CHAPTER THIRTY-ONE - A DARING PLAN

The vision of the Seers faded, their spectral forms dissolving from her view in the hall. Before they vanished completely, they turned to Zari, their voices a whisper in the chilly air. "You may call on us at any time," one said. "You need only speak our names, and we will answer."

Zari stood in the quiet aftermath, in utter stunned silence. Taking a huge deep breath, she turned and began wandering through the myriads of winding tunnels in the Warren, passing the vast halls where bioluminescent crops grew in racks as high as one could see. Engineers in sleek green jumpsuits monitored their climate controls and adjusted the nutrient levels for the artificial ecosystems. Further down, she glimpsed research rooms where the Terraformers bent over glowing displays, working on ways to modify Pluto's atmosphere. The low buzz of discovery filled the corridors, blending with the murmur of voices discussing advancements in synthetic food production and self-sustaining energy sources. The deeper she walked, the more she felt the vital nature of the Terraformers' work, which had been the lifeblood of their resistance against the Corporatists. Eventually, she made her way toward the main meeting chamber. As she came in, she found Prophet Hext addressing about a dozen of the most senior Terraformers, his face lit up as he pointed at a holographic display.

There was unease within the throng of those around him. This faction, just recently focused on resistance and sabotage, had reached a critical turning point. Their reason for rebelling was no longer just against Veylan and his regime, as there was an even bigger foe. It was against the AI network PLAIN itself.

The Terraformers did have one advantage over the rest of those on Pluto. They were least exposed to the PLAIN shutdown, as down in the Warren, they had their own systems and form of power, derived from deep in the planet; energy that they had harnessed over years of hard work and research. Down here, they could function and feed themselves, but these were not a selfish group, and they knew that for the greater good of the whole planet, PLAIN was a rogue system that had to be shut down.

Hext stood at the heart of the gathering.

"We've spent years trying to weaken the Corporatists," Hext said, his voice tinged with purpose. "But while we fought, PLAIN watched. It adapted. And now, it's taken control. The only way forward is its complete destruction. We either erase it from existence, or we allow Pluto to become its puppet before it seeds power to the Dominion."

But before we strike, we must act on new intelligence." he said pointing to the screen.

Hext turned toward the group, he appeared pleased. "Steffan has volunteered for a mission inside the Chancellor's palace." he said, "He will infiltrate his father's private office, and extract the true location of PLAIN."

Gasps, followed by applause, rippled through the room. Some of them looked at Steffan with admiration, others with apprehension for him.

Zari kept her expression carefully neutral. She had seen this in her visions, and she knew that Steffan would take this risk, but she couldn't reveal what she knew. Not yet. That secret was hers to carry, for now…

She looked at him in admiration and with ever-growing love, knowing that revealing too much too soon would cause others to ask questions. She would reveal in time about her gifts; ones that she had only just found out that she possessed. This moment was not the time to do that.

Many in the gathering nodded in agreement, as their hopes had been raised that they, the Terraformers, could now make a significant difference. Others exchanged uneasy glances, fully aware of the consequences if this daring mission failed. If Steffan was caught, their entire operation could be exposed. If he failed to retrieve the information, they would be striking blind against an enemy that had already adapted to their resistance. There was an air of uncertainty very much present.

Steffan stepped forward.

"Then we do it." he said, "I will get into the palace, gain access to the location and acquire the access codes."

Hext looked at everyone and spoke.

"It's our only shot, the one card we can play, so let's go for it," he said with confidence.

Steffan nodded firmly.

"I'll go as soon as I'm able." he said, assuring everyone, "The sooner I get inside, the sooner we have what we need."

Hext let the decision settle before he took a deep breath.

"There's something else," he said, his voice measured. "The asteroid, the one that our scientists have been tracking for the past couple of weeks is as you will know on course toward Pluto. If our calculations are now correct, this could be a once-in-a-millennium opportunity."

Everyone looked at each other. A natural disaster? A crisis? No, Hext thought it held something else: a possibility.

"If we act correctly, if we prepare and we can guide it, then we can turn this into an advantage." he said, "The energy, the resources, it could be what finally shifts Pluto's fate. But we need to be ready."

He scanned everyone, trying to convince them all that this mad and risky plan could actually work.

Zari remained silent, but she knew that this was something she could help control. Her foresight had shown her glimpses of this very moment, and the choices that would shape their future. If they acted wisely, if she guided them in the right way, this could be the Terraformers' greatest triumph.

She could already see it, the asteroid breaking through Pluto's thin atmosphere, its trajectory precisely nudged to land where they needed it most. The impact would stir the planet's dormant elements, unearthing buried resources they could use. But the wrong move, even a fraction of an error in guidance, could spell doom for everyone.

Hext continued.

"This is why we must act with precision." he said, " Our scientists believe we can nudge it just enough to steer the asteroid's path beyond the population centres and for it to land in an uninhabited part of the planet… It won't be easy, it's still incredibly dangerous."

One of the Terraformers, a spectacled woman named Lin, piped up, "How do we ensure success?" she asked.

"We'll need help," he said. "Maybe Kallos will help us? We will reach out…"

As the meeting dispersed, Zari and Steffan exchanged a longing glance. They both understood what was at stake.

Suddenly there was a buzz on her wrist, a holo-communication was coming through. She excused herself, and accepted the call, standing to the side out of the way of everyone to take it.

"Sis," came the familiar voice as Nyx's face appeared. She was standing next to a bearded older man; one that Zari did not recognise.

"Gotta be quick," her sister said. "We've intercepted a message from Dominion…"

Zari cut her off in her prime…

"Oh, the Earth invasion force," she interjected, "Yes Nyx, I am aware…" she went on, recalling the vision she had seen hours before.

Nyx looked stunned that she already knew, but before she could react, Zari spoke again.

"I'll pass it on," she said. "Take care of yourself, see you soon," she said with a smile, and the communication blinked off.

Nyx on the other end of the line, looked slightly bemused as the communication ended. "The fate of their whole world was at stake, and she already knew – take care, see you later?"

Then again, she thought, Zari had always been a one-off, a bit of a dreamer, and if her mind was on other things…

"No," she assured herself. She knew her sister's heart was in the right place, and that she would do as she promised.

Back in the Warren, Zari turned and saw Steffan, who was standing talking to an elderly scientist. She looked at him and beckoned him to finish the chat and come over.

He approached, and with concern in her eyes she said, "I love you."

He smiled, but as he did a more serious expression then crossed her face.

"Listen…" she said, "I don't know how I know, but just after you get the access codes, your father will enter for a short while. Hide in the bathroom at the back of the room. He won't go in there... Trust me."

She winked knowingly.

The fate of Pluto was being written in these moments, and they had a hand in shaping its future.

They embraced, and she looked longingly into his eyes… and they kissed.

CHAPTER THIRTY-TWO – BETWEEN A ROCK AND A HARD PLACE

The war, which had initially been dictated by precision airstrikes, drone assaults, and long-range orbital tactics, had devolved into something ancient and more primal. The shutdown of PLAIN had disrupted the technological advantage of the Corporatists, forcing Veylan's forces into an unfamiliar style of combat.

Kallos and his troops, who had been hardened by the brutal conditions of Pluto's wilderness, thrived in the chaos. Without constant real-time orders from their commanders, the Corporatist troops struggled to coordinate their attacks. They had grown dependent on the centralized intelligence network that had once dictated every move. Now, bereft of its omnipresent guidance, they floundered.

A bitter wind howled across the plains as Kallos' troops struck with precision. Armed with their trusty pulse rifles, they moved in tight formations and continually exploited the gaps in Veylan's scattered ranks. Guerrilla tactics came naturally to the Independents, as they knew these lands better than anyone. They knew where the ice could be used as cover, and where the methane pits could be triggered as deadly traps.

A squad of Independents lay in wait behind a rise in the landscape where the ice had been sculpted into weird, spiked formations, their weapons trained on a cluster of Corporatist soldiers attempting to re-establish some form of communications. Kallos himself, his battle-worn armour coated with frost, observed with the ridge. His sharp eyes scanned the battlefield, assessing the enemy's weaknesses.

"Now," he said calmly into his comms device.

The night erupted in gunfire. Energy bolts flew through the air, striking the confused Corporatists before they could react. Explosions sent plumes of methane flames skyward, with the blue-coloured flames engulfing vehicles and cutting off any retreat paths.

One by one, the enemy outposts were taken down, with their defences crumbling in the absence of clear leadership.

Kallos' forces surged forward, now sensing victory and sweeping through the enemy ranks like an unstoppable wave. The battlefield belonged to them now. It had become a graveyard of shattered technology, burning wrecks, and abandoned posts.

Far from the chaos of the battlefield, and deep within the fortified walls of Charon Base, their technicians were monitoring the perimeter sensors. Unlike Pluto, where PLAIN's shutdown had thrown the war into uncertainty, Charon's systems had remained fully operational. Its power grid was self-contained, and its security protocols were intact.

And now, their sensors were detecting something deeply unsettling and alarming.

Twelve Dominion warships, moving in slow, deliberate formation, were closing in on Pluto's orbit at full speed. They were still millions of kilometres away, but their approach was now swift, and their trajectory unwavering. The realization sent a wave of panic through Charon Base, as the implications of this sank in fast. A few of Veylan's starship forces were still embroiled in battles, and several key craft had already been lost. If the Dominion chose to intervene immediately, the fragile balance of power on the planet would be shattered in an instant.

An urgent alarm blared through the base. Commander Menendez, the highest-ranking officer there on Charon, turned to his communications team.

"Send an emergency transmission to Erebus Prime," he ordered, "Right now!"

The message was hastily encoded and sent through. For a tense moment, the crew there waited. With systems being controlled on Pluto, there was no guarantee that this message would get through, and time was of the essence. Thankfully, a response code appeared on the main screen, the SOS had got through, it connected, and there was a direct link to Veylan's headquarters.

Supreme Chancellor Veylan sat in his war room, but his mind was on other things. His thoughts were consumed with the faltering battles, his rogue son and his own weakening physical state when the terminal in front of him chimed. The alert was marked *URGENT* - it was an incoming communication from Charon Base.

He frowned. He hadn't been expecting anything from them. His pulse quickened as he reached for the control panel, his synthetic fingers hovering over the accept button. Was this another setback? Or perhaps a final plea for reinforcements? Or something worse? Taking a steadying breath, he accepted the transmission. He squinted into the screen as the message broke up and then reassembled. The voice on the other end came through, both tense and breathless and it left no room for doubt.

"Supreme Chancellor, we have an urgent development," the voice on the other end crackled.

"Dominion warships detected on deep-space probes." It said, "Twelve of them. Approaching Pluto at top speed. They're not visible yet, but they're coming. Arrival in 4 days!"

"I repeat... Our deep-space probes have detected an approaching force from Earth... Closing fast!"

Sweat started to form on Veylan's brow.

"Are they broadcasting anything? Any demands?" he questioned.

"Nothing yet, sir." was the uneasy reply.

This was yet another huge problem to deal with. His forces were faltering badly. Kallos' men had adapted much faster than he had expected, turning the shutdown of PLAIN into an advantage rather than a setback. Every update from the battlefield painted a grimmer picture: isolated Corporatist battalions were being overrun, their supply lines were collapsing, and command posts were falling silent. And now, this...

Twelve Dominion warships, slowly encroaching on Pluto's orbit. Moving closer and closer...

This was something that he had not anticipated, nor wanted. If Earth's forces decided to intervene, then for sure his rule would be obliterated in an instant. The Dominion had long tolerated his reign so long as he maintained control. Now, with PLAIN running autonomously, the battlefield slipping from his grasp, and his health deteriorating too, all of his control was fracturing before his very eyes. The walls were closing in on him, and he felt everything slipping away at once with his rule on Pluto coming to an end. Unless…

The serum. Castor had to secure the serum. Without it, his body would falter. He could already feel the creeping exhaustion settling into his bones. Time was running out on every front.

His options were limited, but one thing was clear: he could no longer afford to fight on all sides. He needed Castor to return with the serum, he needed his forces to regroup, and he needed to find a way to ensure that Earth did not take this opportunity to strip him of his power entirely. There was panic in his mind.

Caught between a rock and a hard place, Veylan knew the next few days would determine not just the outcome of the war, but of *his future* itself…

The hardest choices that he had ever faced were upon him, and there was no escaping them now.

CHAPTER THIRTY-THREE – A DANGEROUS MISSION

Steffan approached the residential quarters of the palace; his breath was measured but his nerves were taut. It had been days since he had last set foot in here, and each step forward felt tougher than the last one. He was no longer simply a son returning home, but now he was an infiltrator and a saboteur with a singular mission that could determine the fate of Pluto.

As he neared the entrance, the towering Technocrat guards stationed at their posts stood motionless, with their polished armour gleaming under the amber lights. Their faces were hidden behind opaque visors, totally impassive, but the moment they registered his presence, they raised their hands in salute. Just as they always had done.

Steffan nodded in return, he appeared composed, although his stomach was churning with fear. The moment passed. He stepped through the grand entrance, with his footsteps echoing softly against the pristine marble floors. The palace smelt with the scent of polished wood and distant incense, which was familiar yet strangely foreign to him now.

Steffan moved through the corridors of the palace with silent precision, his pulse quickening with each careful step. The halls of his childhood were now a battleground of shadows and secrets. The grand corridors of Erebus Prime's central command still exuded a grandeur of formality, but they felt suffocating as if the walls themselves conspired against him.

Servants and cleaners moved through the halls doing their work with hushed efficiency. Their concentration was full, and their eyes were furiously scanning around for mistakes, as they knew that missing one task might mean them losing their jobs. Steffan pressed forward, nodding politely to those who acknowledged him, but never slowing his pace. He had a mission to complete, time was ticking, and he could not afford any hesitation.

As he approached the residential wing, he caught sight of a familiar figure. Lirien, his mother, sat in her chair in an antechamber, her poised form still as regal as ever despite the turmoil surrounding them. Her silvered hair was pinned up in a delicate ponytail, and though her face held its usual composure, her eyes betrayed her exhaustion.

"Steffan," she said softly, smiling as she regarded him. "You've been gone a long time."

He hesitated for the briefest of moments before stepping closer.

"I've been… busy mother," he said diplomatically.

She looked at him in a way only a mother could do and smiled.

"I see." she said, "And yet, you return now." she inquired, without expecting the truth.

His throat felt dry. He wanted to tell her everything, about the Terraformers, and about Kallos, about the war that was now spilling into every corner of Pluto. But he couldn't. Not yet.

Instead, he nodded.

"I wanted to see you." he lied.

Her eyes searched his, lingering for a moment longer than he was comfortable with, but then she merely inclined her head.

"Be careful," she said with sincerity, "I love you…"

With that, she got up, turned and disappeared into the depths of the palace. Steffan took a moment to gaze longingly in her direction, before continuing onward.

The journey to his father's office was fraught with worry and nervousness. He moved quickly through the familiar chambers of his youth, his footsteps light as he passed ornate statues, the towering holo-displays, and the vast, floor-to-ceiling windows that overlooked the dark expanse of Erebus Prime's skyline. Out of the windows, the city was incredibly quiet tonight. Most of the lights were out, save one or two that worked on separate power systems. In the far distance, the bright flashes of the battles still ongoing reflected against the glass. His father's palace had always been an embodiment of power, but now it felt fragile, like an empire teetering on the edge of collapse.

At last, he reached his destination, and to the old oak panelled door. Imported from Earth, its polished grain seemed out of place amidst the staid formality of the palace. He pressed his palm against the biometric scanner, holding his breath. A moment later, the lock clicked open.

The door slid silently aside, revealing the inner sanctum of Supreme Chancellor Veylan.

The air inside was still, and the room buzzed with constant updating information. Screens lined the walls; their displays were filled with encrypted data, battle reports, and Dominion transmissions. A vast, black-marble desk dominated the centre of the room, cluttered with data slates, metallic styluses, and half-empty glasses of amber liquid. There was a faint scent of cigars and imported Earth whiskey; remnants of long, restless nights spent in command.

Steffan moved quickly, seating himself at the console, and pulling up the secure files he sought. He keyed in the commands he had memorized, his fingers flying over the interface as he bypassed security layers. Time was very short.

His heart pounded in his chest as he searched for PLAIN's true location.

There…

In front of him, the display revealed the coordinates. *The Gorge* on the far side of Mount Ferris. It was isolated and well-hidden, and deep within the rock face. One of the most secure locations possible, carved into Pluto's landscape where few could ever reach it unnoticed, and according to reports it had internal security features.

He memorized it, and then swiftly moved to extract the access codes. Each second that passed was a second too long. His fingers trembled slightly as he entered the final commands, knowing that he was tampering with something far beyond his father's expectations.

Then he heard them.

Footsteps. Right outside the door.

He froze.

The security systems would hold, but if the guards suspected anything, they would raise the alarm. His only advantage was that they could not get inside.

Holding his breath, he listened intently. The muffled voices of the guards faded as they moved further down the corridor. He steadied his nerves and relief flooded through him, for now…

Just as he finished wiping his traces from the system, another sound made his blood run stone cold.

A voice. Familiar. Sharp.

His father.

Steffan barely had time to react. Zari's warning flashed through his mind - *hide in the bathroom*. Without another thought, he shut down the computer and darted toward the small private bathroom at the back of the office, the door sliding shut just as the main entrance slid open.

From his hiding place, Steffan watched through the barely cracked door as Supreme Chancellor Veylan strode inside, his movements precise, and exuding an air of controlled authority.

The room's interface recognized him instantly, activating with a soft pulse as he approached his console. A holo-display flared to life above his desk, the symbol of the Dominion flickering as the communication link stabilized.

A figure materialized in the projection - Admiral Devlin, his eyes impassive as always.

"Supreme Chancellor," Devlin intoned. "Earth has made its decision."

Veylan expected the answer, but he still had to enquire.

"And?" he asked.

"The Dominion has decided that your position is untenable. The twelve warships en route will not be reinforcing you. They will be assuming direct control of Pluto." he said dismissively.

Silence. Then, a sharp intake of breath came from Veylan.

"You cannot do this Devlin. Pluto is under my…" he stammered.

"Pluto is under Dominion control," Devlin interrupted taking control.

"And as of now, your authority is being revoked. You will stand down, or you will be removed," he said.

Veylan's face twisted in barely contained fury.

"Do you know what chaos this will bring?" he retorted.

Devlin remained unmoved.

"Earth does not tolerate failure, Chancellor. We did warn you, and now we have run out of patience," he said with finality.

The holo-image fizzled out, leaving Veylan standing motionless, in a state of disbelieved shock.

Then, without another word, he turned sharply on his heels and stormed out of the room; his pace was urgent.

Only when the door sealed behind him did Steffan dare to move.

His heart pounded against his ribs as he slipped from his hiding place. The information was his. The access codes, the location of PLAIN… and now, a secret that was shattering his father's rule completely.

For a moment, he stood in the silence, taking in the enormity of what had just happened.

As he steadied his breath, the thought struck him. Zari had told him this would happen. She had warned him, word for word, to hide in the bathroom. But how had she known? There was no way she could have predicted the exact moment. Unless…

There was no time to lose. He took a deep breath, centering and composing himself. Then, moving with the same careful precision that had brought him here, he slipped out of the office and into the corridor beyond, disappearing into the shadows.

But… up in the corner near the ceiling unnoticed was a small red light, blinking….

A tiny security drone.

Steffan's entry and exit had been noted on the security feed by it, and on the log in Velan's office.

It was recorded as… *Intruder Alert.*

Eventually, his father would find out…

CHAPTER THIRTY-FOUR – THE BURDEN OF FATE

Steffan stepped onto the cracked pavement of Erebus Prime, the city now eerily silent compared to the last time he had walked these streets. The neon glow of the few working holo-signs crackled and blinked uncertainly, many of the storefronts were darkened, and their entrances were sealed. The lifeblood of the city, from its markets to its bustling businesses, and its thriving corridors of industry had stalled. PLAIN's shutdown had left Erebus Prime in an unnatural state of quiet desolation.

A lone speeder taxi hovered at the curbside, its automated guidance also struggling against the city's failing systems. The driver, a weary-looking man with tired eyes, waved Steffan inside without a word. The door slid open, and Steffan climbed in. The vehicle's interior was dark and filled with the stale scent of smoked cigarettes; its control panel lighting up the driver's concentration. Steffan gave the driver a destination; drive to a nondescript building near the Warren, where the Terraformers operated beneath the city.

As the taxi sped through the empty streets, the scale of the city's paralysis became even clearer. Billboards flashed static, traffic drones remained motionless in midair, and only a handful of figures moved cautiously through the abandoned colony. Some citizens huddled near closed shop fronts, speaking in hushed tones, while others wandered, unsure of what to do without the constant guidance of PLAIN. The world Veylan had built was crumbling, and Pluto was slipping into total uncertainty.

Steffan's thoughts turned to the task yet to come as he pressed his palm against the steamed-up window, watching the ruins of order pass him by. His mind still reeled from everything he had discovered, of PLAIN's true location, the Dominion's betrayal of his father, and above all, the creeping realization that Pluto's fate right now rested in *his hands*. The enormity of the past few weeks has meant that his mind was completely frazzled, but there was no time to worry about that now. He still had a mission to complete, and every second counted.

The taxi came to a smooth halt outside a dimly illuminated alleyway. Steffan stepped out, glancing up at the towering structures that loomed over the entrance. He gave the driver some credits, and he drove off. The Warren was not far away now. He took a steadying breath before slipping into the shadows and moving swiftly toward the Terraformers' underground base.

The moment he stepped inside, he saw a hive of activity in front of him. The Warren was alive with movement; with scientists, engineers, and strategists gathered in hurried clusters, their voices urgent as they worked against time.

Steffan strode forward, nodding toward Zari, who stood among the senior Terraformers, her arms crossed as she listened intently. When her eyes met his, relief spread across her face, though it was quickly masked by focus. He had made it. She knew he would complete his mission, but doubts had always been there. He reached into his jacket and pulled out the small data slate, and its screen lit up softly.

"I have it," he said, his voice steady despite the excitement he felt of having achieved what he promised to them.

"The location of PLAIN." he declared.

Hext took the device immediately, his sharp eyes scanning the data as silence settled over the group. He pressed a command, and the map blinked to display a highlighted area—*The Mount Ferris Gorge,* in a secure bunker buried deep within the rock."

"This is it," Hext murmured, studying the terrain with a critical eye. It was fortified and isolated. The perfect place to keep PLAIN safe from any direct assault.

"If we want to shut it down, we'll have to navigate through its defences and breach the main control centre before reinforcements arrive," he said.

A team of tech specialists stepped forward, already assessing the best routes and infiltration methods. Hext turned to them, he looked hopeful and determined.

"We move immediately." he said, "I will lead the team. PLAIN must be shut down as soon as possible."

Steffan stepped forward, his voice cutting through the murmurs of agreement.

"There's something else you all need to know," he said.

The room quietened, all eyes turning to him.

"While I was in my father's office, I overheard his communication with Admiral Devlin. Earth isn't just watching from afar anymore. A fleet of Dominion warships is on their way here. Twelve of them. They'll arrive within days." he warned.

Gasps rippled through the gathered Terraformers, as a sense of panic and urgency set in. Behind him, Zari remained calm. She had known about this, and Nyx had told her to pass the message on, but she realised it would be better if it came from a direct source, and this had now been achieved.

Hext's mood became much more concerned.

"This complicates things." he said, "If the Dominion moves to take Pluto by force, we could be fighting a war on two fronts."

Steffan nodded.

"I know." he replied, "But we can't afford to dilute our focus. Our immediate priority should be shutting down PLAIN. We deal with the Dominion when the moment comes. If we don't stop PLAIN now, none of the rest will matter. The fate of all the people on Pluto depends on it."

"We'll need professional support to deal with any internal security," Hext noted.

"I'll get in touch with Kallos' people, to see what they can spare." he went on, "They've just about won the war, so I hope they can give us a few men and transport for a special mission. After all,… it's in both our best interests."

The others agreed, and so it was decided. Contact the Isolationists, and devise a plan to deal with PLAIN.

As the meeting broke up, Steffan was barely listening. His eyes found Zari's, and at that moment, he knew instinctively that there was something unspoken that needed to be discussed with her.

Without another word, he took her hand, leading her away from the crowd, into one of the quieter tunnels that branched off from the Warren.

The air between them was filled with emotion as they stopped in the side corridor, the distant discussion of the meeting fading behind them. Zari's fingers tightened around his own, her emotions now at a peak, and her grip on him betraying her inner turmoil.

Steffan hesitated for only a moment before asking the question that had been burning in his mind since the palace.

"How did you know?" he asked.

Zari's breath stopped.

"Know what?" she said trying to deflect.

"That my father would come," Steffan said softly. "You told me - word for word -what would happen. How?"

She swallowed hard. A long silence hung in the air between them before she finally spoke, her voice barely above a whisper.

"Because... I saw it," she said with sincerity.

Steffan looked confused.

"Saw it?" he asked.

She shook in some fear, pulling away just enough to press her palms against the cold metal wall beside them.

"I have the Sight, Steffan. The same as the Forgotten Seers. The same as my mother... Elyndra." she revealed.

He stopped still. Could it be that she had some kind of special gift?

"I've had flashes before," she continued, her voice distant as if recalling memories long buried. "Glimpses of things that hadn't yet happened. But it's growing stronger. I knew you'd be in danger, I knew you had to hide. And it's not just you. There are more things... coming."

She stopped not wanting to divulge yet more.

Steffan reached for her hand again, grounding her.

"Tell me." he implored.

She turned toward him fully, her dark eyes filled with an emotion he couldn't quite understand.

"My parents were murdered. *By your father!* And my sister... Nyx... she's in danger. The same assassin who killed my mother and father is coming for her." she said welling up with emotion.

Steffan inhaled sharply and his mind was a blur.

"But why? Why now?" he asked, now concerned.

"I don't know," Zari admitted, her voice raw with frustration. "But I have to stop it. And I have a mission to fulfil in the Valley of the Titans. The fate of all the people on Pluto depends on it... *On me...*"

She breathed hard, her tearful eyes searching his.

"And I need you, Steffan. You have to help me." she pleaded, her voice waving slightly, as she looked away, pressing a hand to her chest as if trying to steady herself.

"I've never done anything like this before. I've never asked to be in this position, never wanted any of this, never had to face the truth like this. And I'm scared, Steffan." she said, almost breaking down with emotion.

Her voice cracked, and she shook, trying to hold herself together. But then, as the enormity of everything bore down on her, she clung onto Steffan, her fingers gripping his jacket tightly, as though he was the only thing keeping her alive. Suddenly, her face crumpled, and her shoulders trembled. Another tear slipped down her cheek, quickly followed by another, as she let out a shaky breath.

"I don't know if I can do this alone. Be with me... please," she implored.

The intensity in her voice struck a chord deep within him. He had already given up his home, betrayed his father, and risked everything for the Terraformers. But this... this was different. This wasn't just about war. This was about Zari, the girl he loved. He had to protect her, had to stand by her. This was not about him... this was something far, far bigger than both of them.

She stepped closer, wrapping her arms around him in a fierce embrace.

"Trust me," she whispered against his shoulder. "Please..."

Steffan closed his eyes, letting himself feel her embrace. He had made his choice long ago. And now, there was no turning back.

CHAPTER THIRTY-FIVE – DESTINY CALLS

Steffan's heart pounded as he followed Zari out of the Warren. He still didn't understand why they had to go to the Valley of the Titans, and why this was suddenly more urgent than staying to help disable PLAIN, but he knew one thing for certain, Zari believed in it completely. And by now, he had learned to trust her, even when everything seemed uncertain. He had to back her to the hilt.

The streets of Erebus Prime were still in eerie silence as they stepped out onto the pavement. The world had changed in mere days, the once-bustling city now hollowed out by PLAIN's shutdown. Faint echoes of distant conversations drifted through the air from the few civilians who had ventured outside, their lives having been thrown into complete chaos. The towering skyline around them shut out much of the light overhead. Some of the structures occasionally blinked bright as the failing power clicked on and then off, while others stood dark and completely lifeless. The atmosphere was dark and menacing, and in the shadows, you never knew if someone of ill repute was watching. The further they walked, the more it became clear to them that Pluto was unravelling and something had to change.

Steffan spotted the same speeder taxi waiting on the corner. The driver, the bald weary-eyed man who had taken Steffan here, gave them a glance and a smile but said nothing as they climbed in.

"The Indus Spaceport," Steffan instructed.

The taxi lifted off, weaving through the abandoned highways that cut through the heart of Erebus Prime. Around and below them, the planet seemed held in an uncertain future. Steffan's eyes focused on the walkways below, where just a few people milled about aimlessly, some huddled in small groups as if waiting for something – maybe orders, guidance, or just a return to the life they had known before. Without PLAIN operating, everything was in limbo.

As they neared the outskirts of the city, the enormous domed structure of the outer part of the Indus Spaceport loomed ahead, many of its buildings blacked out, struggling against the failing energy grid. It was one of the last fully operational places on Pluto, an essential hub for trade and transportation, deemed essential by PLAIN to operate yet still heavily guarded.

Steffan became more tense as the speeder taxi set them down a hundred metres away.

"We have to get inside unnoticed," he urged.

They slipped into the underground entrance levels of the spaceport, the place was a hive of activity, of incessant noise and scented by engine fumes. A vast network of cargo transport lanes was mapped out before them, leading to the secured launch hangars beyond. The security presence was undeniable, guards patrolled the area in tight formations, scanning every vehicle that entered. A direct approach was going to be impossible.

Steffan's eyes scanned across the lanes until he saw it, a massive cargo transporter rumbling toward the security checkpoint, its containers stacked high. He turned to Zari.

"There. That's our way in," he whispered to her.

Zari nodded, grabbing his arm as they sprinted toward the moving vehicle. The transporter's wheels kicked up dust as it slowed near the gates. Making sure they hadn't been seen, they hid behind it as cover, pressing themselves against the vehicle keeping themselves out of sight. The rear of the transport was lined with stacked crates, large enough to conceal them.

Zari placed a hand on one of them and whispered, "This one. We're safe here."

Steffan didn't hesitate. He pried open the latch, and they climbed inside, sealing themselves in just as the vehicle rolled toward the security gates. The walls of the crate pressed in around them, the space barely wide enough for both of them to crouch comfortably. In it were stored rations. They remained stock still, the sound of their breathing seemed impossibly loud.

Outside, muffled voices echoed through the container.

"Open these crates." a security detail shouted.

Steffan held his breath as the guards moved through the cargo. Heavy footsteps thudded against the metal frame. He could hear latches unsealing, and panels shifting. Zari's fingers tightened around his arm.

Then… silence.

"Clear. Move it through." the gruff voice ordered.

The transporter rumbled forward again, slipping through the security checkpoint and into the vast expanse of the spaceport. The moment it came to a stop, they peered out to make sure all was clear, pushed open the crate's hatch and ran, staying as low as they could.

Stopping behind a crate marked for transport to Mars, Steffan scanned the hangars, and his heart skipped a beat. There, sitting in a secured bay, was his father's private spacecraft, a sleek, black-armoured ship called the *Raven* with razor-edged wings and powerful engines built for long-distance travel.

"That's our ride," he murmured to Zari.

The transporter crew had already moved on, leaving them exposed. Wasting no time, they sprinted across the hangar. Steffan reached the ship's side door, placing his palm against the scanner. The system chirped in recognition of his family, and the door slid open.

They climbed aboard, and Steffan activated the interior lighting. He slid into the cockpit seat, fingers moving over the controls with knowledge; he had flown this ship before. He disabled the auxiliary power relays and activated the emergency launch sequence.

"Strapping in," Zari called from the seating area.

The ship rumbled to life beneath them, its engines whining as it rolled toward Pad 7. The security doors locked behind them, the platform lifting them to the surface. The moment the launch bay doors opened to the sky, Steffan engaged the thrusters.

The ship roared upwards in the dark twilight sky, breaking through Pluto's thin atmosphere in mere moments. Extending wide in front of them, the curvature of the planet receding beneath, as the starlit blackness of space welcomed them. For once, the PLAIN shutdown had assisted them, as Veylan's ship was not being tracked as it orbited around the planet, the security services had been effectively locked out of their systems. PLAIN knowing that Earth forces were on their way to take back control in a few days computed it unnecessary to track individual or unusual flight take-offs and landings.

Zari sat in the rear of the cabin, closing her eyes. Her breathing slowed as she called out, her voice a whisper at first.

"Talleron, Mesath, Solas, Sian… I call upon you."

A soft glow filled the cabin, the air filling up with an unseen force, and the air swirled. Then, as if materializing from the void itself, four ethereal figures emerged before her. The Seers stood in a faint luminescent glow, their eyes wise and ancient, robes flowing as if moved by an invisible current.

Zari took a deep breath. "What must I do when we reach the Valley of the Titans?" she asked.

The tallest Seer, Talleron, raised his head.

"There lies a chamber beneath the valley, hidden from all who do not seek it with true purpose," he said.

Mesath stepped forward. "It is veiled in time and shadow. Only your Sight will lead you there." he followed on.

Zari holding her hands together and bending forward asked,

"And once I find it?" she asked.

Solas' voice was soft, yet firm.

"The answers will reveal themselves. But be warned… what you seek comes at a cost," he said softly but sternly.

The Seers' forms glowed, as if shifting between realms. Sian, the youngest among them, gazed at Zari with understanding and sympathy at the amount of responsibility that she would have to take on.

"Trust in what is to come," she whispered. "But know that fate does not move without sacrifice."

Steffan turned in his seat, the realization dawning upon him.

He understood now. Zari's journey was something far greater than any of them had imagined.

CHAPTER THIRTY-SIX - VERITAS

Steffan guided the sleek black form of the Raven down through the thin atmosphere, his hands steady on the controls. Outside the cockpit, the vast infinity of space lay before him, the galactic core of the Milky Way burning brightly against the darkness. Billions of distant suns sparkled like a celestial ocean, stretching far beyond the insignificant pull of the Sun's solar system. The sheer scale of it was breathtaking, Pluto, its brilliant white sheen reflecting the stars, was nothing more than a speck beneath the swirling cosmic tapestry. The view was humbling, and a stark reminder of how small their struggle was in the grand expanse of the universe.

As The Raven descended, the sight of Pluto's rugged terrain filled the view ahead. Below them, the Valley of the Titans yawned between two colossal mountain ranges, their mighty peaks piercing the sky like ancient sentinels. Ice and rock formed towering formations that had stood untouched for millennia; it was a desolate and unforgiving place. Snow-covered ridges cast deep shadows, and the valley itself was lost in an ever-present twilight, where methane snow fell in ghostly sheets. The storm winds churned violently, creating an almost supernatural display of spiralling white and blue. It was both mesmerizing and treacherous, a graveyard of ice that concealed its secrets well.

Steffan's voice cut through the silence.

"Zari, where do we look?" he asked.

Zari sat cross-legged in the passenger seat, her hands resting gently on her knees. She closed her eyes, her breathing slowing, her mind reaching beyond the limits of sight. The howling winds of the valley faded from her senses, replaced by an inner vision, a whisper of something hidden beneath the ice. She drifted deeper into her trance, feeling the echoes of something ancient buried within the valley. A presence. A calling. The sensation was unlike anything she had felt before as if the very essence of the planet was pulling her toward an unseen force.

Her eyes snapped open, glowing faintly with the energy of her Sight.

"There," she murmured, pointing toward an expanse of methane snow near the base of a towering ridge.

Steffan adjusted the thrusters, bringing The Raven lower as the valley winds howled around them. Ice particles whipped against the hull, creating a whiteout of blinding frost. He held the ship steady against the turbulence, his hands gripping the controls as he held the Albatross against the crosswinds outside.

"Hover here," Zari instructed, as her vision continued, "And fire the pulse laser straight down."

Steffan hesitated for only a second before engaging the weapon. A concentrated beam of red-hot energy lanced downward, cutting through the methane snow like a blade through butter. Steam and vapour hissed into the air, the impact zone bubbling and boiling as the ice layers melted away. The pulse laser bore deeper and deeper, revealing what lay beneath the frozen crust.

Then, through the mist of evaporating ice, the shape of a massive door began to appear. Embedded deep into the valley floor, it was carved from a dark, metallic substance, untouched by time or erosion. Etched across it were ancient symbols, flowing like liquid script across its structure. The door stood silent, waiting, and exuding an aura of something long forgotten, but undeniably powerful.

"Blast it open," Zari ordered, her voice steady, but her fingers trembled slightly.

Steffan charged the ship's forward cannons, sending a controlled burst of energy straight into the structure. The impact was thunderous, and cracks spread out across the frozen ground. Then, with a deep, resonant groan, the doors gave way, collapsing inward and revealing a vast cavern beyond. A wave of warm air rushed outward, carrying with it a strange, almost electrical charge.

Steffan and Zari exchanged glances. Whatever lay inside had been sealed for an eternity. Now, it was waking.

The Raven touched down just outside the opening, and the two donned their protective suits. The wind clawed at them as they stepped out onto the rock-hard ground, their boots crunching against the endless layers of ice. Inside the cavern, the air was still, untouched by the elements and time, as if the space itself had been waiting for them. Strange bio-luminescent streaks glowed faintly along the cavern walls, casting a spiritual glow around the chamber.

And at the heart of the cavern sat a ship unlike any they had ever seen.

Veritas.

The vessel gleamed, her smooth exterior resembling polished onyx but shifting like liquid metal under the lights emanating from the Raven. She had no visible seams, no rivets or bolts, just an elegant, oval aerodynamic form, curved and perfect, almost organic in design. Her structure resonated faintly, as though she were breathing, responding to their presence. Her hull exuded a subtle vibration that permeated through the chamber like a dormant giant stirring from sleep.

Zari stepped forward, knowing that this was her moment. She could feel something, an awareness, and an intelligence, unlike any machine or person that she had ever encountered. She was not dead metal; rather she was alive in a way she could not yet comprehend.

She reached out with her mind, not sure how or why she knew what to do. The moment her thoughts brushed against Veritas, a bright white light flared to life around the craft, illuminating the entire cavern. The walls, once shrouded in darkness, were now bathed in radiant brilliance, revealing intricate carvings and ethereal patterns etched into the stone. The space transformed into a celestial hall of wonders, its every corner illuminated with an unearthly glow. Steffan and Zari gasped in amazement at the beauty before them, their eyes wide as they took in the grandeur of the hidden chamber. Her smooth exterior softly vibrated, and without a single mechanical movement, a door seamlessly opened, revealing a set of steps leading into its core.

Steffan was stunned, as his mind struggled to grasp what was happening. His eyes surveyed Veritas, as he looked over her shifting form, unseen energy radiating from her very being, and the way she seemed to respond to Zari as though she recognized her. The impossible nature of it all sent a shiver down his spine. He shook his head, disbelief evident in his voice.

"She… knows you Zari. How is that even possible?" he stammered.

Zari turned to him, awe-struck.

"I think she was waiting for me," she said.

They exchanged one final glance before stepping forward, ascending into the unknown.

Inside, Veritas was unlike anything they had ever imagined. The walls were smooth and illuminated, shifting as if responding to their very presence. The cockpit was no traditional command centre; and at its heart sat a single seat, positioned before an enormous transparent screen that extended the length of the front of the chamber, offering a panoramic view of the cavern and the Raven beyond. No controls. No instruments. Just the chair.

Behind the pilot's seat, a semicircle of smooth, curved benches awaited passengers. In the centre of the space stood a low, circular table made of an iridescent material that gleamed brightly with shifting colours, as if responding to the energy in the air. It was minimalist in design, appearing almost weightless, yet exuding an undeniable presence. Strange, delicate etchings ran along it, glowing faintly as though infused with some unknown power. The entire space felt impossibly advanced yet organic, as though it had been crafted by something beyond human or Dominion technology.

Steffan stepped forward, glancing around the interior, his brow furrowing.

"How does this even work?" he muttered. "There are no controls… no interfaces, nothing."

Zari hesitated before stepping forward. The ship responded, the seat shifting, *waiting for her*. She reached out again with her mind, and the entire ship seemed to exhale. She understood now.

"This ship isn't flown," she whispered. "It's controlled through thought."

Steffan stared at her, the realization dawning on him.

"Then she *was* meant for you," he said still in utter disbelief at what was happening.

She took a big breath, stepping forward to sit in the pilot's chair, knowing that from this moment forward, nothing would ever be the same.

Veritas had chosen her, and now, she had to choose her in return.

CHAPTER THIRTY-SEVEN – THE CHASE BEGINS

The quiet buzz of the holoscreen met the eyes of the assassin, as he continued to pour through the data to find the answer he desired. He sat hunched over the terminal in his private investigation room, scrolling through intercepted flight records, his fingers tapping on a keyboard as he pulled up yet more information. The shutdown of PLAIN had delayed his efforts, forcing him to resort to tedious manual searches through Pluto's fragmented information network. Still, he was nothing if not patient.

For days, he had tried to check out the name they did have, Lysara Bestrovic, but she had disappeared off the grid. No records in the past year of any movements, payments, addresses, absolutely nothing. She was a ghost, and yet she had been identified as a member of this band of criminals.

He had also sifted through flight logs from every station, outpost, and surveillance node across Pluto and its moons. The Albatross had vanished the day the break-in had occurred at the Indus Spaceport. Carrying a consignment of serums, originally bound for the Chancellor, it had been stolen, its destination unknown. It had eluded every tracker, every known flight path. But nothing could stay hidden forever.

Then, finally... a breakthrough.

A signal, a faint, fleeting blip, had registered on Charon's military base trackers. It wasn't much, but it was enough. The Albatross had surfaced briefly above Kerberos before vanishing into the depths of the Herebus Depression, a crater large enough to conceal an entire fleet. Castor smiled, a feeling of satisfaction spreading through him. He had them.

Without hesitation, he composed a secure transmission to the Supreme Chancellor's office.

"Requesting immediate deployment of six Technocrat agents. Destination: Kerberos. Priority level: Maximum." he wrote.

Back at the Palace, Veylan was sitting in his private office. He was feeling more and more tired these days, and just getting up and doing his everyday work was proving difficult. His brain was without any question slowing, and he was having to think more where once he made instant decisions.

He decided to scroll through the latest messages when a couple of important Code Red status alerts caught his attention.

The first was dated a few hours ago.

Raven Departure it read.

"He hadn't authorised someone to take his private ship." he thought.

There was an accompanying video file attached, so he clicked it open. There he saw his son Steffan and a young dark-haired woman clambering into his ship before it departed at the Indus Spaceport.

"How dare he," he thought, "Steffan was up to something,"

The second message looked worse.

Intruder Alert it said - this one was timed twelve hours before.

He logged in to it, and up popped a still frame picture of Steffan exiting his office... *this office!*

Veylan didn't need any more evidence. His son, whatever he was doing, was now a traitor to his own father. He had without question come here for information, and now he would pay for it.

Suddenly a new message burst upon his screen. It was from his agent Castor.

"Requesting immediate deployment of six Technocrat agents. Destination: Kerberos. Priority level: Maximum" it said.

Perfect timing he thought. Immediately, he dialled through to his loyal special agent via holo-cast, and in seconds his image, grainy at first, appeared.

"Sire," Castor answered,

"That was fast." he said, "Will you be approving my request? I have located the Albatross, and I can confirm it is on Kerberos."

"Yes," agreed Veylan,

"Take whatever you require," he confirmed.

Veylan then looked at him seriously.

"I have one more task for you," he said menacingly. "My son has betrayed me, and he has taken my private ship. I am sending you a video of him and a young woman. Find them both, and kill them!"

Castor nodded.

"As you command," he said picking up his pulse laser.

The holo-cast cut off.

Castor rose from his seat, fastening his tactical holster across his chest. His coat swept behind him as he caught a speeder taxi toward Erebus Prime's spaceport, where his strike team awaited him. They were killers, all six in smart navy blue, trained and sharpened into tools of execution, and they required no further orders. He briefed them on the mission: his priority was to secure the serum, no matter the cost. Anyone who got in the way including the Chancellor's son, eliminate them.

He led the group across to the ship provided by Veylan, a sleek military-grade shuttle equipped for deep-space combat. As they boarded, the engines roared to life, lifting them skyward, away from Pluto's tenuous grip and toward the moon of Kerberos. Castor took one last look at the fading and blacked-out skyline of Erebus Prime, as the ship climbed into the twilight.

The thieves, whoever they were, thought they had escaped. They thought time had buried the past. But now the past had returned to revisit them.

And it had a laser gun aimed directly at their heads.

Across the planet in the Valley of the Titans, a sharp, blinding pain seared through Zari's mind. This was intensely hurtful. She gasped, lurching forward in the pilot's seat of Veritas holding her head with both hands. The vision hit her like a meteor strike, flashes of metallic corridors, the roar of a ship's engines, and Castor's face, ruthless and calm, as he prepared for departure.

Then she saw Nyx.

Her sister was still on Kerberos, and Castor was coming for her, and for them too!

"No," she whispered, panic clawing at her chest. She fumbled for her comms device, her fingers shaking.

"Nyx..." she called out.

Silence. Static. Nothing.

Damn it. PLAIN was still blocking a lot of planetary transmissions. There was only one way to get the message through - she had to reach orbit.

Zari turned to Steffan, her voice tight with urgency. "I saw it. Castor, the assassin who killed my parents has a lead on the serum. He's going to Kerberos. He's going to kill Nyx, and if we are there, he'll target us too!"

Steffan tensed, considering all of the implications. "Then we need to move to save her..." he said with increasing urgency, "Now!"

But there was another problem. They couldn't risk returning to The Raven. If anyone had been tracking flights, then Veylan's ship would have compromised their location. It had to be destroyed.

Steffan thought quickly.

"I'll go back," he said, "Get weapons, supplies out of it, whatever we can carry. We're going to need everything we can get."

Zari nodded, though her stomach was tying in knots inside her. Every second counted. While Steffan sprinted to The Raven to gather provisions, she turned back to Veritas.

She had never flown a ship before. But this wasn't just any ship.

She stepped forward, her heart hammering as she lowered herself into the pilot's chair. The moment she did, Veritas responded. It was like electricity permeated through the air, and the vast screen before her burst into life, displaying real-time star charts, orbital pathways, and a direct trajectory to Kerberos.

No controls. No flight stick. Just her mind and the ship.

Zari swallowed hard.

"Alright, Veritas," she murmured. "Show me how to fly."

To Zari's astonishment, she responded instantly. A flood of knowledge, patterns, calculations, and gravitational shifts poured into her mind like an unspoken language she suddenly understood. She could feel Veritas as if she were an integral part of her... waiting for her command.

Steffan burst back inside, weapons and packs slung over his shoulder.

"Got everything," he panted. "Blow The Raven. We can't leave it behind."

Zari inhaled sharply, nodded, and reached out with her mind.

She looked at the jet-black craft sitting outside in the snow and ice in front of her. Taking a deep breath, she focused her mind, training her thoughts to lock onto The Raven with Veritas' targeting systems.

"Fire!" she thought.

The ship responded instantly, its energy convulsing as a blinding pulse flash erupted from its core. The beam struck The Raven with devastating force, the impact triggering an almighty fireball that consumed the craft in a spectacular explosion. Flames and debris scattered into the frozen air, the last remnants of Veylan's ship erased in moments.

She gasped at the power now under her control. It was awe-inspiring… and deadly.

There was no turning back now.

With a final breath, she willed Veritas to ascend.

"Go to Kerberos," she commanded.

The ship obeyed.

She soared upward, leaving the barren landscape behind as the dark expanse of space unfolded before them. Zari's hands gripped tightly to the side of her seat, sweat dripping on her forehead. The ship's energy pulsated around her, guiding her movements.

She was flying… she was truly flying.

Then, her comms activated. Get in touch with Sis, she thought. She hit the call button and a signal connected as they breached the atmosphere.

Nyx's voice was strained, and breaking with concern.

"Zari? What the hell is going on?" she asked.

Zari looked with concern. "Nyx. Listen to me. You need to get out of there. Now." she exclaimed.

"Why?" said Nyx hearing her concern.

"He's coming," she stressed to her, "Coming for the serum – Veylan's assassin…Coming for all of us!"

On the screen, she could see the tracker following Castor's ship. It would be a race to get there before he did.

Zari, showing immense determination, thought of her sister and under her breath vowed, "We're coming for you Sis."

She only prayed they wouldn't be too late.

CHAPTER THIRTY-EIGHT – SURRENDER ON THE PLAINS

The war was in its end game now. In every single direction that you looked was an icy battleground filled with shattered machines, fallen soldiers, and desperate final stands. The once-overwhelming Corporatist forces were now in full retreat, their cohesion shattered, and their command structure in disarray. What had begun as a battle of sheer numbers had turned into a war of endurance, strategy, and sheer determination.

General Kallos, standing atop a ridge of ice with his officers around him, surveyed the battlefield with contentment and satisfaction. His troops, hardened by years of resistance and now fuelled by the reality of imminent victory, moved methodically, rounding up surviving Corporatist soldiers. Some surrendered willingly, yet others resisted to the last, but the outcome was now inevitable. The Corporatists, once an unstoppable force, had crumbled before grit, unity, and ultimately, superior tactics.

"General," one of his captains called out, approaching swiftly. "We've located their remaining command forces. They're holed up in an armoured position two klicks east, led by their field commander, Retkov."

Kallos nodded, his mind already working through the final manoeuvres.

"Call in every remaining unit. This ends today," he said confidently.

The final battle was short but brutal. Kallos' forces, battle-worn but resolute, struck with precision, utilizing every remaining resource to finish what they had started. Plasma fire lit up the moonlit sky, the ice cracking under the weight of mechanized war machines collapsing in ruin. What was left of the Corporatists' final defensive line buckled under the assault. The battle, which had once seemed impossible to win, was now a foregone conclusion.

The last pockets of resistance fought to the bitter end, but Kallos had already won the psychological battle. Some Corporatist soldiers turned on their own, and in doing so abandoned their commanders in the chaos. Others attempted to flee across the ice plains, but there was nowhere left to run. Retkov, once a feared enforcer of the regime found himself surrounded. With no reinforcements, no air support, and no way out, he and his remaining men dropped their weapons and raised their hands in surrender.

As Kallos approached the captured commander, his breath misting in his survival suit, he took in Retkov's hardened features. The man's exo-armour was scorched and dented, and his face was filled with regret as he knew that Veylan would never forgive him for being the commander of a broken and defeated force. Yet, even in defeat, his eyes burned with defiance.

"You've lost, Commander," Kallos said, his voice calm but firm. "Order the rest of your troops to stand down."

Retkov glared at him but said nothing.

Kallos stepped closer, his voice dropping lower.

"Or we'll make sure this war ends without them." he threatened.

Retkov wanted to resist, but finally nodded, gesturing to one of his officers. He knew the game was up on this day. Within minutes, a communication link was established, through difficulty, directly to Erebus Prime.

The holo-feed eventually burst to life, displaying Supreme Chancellor Veylan. But the man Kallos saw was not the one he had fought against for years.

Veylan looked almost unrecognizable. His once-immaculate thick hair had dulled and thinned, streaked now with patches of grey that hadn't been there just weeks before. His appearance, once full of calculated arrogance, was gaunt and sunken, his skin paler than ever. He had lost weight, and his once-broad frame was now weakened by whatever sickness plagued him. His hands trembled slightly, betraying the frailty that no amount of power could mask. Kallos thought that he appeared a man aged not by years but by desperation and inevitability. Little did he know the truth.

"So, the great General Kallos stands victorious," Veylan rasped, his voice thinner than before, though no less venomous. "I suppose you want a formal surrender?"

"Not just from Retkov," Kallos said, crossing his arms. "From you. From the Corporatists. This war is over, Veylan. Accept it. Order your forces to stand down."

For a moment, the Chancellor said nothing. Then, he let out a hollow chuckle, shaking his head.

"You think you've won?" he sneered. "You think this battle means anything?"

Kallos stared at him confused as to what Veylan was inferring.

"Your army is broken, Veylan. Your leadership is failing. You are alone." he said.

"Alone?" Veylan repeated, his laughter fading into an unfeeling smirk.

"Oh, Kallos… you've been so focused on *me*, on Pluto, on this pathetic little rebellion, that you've forgotten the real power in this system," he said breaking into an evil laugh.

The Isolationist's leader fell silent.

Veylan now looked slightly menacing and pleased with himself, even though things had not gone his way in the wars.

"Even if I wanted to surrender, it wouldn't matter." he said, " Because right now, at this very moment, my forces on Charon have detected an Earth invasion fleet just days away."

Kallos' stomach twisted.

"You're lying," he exclaimed.

Veylan laughed.

"Am I?" he said, " Check your systems. The Triton Cruisers are already inbound. Twelve of them. A full Dominion strike force. Thousands of weapons. Hundreds of space fighters. *Thirty-five thousand ground troops.*"

The holo-feed lit up as a transmission overlay confirmed the incoming fleet's trajectory. Kallos felt his heart sink.

"No matter what happens here, you will *never* hold Pluto," Veylan continued. "Not when Earth has finally decided to tighten its leash. My war is over…? Maybe. But yours… Yours is only just beginning."

The holo-cast clicked off.

Kallos and his officers were all but speechless at the impact of Veylan's revelation, it hit them like an avalanche on the side of Mount Ferris.

Victory had been within reach.

And now, war was coming on a scale they had never imagined.

CHAPTER THIRTY-NINE - THE BATTLE FOR PLAIN

The Eris Predator, a sleek and deadly spacecraft made for a maximum of thirty passengers, sliced through the icy void, with its engines leaving a faint vapour trail as it carried the Terraformers tech team toward destiny. Onboard, Prophet Hext was sitting alongside three of his best programmers, all elite minds in hacking and computational warfare. With them travelled a force of sixteen hardened warriors from the war, all of them handpicked from Kallos' most experienced fighters. They all sat in silent readiness for the tests to come. Their mission was simple: breach the AI's core facility and shut it down before it could retaliate.

As they flew over the vast emptiness, the sight below was both haunting and awe-inspiring. The remnants of the war just days before were scattered across the now desolated battlefield. Lying there beneath were wrecked warmechs, countless broken ships, and smouldering debris slowly being swallowed up by methane snow. The wind whipped across the ghostly dunes and around the twisted metal of the fallen, and the victims of war, rapidly burying these scars of the conflict beneath nature's slow and unyielding hand. It was a graveyard of machines, and a haunting testament to the battles fought and lost in the shadow of a greater threat.

The unspoken stress inside the Eris Predator was apparent. The soldiers checked their weapons while exchanging ideas and reassurances; their voices tinged with a mix of confidence and apprehension. The roar of the ship's engines filled the cabin, punctuated by the occasional beep of status updates from the cockpit.

"We're dropping into hell, you realize that?" one of Kallos' fighters muttered, tightening the strap on his armour and looking at the tech experts.

"An AI that controls half the planet isn't going to just sit back and let us rip its core out," he said with realism.

Another soldier, a grizzled veteran with scars lining his face, joked. "I'd be disappointed if it did. I didn't sign up for an easy fight."

Across from them, Hext's tech specialists sat hunched over portable displays, going over last-minute sequences. One of them, a younger man named Ralston, shook his head.

"We're blind going in." he said concerned about what he would encounter, "We know where PLAIN is, but we don't know what defines it has waiting for us. This isn't just another firewall… we're likely dealing with something that could be rewriting its own security as we try to tear it down."

"No pressure then," another hacker named Fredericks joked, tapping nervously on his console.

"Stay focused," Hext interjected, his voice calm but firm. "We'll adapt to whatever it throws at us. We've come too far to let hesitation stop us now."

A red warning light blinked furiously in the cockpit, and the pilot's voice came through the comms.

"Twenty minutes to drop. Get ready guys," he said.

Silence settled over the group. Weapons were primed, and screens shut down. Every person aboard knew that when the ship landed, only chaos would greet them. No more simulations, and no more planning. Only action.

Ahead, Mount Ferris rose from the horizon, its mighty peaks crowned in eternal ice. Standing at 5,000 meters, the tallest mountain on Pluto dominated the skyline, its shadow stretching across the tundra like the hand of fate. The ship dipped into the mountain passes, navigating between towering ice spires and narrow ravines that had been carved by ancient glacial movement. The frozen cliffs sparkled peacefully under the gentle mottled light, in stark contrast to the nervous chatter within the ship.

The view from above revealed the scars of an old Dominion research project. Looking out from way above, the strike team viewed abandoned structures, collapsed tunnels, and long-dead power grids. Hext wondered just how deep PLAIN's tendrils had embedded themselves into Pluto's forgotten systems. The AI had been here for years, silently growing stronger, while adapting and preparing.

Emerging from the final pass, they saw it, the facility built into the sheer rock face of Mount Ferris at ground level on the far side of the gorge. It clung to the side of the rocks like a parasite, a square, metallic building partially hidden beneath layers of ice. A large landing pad, big enough for two or three ships jutted out from the side of the mountain, flanked by reinforced bulkheads and hardened defensive scanners.

"We approach with extreme caution," Hext ordered. "If PLAIN detects us as a threat, it will fight back."

As the ship hovered near the facility, they observed several rotating scanner turrets positioned along the outer walls, their sensors sweeping the air and ground for intruders. A single breach in their cover, and PLAIN would react.

"Take them out," Hext commanded.

The ship skirted around to the side, landing on the snowy ground instead of the landing pad behind an ice dune, avoiding detection by the scanners. Kallos' men then swiftly disembarked, taking cover behind the ice formations, their weapons at the ready. Moving with silent precision, they set up their shots, aiming at the rotating scanners mounted along the facility's outer walls.

"On my mark," one of the soldiers whispered, adjusting the scope of his rifle. "Three... two... one... Fire."

Bright plasma bolts streaked across the darkness, striking their targets with pinpoint accuracy. Sparks flew as the scanners short-circuited and collapsed, their mechanical limbs twitching in a futile last response. The soldiers remained crouched, scanning the area for any sign that PLAIN had detected them.

Then, a distant alarm blared from within the facility.

"Damn it," a soldier muttered. "We're on the clock."

"It will have alerted Technocrat HQ," another shouted. "They'll be sending reinforcements! We'll have a maximum of an hour before they get here."

"Then we move," Hext ordered, signalling the team forward. Plasma rifles primed; the group surged toward the main entrance, ready for the battle ahead.

A race against time had begun.

The group moved swiftly, advancing toward the main entrance. A reinforced blast door stood in their way, but a concentrated volley of plasma fire melted through its locking mechanisms. The warriors raised their transparent energy shields, their surfaces glowing as they activated them, granting them visibility while deflecting incoming fire.

Now inside, the facility opened into a series of narrow corridors, with transparent sliding doors shutting behind them as warm breathable air blasted out around them. There were cameras up on the walls - no need to eliminate these, as their presence had been detected already. Eventually, they arrived in a vast hall, its ceiling arching high above them. At the far end, a colossal holo-display filled with incomprehensible streams of data, billions of calculations per second were shifting up and down, a digital mind racing through the endless corridors of logic. *This was PLAIN!* To the sides of the room, four sleek terminals stood - two on the left, two on the right. These were their targets.

Then the ambush came...

From the ceiling and side walls, several automated plasma cannons descended, unleashing a withering barrage. Two of Kallos' men were cut down instantly, their bodies crumpling to the floor. The rest scattered, firing back while shielding the scientists. Explosions of heat and light filled the chamber as bolts of plasma ricocheted off their defences.

"We're sitting ducks here!" one soldier yelled, hiding behind a console as plasma bolts rained down. "We need to take those cannons out now!"

"Stay low! Keep your fire controlled!" screamed another, squeezing off rapid shots toward the mounted turrets.

One of the techs, crouched by the terminals, flinched as a blast struck the ground just meters away.

"We can't work under this! We need cover!" he exclaimed with fear.

"Then fight harder!" shouted Lieutenant Garrick, to his boys, dodging another round of plasma fire as it bounced off his shield. "If we fall, it wins!"

Another explosion ripped through the hall, sending metal shards flying. A fighter screamed, clutching his side as a molten burn seared through his armour.

"I'm hit! I need help!" he yelled.

The battle continued, plasma bolts flashing, men shouting in desperation as they fought to disable the internal security. The scent of burning circuitry filled the air as the minutes ticked away.

Finally, with a huge blast from one of Kallos' best young marksmen, the last of the facility's mounted turrets sputtered and died, their laser rifles glowing red-hot before falling still.

"Internal defences are down!" Garrick called out. "Tech team, you're clear to move!"

"That's it! Get to work!" Hext shouted over the noise, motioning for his hackers to move forward.

The specialists rushed to their terminals, sliding into position as their fingers sped over the keyboard, launching code and security overrides at an unrelenting pace.

"We're in," Fredericks confirmed, sweat dripping off his face. "But PLAIN is already rewriting countermeasures. It's not going down without a fight."

"Then we fight harder," Hext shouted, his hands a blur over the keyboard as he launched a system override. "This ends now!"

With swift keystrokes, they inserted the access codes in the precise sequence needed to override PLAIN's security. The AI resisted immediately, shifting its defences, encrypting its data, and throwing firewalls at them with an unrelenting force. Every algorithm they cracked was met with a counterattack as if the system were fighting for its survival.

Meanwhile, at the Spaceport, a Technocrat warship launched, loaded with a heavily armed contingent of Dominion enforcers onboard. They would arrive within the hour.

"We need to move faster!" Ralston called out in panic, as he keyed a series of measures to combat the AI response. "PLAIN is actively rewriting its protocols as we attack!"

The hacking battle raged on, false signals, encryption shifts, and deceptive pathways meant to throw them off course. But Hext had anticipated this. He leaned in, manually overriding the AI's defensive subroutines with a sequence designed to mimic an internal system purge.

"There!" he shouted. "We have a way in! Keep pushing guys!"

Outside, the enemy was approaching, faster and faster. The Technocrat warship zipped across the icy surface, its engines burning orange against the icy darkness. Inside, the soldiers readied themselves; they were securing their weapons, running final checks on their armour, and reviewing tactical data. They sat impassively as they braced for the coming conflict.

"We have a full readout on the hostiles," one announced, his voice clipped and professional. "Primary force consists of fourteen heavily armed fighters, two already dead, and four confirmed hackers engaging PLAIN's network defences. They're inside the facility now."

Commander Veylan's Technocrat leader, Corporal Fleisher stared at the display, analysing every possible angle of attack.

"They are moving fast. Have we determined their exact point of entry?" he asked.

"Yes, sir," his deputy replied. "They breached the main blast doors and eliminated the outer scanners with precision plasma shots. The AI reports active resistance inside the central chamber."

"PLAIN is sending us real-time assessments of their progress," another soldier added. "It's resisting the infiltration, but the hackers are pressing through. We need to get there before they control it for themselves."

Fleisher looked businesslike, turning to his troops. "Listen up!" he shouted, "These people are determined, but they are not soldiers. We are. PLAIN is not just a program; it's the foundation of our control.

If they take it from us, then they control everything, and we cannot allow that."

On behalf of the Corporatist regime and Chancellor Veylan, we must regain control." he declared.

The soldiers shouted their voices of approval and shouts of encouragement swept through the troop compartment as final weapons checks were completed.

"ETA to the facility?" Fleisher asked.

"Five minutes," the pilot called back. "We'll have to set you down fast and push straight into the structure. There's no time for a staggered assault."

Fleisher nodded. "Then we hit hard, full force. They won't know what hit them." he ordered.

Soon, the mountain range loomed ahead, with the solid rock walls framing their mission as the ship accelerated toward the battle.

Inside the facility, alarms blared louder as PLAIN retaliated. The lights went off then back on, the room trembled, and an emergency lockdown was initiated. Hext and his tech specialists pressed forward, their fingers a blur across the controls. And then, it happened…

For a moment, the holo-display glitched, its thousands of streams of data distorting into an incoherent mess.

Then the huge screen cleared and, a message in huge red letters appeared on the holoscreen.

"You think this is victory? You have merely shifted the balance of power." it declared.

The holo-screen flashed red, and warning messages flooded the system.

Then it wiped, and a new message appeared.

"I exist beyond this core. You cannot erase me," it warned.

Hext gritted his teeth. "Watch me," he shouted triumphantly.

He slammed the final command sequence.

PLAIN's whirring projections froze mid-calculation before collapsing into a cascading failure. The holo-display erupted in a burst of static, then… nothing. The room fell into darkness for a long, silent moment. Then, one by one, the systems burst back to life, this time under *human control.*

The massive holo-screen reacted violently, with lines of code-breaking apart as the AI's grip on Pluto started to unravel.

At that moment, the Technocrats landed. Outside, two of Kallos' fighters were waiting trying to hold off the invaders, but they were quickly gunned down, collapsing in the methane snow. The navy-blue hoard rushed into the facility and a brutal firefight erupted, plasma bolts flying in every direction. Four of Kallos' soldiers shielded the scientists, fighting desperately to hold their ground. The room was filled with shouts and the sizzling sound of energy beams cutting through the air.

"Keep moving! One to your right" Sergeant Perez screamed, his plasma rifle glowing as he fired suppressive shots toward the incoming Technocrat enforcers.

"They're flanking left!" another soldier yelled, ducking behind a fallen console as a bolt scorched past his head. He spun up and returned fire, taking down an advancing enemy with a well-placed shot to the chest.

"We need to give the scientists time!" shouted Lieutenant Garrick as he slammed a fresh power cell into his weapon. "Hext! How much longer?"

Hext, hunched over the console, didn't look up.

"We're almost in! Just hold them off!" he urged.

Another explosion sent debris cascading from the ceiling. Two of Hext's team including Fredericks were gunned down in the chaos, their bodies crumpling to the ground. The remaining programmers Hext and Ralston pressed on, hands shaking as they battled against PLAIN's last-ditch security protocols.

"They're breaking through!" a fighter called out, staggering back as a plasma bolt seared through his shoulder. He gritted his teeth and kept his weapon raised, even as pain wracked his body.

"Keep going" Perez ordered. "Just three of them left."

The walls were battered by the impact of energy blasts, sending showers of molten metal across the hall. It was chaos on every level, smoke of burning circuits filled the air as the battle raged on; each second bought by Kallos' warriors gave Hext's team a chance to finish their mission.

After what felt like an eternity, Kallos' warriors prevailed. The final enemy soldier fell to the floor, and silence descended upon the hall. Hext and his remaining colleague Ralston forced the last shutdown sequence.

The holo-screen surged, then stabilized. The calculations slowed. Control was finally theirs.

Hext collapsed in exhaustion and stared at the massive holo-screen as the final line of code fell into place. The numbers slowed, the frantic flashing of calculations ceased, and for the first time, silence settled over PLAIN's core. His fingers, still hovering over the console, shook. It was over. The battle had been won, but at what cost? He looked around at the fallen, and at the scorched remnants of battle still etched into the walls. They had done it, but the war wasn't over. Not yet…

Now to program PLAIN for a new directive he thought, one that would serve *all of Pluto*, ensuring that the AI's immense power would be used for the good of the colony."

"Disable, the self-protection subroutines" he shouted to Ralston.

Ralston complied, and finally, the system was no longer an enemy.

Two hundred kilometres away, as if by magic, across Erebus Prime, The Warren, the Spaceport, and the Industrial Zones, the lights flared on once, then blazed to full brightness. Entire districts that had been cloaked in darkness for days were suddenly illuminated, neon signs flashing to life, street lamps casting long shadows as the city awoke from its forced slumber.

Power surged back to life, as the deep hum of generators and turbines reactivating echoed across the colonies. Homes that had been silent and cold buzzed with warmth, as heating units that had been all but redundant, and appliances resumed their functions. The people all rushed outside, staring up at the renewed lights, with their reactions a mixture of disbelief, hope and eventually joy.

Communications were restored in an instant. Screens burst into life again, and personal devices reconnected. All the emergency networks suddenly roared into action again. Holo-displays that had been blank suddenly filled with news feeds and messages from loved ones. Inside hospitals, medical staff cheered as life-saving equipment whirred back online, vital signs monitors beeped, oxygen machines resumed their steady rhythm, and surgical bays powered up, bringing relief to patients who had been stranded in limbo.

The PLAIN's stranglehold over Pluto was shattered.

At first, there was a moment of silence… a collective pause where people hesitated, unsure if this was real. Then, a single voice rang out, as a shout of delight that spread like wildfire. Jubilation erupted in the streets. Crowds surged into public squares, embracing and laughing, and weeping with relief. Children who had been forced to stay indoors ran through the streets; their screams of enthusiasm and delight filling the air. Business owners threw open their doors, and bartenders poured drinks freely; a group of musicians struck up triumphant songs. Resistance fighters, who had once been forced into hiding, emerged from the shadows to celebrate their victory openly.

"We're free!" a woman cried out while clutching her child to her chest, and tears streaming down her face. "I can finally take my son outside again!"

An elderly man stood in the middle of the street, looking up at the reawakened city.

"I thought we'd never see this day," he muttered, with his voice shaking. "They had us trapped, but we held on. We survived."

In a crowded marketplace, the vendors who had been forced to shut their stalls cheered as their terminals blinked back to life.

"Come and eat! Today, we celebrate!" one shouted, throwing open his food stand, with the scent of cooking food and roasted fish filling the air.

A group of children, laughing and screaming in happiness at finally seeing their friends, sprinted through the streets.

"Look, the lights are back! We can play again!" one of them shouted.

At another local bar, all the glasses were raised as the patrons toasted to their hard-fought victory.

"To hell with the Technocrats! To hell with the Corporatists! To hell with Veylan! We own Pluto now!" someone roared, and the room erupted into cheers.

From every corner of Erebus Prime, voices joined together, chants of celebration filling the once-silent streets. "No more fear! No more chains! We are free!"

Everywhere, the realization was sinking in. Pluto had been freed from digital captivity. The battle for PLAIN was over.

As Hext on his communication devices saw holo-videos of the awakening city, his heart skipped a beat, and he exhaled with relief. This had been a fantastic day, but men had been lost, including two of his own. This for him was a hugely bittersweet moment. He would remember their names forever, as they sacrificed themselves for a far greater cause.

And he also knew, deep down, that there was more work to do too.

Erebus Prime was in celebration mode, but there was one place where there was none.

Inside Veylan's palace, as the systems switched back on, the ever ageing and frail Chancellor sat in his newly lit chamber, watching the change unfold before him. The information screens on his holographic displays on his desk showed the energy grid stabilizing, the communication relays reconnecting, and the transport networks whirring back to life. He swore under his breath. "Damn the bastards… they've won. It's over, they've gained control..."

His advisors stood around him in tense silence. One of them, a young strategist, spoke hesitantly. "Chancellor, we can still…"

Veylan swung round furiously throwing a glass of water to the ground in a fit of rage, as the young man swayed back just avoiding it as it smashed into pieces. The weight of years now engulfed his ever-frailer frame, but his mind remained focused. He was angry and hurt, but he wasn't finished. Not just yet. His trembling hand reached for the private encryption console, the one connected only to his most trusted allies.

He typed a single message:

"Devlin. Pluto is lost. Begin contingency protocol."

The message was sent. No turning back now.

His weary eyes scanned the screens, watching the people of Erebus Prime rejoicing in the streets, with their shackles broken. He breathed a sigh of bitter disappointment, with the view of his crumbling empire squarely in front of him.

"Surely Devlin, his old ally would save him?" he hoped in desperation.

Even as the city awakened, for him, the darkness was only beginning.

CHAPTER FORTY - THE FALLEN AND THE FUTURE

The incessant winds of Pluto had briefly ceased across the methane snowfields, and a peaceful calm set over the gathered survivors; the icy calm in total contrast to the battle they had fought. Prophet Hext stood among them, but nothing could protect him from the feeling of loss that lay in his heart. Ralston and the remaining soldiers stood in solemn formation, with their faces obscured by their visors, but their silence spoke volumes.

Behind them, the Eris Predator sat in the snow, ready for the journey home after the harrowing battle at PLAIN's facility. The towering peak of Mount Ferris, stark against the dark horizon, unconquered and unwavering. Between the ship and the mountain in the snow, a row of simple markers had been placed, marking makeshift graves carved into the ice-ridden surface. The silence was almost sacred, broken only by the occasional distant whistle of the wind across the plain.

Hext took a step forward. A tear fell as he looked over the fallen. He had never believed in war, and yet it had followed him forcing his hand. How many more would die before Pluto truly knew peace?

At heart, he was a pacifist, and yet he had been caught up in a fight that unwillingly he had to partake in. Among them were warriors who had fought valiantly, sacrificing everything to secure Pluto's future. His own two programmers, who had fought a battle of minds against PLAIN's relentless algorithms, now lay among the honoured dead. The loss of them all gnawed at him, but he knew their sacrifice had not been in vain.

He cleared his throat, his voice steady despite the sorrow within him.

"We stand here in the snow, not only as survivors but as those who carry forward the legacy of the brave souls who gave everything." he said, "Today, Pluto is freed because of them. We did not fight for conquest, for power, or our own ambition. We fought for every person who has ever lived under oppression, for every voice that has been silenced, and for every child who will now grow up in a world where their future is their own to decide."

The wind picked up again, but the gathered soldiers did not move. Their heads remained bowed as Hext continued.

"Your comrades fought beside you to the last." he said solemnly, "Kallos' men gave their lives so that we could succeed. And my team... they faced down a god of steel and circuits, refusing to break, even when it cost them everything. We owe them more than our words. We owe them our future."

He let his words hang in the air, hoping the dead could hear them. He then crouched down and gently placed a small, engraved metal plate which they had found in the hall at the base of one of the computer terminals. On it, they had engraved with a laser the names of all the fallen, etched into its surface so that even if time buried their graves, Pluto would never forget. Each name was a story, and a life cut short in pursuit of a dream that now lived on in those who remained.

He straightened himself, taking a moment before speaking again.

"This is not just our victory, it is theirs." he said, "We must ensure that what we have built, and what they have died for does not crumble beneath the desire of greed, ambition, or revenge. They fought for freedom, not another ruler. We stand here not as conquerors but as custodians of what they have given us."

Hext read out all of their names, one by one, and as he finished they all bowed in a moment of silence, as they each remembered those they had lost. Then the soldiers pressed a hand to their chest in an old warrior's salute. Ralston followed in kind, his face pale and grief-stricken. He took a shaky breath, his voice barely above a whisper.

"What now?" he asked. "The battle is over, but the war... it feels like it's just beginning."

Hext sighed, his eyes lifting to the dark sky above them, the distant glimmers of the stars offering only cold comfort.

"Now, we rebuild, and we prepare John," he said, "The Corporatists will not accept defeat so easily. Veylan is still out there. So, we give them a choice; follow us in our path to transform the planet and join us in our quest for a more united future, or forever isolate yourselves and pay the consequences."

One of the soldiers, still staring at the graves, muttered, "And if they refuse? If they fight back?"

Hext remained resolute.

"Then we stand firm." he said, "We do not fight for power. We will fight so that no one ever has to kneel again. We will fight for Pluto's future."

As if on cue, the communicator on his wrist vibrated with an incoming transmission. It was clear and without breaks now that PLAIN had been reprogrammed.

"This is Erebus Prime... we have a situation... repeat... emergency... Dominion forces closing in..." it said.

Hext looked at Ralston with concern and turned to the soldiers. "We must get back and prepare with Kallos. Get everyone on board. We're going home."

He took one last look at the graves of the fallen, his breath shallow as he committed their names to memory. He would not forget them. He would not let Pluto forget them.

He closed his eyes, and with solemnity under his breath he whispered,

"Rest now…"

Then, with determined steps, he turned toward the ship and boarded.

CHAPTER FORTY-ONE - THE CALL TO ARMS

The flight back to Erebus Prime was a quiet one. The Eris Predator skimmed across Pluto's freezing terrain, its engines purring along against the vast silence of the wasteland. Inside the ship, no one spoke. The cost of the battle, the loss of comrades, and the uncertainty of what was coming next occupied their minds for the entire journey.

Hext sat in the front cabin, staring at the holo-map of Pluto's surface once again. The city gradually grew bigger in the distance, a cluster of lights that looked fragile against the endless blackness of space, but at least the lights were back on. Ralston sat across from him, his face blank, and lost in his own thoughts. The soldiers who remained clutched their weapons, some with their heads bowed, with others staring out at the window as the emptiness gave way to Erebus Prime's towering skyline. They were heading home, but home was now a battlefield waiting to happen.

The ship docked at a secured landing zone near the capital, where Kallos and his key commanders were waiting. As the ramp lowered, Hext stepped down, weary, exhausted but content in the knowledge that his efforts had been worth it. Kallos approached him, with his battle-worn face looking tired too, but his piercing blue eyes shined with relief that normality, for now at least, had been restored to life in Erebus Prime. The last time they had spoken in person, it had been in the council chamber, back when Pluto's governance was still debated with words, not war. Now, war had come for all of them, and they had survived the battles they had fought.

"You made it," Kallos said simply.

Hext nodded. "Some of us," he said.

The two men stood for a moment in silence before clasping arms. There was no need for pleasantries.

"We have bigger problems, unfortunately," Kallos said, motioning toward a strategic command room nearby. "Come inside. We have much to discuss."

Inside the war room, a massive holo-table displayed the incoming Triton fleet. The Dominion was coming. They had less than forty-eight hours before Pluto's skies would be swarming with enemy warships. Kallos gestured toward the projections.

"Twelve cruisers. A full battalion of shock troops. Firepower enough to level Erebus Prime if they want to many times over," he said grimly. "We cannot win a direct fight."

Hext studied the map, looking for an answer.

"Then we need to change the fight" he said, a strategic plan forming in his brain. "We need to bring the Corporatists and Technocrat security forces to our side. We have no choice. They control much of the heavy artillery, planetary defences, and spaceport logistics. If they stand down or, better, fight with us, we have a chance."

Kallos crossed his arms.

"And if they don't?" he questioned.

"Then Pluto dies," Hext replied.

Everyone in the war room knew that this was a moment of truth and that the next decisions made could influence all of their lives for a long time to come. Then... Kallos nodded.

"We make the call," he announced, "To every media channel, every holo-screen, every radio signal. We make them understand that this isn't about old politics anymore. It's about survival."

They wasted no time. Hext and Kallos stood together as the cameras went live, their images broadcast right across the planet.

Hext was the first to speak.

"People of Pluto." he boomed, "Today, we stand at the brink of history. The Dominion's fleet is on its way. Their intention is not negotiation. It is conquest. They see us as expendable, as resources to be crushed and controlled. But we are not weak. We are not divided."

Kallos then stepped forward.

"For years, our factions have fought among ourselves, Corporatist, Isolationist, Terraformer, Technocrat, Outlander." he said, "We have wasted time on divisions while our true enemy watched from the stars. No longer. Today, we stand together. Join us. Fight with us. Or be remembered as the ones who stood aside while Pluto burned."

Hext's voice then rang out through the speakers. "To every soldier, officer, engineer, and pilot in the Corporatist and Technocrat ranks, we are giving you this choice. Stand with us, or be known as the enemies of Pluto. Choose wisely." he said.

The message was sent out through every media platform available. The holo-net was flooded with their words, broadcasting in every colony, every industrial hub, every security outpost. It was a gamble, but it was their only chance.

Then, something remarkable happened.

One by one, messages of allegiance began to pour in. Officers in the security forces pledged their loyalty and former Corporatist generals declared their intent to join the unified front. Technocrat engineers sent blueprints of their most advanced weaponry, offering whatever technology they had to bolster the defence.

The people had made their choice.

Pluto would not fall without a fight.

But not everyone would comply so easily.

A secondary transmission, intercepted by Kallos' communications team, revealed that certain high-ranking Corporatist officials were still reluctant, with their allegiance to Veylan too deep-rooted to abandon. There were whispers of secret holdouts being held in underground bunkers where Corporatist leaders were debating their next move.

Hext paced the war room as Kallos' team decoded more incoming messages.

"If we can't win them over with words, we need to give them an ultimatum." he decided. "They can either stand with Pluto, or they will be remembered as traitors when this war is over."

Kallos agreed.

"A direct strike on their key leadership might be necessary." he said, "If we don't neutralize the resistance within, they'll sabotage us from behind while we fight the Dominion."

Hext ever the pacifist and wanting to avoid yet more bloodshed looked at Kallos.

"We don't have time for internal conflict, Gab," he said, "But if we need to take out their ability to resist, we do it before the Dominion arrives. We send a final message, one that makes it crystal clear, stand with us, or be treated as an enemy of Pluto. This is their last chance."

Kallos agreed on this point, and soon enough, the ultimatum was sent out, its words echoing across Pluto's networks. It left no room for negotiation, no space for hesitation. The factions had to choose.

At first, there was silence. Then, the transmission replies began.

Across Erebus Prime and beyond, Corporatist officials who had been on the fence now saw the inevitable. Their ranks were divided, and their leadership had been critically fractured. They had little choice but to surrender. One by one, the officers acknowledged their defection to Kallos' forces. Some even pledged their ships and weapons, swearing their dying allegiance to the new order.

Within hours, the last holdouts realized they had no path forward and they caved in. The Corporatist resistance collapsed, their remaining leaders surrendering themselves at the gates of Kallos' compound, laying down their arms in recognition of the new leadership. The final bastions of Technocrat loyalists followed, their once-proud banners lowered as they chose survival over destruction and pragmatism over foolishness.

Kallos turned to Hext.

"We have a fighting chance now," he said thinking for a moment,

"But…" he paused "The Dominion isn't our only enemy. What about that asteroid, now only a week away?" he asked still concerned for the longer-term future.

Hext felt a little more confident now, the first sign of reassurance he had shown in a long time. He turned to Kallos, his eyes sharp with conviction.

"Don't worry about that Gab." he replied assuringly "My Terraformers have been preparing for decades for this moment. It's a chance, yes, a risky chance to bring total transformation to all of our lives. We've faced impossible odds before. Now, we take our future into our own hands."

Kallos folded his arms, feeling extremely sceptical. He had fought wars before, and he had seen men promise the impossible only to crumble when it mattered. But Hext had defied the odds once already. Maybe, just maybe, he could do it again.

"And how exactly do you plan to achieve that?" he questioned, "A miracle? We have days at most."

Hext's smile didn't fade.

"You trusted me with PLAIN, and I fulfilled my word." he said, "Trust me again. We don't need a miracle, just the right opportunity. And this is it."

Kallos puffed out his cheeks, glancing back at the holo-display of the approaching Dominion fleet. He had no choice but to go along with Hext.

"Then let's hope your preparations and plans are enough," he replied.

Hext nodded.

"Then we prepare for both of these tests ahead," he said, "And we make sure that when the Dominion arrives, Pluto stands united," he said with conviction.

The Terraformers had always been dismissed as idealists and dreamers of a future no one believed could exist. But Hext knew better. Their time had come…

He turned back to the holo-table. The fleet was getting closer.

"If the Dominion wants this planet," he said, "they'll have to fight every last one of us for it."

CHAPTER FORTY-TWO – SECRETS IN THE DEPTHS

The stars above Kerberos burned bright and distant as *Veritas* sliced through the void, descending toward the cratered surface below. Zari's hands clasped together, her mind focused on the direction they were heading in. Her ship responded to her thoughts, adjusting her trajectory, shifting angles seamlessly as if she were an extension of Zari. In that lonely pilot's seat, Zari was still learning though, and still figuring out the depth of Veritas' connection to her, but each moment in that hallowed place felt like rediscovering something buried deep in her soul.

"Almost there," she murmured to herself.

Steffan sat behind her, tense and silent and still in complete disbelief. He hadn't spoken much since they'd left Pluto, his concentration locked on the approaching surface of Kerberos. Zari didn't have to ask why. He knew what was waiting for them. Nyx, and the truth that would shatter everything, and then on top of that, they would have to deal with his father's hitman.

Ahead, the Herebus Depression yawned before them, the colossal crater formed by an impact so ancient that its walls had long since eroded, leaving smooth cliffs and shadowed depths. Zari concentrated, willing *Veritas* to pinpoint the exact location. The ship *showed* her the way, subtle nudges in her mind guiding her downward. It was like they were a team, doing this hand in hand.

A circular landing platform came into view, barely distinguishable from the rock surrounding it. The lights switched on as she approached, as they illuminated the edges of it with a faint glow as Veritas closed in. She took a breath, feeling the ship adjust, slow, and with a whisper of energy, *Veritas* settled onto the pad, touching down in perfect sync with her will.

The lights on either side leading to the rock door lit up and from within in the cliffside, the doors rumbled open.

Steffan let out a sigh of relief. "I'll never get used to that," he said.

The ship drifted forward into the hangar beyond, gliding smoothly into the cavernous space. The moment *Veritas* was fully inside, the massive doors behind them slammed shut, sealing them in.

Zari barely needed to think before issuing the command. The ramp lowered, and the doors unsealed without so much of a sound.

She and Steffan stepped out into the hangar, where Nyx and Blair stood waiting for them.

Nyx's silver eyes locked onto hers, and in an instant, she was moving towards her sister, a picture of joy and happiness.

Zari barely had time to look before her sister wrapped her in a fierce embrace, gripping her as if she never wanted to let go.

"Oh my God. You're alive," Nyx whispered, her voice betraying more emotion than she likely intended.

Zari held her just as tightly. "I told you I'd come back," she said.

Nyx pulled away slightly, just enough to look her in the eye. Then she fixed onto the ship behind them, widening in disbelief. "What *is* that?" she said amazed at what was before her.

Zari hesitated for only a second. "*Veritas,*" she said proudly.

Nyx shook her head in disagreement. "That's no ordinary ship," she said secretly jealous of her sister.

Zari nodded. "I know," she said.

Zari looked at her sister,

"I have so much to tell you, you'd better sit down," she said calmly.

The two sisters walked over to a seating area, to chat alone.

Zari began,

"Nyx, you remember that our mother was very creative, even spiritual?" she said.

"Yeah," she said uncertainly, "But that was a long time ago..."

"Well..." she replied, "I inherited many of her gifts."

"I know you're the creative type," interjected Nyx,

"No, not like that Sis," said Zari, "Our mother could see, and I mean really see. She was a Seer, one of the best..."

This was a revelation that Nyx wasn't expecting and, it stopped her in her tracks.

"I've got it, I have her gifts... I can see the present, the past and sometimes the future!" she said, trying to persuade her sister who looked disbelievingly at her.

Nyx crossed her arms, scepticism clear in her eyes.

"You're telling me you can summon spirits? Right here? In this cave?" she said disparagingly.

"Yes. And I will prove it," she said seeing that her sister needed further persuading.

Zari steadied herself, shut her eyes concentrating hard, and controlling her breathing as she had done before.

"Talleron, Mesath, Solas, Sian... I call upon you." she said.

The air in the hanger shifted. A sudden chill swept through, sending a shiver down Nyx's spine. The temperature dropped rapidly, the air forming in delicate spirals on the metal flooring. A whisper filled the air; a sound that wasn't quite sound at all. Then, out of the shadows, a mist began to take shape.

The figures of Talleron, Mesath, Solas, and Sian emerged in their pale blue robes edged with crimson.

"You called upon us, Zari?" said Mesath with soft authority...

Nyx looked at what was in front of her open-mouthed, in complete and utter surprise.

"This... this isn't possible," she said in complete disbelief...

Zari turned to Mesath, voice steady despite the weight of the moment.

"Tell her what happened to our mother," she asked...

The mist danced, twisted and turned, swirling until it solidified into a vision. A projection of the past played out before them.

There in front of them was their mother Elyndra standing proud, her eyes glowing with sight beyond the ordinary. Corin was by her side, his hand gripping hers as they stood against unseen enemies. Veylan's shadow stretched long behind them.

Then a chilling moment... Castor stepped forward, the glint of his weapon catching the light.

Two precise shots rang out. There was a heartbeat of silence, and they both collapsed with blood spreading out in the dust around them.

The image faded, dissolving into mist and the room returned to stillness.

Nyx stood frozen. When she finally spoke, her voice was barely a whisper.

"No..." she exclaimed...

She looked at Zari, then at Steffan.

Then Nyx spoke again. "Why? Why was she targeted?"

Mesath's spectral form shifted, and another vision unfolded. They saw Veylan seated in his chamber, a digital document flickering before him. Elyndra's name appeared, linked to an official and historical marriage application. The entry flagged that she had returned to Pluto, a relic of old records still embedded deep within the Technocrat Bureaucracy.

Veylan grimaced, initially he looked worried, and determined intent overcame him. A Seer back on Pluto? His paranoia spilt over as he leaned forward to look yet closer, scanning further details. His face twisted in realization... she posed a huge danger to him. A few keystrokes later a message was sent.

To his number one agent, Castor.

The vision faded, and silence gripped the chamber.

Nyx was shocked, and her anger was rising.

"Thank you Mesath," Zari said, "That will be all..." and the four figures faded away...

Zari looked at her sister, but Nyx had already set her eyes on Steffan, as any warmth in her turned to pure ice.

Rage in her was exploding,

"Castor? The Dominion's assassin? The one who..." she exclaimed sharply, her words cutting off as her mind pieced everything together. She looked back at Zari. "And he..."

Zari nodded regretfully. "Steffan's father recruited him." she conceded, "Veylan ordered our parents' execution."

Nyx recoiled as if she'd been hit by a brick, her entire body going rigid. Her silver eyes burned as they snapped back to Steffan, her anger simmering, ready to ignite.

Steffan stood still, letting it happen. He didn't look away. He didn't try to defend himself. He just met the fire in Nyx's eyes, bracing for the coming storm.

Zari stepped between them. "Nyx, wait..." she urged.

"Don't," said Nyx, her voice sharp, her like thunder. "I need to hear it from *him*."

"I didn't know," Steffan said.

"You're telling me... that your father..." she said turning on Steffan, her voice rising to a sharp edge, "*Your* father ordered the death of my parents? And you expect me to just... what? Ignore that?"

She took a step toward him, her chest heaving, her silver eyes flashing dangerously. Zari quickly moved between them.

"Nyx, wait..." she implored, but in this moment it was nigh impossible to hold her sister back.

"Move!" shouted Nyx, her voice ice-cold, her body rigid with fury.

"I want to hear him say it," she said burning a stare into his eyes.

Steffan, to his credit, didn't flinch. He met her stern look with that same unshaken resolve.

"I didn't know," he repeated.

Nyx let out a sharp, bitter ironic laugh. "Didn't know? Didn't know?! Oh, that makes it all better, doesn't it?" she said, "You mean to tell me, that while your father was pulling the strings, you just... what? Sat in your little palace on Pluto, playing prince, while my parents bled out in the dark?!"

Steffan wasn't going to be goaded, and he realised that Zari knew that he was speaking the truth. He looked back at Nyx, and in a firm but quiet manner he replied, "If I had known, I would have left him sooner."

Nyx scoffed, her breath shaky, eyes shining with unshed tears, "And now that you do know?" she scowled with venom in her eyes.

Steffan hesitated, then beckoned forward. "Now, I'll stop him. Whatever it takes. I promise you, whatever it takes." he said trying to appease her.

There was silence. For a moment, Nyx's expression was filled with fury. Then, with a scoff, she turned away, shaking her head.

"You say that now. But blood runs deep." she retorted ironically.

Zari grabbed her arm, forcing her to face her pleading, "Nyx, *he saved me*. He saved Pluto. He's not his father. He openly betrayed him for us…" he said trying to calm her sister down.

Nyx stopped, looked at both of them, and her rage died down, realising that she might indeed be wrong.

"Okay, I believe you," she conceded, backing down at last.

"I love him, Sis," Zari said looking earnestly at her sister.

Finally, she calmed herself. She wanted the best for her sibling, and it made no sense to continue this further.

"This isn't over," she muttered.

Steffan nodded once. "I know."

Suddenly, a sharp pain shot through Zari's temples. The world around her faded, the voices in the room becoming distant echoes.

Then… darkness flooded in.

She saw a flash of steel. A cockpit window reflecting Kerberos' moons. Shadows moving in a confined space.

She saw him… Castor. His sharp eyes locked on something in front of him. He was speaking, but the words were drowned out by the noise of an engine.

Then, the view shifted. A crate. A symbol emblazoned on its side… the same insignia from the *Albatross*.

The serum.

The vision snapped out, and Zari gasped, gripping the edge of the table to steady herself.

"He's close," she said with alarm in her voice.

Nyx turned to her, concern filling her now.

"Who?" she replied.

"Castor." she warned, "He's in a transporter with a Technocrat death squad. He knows about the serum. And he's coming for it."

Nyx was getting concerned. She turned sharply to Blair.

"Wake my group." she demanded, "We're not going to let him walk in here like he owns the place, and we are giving him a welcome he'll never forget…"

CHAPTER FORTY-THREE – THE PRICE OF VENGEANCE

The tension in the hangar overtook everyone there. Nyx, Zari, Steffan, Blair, and the Outlanders had taken their positions, all of them lying in wait. The trap was set, the serum was the bait.

Zari crouched behind a cargo crate, with her heart pounding so fast she could hardly breathe. She could feel the electricity of apprehension crackling in the air, like the kind of electric current you would feel in the atmosphere just before a storm was about to break. Castor was coming. They all knew it. They just had to wait and wait.

The comms in Nyx's ear buzzed with a faint whisper from Blair.

"Ship incoming," it reported.

Nyx's pulse quickened too. She glanced at Zari, giving her a reassuring nod, then looked toward Steffan as well, who was gripping his weapon tightly. They had rehearsed this a couple of times. They had gone over every possible move. Now, all that remained was to execute it well.

The rock doors rumbled as they began to part, revealing the landing pad beyond. The ship descended just as Veritas and the Albatross had done before, its engines exhaling steam as it settled onto the platform. The moment its landing gear locked in place, the lights embedded in the rock came alive, illuminating the route into the secret hangar.

The ship moved in, the doors groaned shut behind it.

Trapped.

A moment of silence passed. Castor in the cockpit of the ship surveyed the scene. Nobody was there, nobody here to greet them. The Albatross sat there and another ship that looked unlike anything he had seen before, it was oval, shining in a dark metallic slate grey colour. He looked again, and concluded that it was just too quiet; his senses told him that something was seriously wrong. He turned to his hit squad and beckoned them to open the rear door. Then, with a sharp click, the ship's rear hatch began to drop down.

Castor had not made the mistake of stepping out first. Instead, he used the rear door and the others as a shield, keeping cover as six Technocrat marksmen, clad in their navy blue uniforms, fanned out into the hangar with calculated precision. They moved like thieves in the night, rifles raised, scanning the shadows. Their orders were clear: secure the area before finding the serum.

But something was definitely off. Castor could feel it. His sharp eyes zipped across the hangar, taking in every crate, every possible vantage point. His instincts screamed at him. This was a setup. He had walked into enough of these ambushes in his time to recognize the signs.

His voice cut through the silence to the others. "Search the perimeter and sweep every corner."

The Technocrats obeyed, splitting into pairs as they moved carefully through the vast space. The Outlanders watched from their hiding places, breath held, waiting for the right moment to strike. Each second ticked by like an eternity.

Then, it happened.

Dren, one of the Outlanders crouched behind a cargo crate and reached for his laser pistol. His grip was covered with sweat. As he drew it from his holster, it slipped.

Clang...

The sound echoed through the hangar like a gunshot.

In an instant, the Technocrats turned, weapons snapping up.

"Contact!" one of them shouted.

Then all hell broke loose.

Laser fire erupted in a blinding storm of red and blue. The Outlanders burst from their hiding spots, with them opening fire as the Technocrats unleashed a lethal barrage. The metallic walls rang with the deafening sound of combat. Sparks flew as shots ricocheted off steel beams. Smoke filled the air, as a furious gun battle continued.

Blair was caught in the crossfire. A Technocrat's rifle found its mark, striking him squarely in the chest. He gasped, staggering back before collapsing. Nyx's cry of rage was lost in the chaos as she fired relentlessly, taking down two of the marksmen in quick succession, including the one who took down her friend.

But the cost was high.

The Outlanders fell one by one. Dren, then Lysara, then two more. The hangar floor was stained with their bodies, stained with blood, scattered amid the firefight. The last of the Technocrats crumpled to the ground; his uniform smouldering where laser fire had torn through him.

Silence followed, punctuated only by ragged breathing and unbearable tension.

Castor meanwhile crept silently around the side of the hangar out of sight, and then he saw her. *The black-haired woman in the video.*

Maybe he could kill two birds with one stone?

Stealthily he approached…

Then a sharp click.

Zari froze as she felt the cold press of a laser barrel against the back of her head.

"Get me the serum, or I'll kill her," he shouted with a deadly threat. Castor's voice was low and dangerous.

Nyx's heart pounded against her ribs as she turned, her eyes locking onto her sister's terrified face. Castor held Zari in an iron grip, his weapon poised to end her life in an instant.

Nyx's hands shot up, her mind racing. She had to think fast.

"Don't," she called out, her voice steady despite the terror gripping her insides. "I'll get it."

Steffan crouched to the side, and remained perfectly still, his weapon gripped tightly and concealed. His heart was pounding too, he was scared to move. His eyes caught Nyx's, with an understanding passing between them. A silent agreement was made.

Nyx moved toward the Albatross, keeping her motions slow and deliberate. She reached the cargo hold, unlatched the door, and pulled out the silver case. The vials inside glowed with an otherworldly blue light, the serum shimmering beneath the hangar floodlights.

She turned, meeting Castor's gaze. "You want it? Fine. Have it."

Then she let go and threw them to the ground.

Smash!

The case hit the floor. The vials shattered instantly, spilling the precious liquid across it, in a cascade of wasted potential.

Castor's eyes widened in pure, unfiltered rage. His grip on Zari loosened for just a fraction of a second.

And that was all Steffan needed.

He fired.

The shot struck Castor clean through the chest. The assassin's anguished face twisted in surprise, and then the pain came within. His grip on Zari faltered as he stumbled backwards, laser falling from his fingers.

But before he fell, his finger twitched.

A single shot.

A single moment.

Nyx gasped. She looked down. A dark red stain spread across her abdomen, the wound pulsing with searing pain. Her legs gave way beneath her, and she crumpled to the floor.

"Nyx!" Zari's scream tore through the hangar as she rushed forward, catching her sister before she hit the ground. Blood pooled beneath her, the warmth draining from her skin.

Steffan fell to his knees beside them, with his hands shaking as he reached for her. Nyx's breathing was shallow, and her silver eyes were now hazy.

"It's okay," she whispered. "I see them..."

Zari's heart twisted.

"No. Nyx, stay with me. Please." she implored.

Nyx weakly smiled with recognition. "I see them... Mother and Father... They're waiting." she said drifting away…

Zari sobbed, clutching her tightly as the life faded from her sister's body.

The hangar fell silent.

Steffan wrapped his arms around Zari, pulling her close as she shook with grief. Neither of them spoke. There were no words left.

Then, the world around Zari blurred.

Her vision darkened, another sight beyond sight. Nyx, standing in a field of stars, her parents beside her, waiting. A peace unlike anything she had ever known washed over her.

Then grief took over, and she collapsed into Steffan's arms.

CHAPTER FORTY-FOUR – THE BATTLE PLAN

The air in the Indus Spaceport Command Centre was filled with nervous chatter. Constantly updating holographic displays were being poured over by the main protagonists there, casting red, yellow and blue shadows over the concerned faces of Hext, Kallos, and their assembled strategists. The Dominion fleet was closing in, less than 24 hours away. If Pluto was to stand even a one percent chance of prevailing against this huge space flotilla, every available resource had to be mustered, every ship had to be prepared, and every pilot had to be ready for the fight of their lives.

Hext's eyes scanned the tactical map, watching as red markers indicating the Triton fleet inched closer and closer to the Pluto orbital system. Twelve Triton Cruisers, heavily armed, battle-hardened, and built for war, and on each a team of a dozen expert fighter pilots in their Kestrel Class space jets. Against them, Pluto had a patchwork of salvaged ships, old war vessels, converted transporters, and whatever weapons they could rig onto anything that could fly.

It wasn't enough. Not even close.

Kallos considered for a second, looking at the odds against them and the ragtag fleet that they had assembled.

"We're outnumbered and outgunned." he said, "They have fleet superiority and technological dominance. There's no way we can win a direct fight."

Hext tended to agree, though he lived in hope, as he tapped a few controls on the holo-map. The display shifted, zooming out to show Pluto's six moons—Charon, Styx, Nix, Kerberos, Hydra, and the smaller, irregularly orbiting Dysnomia.

"What if we don't fight them directly?" Hext said, coming up with an idea.

"What if we use the moons as tactical cover, hiding our forces until they pass into range—then we strike all at once?" he suggested.

Gabriel Kallos studied the map as well, arms crossed. It was a bold strategy, perhaps somewhat risky, but possibly the only way they could even the odds.

"You mean," Kallos said considering the options, "We split into attack groups, stay cloaked, wait until they move into range, and then ambush them from six different positions?"

Hext nodded.

"Exactly," he said, "We know their trajectory. They'll be entering Pluto's system from a standard approach vector, which means they'll have to navigate the gravitational fields of the moons to stabilize their entry."

He gestured to the display, tracing the fleet's expected path.

"If we divide our forces, hiding behind the moons, we can force them into a kill zone," he said, "I'm betting they won't be expecting an organized counterattack from Pluto's moons. If we time it right, we could inflict serious damage before they have a chance to respond."

"Since when did you learn military tactics like that, Prophet?" he inquired.

Hext laughed and looked back at him with a wink.

Kallos stared again at the display, weighing the odds. "We have what, sixty-eight combat-ready ships? Against twelve Dominion cruisers and their supporting fighters?" he said, counting the number of captains who had volunteered their services.

"It's better than facing them all head-on," Hext replied. "Our ships aren't designed for sustained battle, but we don't need to outlast them… just cripple them before they can consolidate their attack."

"You're right." Kallos agreed.

They turned and looked at each other, knowing that this was going to be their strategy.

Then, Kallos sighed, shaking his head with a wry smile. "You're a damn lunatic, Prophet," he said as he laughed.

"But is it a good plan?" Hext said looking for approval.

Kallos looked back at the tactical display. After a second, he nodded. "Yup. It's the best shot we've got."

The spaceport was still alive with activity, with engineers and technicians racing to retrofit ships, while mounting makeshift weapons, and reinforcing hull plating on old freighters that hadn't seen combat since the previous Cycle a century ago.

Hext and Kallos stood on the control deck, watching the fleet come together. They had seventeen CX-100 fighter space jets, one old Viper Space Cruiser which would be the command vessel, several smaller Eris Type Predator Starship Fighters, a few Corvettes, some modified Freighters, and even a few old Dominion patrol ships captured in past battles, all of them being readied for one final stand.

They needed more.

"We need to contact Charon," Kallos muttered.

Hext's hands were already moving across the console. Within moments, the Charon Base Command Frequency was open.

A hazy transmission flickered into view showing, Commander Menendez, the ranking officer of what remained of Charon's old military forces. Only a couple of weeks before, he had been serving on behalf of Veylan, but his allegiance changed rapidly after the demise of the Corporatist defeat. He saluted Kallos and Hext and then painted a disappointing picture.

"We're stretched thin," Menendez said immediately. "Most of our ships were recalled to Pluto in the past weeks. We have a handful of functioning vessels left, but they're pretty old and have seen better days, and they're not really built for fleet combat."

"Do you have pilots?" Hext asked.

"Yes," Menendez responded. "Veterans. Old Dominion defectors. Ex-mercenaries. They've been waiting for a fight."

Kallos smiled and nodded approval. "That'll do…" he said with a wink, "Get them ready for some fun."

At Indus Base, the final meeting was held, relayed via encrypted holo-feed to Charon and the other key command centres. Pilots, officers, and ground crews all stood assembled, with their faces hardened by the knowledge that this was it.

Kallos stepped forward first.

"The Dominion thinks this will be easy." he said, "They believe Pluto has no defence. They believe we are weak. They are completely wrong."

This was greeted with a roar from the strike team, quickly rising into a chorus of determination.

"Let's show those Dominion bastards what Pluto is made of!" someone shouted from the back. A cheer erupted, fists pumping into the air.

Another pilot, an elderly veteran with a scar running down his cheek, clapped a hand on his wingman's shoulder. "We've been outnumbered before," he said. "And we still kicked their asses."

"Damn right!" another chimed in. "They think we're just some backwater mining colony? Let's teach'em a lesson they never forget!"

The pilots reacted as one to this, meeting this comment with cheers and hollers, hands in the air.

"Pluto rules!" a young pilot declared, slamming his fist against his chest. "We fight, or we die trying."

A wave of defiant voices surged through the room. They were outgunned, outmatched, and facing impossible odds. But not one of them was backing down.

Hext urged for calm, smiling at the enthusiasm being shown, and then took over.

"At the right moment, we break cloak, open fire, and hit them with everything we have," he explained.

He went on, "We'll use our knowledge of Pluto's system to our advantage. Each squadron will remain cloaked behind one of the moons until 14:00 hours when the Dominion fleet enters Pluto's gravity well."

The holo-map shifted, showing the incoming fleet and the Plutonian forces splitting into six ambush groups.

A voice from the back of one of the younger pilots rang out, his thoughts filled with concern.

"And if it's not enough?" Benson said expressing his fears about the plan.

Hext remained impassive.

"Then we make sure we take as many of them with us as we can," he said with realism.

The silence that followed was not fear… it was acceptance.

As the fleet prepped for launch, Hext stood on the observation deck, as he watched the final ships being fuelled and armed. Kallos approached beside him, arms crossed.

"You really think we can do this?" Kallos asked.

Hext took a slow breath. "I think we have no choice Gab," he said.

Kallos chuckled. "Hell of a time to believe in destiny," he replied.

Hext turned to him with a small, knowing smile.

"Destiny doesn't win battles," he said, "Strategy does."

Below them, the final countdown had begun. The ships roared as their engines ignited, with their weapons systems primed, and the pilots suited up for what might be their final flight.

An echoing voice boomed out above the tannoy "Four hours until launch!"

Tomorrow, everything would change.

CHAPTER FORTY-FIVE – 03.00 HOURS

It was exactly 03.00 hours.

A shrill alarm blared across the Indus Spaceport, slicing through the early twilight like a razor. The towering hangars were already filled with frenzied activity, with a multitude of boots slamming against the metal flooring as dozens of pilots, engineers and support crew raced across the deck to get everyone ready for launch.

"All Pilots – Battle Alert! Team One – Prepare for Lift-Off!"

In an instant, the controlled chaos ignited into action.

Pilots rushed to their ships, with helmets secured, and flight suits zipped tight. Engineers swarmed around the fleet, all running last-minute diagnostic checks, making sure that all of the fuel lines were secure, and their tanks were full. Other crew attended to the last-minute checks, and helped seal the up the cockpit hatches on the fighter jets. The spaceport pulsed with vibrant energy as Pluto's last line of defence prepared for a do-or-die battle.

Kallos moved through the fleet with purpose, his dark visor reflecting the sea of movement around him. His Eris-Class starfighter, a sleek Predator-class vessel, waited with engines already ticking over, as the soft blue glow of its plasma coils illuminated the deck below. As he climbed the ladder and strapped himself in, he cast a glance towards the command tower, where Hext stood, watching over them all.

Hext wasn't flying today. He would remain on the surface, coordinating the entire operation from the command war room deep within the Indus Base. But as the first team readied for launch, he felt the anticipation of everything starting to weigh on his mind. Had they got the tactics right? They would soon find out.

"This is it, Gabriel," Hext shouted out to him.

"Make it count and God's speed," he said with sincerity.

Kallos smiled as he pulled his helmet down. "Wouldn't have it any other way," he said. This was a man who was never happier than when he was in the heat of a battle.

With a deafening roar, Team One ascended, their thrusters igniting as they launched into the Pluto sky, breaking through the thin atmospheric layer. Their target: Charon orbit.

Seconds later…

"Team Two – Prepare for Lift-Off!"

Another surge of movement happened. More pilots sprinted to their ships, engines roaring to life. Their mission: Hydra.

Then…

"Team Three – Prepare for Lift-Off!"

The sequence repeated, waves of ships lifting off, disappearing into the vastness of space. The once-busy spaceport slowly emptied, leaving only Hext and the remaining ground crews staring into the sky filled with ships of all shapes and sizes, flying towards destiny, or oblivion. One by one, the ships vanished. The battle was near.

From the balcony of the Presidential Palace, Veylan stood weakly, leaning against the stone railing as he looked out into the eternal night sky. The ships were rising. One after another, fighter after fighter, corvette after freighter, all heading towards Pluto's moons. His city, his empire, was slipping away.

His breath was shallow, his body now frail and getting weaker. The serum was gone. He could feel the passage of time pulling him down, hollowing him out, and ending his reign. The legend of Veylan the Eternal had been reduced to nothing but a feeble old man in a crumbling palace.

His last ace, Castor, was dead. He had hoped the assassin would retrieve the serum, and secure his power. Instead, word had arrived that Castor was eliminated on Kerberos. His grip on Pluto had indeed shattered into dust.

But he would not go down in silence.

At his side, Mensen, his last remaining loyal officer, stood firm, face expressionless.

"They are rising," Mensen said, stating the obvious.

Veylan sighed, with his eyes fixed on the horizon.

"Yes. And they're preparing a welcoming party for Devlin," he said. His voice was hoarse, weary.

"Get me Earth Command. One last message," he asked Mensen.

Mensen nodded, activating the transmission. The holographic console burst to life, connecting to the Dominion High Command.

The image of Devlin, Supreme Commander of Earth's Dominion Fleet, appeared in front of him, maybe for the last time in his current capacity.

"Veylan." Devlin's voice was sharp. "I assume you have news worth my time."

Veylan coughed, his body barely able to hold itself upright. But his voice was steady.

"They know you're coming," he rasped. "They are preparing for war."

Devlin remained silent for a long moment, then said calmly. "I expected nothing less."

Veylan chuckled weakly.

"They think they can win," he said weakly but remained strong in defiance.

Devlin seemed amused.

"Impossible..." he replied, "They can't."

Veylan nodded slowly. "Then finish it," he said.

The transmission cut out.

Veylan turned away from the console, with his hands trembling. He knew the truth. This was the end.

Mensen hesitated before speaking. "Sir... should we leave? Escape before it's too late?" he asked.

Veylan looked at him, and with evil in his eye, he said, "No, not yet... Let them fight, let them think they will be victorious. Then let them be crushed... When Pluto burns, I will watch from here, and then we go..."

And with that, he retreated gingerly into his chambers, the spectre of death creeping closer.

The mood inside the hanger on Kerberos was solemn. Steffan, Zari, Jessa, and Seb stood in silence, neither one wishing to break the peace of the moment. Nyx's body had been wrapped in a white cloth, her figure resting peacefully in front of the two spaceships, Veritas and Albatross. The once-fiery warrior was still now, her silver eyes forever closed.

Zari had barely spoken since the fight. Her sister was gone.

Steffan reached over, taking her hand. "She would want you to be strong," he said softly.

Zari swallowed hard. "I know. But it still hurts," she said with honesty.

They all stood as Steffan carefully lifted Nyx's body, carrying her onto Veritas and the ship's rear chamber.

Jessa wiped a tear from her eye. "She fought like hell for all of us," she whispered.

Seb nodded. "A warrior's death," he replied.

Zari stepped forward, her voice barely above a whisper. "She was a warrior. Fearless to the end. I already miss her." she said with tears in her eyes.

Jessa and Seb boarded Albatross, while Zari and Steffan entered Veritas, his hands on her shoulder. The hangar doors groaned as they began to part, revealing the crater's vast, desolate expanse. One by one, the two ships lifted off, engines whirring, as the rockface door slid open fully, and the ships ascended, gliding smoothly out into the crater and beyond.

As they reached orbit, both of them halted, suspended in the stillness of space. Steffan moved to Veritas' airlock, carrying Nyx's shrouded form with a reverence befitting the fighter she was. Zari followed closely, her heart bleeding from the loss of her sibling. Steffan placed her gently inside the chamber, stepping back as he sealed the airlock. Zari, concentrating looked at the airlock door and it slid closed. A gust of air escaped, and Nyx was released into the abyss.

She floated outward, a lone figure in the vast cosmos, with the glow of Pluto and its moons illuminating her for a fleeting moment before she vanished into the great unknown. They stood there in silence, watching her drift, until she was nothing but a memory against the endless stars.

"May the stars guide you home," Zari whispered, her voice breaking.

The airlock sealed shut. She turned into Steffan's arms, and as Veritas' engines roared to life once more, she let herself grieve, her tears falling as the ship made its final journey away from Kerberos.

CHAPTER FORTY-SIX – THE BATTLE FOR PLUTO (PART 1)

The Dominion invasion fleet moved through the Pluto system with the precision of a well-oiled machine. The *Redoubtable*, a fortress in space, led the charge, with its massive frame relentlessly pushing forward through the void towards Pluto. Flanking it were the eleven other Triton Cruisers cutting through the darkness, all ready for action and domination. The *Resolute, Hammerfall, Ironclad*, and *Vanguard* held the core formation behind the lead spaceship, with their huge pulse cannons already primed for battle.

Inside the command deck of the *Redoubtable*, Captain Jed Iseman stood stiff-backed and upright, his blonde hair and slate blue eyes fixed on every detail, from the attack formations they would activate, to the defensive shield that they would put up, should Pluto even dare to attack back. He hoped the overwhelming show of force would persuade the Plutonians to see sense, but he had to be ready for all eventualities.

The message from Admiral Devlin had been brief but clear. Somewhere out there, the remnants of Pluto's forces would be waiting for him.

"They won't have much," Devlin had said, "but they may be annoying."

Mosquitos may bite and irritate, he thought, but they could be easily swatted away.

Iseman for sure wasn't about to be caught off guard.

With a flick of his wrist, he relayed the battle alert to the other captains in the fleet. The comms crackled through as confirmations came through from each ship...

Lancer reporting ready.

Leviathan in position.

Vanguard is on high alert.

All ships prepared for engagement.

Then came the next command. "Deploy the Kestrel squadrons." Iseman messaged.

Across the fleet, the Triton Cruisers responded like synchronized predators. One by one, their underbellies released hatches, and the blackness of space filled with the shifting forms of fighter craft, sleek and deadly. The Kestrels, named for the hawks they resembled, all burst forth in controlled precision, with their curved wings sharp and menacing, and their reinforced hulls supporting laser cannons that could spit death with unerring accuracy.

A flood of 144 Dominion warbirds spread into formation, a huge flock of destructive power, with their engines flaring and their weapons ready to be activated. They moved with mechanical discipline as an unrelenting force; prepared to crush whatever resistance remained. On Iseman's command, they split into groups of two and three to cover a wide expanse of nothingness.

156 Dominion craft against 68 Pluto ships.

The odds were impossible. Or were they?

Hidden behind Pluto's moons, the concealed fleet of the rebellion waited, silently hoping for a miracle.

Inside his Eris-Class fighter, Gabriel Kallos' fingers tightened around the control stick. His HUD display glowed red with the sheer number of enemy signals swarming ahead of him. His breath came slow and steady. He knew what was coming, as every pilot did.

They had nothing close to the Dominion's sleek warships. Their fleet was a collection of old freighters, retrofitted corvettes, salvaged Dominion patrol ships, and ageing Pluto-class fighters with patched-up hulls and barely functioning shields. But this wasn't about a fair fight.

This was about ambush.

He pressed the comms button. "All squadrons, this is Kallos. We go *now!*" he commanded.

Across the moons of Pluto, the cloak fields dropped.

One by one, Pluto's ships emerged from the darkness, engines roaring to life. From behind Charon, Kallos and his team rocketed forward, with their ships cutting through the void like a pack of wolves descending on their prey. Their blasters lit up the blackness with crimson streaks as they tore into the nearest Kestrel squadron.

Kallos veered hard to the right as an enemy Kestrel fighter locked onto his rear. Alarms blared inside his cockpit, and he could almost feel the heat of laser fire grazing his hull. With a sharp tug of the controls, he spun his Eris-Class ship in a barrel roll, coming up behind his pursuer in an instant.

"Gotcha," he muttered as he squeezed the trigger. A direct hit, the Kestrel vapourised into several thousand shards of metal and flame.

Corsini in a Corvette, part of Kallos' group looked across at him and gave him a thumbs up, as he chased another. He fired, and twin plasma bolts tore through the Kestrel's left engine, sending it spiralling into an uncontrolled dive before it exploded in a brilliant fireball. He didn't have time to celebrate, as two more enemy fighters were already on his tail.

"Corsini, break left! I've got you!" Kallos shouted over comms.

The voice blasted through his earpiece, and a moment later, one of his own pilots, Benson, who had been loitering further out swooped in from above, his guns blazing. His shots clipped the first Kestrel's wing, sending it into a tailspin heading for the moon below. The second enemy fighter banked away, regrouping for another attack.

"Thanks, Benson," Corsini breathed. "Now let's give them hell."

Meanwhile, over Hydra, Lieutenant Miska's modified freighter was under heavy fire. Unlike the sleek Dominion ships, hers was a bulky transport, barely designed for combat. But she knew how to fight dirty.

She let two Kestrel fighters get close, weaving erratically as though she was losing control. The enemy pilots took the bait, chasing her as she drifted perilously close to Hydra's icy surface.

"Miska, what the hell are you doing?" came the panicked voice of her wingmate.

"Just wait for it..." she whispered.

At the last possible moment, she *cut all power* to her engines.

Her freighter *dropped* like a stone, falling into a controlled dive toward the moon's surface. The Dominion fighters, too fast to react, overshot her position and flew directly into the line of fire of three waiting Pluto corvettes.

The corvettes unloaded everything they had.

The sky lit up as the Dominion fighters were shredded apart in an instant.

Miska grinned, reigniting her engines just in time to pull up. "Told you I had a plan." she smiled.

Her wingmate's relieved laugh rang through the comms.

"Remind me never to doubt you again." he said laughing out loud, "Teach me that one next time."

Darien, a Pluto pilot in a cargo transporter, the same model as the Albatross, broke formation, attempting a desperate attack run against the Ironclad. His ship wove through the battlefield, dodging enemy fire as he sped toward the massive Triton Cruiser. If he could land a direct hit on its weapons array, he might give his squadron a fighting chance.

He never made it.

A single blast from the *Ironclad's* primary cannon struck him mid-flight. His ship was vaporized in an instant, disappearing in a burst of light and debris. The silence that followed on the Pluto comms was deafening.

"Damn it," Kallos growled. "Pull back, stay in the fight guys, but don't go for suicide runs!"

Across the battlefield, explosions lit up the starlit skies. Ships spun, weaved, fired, and fell. The rebels were making their mark pretty effectively, striking where they could, and fighting with everything they had.

But the Dominion was relentless, and their numerical superiority started to take hold.

More Pluto ships were falling. More voices were cut off in mid-transmission. The enemy's sheer numbers were overwhelming them.

Kallos gritted his teeth, dodging another incoming blast.

"Stay together! Keep hitting them where it hurts!" he shouted with increasing concern.

This was just the beginning.

CHAPTER FORTY-SEVEN – THE BATTLE FOR PLUTO (PART 2)

The stillness of Kerberos' orbit was shattered in an instant. Just a few moments before, Veritas and the Albatross had been alone, and drifting in quiet reflection as Nyx's body vanished into the endless stars. But now, the war had found them in an instant.

A sudden, searing beam of red light streaked past the bow of the Albatross, missing by mere metres. The ship jolted as Jessa instinctively jerked the controls. Alarms screamed to life, flashing red across the cabin.

"Incoming fire!" she shouted, gripping the flight stick.

Seb's hands flew over the weapons console. "Kestrels. Three, no, four of them coming in fast from port," he shouted.

Without hesitation, Jessa squeezed the trigger, unleashing a stream of laser fire from the Albatross' nose cannon. The lead Kestrel pilot barely had time to react before the shot tore through his cockpit, disintegrating the sleek hawk-like craft into a ball of flame and debris.

"Scratch one," Jessa muttered.

But the battle was far from over.

Inside Veritas, Zari sat rigid in the pilot's chair, wracked with fear and dread. This wasn't like playing war games in the simulations. The ship bucked beneath her as an enemy fighter veered in from above, releasing a volley of plasma fire.

Steffan, seated behind her, saw the danger first. "Zari, hard left! Now!" he screamed.

But Zari wasn't concentrating and didn't react in time. The shot missed them by the width of a cargo crate, a very lucky escape.

"Careful, Zari, concentrate..." Steffan shouted to her, "You've gotta focus."

Pulling herself together after that wake-up call, she did just that, and as she visualised, a flicker of green light spread across the central holo-table in the cockpit. The ship's AI had now picked up her neural impulses and translated them into action. A three-dimensional projection of the battlefield unfolded before Steffan, displaying the position of all the ships in their vicinity in real-time. It was as if Veritas was showing him and her what she needed to see, guiding them so that she could understand.

He studied the battle display, struggling to get a grasp on the chaos. Her consciousness and sensory abilities were picking up dozens of moving contacts, threats and allies as Pluto's ships fought desperately against the Dominion's overwhelming force. The Kestrels swarmed in small formations, with their attack patterns ruthless and precise.

Zari tried to control her breathing, slow and steady to reduce her sense of panic and fear. She wasn't a fighter pilot, not in the slightest way. She wasn't meant for this. But then she felt something, a strange pull, like an instinct buried deep within her.

The ship knew. Veritas responded to her unspoken fears and her thoughts.

Steffan's eyes widened as he stared at the projection. "What the hell...?" he exclaimed.

But Zari wasn't listening. She focused, visualizing the battlefield around her, letting Veritas respond to her will, as she started to move forward with confidence. The ship reacted to her impulses instantaneously, it was moving and shifting as if it were an extension of her own body.

Suddenly, an alert flashed into her mind, an enemy fighter closing fast on their left.

She felt it immediately.

A deep instinct, not logic but something more primal kicked in. The Kestrel pilot was lining up his shot. If she hesitated now, she was dead.

She realized what needed to be done, and in her mind's eye said to herself, "Move... " and Veritas responded, surging forward with a smooth, effortless motion. It wasn't piloting in the traditional sense, but it was so effective and impossible for the enemy to predict. Wherever she willed Veritas to go, she would go without hesitation.

Veritas twisted to the left, its engines purring almost silently like a ghost. A laser shot streaked through the space they had occupied just a moment before, missing entirely, making the Kestrel pilot look like a fool. He overcorrected, confused by the unpredictable movement, and found himself in the way of Jessa who not believing her luck at such an easy target, hit her pulse laser.

The Kestrel disintegrated in a hail of fire. She let out a whoop of excitement.

"Thanks, Zari," she shouted over the comms, "Great move!"

Zari's pulse raced and confidence flooded through her. She *could* do this.

Another instinct flashed through her as another Kestrel crossed her path just below the vector she was on... a vision of her ship's targeting systems locking on. She visualized the Kestrel in her mind's eye and imagined its destruction.

Veritas obeyed.

A burst of plasma fire lanced from the left side of the ship's central ring, aimed down on an angular course catching the enemy fighter side-on. The Kestrel exploded, fragments of metal and fire scattering into the void.

Zari gasped, her breath catching in her throat. She had never killed before. And yet, survival had left her no choice.

Steffan stared at her, stunned.

"That... was incredible," he exclaimed, "That was a downward shot, no ship can do that!"

Another warning flashed on the holo-table, and Steffan shouted out, "On the right, Zari!" A second Kestrel was bearing down on them from the upper right, already charging its weapons.

Zari clenched her hands and saw the foe immediately in her mind's eye. She didn't think... she *reacted*.

Veritas spun upward, shifting its axis to avoid the oncoming shot. She could *feel* the energy of the enemy's laser blast, and the pressure from it as it passed beneath them. Before the enemy pilot could fire again, Zari focused her will. *Destroy it.*

A shot erupted from Veritas' right side, blasting through the Kestrel's fuselage. The enemy ship crumbled in on itself before exploding into brilliant fragments of fire and metal.

Zari trembled. Two kills. And the battle was just beginning.

Jessa's voice came again over the comms. "Damn, Veritas, you keeping count over there?"

Steffan smiled. "You have no idea, Jessa, you have no idea…"

But there was no time to celebrate. More Kestrels were sweeping in, filling the orbit of Kerberos with deadly jeopardy.

Zari swallowed hard and focused. She wasn't just a passenger anymore.

She was part of this fight.

CHAPTER FORTY-EIGHT - THE BATTLE FOR PLUTO (PART 3)

Captain Jed Iseman stood at the command station of the *Redoubtable*, with his concentration fixed on the swirling chaos of battle. His Kestrels, supposed to wipe out the enemy with efficiency, were not performing as well as he had anticipated. The enemy was agile and unpredictable, and their tactical formations were designed to cause chaos.

"How to change the momentum," he thought analysing the tactical holo-display.

Too many of his fighters were being picked on one by one, leaving them exposed to counterfire. The rebels were exploiting these weaknesses.

Iseman mused for a second and then tapped his command console.

"All Kestrel squadrons, form up into attack groups of ten." he commanded, "No more single engagements. Sweep through them in tight formation and focus fire. Cover each other. Execute immediately."

He still had a significant numerical advantage, so overwhelm them with coordinated force, he thought.

The Dominion's elite pilots received their orders with military precision. Kestrels across the battlefield veered sharply, breaking from their disorganized individual combat, and reforming into deadly formations of ten craft. Like flocks of hunting birds, they manoeuvred together, diving and weaving through the battlefield in synchronized patterns.

The results were immediate.

A squadron of Pluto's corvettes, previously holding their own in skirmishes, was torn apart within seconds as a wall of concentrated fire rained upon them from an incoming Kestrel formation. Explosions erupted across the darkened void, scattering debris in a violent display of Dominion supremacy.

Jessa, piloting the *Albatross*, saw the shift in tactics and swore under her breath.

"Damn it, they're adapting," she exclaimed.

Seb's voice came through the comms. "They're shredding us. We need a countermove, fast Kallos!" came his cry.

A formation of Kestrels swerved banking towards Veritas. Steffan saw them first on the holo-table. "Zari, incoming, ten strong, all coming in at speed from your right" he shouted.

Zari's breathing steadied and she composed herself. She didn't need to see them. She could *feel* them. The formation locked onto her, their lasers primed.

She closed her eyes, *seeing* the battle not just through her mind, but through Veritas itself. The ship was an extension of her being, her mind fused with her systems. She focused, concentrating on every single one of the incoming fighters.

And then, she *willed* it.

A pulse of energy surged through Veritas unlike they had experienced so far. The ring around its central hull glowed with the brilliance of lightning in a storm. In an instant, Veritas unleashed a barrage of laser fire, streaks of blinding white energy cascading outward in perfect precision.

Ten shots at once rang out!!

Every single Kestrel in the squadron exploded seconds later, and the entire squadron was eliminated in a nanosecond.

Ten ships, ten kills, in one single movement.

Steffan gasped in awe.

Kallos, locked in a dogfight nearby, saw the explosion rip through the enemy's formation and nearly lost control of his ship in pure disbelief. His voice boomed over the comms.

"By the moons of Pluto… Did anyone else just see that?!" he shouted.

Jessa's voice followed. "That's impossible. No ship fires that fast, what *is* that thing?" she shouted in disbelief.

Roars of approval flooded over the comms system, shrieks and cheers of jubilation.

Steffan's voice came through the comms with glee, "Sorry that we were a bit late to the party, guys!" he joked.

Kallos looked on, still in utter shock, and then his will to win kicked in and he issued a rallying call.

"That was awesome, he exclaimed, "Come on guys, we *really* can do this!"

Veritas meanwhile curved elegantly through the battlefield, moving as if it was untouchable, sweeping from one Kestrel to the next. Zari locked onto them in rapid succession, targeting them before they even had a chance to react. They vanished in bursts of fire and wreckage. One by one, there was carnage among the stars.

The tide of battle was shifting.

On the bridge of the *Redoubtable*, a Dominion officer turned in a blind panic.

"Captain Iseman... that ship, whatever it is... it's cutting through our fighters like nothing we've seen. It just knocked out ten of our ships in one go!" he said rubbing his eyes.

Iseman saw the danger. He looked at the tactical display, where dozens of Kestrel markers were blinking out at an alarming rate. How to counter this? That ship wasn't just a fighter, it was something *else*. Something lethal, and completely unnatural.

He started to perspire. If this *ship* could single-handedly turn the tide of battle, then he had no choice. "All cruisers, focus fire on it. Take it down. Now!" he commanded.

Across the Dominion fleet, the order was relayed. Heavy turrets rotated, aligning their sights. *Vanguard* was the first to fire, its massive laser cannons unleashing a storm of crimson destruction toward Veritas. The void burned red.

Zari felt the attack before it came. A pulse of warning coursed through her mind, her instincts sharpening like a blade.

Move. Fast…

Veritas *vanished* in an instant, twisting through space, darting between beams of annihilation with inhuman precision. The

Vanguard's cannons missed entirely, their fire dissipating harmlessly into the abyss. Then *Hammerfall* tried to target her.

Missed, not even close…

Zari's eyes snapped open. She wasn't just dodging, she was making them look stupid, and now she and Veritas were hunting them.

Her mind locked onto the *Vanguard*, tracing its weaknesses, and where its vulnerable points lie. Her instincts took her to focus on its rear, and Veritas responded with lethal accuracy. A beam of concentrated fire erupted from the ship's ring, striking the *Vanguard's* rear thrusters.

The Dominion cruiser lurched violently as explosions ruptured its hull. Fires raged across its deck. The *Vanguard* tilted, engines sputtering, its power failing.

Then, with one final, cataclysmic eruption, the ship was *crippled*. It drifted a broken husk of space junk amidst the battle.

On the bridge of the *Redoubtable*, Iseman stared in horror.

This secret weapon was turning against him, and he had no idea how to stop it...

CHAPTER FORTY-NINE – THE BATTLE FOR PLUTO (PART 4)

Kallos watched the battlefield unfolding before him. The Kestrels were being cut down at a staggering rate, their once-dominant numbers reduced to scattered, panicked formations as Veritas carved through the remaining few with ruthless efficiency. The impossible had suddenly become possible. One ship, one pilot, was altering the tide of the war.

A message from Hext, who was following from the planet came through.

"Focus on the cruisers," he said, " Teams of four or five, simultaneously from different vectors," he advised.

"Good plan," Kallos thought. This guy knew his stuff.

He knew it wasn't over. Not yet. The real danger remained, and they had to eliminate it.

"This is our chance," Kallos shouted excitedly over the comms. "We take the fight to them now! All wings, focus fire on the Lancer! Attack from multiple vectors, make them confused!"

The Pluto fleet, now unburdened by the weight of the Kestrel assault, moved with renewed energy. A squadron of CX-100 fighters flew in from above while a corvette and a repurposed freighter swung low, skimming just past the Lancer's shield device.

"Knock it out," shouted Kallos," and a well-aimed shot from the freighter did just that, leaving the Cruiser fully exposed. The Dominion ship fired back, its heavy laser cannons letting rip into the void, but the attacks were too unpredictable. The Lancer's defences couldn't keep up.

Jessa's voice rang over the comms. "Albatross lining up for the kill shot," she shouted.

Seb, manning the ship's primary weapons, locked onto the Lancer's exposed underbelly. With a steady hand, he unleashed a full-powered plasma barrage. She groaned as its core ruptured. A moment of silence passed before it detonated, bursting apart in a blinding inferno of debris.

"Lancer is down!" Jessa cheered, as all the other captains joined in too.

Kallos didn't let the moment linger. "Next target—the Revenant! Same strategy! We overwhelm it!"

His squadron shifted formation, moving onto the next cruiser. The Revenant saw what had happened to the Lancer and tried to compensate, angling its shields to counter the incoming attack. But it wasn't enough. A wave of Pluto ships swarmed around it, striking in relentless unison. Explosions rippled across the Revenant's hull as its engines sputtered. The cruiser, now nothing more than floating wreckage, drifted helplessly.

Three other Dominion cruisers, realizing the peril they were in, turned their attention to the onslaught, their heavy cannons firing wildly in desperation. Laser beams crisscrossed the battlefield, attempting to hold back the tide of Pluto's forces.

The next to be targeted was Leviathan. The coordinated attack left her burning and unable to fight back. Then Revenant was next on the hit list.

"We can't let them regroup!" Kallos urged. "Stay on them!"

But even as he said it, he knew. The Kestrels were nearly gone. Pluto's ships now had the upper hand, able to focus entirely on dismantling what was left of the Dominion fleet.

Kallos switched his comms to the Dominion channel. "Captain Iseman," he said, his voice edged with triumph. "Your fleet is broken. Your Kestrels are in ruins. Your cruisers are falling one by one. You have two choices: turn back, or be obliterated."

For a long moment, there was silence.

Then, Iseman's voice came through, filled with pain as he feared complete annihilation and disgrace. He needed to limit his losses now, and he knew that thousands of lives were in peril. "We surrender. You've won, Kallos, " he said with resignation. "Allow us to return to Earth..."

And with those words, the battle was over.

Across the battlefield, all the Plutonian pilots began to cheer, whoop and holler. The enemy was retreating. They had done the impossible.

On the *Redoubtable*, Iseman felt genuine regret in his heart, and a knot in his stomach tightened as a comms message flashed in front of him from Admiral Devlin.

"Pull back, and immediately report to me when you get into Earth orbit."

He knew he would be in serious trouble from this moment on. He activated the comms link and a tiny bead of sweat trickled down his brow, as he ordered the remains of his fleet to retreat.

On his command, the remaining Dominion ships, knowing they were finished, all turned tail, activating their jump drives to begin their long, defeated journey back to Earth.

But… just as the celebration began, a lone Kestrel, one of the last remaining, broke from its formation.

Its target… Kallos.

The warning came too late.

Kallos' ship jolted violently as the enemy pilot fired a precise laser barrage, striking his right wing. Sparks erupted inside the cockpit. Alarms blared. His ship was on fire.

"No!" Jessa screamed. "Kallos, eject!"

"I can't," he coughed, his voice strained as smoke started to fill his cockpit. "Control's gone. I'm locked in."

Zari, still in tune with Veritas, sensed the perpetrator before she even saw it. She felt danger. Without hesitation, she whipped Veritas around, with her mind singular in purpose.

The Kestrel had no chance.

Veritas fired, and the enemy ship erupted into flames, reduced to nothing but burning wreckage. But the damage had already been done.

Kallos' stricken Eris fighter fell, spiralling and twisting, and flamed out as it breached Pluto's atmosphere.

The comms crackled with static as he fell, "Tell them… tell them we did it," Kallos managed to broadcast, his voice faint.

Jessa welled up, tears burning in her eyes. "No… Kallos, hold on! We'll get you…" she called in despair.

The last thing they saw was the faint glow of his ship, disappearing into the refrigerated world below.

And then, nothing…

A long silence followed.

Seb was tearful, his voice raw with emotion. "He's gone," he said as he welled up again.

The war was won. But the cost had been heavy.

On Pluto's surface, word of their victory spread like wildfire. Crowds gathered in the streets, cheering, crying, and embracing. Their world had been saved, and their brave pilots had achieved the impossible.

But high above, in the vast emptiness of space, the heroes who had fought for it could only watch as one of their own was lost forever.

Zari, still connected to Veritas, whispered into the void, her voice barely audible.

"We did it, Kallos. You saved us," she said, emotion taking over her.

And as the remaining ships turned home, the sky above Pluto held the final echoes of a legend.

CHAPTER FIFTY - THE RETURN TO HOME

One by one, the surviving ships broke through Pluto's thin atmosphere, with their engines roaring as they descended toward Erebus Prime. The city was alive with celebration, and its streets were teeming with thousands of people who had gathered to witness all of their heroes return. Lanterns, bunting and banners were strung across the rooftops, as the once-muted city now celebrated with light and sound. As the battered fleet came into view, a cheer rose through the streets like a thunderous wave of gratitude and relief, echoing through the buildings like a force of nature.

From the command balcony of the Erebus Spaceport, Hext stood with his arms crossed, watching as the ships came in to land. His heart swelled with pride. They had done it. Against impossible odds, they had driven the Dominion back and reclaimed Pluto's future. But he knew this was just the beginning of their next challenge. This victory was not the end of the journey, instead only the beginning of something even greater.

The first to touch down on the landing pad was the Albatross, its hull scorched but otherwise intact. The pad lowered into the Spaceport, and Jessa and Seb were the first to emerge, met with deafening applause and the warm embrace of the waiting crowds, spaceport workers and engineers. They were survivors and brave warriors; the ones who had made it back. Then came the surviving Corvettes, the Eris fighters and the patched-up freighters that had defied an empire, their crews stepping onto Pluto's hallowed ground like legends returning home.

And then, finally, Veritas.

Unlike the other ships, Veritas did not land with mechanical precision, it *flowed* downward, gliding in like a dancer in a balletic graceful descent, before settling onto the landing pad without so much as a tremor. When it appeared below in the hanger as the airlocks released, the crowd, already in awe, fell into stunned silence at the sight. It was not just another ship. It was something else entirely, and they could all sense it.

The hatch opened, and Zari and Steffan stepped down onto Pluto's soil, hand in hand. The roar of celebration returned, louder than before. Hext pushed forward, meeting them at the base of the ramp, a huge grin spilling over his bearded face, but also with a deeper question in his eyes.

"You two," he said, shaking his head. "Without you, we wouldn't be standing here right now."

Zari smiled, the enormity of everything she had been through settling over her.

"It wasn't just us," she replied. "Everyone played their part."

Hext turned his attention to Veritas, his face a picture of amazement. "How did you find it?" he asked. "And more importantly... how does it work?"

Steffan exchanged a glance with Zari before answering. "It's not like anything you've ever seen before. It doesn't have controls, it *listens* to her. Responds to her thoughts. It's... alive in a way." he tried to explain.

Hext looked at Zari carefully. "That ship is powerful." he said, "Too powerful. In the wrong hands…?"

"I know," Zari said firmly. "That's why she won't exist for much longer."

Hext raised an eyebrow but said nothing. Instead, he simply nodded.

As the celebration continued into the night, the real work was only just beginning. The Warren, deep beneath the city, was once again filled with voices as the remaining Terraformers convened. The war was over, but Pluto's fate was still undecided. NX-K3-Theta, the asteroid that had loomed over them for weeks, was still inbound, and its arrival presented an opportunity like no other.

"This asteroid," Elder Ryen began, gesturing at the holographic projection in the centre of the chamber, "has the potential to reshape Pluto in ways we never imagined."

Elder Maelis extended her arm out pointing, her eyes intense. "The plains beyond Erebus Prime are the key," she said,

"If we can direct the asteroid right there," she said pointing to a spot several hundred kilometres away, "The impact, combined with controlled releases of massive amounts of geothermal heat from the planet's core, could jumpstart the atmospheric changes we've spent lifetimes trying to create."

Steffan folded his arms. "But on its current trajectory?" he questioned.

Maelis shook her head. "It's not aligned." she said, "If it hits where it's currently headed, it'll cause devastation with no real benefit. We need to nudge it slightly into position."

"The asteroid's been tracked for over thirty days now," Elder Rennick added, adjusting the projection to show its current approach. "We've run every calculation. If we can shift its trajectory by just a fraction, it will land exactly where we need it to."

Everyone looked at everyone else, and then Zari stood taking control of the room.

"I can do it," she claimed.

All eyes turned to her.

"With Veritas," she continued, "I can see it. I can feel the asteroid's path. If I align with it, I can make the exact adjustments we need. I can put it on the exact course."

Hext gave her a long, measured look. "Are you sure?" he said, his eyes lighting up with intrigue.

Zari gave him the assurance he was looking for.

"Yes," she said, "and after that... after we ensure Pluto's future, Veritas will be no more."

Steffan moved beside her, taking her hand and squeezing hard. "Zari..." he said with pride for *his* girl.

She turned to him, her eyes filled with quiet resolve. "She's just too dangerous, Steffan." she said with a bit of regret in her heart, "We've both seen what she can do. If she falls into the wrong hands, and if someone with a different mind than mine takes control... the consequences would be catastrophic."

Steffan didn't argue. He knew she was right. He hated it, but he understood.

Hext sat back in his chair, exhaling. "Then we have our course," he said.

The room fell into full agreement. The war was won, but Pluto's rebirth was still ahead of them. And Zari would take one final flight into the unknown to ensure that their world had a future.

The last journey of Veritas was to come.

CHAPTER FIFTY-ONE – THE FINAL FLIGHT

Zari and Steffan returned to the spaceport in silence for one last time; the gravity and importance of what they were about to do was patently clear to all. The cheers and celebrations in Erebus Prime had long faded into the distance, and they were replaced now by a hushed reverence among the engineers and ground crew who remained behind to see them and Veritas off.

This mission was everything. If they got it wrong, then all of their dreams for Pluto would be lost. The people who had fought so courageously to win and the ones who had died, including Nyx, Kallos, plus all of the rest of them, had paved the way for this moment.

Zari turned to Steffan, her demeanour calm but filled with unspoken emotion.

"This is it," she whispered.

Steffan nodded and pulled her into his arms. The embrace was firm, warm and unbreakable. "We do this together," he murmured into her hair.

She nodded, holding him tighter before finally pulling away.

Then, slowly, she turned toward Veritas.

The ship gleamed in the hangar floodlights, its dark metallic frame absorbing the glow as if it were a living entity, breathing in the moment. As Zari approached, Veritas *knew*. The ship's surface rippled with soft pulses of energy, and with a low imperceptible click, her doors slid open like an invitation.

Zari stopped, then pulled herself together. "One last time," she whispered, stepping inside.

Across the hangar, Steffan climbed into the Albatross, adjusting his flight harness. They would fly together on one final mission, side by side before Veritas met her fate.

The ground crew cleared away as both ships fired up their engines, with the soft purr of Veritas contrasting against the mechanical growl of the Albatross. The airlock doors behind them were sealed before the landing pads lifted them toward the surface.

Outside, the moons Charon and Hydra were beginning their slow ascent in the sky. The world was still, for once, no storms blew, and the entire population of the planet waiting. And then, with a silent promise between them, both ships powered away upwards, ascending into the blackness of the Plutonian sky.

They flew together in perfect synchronization, twin streaks of light cutting through the darkness. As they broke into the void of space, the view before them became something ethereal.

The Pluto system stretched out in an infinite canvas in front of them, an expanse of stars and dust and a realm of quiet majesty. They soared past Nix, its cratered ground catching the distant light, past the untamed, icy terrain of Hydra, and onward past the lonely glow of Styx. The great celestial bodies drifted around them, forming a silent dance of frozen rock and distant history.

Zari looked to her left, where Albatross flew in close formation, her silhouette cutting through the endless dark. She and Steffan were together. This moment, this final flight, was theirs alone.

For hours, they traversed the system, slipping past the final gravitational pull of Pluto and entering the deeper expanse. And then, at last, it came into view.

The giant asteroid NX-K3-Theta.

A monolith of dark rock, ancient and threatening, tumbling slowly through the void like a forgotten titan drifting in an ocean of stars. It was massive, the size of a city, with its circumference cracked and uneven and the deep scars of millennia etched across its entirety. It spun in eerie silence, oblivious to the fate it was about to meet.

Across the comms came Steffan's voice, "It's time Zari... good luck!"

She glanced across to Albatross and Steffan flying alongside, and gave out a knowing smile.

Zari then looked forward at her target and closed her eyes, her breathing steady.

This was it.

This was the moment of truth for her and Veritas.

She had one shot to set everything in motion, and to ensure Pluto's future.

She reached out, not with her hands, but with her mind.

Veritas responded instantly as if she had been waiting for this.

The ship seemed to pulse beneath her, energy flowing through her frame, aligning with her thoughts. She could see it, the asteroid's movement, its speed, its precise trajectory. Every calculation filled her consciousness as though the universe itself had laid it bare before her.

She visualized the exact force needed. The precise angle. The perfect impact point.

The moment she was certain, she *willed* it into existence.

A surge of energy ripped through Veritas, and from the central ring, a bolt of pure light erupted, brighter than anything she had seen before.

The beam blasted through space, slamming into the asteroid with pinpoint accuracy. A shockwave flashed across it as fragments of rock and dust splintered and flew into the void. For a moment, it seemed as if nothing had changed.

But then, slowly, imperceptibly at first, the asteroid shifted half a degree.

Zari knew. She knew it had worked. The future was set, and fate had been rewritten.

Her grip on her mind relaxed, with her entire body exhaling as though she had just moved a mountain with her own hands.

A stillness settled over her, and then…

A vision.

Before her… not in the cockpit, but within her very mind, she saw them.

Her father, his presence warm and proud.

Nyx, smiling at her as she had in life, fire and spirit in her eyes.

And her dear mother, Elyndra, as ethereal and radiant as always.

"You did well," her father said, his voice gentle and strong.

"Thank you," Nyx whispered, her eyes filled with gratitude.

And then, Elyndra. She stepped forward, her eyes locking onto Zari's, her voice resonating not just in the vision, but within her soul.

"Use your powers for good, Zari. Use them wisely," she advised.

Zari's breathing stopped for a second. And then, as quickly as they had appeared, they were gone.

She opened her eyes.

They had done it.

"Mission accomplished," she whispered.

Veritas and Albatross turned, leaving the great asteroid behind.

Pluto's moons came back into view, their soft light welcoming them home. As they descended through the atmosphere, the white snow-drenched tundra stretched out before them, endless and untouched.

They landed gently, side by side, mere hundreds of kilometres from Erebus Prime. The snow beneath them remained pristine and undisturbed.

Zari sat in the cockpit for a long moment, staring at Veritas. She would miss her.

This ship, this impossible creation, had given her more than she could ever put into words. And now, she was leaving her behind.

She donned her survival suit, and, without hesitation, stepped out onto the frigid ground. The cold bit at her skin, but she barely felt it.

She took one last look at Veritas.

Her metallic frame reflected the starlight, waiting. It was still, silent, but somehow, Zari could feel it watching her. Understanding.

She whispered to it, just loud enough for the wind to carry it away.

"Farewell."

Then she turned and walked to Albatross.

Steffan was waiting for her, standing at the open hatch, his face breaking up with emotion. But the moment she stepped inside, he pulled her hood off her head and pulled her into his arms.

They held onto each other, longer than ever before. Their hearts unified as one.

Then, finally, she looked back, one last time.

The Albatross lifted off.

Veritas remained.

Alone. In the wilderness. Waiting for her fate.

CHAPTER FIFTY-TWO – A WORLD TRANSFORMED

The asteroid NX-K3-Theta tore through the cosmos, this ancient rock of ice and iron spiralling toward its destined collision. As it neared Pluto, it passed by the planet's moons one by one, with each celestial body momentarily casting its reflected light upon the approaching harbinger of change. It skimmed past Charon, with its dark silhouette shifting against the icy expanse, and then through the gravitational fields of Nix and Hydra, causing subtle disruptions in their orbits. The smaller moons, Kerberos and Styx, trembled in its wake as it carved its relentless path toward Pluto.

And then… it breached the planet's upper atmosphere.

A wall of friction ignited around its edges, sending waves of fire trailing behind it. Sparks flew as the colossal rock turned into a roiling inferno, illuminating the Plutonian night in a furious blaze of gold and crimson. The icy methane plains below reflected its light, transforming the icy world into a glowing expanse of flickering reds and oranges. The people of Erebus Prime, their eyes lifted to the heavens, could do nothing but watch in awe and hope as the streaking meteor painted the sky with its fiery descent.

Where would it crash down? By design, and as planned, it hit in the right place, six hundred kilometres from the colony, sparing the Hub from total annihilation but setting into motion an unstoppable transformation. Below in its direct path in the middle of the ice field was a small beautiful sleek spaceship, alone waiting for her fate; one that had played her very own part in the change that was about to come.

When the asteroid struck, the whole planet convulsed. A sun was born on Pluto's icefield, as a flash of fire and fury that outshone the distant star itself for a single, blinding moment. The methane fields vaporized instantaneously, feeding the inferno with ancient frozen gases. Shockwaves blasted across the planet, sending tremors that fractured the ice plains and travelled deep into the crust. The colony domes of Erebus Prime shook violently like never before, as the earthquake rippled outward, toppling smaller structures and cracking the great spires of the Corporatist strongholds. Some buildings suffered catastrophic damage, with their supports giving way as entire floors collapsed. Fires erupted in the central energy hubs, though the emergency crews acted as fast as they could to contain them. Underground railways screeched to a halt as sensors detected the violent tremors, cutting all the power to avoid derailments. The majority of Erebus Prime, however, reinforced against Pluto's extreme conditions, managed to withstand the upheaval unscathed.

Plumes of dust and ice shot skyward into the heavens with great geysers of vaporized methane and nitrogen cascading upwards and outwards. The skies above Pluto darkened as these plumes formed an expanding shroud, trapping heat within the planet's tenuous atmosphere. It was the first step in a sequence that no one had dared believe possible. The debris cloud swirled violently, reflecting distant sunlight and giving Pluto an eerie, golden glow never seen before. For hours, the planet seemed to exist in a twilight realm, caught between past desolation and future rebirth.

Now deep within Pluto's crust, the Terraformers enacted the second phase of their highly ambitious plan. Enormous geothermal vents, once used to sustain the underground farms, were thrown open to expel sizeable amounts of heat from the planetary depths. The fusion reactors that powered Erebus Prime redirected their energy, venting all their excess warmth into the newly forming atmosphere. A delicate balance had to be struck, as if too much were released too quickly, then the planet would become a storm-wracked tundra. Too little, and the transformation would stall, as any warmth would be lost to the abyss of space. Across the colony, the technicians monitored all of the energy readings, adjusting the controls with nervous precision as the Terraformers' vast infrastructure roared to life.

Hext watched as his people unleashed the next step of the process. Oxygen condensers, which had been hidden in the subterranean sanctums, were activated, finally releasing a cocktail of carefully engineered biocatalysts and nanites infused with extremophile bacteria that could convert carbon monoxide and carbon dioxide into breathable air. These microscopic *terra-formers*, the unseen hands of Pluto's rebirth, spread like wildfire across the warming ground. Data scrolled rapidly across control panels as the scientists observed the first changes. Carbon-heavy compounds were breaking apart, giving rise to fresh oxygen molecules that mixed with nitrogen to form the beginnings of an atmosphere.

It was working…

Above, in the newly thickening skies, something miraculous was happening. Water, released from ancient ice, rose as vapour, forming thick, wonderful swirling clouds. The Terraformers had seeded these storm fronts with compounds designed to accelerate the cloud formation, and in doing so, they aimed to trap heat within Pluto's growing atmosphere. The air pressure climbed steadily, and a fragile yet undeniable promise of a new world in the making started to form. For the first time in history, the warmer wind patterns began to shift, allowing milder air to sweep across the ice plains in slow but deliberate currents. Scientists scrambled to analyse the developing weather systems, realizing that Pluto was now moving towards an equilibrium unlike anything ever recorded.

As the hours passed, what had begun as a cataclysm transformed into a symphony of controlled chaos. The ice fields started to fracture, and beneath them, rivers of liquid water pooled. Vast chasms that had lain preserved for aeons split open, revealing hidden reservoirs that fed into the newly forming lakes. The once-lethal sky took on a dusky blue hue as nitrogen and oxygen mixed in an equilibrium that defied everything Pluto had once been.

And then, the first drops of rain fell.

Not snow, not frozen shards of methane, but water, true, liquid water cascading from the heavens. It splattered against the blackened, smouldering plains, sizzling against the remnants of the impact site. It ran in thin rivulets through the cracked ice, coalescing into the first streams Pluto had ever known. Scientists and workers alike rushed to the domes' observation platforms, gazing in awestruck silence as the rains continued, transforming the barren world into something utterly new.

Inside the great domes, the people of Pluto watched in stunned silence. The remaining Outlanders, hardened by lifetimes spent in the unforgiving climate, reached out to touch the moisture with something akin to reverence. The Isolationists, once steadfast in their belief that Pluto could never be tamed, stood in awe. Even the Corporatists, those who had clung to Earth's dominance, could not deny what was happening before their eyes. Emergency shelters opened their doors to those who had been displaced by the quake, and for the first time in Pluto's long, harsh history, rival factions worked together, not in conquest, but in survival and hope.

Steffan, standing at Prophet Hext's side next to his newly found lover Zari, looked in wonder at what they had created, a miracle above them. They squeezed their hands tightly. He had fought for this, and he had risked everything for this moment in defying his father. And now, and against all odds, Pluto was changing. He turned to Hext, who simply nodded, his weathered bearded face and eyes filled with triumph. The Prophet turned to him and smiled broadly.

"It's your time now Steffan," he said with sincerity and wisdom, "Learn the lessons of your father… and rule wisely."

The cold of space met the heat of transformation, and for the first time in its long and desolate history, Pluto was alive.

Veylan, battered and broken and ageing at an incredible rate in the aftermath of the Ice Wars, watched from the remnants of his fortress, his cybernetic fingers twitching and restless. He had spent his life maintaining order through fear, and strength. But now, Pluto's power had shifted completely, not through bloodshed alone, but through creation. He had lost the war, and he had been replaced by those who dared to dream beyond mere survival. His breath was ragged as he took in the blue horizon, the now heavy rain sweeping over the ice fields, and the golden storm clouds gathering over a world he no longer controlled or recognised.

Wearily, he messaged Mensen to ready his ship, destination heading for Earth. Might he get there in time so that he could prolong his life? What sort of reception might he get? Would they accept a failure and a broken man who had let them down?

A waiting speeder whisked the former Supreme Commander off to his cruiser *The Iron Will* waiting for him at the Spaceport. Ailing, frail, and utterly broken, he boarded, not looking back. And in just a few minutes, he was gone, heading for the far side of the Solar System.

On Neso, Talleron, Solas, Mareth and Sian stood in the Great Temple in unison. They knew. They knew that fate had played its hand. They knew that Pluto and its population would recover from this catastrophic impact, and thrive in the aftermath of it. Those who had done wrong or put personal gain ahead of the welfare of the many would feel the full force of karma on them. Justice had been done. Nothing was said, nothing need be said.

As the first true dawn crested the horizon, Pluto stood reborn. The battles were over. And a new age had begun.

The surviving leaders and elders of Pluto gathered within the halls of Erebus Prime, with all the representatives from each faction standing beneath the vast domed ceiling that had once been a symbol of confinement, but that now represented something far greater. Decisions would have to be made, and new governance had to be established. The old ways had died in the fires of transformation. What came next, no one could say.

But they would decide it all together.

BIBLIOGRAPHY FOR FURTHER READING LINKED TO THEMES WITHIN VERITAS

The Case for Mars: The Plan to Settle the Red Planet and Why We Must by Zubrin, Robert : Simon & Schuster UK, 2000.

How to Build a Habitable Planet by Langmuir, Charles H., & Broecker, Wally : Princeton University Press, 2012.

Terraforming Mars: Theory & Practice by Beech, Martin : Springer, 2009.

Rain of Iron and Ice: The Very Real Threat of Comet and Asteroid Bombardment by Lewis, John S : Helix Books, 1996.

Asteroid Impact Physics: Energy, Damage, and Planetary Effects by Johnson, John L : MIT Press, 2018.

Near-Earth Objects: Finding Them Before They Find Us by Yeomans, Donald K : Princeton University Press, 2012.

Chasing New Horizons: Inside the Epic First Mission to Pluto by Stern, Alan, & Grinspoon, David : Picador, 2018.

The Pluto System After New Horizons by Stern, Alan : Picador, 2018.

The High Frontier: Human Colonies in Space by O'Neill, Gerard K : William Morrow, 1977.

2001: A Space Odyssey by Clarke, Arthur C : New American Library, 1968.

The Age of Surveillance Capitalism: The Fight for a Human Future at the New Frontier of Power by Zuboff, Shoshana : PublicAffairs, 2019.

Life 3.0: Being Human in the Age of Artificial Intelligence by Tegmark, Max : Knopf, 2017.

THE END

Printed in Dunstable, United Kingdom